Praise for *Local Knowledge*

"Gripping and deeply perceptive, this powerful debut novel reveals the pleasures and struggles of true friendship and the painful decisions we often make for acceptance and love. Small-town life and work are rendered in vivid detail, as are the memorable characters who come alive in the hands of a gifted new writer." —Ben Sherwood, author of *The Death and Life of Charlie St. Cloud*

"A powerful and deeply moving novel about the lies we tell ourselves, the moral corners we cut, and the loved ones we betray to get what we want. Gyllenhaal has X-ray vision into the human heart and a sharp eye for contemporary mores and social maneuvering. She knows women and men and children, and pins them to the page with some of the most dazzling prose I've read in a long time."

—Ellen Feldman, author of *Lucy,*
The Boy Who Loved Anne Frank, and *Scottsboro*

"Liza Gyllenhaal's new novel invites instant immersion. *Local Knowledge* delves into the inner lives of the residents of a small town where the native families struggle with a failing economy and the loss of their land; the newcomers buy up the land and build lavish houses; and those in the middle profit and suffer at the hands of both. With insight and sensitivity Liza Gyllenhaal deftly draws the reader of *Local Knowledge* down through the layers and layers of intimate entanglements her characters have with each other, the land, and the new and old ways of life. I highly recommend *Local Knowledge* to anyone who loves good writing, a good story, and hopes to come away from a book with a deeper understanding of others' lives and choices."

—Tina Welling, author of *Crybaby Ranch* and *Fairy Tale Blues*

Written by today's freshest new talents and selected by New American Library, NAL Accent novels touch on subjects close to a woman's heart, from friendship to family to finding our place in the world. The Conversation Guides included in each book are intended to enrich the individual reading experience, as well as encourage us to explore these topics together—because books, and life, are meant for sharing.

Visit us online at www.penguin.com.

LOCAL KNOWLEDGE

LIZA GYLLENHAAL

NAL Accent
Published by New American Library,
a division of Penguin Group (USA) Inc., 375 Hudson Street,
New York, New York 10014, USA
Penguin Group (Canada), 90 Eglinton Avenue East, Suite 700, Toronto,
Ontario M4P 2Y3, Canada (a division of Pearson Penguin Canada Inc.)
Penguin Books Ltd., 80 Strand, London WC2R 0RL, England
Penguin Ireland, 25 St. Stephen's Green, Dublin 2,
Ireland (a division of Penguin Books Ltd.)
Penguin Group (Australia), 250 Camberwell Road, Camberwell, Victoria 3124,
Australia (a division of Pearson Australia Group Pty. Ltd.)
Penguin Books India Pvt. Ltd., 11 Community Centre, Panchsheel Park,
New Delhi – 110 017, India
Penguin Group (NZ), 67 Apollo Drive, Rosedale, North Shore 0632,
New Zealand (a division of Pearson New Zealand Ltd.)
Penguin Books (South Africa) (Pty.) Ltd., 24 Sturdee Avenue,
Rosebank, Johannesburg 2196, South Africa

Penguin Books Ltd., Registered Offices:
80 Strand, London WC2R 0RL, England

First published by NAL Accent, an imprint of New American Library,
a division of Penguin Group (USA) Inc.

First Printing, January 2009
1   3   5   7   9   10   8   6   4   2

Copyright © Liza Gyllenhaal, 2009
Conversation Guide copyright © Penguin Group (USA) Inc., 2009
All rights reserved

ACCENT REGISTERED TRADEMARK—MARCA REGISTRADA

LIBRARY OF CONGRESS CATALOGING-IN-PUBLICATION DATA:

Gyllenhaal, Liza.
Local knowledge./Liza Gyllenhaal.
p. cm.
Conversation guide included.
ISBN 978-0-451-22578-8
1. Women real estate agents—Fiction. 2. New York (State)—Fiction.   I. Title.
PS3607.Y53L63 2009
813'6—dc22   2008016473

Set in Minion • Designed by Elke Sigal
Printed in the United States of America

PUBLISHER'S NOTE
This is a work of fiction. Names, characters, places, and incidents either are the product of the author's imagination or are used fictitiously, and any resemblance to actual persons, living or dead, business establishments, events, or locales is entirely coincidental.

The publisher does not have any control over and does not assume any responsibility for author or third-party Web sites or their content.

Acknowledgments

I'm indebted to Scott Wilton and Bonnie Benson for sharing their memories of growing up in a place not unlike Red River. I'm deeply grateful to: Ellen Feldman, my adopted older sister and ever-generous mentor, for her wisdom and wit; Julian Muller for his advice, affection, and unqualified support; Susan Cohen, friend and agent, for making it all fun; Tracy Bernstein, for her smart, incisive editing; and, not least, to my husband, William Bennett, for being my first reader, sharpest eye, toughest critic, and staunchest ally.

Part One

1

It's a beautiful part of the world. You tend to forget that when you've lived here all your life. I was thinking about that on the drive over. How you stop seeing things after a while. Things and people. Even those you love. Maybe especially those you love.

Along the banks of Evers Creek, running high with the last of the snowmelt, bright yellow coltsfoot flowered among the rock rubble and mud. The underbrush was thickening with a reddish haze. And there, in the middle of the long pasture that had once been part of the Thornsteins' farm, two eager robins pecked at the soggy field. All harbingers of spring. New beginnings. I realized I was looking at things differently that afternoon. Through the eyes of the Zeller family, who were driving up from Manhattan to meet me at the house on Maple Rise. Primarily from Mrs. Zeller's point of view, I suppose, as it tends to be the women who decide these things. Anne Zeller. As usual, Nana's notes were detailed and precise.

It must have been the first or second week of daylight savings time. I remember how strong the sun seemed at five o'clock. I turned the visor down against the glare and caught a glimpse of myself in the clip-on mirror. I was nervous. Of course I was. This was my first big break. A chance to prove I could be trusted with more than the quarter-acre in-towns or the condos at Silver Acres. Though I knew it wasn't a question of what I was selling—but to whom. Nana's agency was booming because of the influx of city people in the market for weekend places, second homes. She'd opened up shop after 9/11 and hadn't stopped growing since. But I'd been taken on because I was born and raised in the area. The only one in the office who knew the difference between Paxter Hill Road and Paxter Mountain Road— or that there even was one. And I'd been groomed primarily to handle the local clientele, even though Red River Realty doesn't have much interest in that end of things. The low end. Nana made the papers here when she sold the county's first $3 million home six months back.

"Allergies. I can barely breathe," she told me when she phoned in sick that morning. "Is Heather in yet?"

"No. She just called. She's on her way to Boston. Her mom took a turn for the worse. She's not sure how long she'll be away."

"Damn. And Linda has the Meyerhauser closing. Okay, sweetie, it's going to have to be you. The Zellers are expecting to be shown the Maple Rise house this afternoon at five thirty. The file's somewhere on my desk. Call Frank and get the plans from him. And don't let him give you a copy. It's much more impressive to whip out a full-sized blueprint. Get him to prime you, or better yet, ask Paul to drop by for lunch and go over all the details. And take notes. You'll want to have this stuff in your head, or at least at your fingertips. The asking's $775,000, though Frank told me he and Nicky would settle for $725,000. But for God's sake don't let them know that!"

"Nana, please," I told her. "I'm not an idiot." I could tell from the way she was talking that she was worried about me taking this on. My biggest sale up to that point had been a $250,000 Colonial in the new development in Harringdale. And that was to a second cousin of Paul's who'd gotten a job at Walco Propane. The Zellers were Nana's kind of people. Wealthy. Professional. Upper East Siders. He was a management consultant. She, something creative in advertising. The requisite two children. That was the only part of their résumé I knew anything about. Kids. I have three girls. And I know from experience that if all else fails you can usually warm up even the most forbidding female by getting her going about her offspring. I had definitely put together a mental picture of what I was going to be dealing with. I met Paul at home for lunch to go over the specs and change into my best pantsuit; it has velvet-covered buttons and sateen piping on the collar and sleeves. But it was black on black, what I figured were the national colors of Manhattan.

I hadn't seen the house finished, though I'd been hearing about it from Paul for over a year. He had been foreman on the job, and it was one of Frank Miles's extravaganzas: an enormous teak contemporary with wrap-around decks and balconies jutting from the upper floors, five bedrooms, pink travertine marble in the bathrooms, a Jacuzzi in the master suite—all your luxury bells and whistles. It was too big for the sloping hillside and looked something like the *Titanic,* atilt and about to go under; that was Paul's take on the final result. But by then, of course, he'd been through hell over its construction. Paul's the first one to admit that every new house has its own unique set of problems, but the Maple Rise place had taken more than the usual out of my husband. Some of which I knew about. The rest I only got to sense, like sudden cold eddies, beneath the deceptively smooth and temperate surface he presents to the world.

River Road meets Maple Rise at the old graveyard, a weedy hillock of cracked headstones and sunken graves, once the final resting place for the Barnett and Hughes families, the earliest English settlers in the territory. It's hidden behind a lichen-covered stone wall and obscured most of the year either by snow or the shade of the ancient maple trees that line the roadway. Today, though, the little cemetery was quite visible in the late-afternoon sun, and, as the land's subdivision had put more than half of it inside the Maple Rise property, I knew I had to be ready to sell its somewhat spooky charms to the Zellers. But that would be easy compared to trying to explain what I passed on my right as I made the switchback up the steep hill. I glanced down at the bizarre landscape, and then back to the graveled road ahead of me. Soft-pedal it, I told myself. Make it an inside joke, a humorous anecdote. They won't even see it by early May when the trees leaf out.

I'd given myself half an hour before the Zellers were due to open the house and get acquainted with the interior. But when I crested the top of the hill, I saw I wasn't going to have a chance to get my bearings after all. A white Lexus SUV was already parked in front of the two-car garage. A woman and two children were perched on the back bumper, their heads turned westward toward the sun, eyes closed. They roused themselves at the sound of my car. The kids—a boy and a girl, roughly five and three, the ages of my two youngest—hopped off the bumper and fell against each other, laughing, as I pulled up. The woman uncrossed her arms and slid her hands into the back pockets of slim-fitting black jeans. She was wearing cowboy-style boots and a well-worn leather bomber jacket. She looked towheaded like her kids, though as she came up to the car I realized that her short-cropped hair was actually prematurely white. I rolled down the window, but she started talking before I had a chance to say a word.

"Hey there. We got up here a lot faster than we thought we would. The

Taconic was absolutely beautiful, by the way. Fantastic. We've just been sitting here soaking up these incredible views. This is Max and Katie. Come on, guys, stop that, and say hello." She had the husky voice of an adolescent boy, and a rapid-fire, near monotone delivery. I felt like I was on some sort of remote video delay, understanding what she was saying about half a beat after she'd said it.

"Hello, Katie and Max," I replied. I reached behind me to get the plans and files.

"Oh, great," she said, when I climbed out of the car with the blueprint under my arm. "That will make Richard's day. He's in the car on his cell phone, of course. I think eventually he'll just have the thing surgically attached to his head. By the way, I'm Anne. And you're . . . Nana Osserman?" There was something in her tone that let me know she suspected I wasn't. I immediately assumed it was my overly dressy outfit. Of course, I should have known better. I looked exactly like what I felt: ill at ease and trying too hard.

"No, I'm sorry, I thought Nana called your husband to tell him. She's sick today and asked me to show you around for her."

"Oh, thank God!" She laughed, nudging me with her elbow as we walked side by side back toward the Zellers' car. She lowered her voice. "I've met Daniel Osserman, but not her. He's got to be at least in his midseventies. And I have this weird, totally non–politically correct bias against May-December unions. It must be some sort of automatic self-defense system that kicks in with women over a certain age, do you know what I mean? And Nana probably did talk to Richard on the way up. He's been on his cell since Poughkeepsie without coming up for air. Let's get him off." She stopped by the driver's side and knocked on the window. We waited. She knocked again and began to make funny faces, finally smooching her face up against the glass. Her children started laughing, and I realized I was smiling. My real smile, not my professional one.

Richard Zeller was still talking into his phone as he got out of the car and slammed the door.

". . . So we fly from Cleveland to San Francisco Tuesday afternoon. What's the problem? No, I don't mind teleconferencing Greensboro in. It's just the plant, right? They don't give a damn what we're trying to do anyway.

Listen, I got to go. I'm at the place. Yeah. Just make it work." He clicked off and then started scrolling through his messages, frowning.

"Richard?" Anne said. "You are totally missing the magnificent sunset here."

"Right," he said, flipping his cell shut. He was tall and heavyset, his unwieldy bulk encased in a beautifully cut dark blue suit. His face was fleshy, the eyes pouched, but the gaze that took me in was avid and quick. He didn't hold out his hand.

"Dan Osserman and I go back about a million years," he said. "Nana's the only one to see up here, I'm told."

"I'm sorry she couldn't be here to do this personally, but—"

"Yeah. I know, we talked," he said, finally turning around to take in the fading sun and distant hills. "Okay, let's see what we've got. You know the acreage?"

"Nine-plus," I said. "Woods on all four sides so you're totally protected. In the summer, the trees will screen out a great deal. Though, of course, it's up to you if you want to do some more selective cutting. The possible views are quite stunning, obviously."

"Not much thought put into landscaping," he said, as we started down the flagstone path to the front door. He was right. The house sat on mud and straw. Up until a few weeks ago, most of the county had been covered in snow.

"Construction was just completed this month, and it's a bit early in the season to plant," I told him, getting out the keys. "I did bring along some drawings that one of the area's top landscape design firms prepared. Some clients have their own ideas, of course, about what they would like. But I imagine you'll want to at least take a look—the plans come with the house." Was I babbling? It felt like it, though the Zellers didn't seem to notice. The kids raced around me into the house before I'd gotten the door half open.

"Be careful," I called after them. "The floor's just been polyurethaned. It's very slippery." Paul had warned me about this. One of the workmen had taken a fall and twisted his ankle.

"Oh, don't worry about them, they're made out of Silly Putty," Anne said, walking into the middle of the living room and looking up at the soaring cathedral ceiling. Pink-tinted sunlight flooded the room, creating a kind of halo around Anne's upturned head. I'd never been in that house until that moment, and I'd just met this woman, so it seemed very odd to me that I should be experiencing a déjà vu. But there it was: that ministroke of time flashing backward—or forward, I'm never sure which. But simultaneously, I felt as though I'd lived through that exact moment before and would do so again.

"I love this room!" Anne said, turning in a circle, arms outstretched. "All this light! And that fireplace—my God, we could all just move in there and live—it's so enormous, do you know what I mean?"

"The caulking hasn't been finished here." Richard pointed to the hearth, where firebrick didn't quite join white marble.

"And the flue's not in yet," I said. "It's being specially fitted by a firm in Springfield. I've a list of things that still need to be finished. All final details, I assure you. I'll give you a copy if you like."

"You certainly have an answer for everything, don't you?" Richard said. It felt like he'd just turned around and slapped me across the face. As Nana had suggested, I'd memorized a lot of facts and figures, and then brought along copies of backup materials I thought might be of interest to the Zellers. But instead of coming across as competent and in control, I'd seemed—what? Officious, maybe. Nana's inexperienced and nervous assistant. But then I realized that he'd known that all along. That Nana had said something to him about me. I could just hear her:

"And I'm so, so sorry! But I'm short-staffed today of all days. I'm going to have to have one of my junior people let you in. She doesn't really know anything about this listing. But the first time around I believe the only important thing is for you to see the place through your own eyes and get a feeling for it. It's like a blind date, don't you think? And I'm positive that you're about to fall head over heels in love."

I didn't blame Nana; she was just trying to protect her backside and a possible sale. I did resent him. Putting me through my paces, seeing how far and fast I could jump. And I sensed he enjoyed playing the bully. But I wasn't about to let him see that he'd gotten to me. Without changing my upbeat tone, I said, "Well, I sure hope so. I have the blueprint, too. Shall we spread it out in the kitchen and take a look?"

Paul had assured me that the kitchen alone would sell the house. He loved carpentry work and had lavished a great deal of his own time on the cherrywood cabinets and cupboards, the dark walnut island topped with gray-veined white marble.

"The architect visualized the kitchen as the house's hub," I said, stepping up to the raised dining area. I was parroting what Paul had told me about what Frank had explained to him. "You may not have noticed, but you get a view of it when you come in the front door. And it communicates one way or the other with every room. Whichever way you enter—from the deck or the back hallway—it really welcomes you in, don't you think?"

"Oh, yes, it's absolutely fabulous," Anne said. She walked around the room, touching the brand-new top-of-the-line appliances: Sub-Zero refrigerator, Miele dishwasher, La Cornue range. The brushed-aluminum handles for the stove top were still wrapped in protective plastic. I unrolled the blueprint on top of the island, as Richard came up behind me.

"Let me take a look at that," he said. Instinctively, I stepped back.

"Come show me the deck," Anne said, grabbing my elbow. "I want to see the view again while we still have some light." I sensed that she wanted to get me away from Richard, give him time to study the designs without my running commentary.

"It's so peaceful here," she said, as I slid the double-hung Andersen door shut behind us. Foolishly, I'd decided I wouldn't need my winter parka, a faded and thoroughly unstylish navy blue down, when I set out earlier. But now the temperature was dropping as the sun sank lower, and I felt goose bumps rising up my legs and arms.

Suddenly a load of pine needles and other debris showered down on us from above. I heard shuffling and giggling and looked up to see that Katie and Max had somehow gotten out on one of the upper bedroom balconies.

"Oh, God," I said. "I'm so sorry. I thought the upstairs doors were locked. You better tell them to get in. I'll run up and—"

"Don't worry. They're not about to jump or anything," Anne said with a laugh. Then she called up to them: "Come on down here, guys. I want you to see the incredible kitchen and this amazing, enormous deck. I'm thinking this would be the perfect place for a Ping-Pong table."

Richard stepped outside with the children. The dying sun reflected off a low-lying bank of clouds, washing the woods in front of us with a reddish glow. Something glinted through the trees.

"What the hell is that? I saw it when we drove up before—a junkyard or something?"

"You mean the—well, I guess—sculpture garden?"

"I mean that load of crap at the bottom of the driveway."

"Richard," Anne said.

"Okay, so I don't mince words. And I expect the same in return."

"That farmhouse and about ten acres around it belong to Luke Barnett," I replied. "His family used to own all this land—for about as far as the eye can see. They were given the original land grant for the territory. The Barnetts were once a pretty powerful force around here, but now. Well. Luke's had to sell off most of what he owned to keep himself going. He makes those sculptures out of things he scavenges from around town. Tourists sometimes buy them."

Though more often they don't. Most of the time now, the world just passes Luke by. Which is how I think he wants it, or at least that's what I tell myself. Paul and I haven't spoken to him for—how long has it been? Months. No, actually more like a year. How odd that the last time I saw him, in person, was not far from this very spot, looking down on what was then a bulldozed, treeless, rubble-strewn hillside. He blamed me, of course, for everything. Just as I blamed him. The truth is, we've been adversaries almost from the start, forced to face off against each other at every important juncture of our lives. Even now, a year after the big blowup, after all those months of silence, I had the sense that we were still circling each other. Angry and wary. Waiting to see who'd give first.

Oh, there was more, so much more, I could say about Luke. But I wasn't about to share it with the Zellers.

I knew, shivering out there on the deck in my cheap black suit, that on an important level I'd failed. Though Nana would have nothing to complain about. I'd done what she asked and shown the Zellers the house for her. But I knew they'd be calling her, not me, for the follow-up. What had I been thinking, trying to impress someone like Richard Zeller with my quickly memorized facts and figures? And Anne? Though she seemed so open and enthusiastic, I knew that she could very well just be stringing me along, judging my every move. I could easily imagine her and Richard picking me apart—"Oh, my God, did you see what she was wearing?"—on the way back to the city. In fact, I was positive that Richard Zeller had seen through me in an instant: a small-town nobody. I sometimes think that every single mistake I've made in my life is a result of believing that I had a shot at becoming something better than that.

"Well, it's a real eyesore, whatever it is," Richard said as he turned away, and we all followed him back into the house.

2

"**Y**ou think Rachel would want to lend a hand around here again this summer?" Kathy asked me when I dropped Lia off with her the following Monday after lunch. Kathy is married to Paul's younger brother, Bob, and she's been helping to make ends meet at the farm for the last several years by running a day-care center out of their finished basement. She comes across as such a positive person: even-tempered, sympathetic, seemingly content under the layers of extra fat that circle her waist and dimple her cheeks when she smiles and laughs, which is often. In-laws in the close-knit Alden family, we are frequently in each other's company, in and out of each other's houses, so you would think I'd know her about as well as anybody. But I was totally taken by surprise when she had to go up to Albany Psychiatric last summer. Bob said it was postpartum depression after Danny, but that was really about as much as I was able to get out of either one of them. Paul told me not to pry. But since then I can't help but see the shadow cast by Kathy's determinedly sunny disposition, the way her gaze doesn't quite meet mine when we talk.

"I'll ask her. I know she enjoys helping you out, but she's looking to make some real money this year," I told her before calling across the room for Lia to come back and give me a good-bye hug. Lia, who's still half days at the pre-K in town, treats Kathy's place like a second home. She was already organizing her two cousins and a couple of the other kids into some kind of game involving Kathy's plastic bowling set. My youngest was born bossy and utterly self-assured. We call her the Little General.

"Bye, Mommy!" Lia shouted, and I knew that was all I was going to get from her. Beanie, my shy, willowy five-year-old, still clings to me every morning when I drop her off at school and will curl up in my lap at night and tuck her head under my chin. She has so little armor, whereas Lia is a walking arsenal of self-confidence. Sure, they're both still very young, but I've grown to believe that we come out of the box fully assembled for the most part.

"I mean to pay her, of course," Kathy said, sounding a little defensive. "Whatever the going rate is. She can tell me, within reason, you know. But I'm already getting six new kids from that ad I put in the *Rambler* last month. And I'm sure to be picking up drop-ins from all the summer rentals. I could just really use her."

"I'll ask her tonight. She's going to be applying for her driver's permit in January, and she's already talking about saving money for her own car. I hate to even think about it. She'll be gone before we know it."

"All I want to do is make it through the summer in one piece," Kathy replied with a self-deprecating laugh. She used to be such a good listener, but I'm not sure she'd even heard what I said about Rachel.

"Okay, I'll talk to her about it. But if not Rachel, I'm sure you'll be able to find someone pretty easily. It's not like there's a lot of work around here in the summer for girls Rachel's age."

"I know, but I'd really love it to be her. She's so great with the little kids, and I trust her. And not just because she's family. She's a good person. You guys are doing something right."

"Thanks," I said, warmed by her praise for my eldest daughter. But in fact I think we all know that I had very little to do with Rachel's inherent sweetness. It flows like strong rich sap through Paul's side of the family, every generation producing one or two offspring who are just naturally kind and generous. And unlike Beanie, Rachel's gentleness can bend with the wind, snap back after duress. At fifteen, Rachel is plagued by erratic spurts of acne, but other than that she's showing few external signs of teenage hormonal imbalance or rebellion. Both Paul and I, remembering ourselves at her age, are holding our breaths. Maybe, if we're careful, if we treat her with respect and understanding, she won't turn against us—as we turned against our own parents. That's why I didn't want to commit her outright to working for Kathy. This was just the sort of thing, Paul and I agreed, that Rachel should be allowed to decide for herself.

The Red River Realty office is on the north end of town, the last clapboard Colonial before Route 198 straightens out and picks up steam heading eastward toward the busier, more built-up areas and River Road

branches off to continue its meandering journey to nowhere along what
had once been an old stagecoach route. Nana had the building repainted inside and out when she bought it five years ago, hung window boxes that we
keep filled with geraniums and English ivy, and landscaped the parking lot
with split-leaf maples and evergreen shrubs to screen it from the highway.
A stranger, driving past, wouldn't actually register that it's a place of business unless they happened to notice the elegantly lettered sign to the right
of the red-painted front door. The building and grounds are meticulously
maintained, discreetly welcoming. "For people of means," Nana likes to say,
though in truth she's far less picky than she pretends.

"Well, I would say that at the very least he's intrigued," Nana told me
when she'd called me at home Friday night. "He seems especially taken by
how close the house is to the Taconic. I've a feeling that money is not the
issue, though I also have the sense he's holding something back. Not in a
calculated way—you know, 'I want it but you're going to have to work to
sell it to me.' But he's hesitating for some reason. Any idea what it could be?
What were you picking up?"

Over the past two years of working for Nana, I've heard her endlessly
discussing and analyzing prospective buyers with Heather and Linda, the
other two Realtors at the agency. Though Nana can come across as totally
professional, perhaps even slightly detached when she's face-to-face with
clients, as soon as they're off the phone or out the door she starts a minute
and often ruthless dissection of their probable net worth, seriousness *vis-à-
vis* the Red River real estate market, and possible hidden character traits that
will make selling a home to them either a happy rush to the altar or a slowly
disintegrating relationship that leads only to acrimony and broken vows.

Nana's often making the point that the relationship is like an engagement—
and that there's going to be a big beautiful wedding cake of a house waiting for you at the end. But like any bride, she's constantly monitoring her
fiancé's commitment and interest, maneuvering behind the scenes and worrying the details in a way that would probably come as a surprise to most of
her clients. Friday night was the first time she had ever included me in one
of these fraught, secretive machinations, which, I believe, are a big part of
the reason Nana and the firm can appear to be so effortlessly successful.

"Well, the look of Luke Barnett's place bothered him, I know that. I
tried to joke about it, but he didn't go for it. Also I don't think he likes to feel

he's being sold on anything. He just wanted the facts—no frills. He wants to feel that he's making up his own mind. He's totally his own man."

"Very interesting," Nana said. "Very *good*, Maddie," she added. "I see exactly what you mean. I was going on about how lucky we were to have an architect of Frank's caliber in the area, et cetera, et cetera, and I could tell he almost resented hearing about it. He needs to come to these conclusions by himself. That's it. We just have to keep him on track, keep the information flowing in his direction, and try not to get in the way."

I could hear the phone ringing in the big office down the hallway on the left when I walked in that afternoon. This is where I work at an open-plan cubicle across the room from Heather and Linda, who share most of the space, with soundproofed dividers giving them some privacy. Nana has the smaller, private office on the right, decorated with a few simple Shaker pieces and a large framed topographic map of the county. Nana looked up as I walked past. She was on the phone, frowning.

". . . I understand your frustration," she was saying. "But that's what happens when inventory is tight. It's like any other commodity. Scarcity means you have to pay more for what you want . . . yes . . . right . . . "

I recognized this as one of Nana's conversational set pieces. She'd been a high-powered television producer in the city before moving up here, and she still loves business jargon, though she'd die before coming right out and saying what every Realtor in the area knows: There are fewer and fewer decent homes available to show. Lately, in fact, some brokers are creating their own inventory by partnering with the developers to put up spec houses and splitting the profits. Though I'm not privy to any of the financial details, this is the kind of arrangement Nana put together with Frank Miles and Nicky Polanski for Maple Rise and the other houses on the old Barnett land. By the time I reached my desk, the ringing had stopped but the line was lit up, indicating that someone was leaving a message. It was the main line, not my direct one, so I didn't bother to pick up. I'd check the messages later. I tucked my shoulder bag under my desk. Linda was on the phone and Heather was at her computer.

I checked my e-mail and logged on to Promatch to keep an eye out for new listings and changes in inventory, and then made a few calls to clients. Nana has taught me to stay in touch with people as much as possible, even if it's just to confirm an open house or double-check a closing date.

Make it seem like they're all you're thinking about, that they're the top of your list, Nana insists. And what amazes me is that though she's juggling dozens of clients, she's still able to give each and every one of them the impression that she's dropped everything else just to take their call. It was nearly three o'clock by the time I checked the messages for the main office number. There was only one.

"Yes, hello, this is Anne Zeller. We were shown a lovely house up there this past Friday and my husband has a few questions that he's asked me to handle since he's on a business trip. Unfortunately, the woman who showed us the place never told me her name, as far as I can remember. And I don't think she gave us her card. In any case I couldn't find it in the paperwork she gave us. So, could someone double-check which Realtor showed us that house—it was, let me see, on Maple Rise? And have her call me back at my office. The number here is . . ."

I felt a lift hearing her voice again—it had a compelling intimacy about it, as though she was whispering a secret in my ear. I played the message again, jotted down Anne's name and number on one of our pink While You Were Out slips, and took it in to Nana's office. As usual, she was on the phone. But when she saw who the message was from she gave me a toothy grin and a thumbs-up signal with her free hand, and then I went back to my desk, taking with me the stack of paperwork Nana had left in her out-box. I'm able to do most of the routine filing and word processing by rote now, freeing up my thoughts.

"What was that about Luke?" Paul had asked me when I hung up the phone after speaking to Nana on Friday night. We'd been in the kitchen when she called, finishing up dinner. The girls had retreated into the living room to watch television and Paul had quietly started to rinse the plates and load them into the dishwasher. I could sense him listening to me, weighing my tone of voice, the direction of the conversation. He knew how much the showing meant to me, how important it was for me to do a credible job. Paul wants me to succeed at Red River Realty as much as I do; he's my biggest supporter, as I am his. I think this comes from us having been so close to the abyss during our early years together. We've been pulling each other back from an edge only we can see—and know is still there—for longer than I care to remember.

"The client commented on Luke's place. He called it an eyesore."

"Christ, Maddie. I hope this isn't going to turn into a real problem."

"You mean any more than it already is? I don't know. They'll be week-enders, if they buy the place. I doubt they'll have the time or interest to get too involved with neighbors."

"From your lips . . . ," he said, as I started to brush past him with the garbage bag, but he pulled me into his arms. We held each other for a long time without talking. But in that silence I couldn't help thinking about Luke. And Paul. And me. If only I could rewind the tape of our life together. If only we could start over again. What wouldn't I give *not* to have Luke's shadow hovering over us! Not so much coming between us as forcing us to see each other through his eyes. Though I've tried to banish him from my thoughts for many months now, it seems that I've allowed him—or some imagined form of him—to assume a kind of mythic stature in my mind.

The intercom buzzed. Nana asked me to come into her office.

"I'm losing it, sweetie. Time to put me out on an ice floe," she told me as she waved me into one of the chairs that face her desk. She did look tired, I thought, and irritated about something.

"You say that at least twice a week," I reminded her.

"Do I? Well, this time I really mean it. I very nearly blew that call. I can't believe it! That was Anne Zeller. I called her back. She's at Freiling and McDuffy, by the way, the ad agency. In my day, a very hot creative shop. I had to go through two assistants before getting through to her. So, she's some-thing in her own right, okay? By the time we finally connected, I was in full selling mode. I know these kinds of women. You don't get to where she is by being a softy. But she seemed surprised that I'd called."

"That's weird. I heard the message."

"No, that *I* had called her. I explained that I was the principal owner of this agency. I was calling mano a mano, so to speak. She asked me who *you* were, what *your* name was. I told her, of course, then asked what her ques-tions were, how I could help. But she seemed reluctant to get into it. She's got this breathy voice—and she was literally kind of humming to herself, not a good sign. I'm such an idiot! Finally, I asked her if something was wrong, you know, if perhaps this wasn't such a good time to talk. And then she came right out with it."

Nana leaned back, threw her arms up in the air, and cried, "Take me now, God, before I do any more harm! She wants to work with *you*. She likes *you*. What? So the two of you bonded the other night? You could have had the decency to tell me, sweetie, before I made such an utter fool of myself."

"I'm so sorry, Nana. I didn't know. I mean, I liked her. A lot. But I would never take a client of yours—"

"You're damned right you wouldn't," Nana cut me off. "But I understand now that this is a special situation. I was thinking about what you said about the husband, Richard. That he doesn't like to feel hustled. I think he's pushing this off on his wife for that reason. He wants it, but he doesn't want to have to get down there and hondle. So he wants her to do it—but she, who knows?—for some reason she feels more comfortable dealing with you. Thinks I'd put on the pressure or something. So, here's what we're going to do. You're going to handle it. Call her back. Get her list of concerns. Love her up. And make her feel good about choosing you over me, okay? You're best friends, or whatever. Then you come to me and I help you every step of the way on this."

"Nana, that's—so kind of you. So generous."

"And we split the commission fifty-fifty."

3

"I'm sorry. She's in a meeting. Who's calling, please?" It was the gum-chewing assistant, the junior one; the other one already recognized my voice.

"Maddie Alden from Red Riv—"

"Oh, sure, wait. She told me to put you right through. Hold on, please." Jazz—the real thing, not Cool 100—briefly filled my ear. Then Anne picked up, though she was in the middle of a conversation with someone else in the room: ". . . let them try, as far as I'm concerned. It's total bull. Right, exactly. He's just hoping to score off the situation, do you know what I mean? Sure. Thanks. See you at the meeting. Okay, what have you got? Maddie, are you still there?"

"Yes, sorry. I have the soil suitability assessment and Northridge Land Design's Test Pits and Perc Testing reports. It's—let's see—about eight pages altogether. Do you want me to fax it?"

"That was fast. God, you're terrific. What I really want is for you to come down and reorganize this damned office. I have a couple of total idiots working for me right now. I'd give anything to have someone like you here. Trippers and askers surround me. That was Whitman, I think. I used to know him by heart. What happened to all that wonderful, useless knowledge that seemed so all-important to us in college? This place is a total madhouse today, in case you couldn't tell. Everything adds up?"

I was getting used to Anne's way of jumping from one subject to another without apparent logic, though I was beginning to see certain patterns in her thinking. Like a cat, she preferred to reach her destination indirectly, taking her time and the long way around to land, suddenly and unexpectedly, exactly where she intended to from the start.

"Yes. The readings are fine. Frank wouldn't have sited the house there otherwise. He's totally reliable."

"Oh, of course. I'm sure you're right. As I already told you, this is all just an exercise in pandering to my husband. He adores paperwork, busywork, forcing people to run around in little circles for him. You would not believe the hoops he's making our bank jump through before he deigns to allow them to give us a mortgage. It's embarrassing. For me, at any rate. Richard claims people like to be pushed. That's fine for him to say, but I'm the one who's having to do the pushing."

"Actually, these are exactly the sorts of things you should be asking about. I'm still working on the school tax question. I've a call into the board commissioner, but it might take another day or—"

"That's fine. What's it like up there this morning? This city is an absolute sauna. No, that's too kind an image. It's more like an open cauldron. The streets are already getting that kind of slimy look they get in the summer—and the smell? God, wouldn't it be wonderful to be up on that deck with you right now, having a glass of iced tea?"

She'd done this to me a few times over the past few weeks: suggesting that, once the Zellers bought the house, the two of us would naturally become friends. Of course, it wasn't going to happen. She was making all sorts of assumptions about me—that I'd been to college, for starters—that I wasn't about to correct while we were still hammering out the details of the sale. Still, I was hoping that we could at least stay friendly. That we'd chat for a moment or two when we ran into each other at the post office or general store. So many of the weekenders stare right through me and Paul or, much worse, treat us with overly polite condescension. Sometimes I wonder how they seem to know automatically that we're locals, which to most of them means the same thing as hired help.

"Live with it," Paul tells me when I get upset that some client has called him on a Saturday night to come over and fix a sliding door to the deck. Or broken light dimmer. Or—and this was my favorite—door handle to the utility closet. On the weekend!

"So, they're not thinking about me, about us. They're only up for a day or two and want it taken care of. You can't take this stuff so personally, Maddie."

But Anne wasn't like that at all. She would actually bend over backward to thank me for things that were just a routine part of my job and then compliment me on my speed and efficiency. But it wasn't just that;

from the beginning she acted as though—and made me believe that—we shared a special kind of understanding. She seemed to enjoy talking to me, lingering on the phone long after we'd finished the business part of our conversation.

"You like working in real estate, don't you?" she asked me at one point. "I could tell that when you took us through the house. Like it was yours— and you were so proud to show us around. I wish I could feel that in my job. That kind of ownership—that joy. Listen, Maddie, the truth is"—her voice sinking lower—"I think maybe I'm reaching a kind of burnout here. There's this continual push for something new, something different. If I hear one more time, 'I don't know what I want. Surprise me!' I'll have to kill someone. These people don't seem to realize that there's a limited number of creative approaches you can take to selling sporting equipment, do you know what I mean?"

"Honestly, I don't know that much about advertising. What does a"—I had her card taped to the inside of the file on the desk in front of me— "Senior Creative Director actually do?"

"You mean besides prostituting her artistic and moral integrity in order to stimulate consumer interest in some shoddily made and overpriced pair of in-line skates?" she asked with her throaty, adolescent boy's laugh and then, perhaps realizing that I was serious, she hesitated for a moment and then went on: "I conceptualize. That is, I try to think of extraordinarily fascinating ways to strengthen Haverford Athletics' flabby bottom line and anemic public image. I'm also in the middle of a pitch right now for a new line of cookware supposedly designed and regularly used by Lucinda d'Annuzio—you know, that Italian chef on the cable food network? Although, since we've only been able to see prototypes and the stuff is being produced somewhere in Malaysia, I doubt that Lucinda herself has done much actual cooking with it. But these days, none of that matters. These pots and pans could be made out of aluminum foil for all that quality matters. It's about branding. Name recognition. God, I sound so cynical, don't I? What a pathetic cliché—a disillusioned advertising executive! At least you get to sell something valuable, Maddie, something quantifiable."

"Yes, I guess you're right," I said, looking around my crowded little cubicle and imagining the view that someone in Anne's position enjoyed. The Freiling & McDuffy offices were on Hudson Street. I'd looked the address up on MapQuest. It's about ten blocks north of Ground Zero in the midst of some of the most desirable residential real estate in the world. The agency was probably in one of those renovated cast-iron buildings. A floor-through loft with exposed brick and ductwork, eighteen-foot-high ceilings, views of the Hudson River or a resurgent downtown. Nothing special to someone like Anne Zeller. But for me, who has been to the city only three times in my life, a world as exotic and foreign as a Turkish seraglio. When Anne said that about wanting me to come down there and reorganize things, although I knew she was kidding, I still felt a little flutter in my stomach. Like when I was pregnant and the baby would kick me. Without warning, there it was: a glimpse into another dimension, a new way of seeing the possible.

"I had to arrange the meeting with the engineer for eleven Saturday morning, by the way," she told me then. "I tried to make it earlier, but that's the best he could do. I hope that won't be a problem for you."

"No," I said, though it was. I was going to have to let the Zellers into the house at the same time I was supposed to be taking Rachel into Northridge to see my gynecologist. She'd been complaining about cramps during her period for the last few months. It would be her first visit to an ob-gyn. This was not something I could ask Paul to handle for me. And I knew I couldn't easily reschedule; it was tough enough getting the Saturday morning appointment. On the other hand, I didn't want to turn the Zellers over to Nana or anyone else. I'd put a lot of time and effort into the Maple Rise sale over the past few weeks. And though the Zellers' offer had been accepted, Nana warned me that things often went wrong on the bigger deals at the last moment.

"Don't let anything slip," she said. "Get them answers before they even know they have questions. Remember the kids' names. Keep in mind every last little like and dislike you know they have. Let him alone, as we agreed. But her? Stick to her like glue. You're her biggest fan. Her best buddy, okay?"

"Margaret says they put this flashlight up you." Rachel was nibbling the edge of the rilled round of paper, the only thing left of the cranberry walnut muffin we'd gotten for her at the general store when I picked up the newspapers. Sometime during my first year with Nana, I started getting the *New York Times* as well as our local paper. I told Paul it's because they have good real estate coverage, which is only partially the truth. To me, it automatically confers a kind of status, and I enjoy tossing it into the backseat of the car when a client gets in on the passenger side. I was pleased to see that Rachel had it in her lap, and I realized that was because I imagined Anne might see it there when we drove up and think—what? Better of Rachel than she already deserved?

"No, honey, I've never heard of that," I said, glancing over at her. She has my hair, though she wears it much longer: dark blond and thick as a horse's mane, a beautiful burden that takes her half an hour to blow-dry every morning. Today she had it partially up in what we used to call a Mary Jane, the velvet scrunchie already listing under the weight of the heavy swags. Her upturned Alden nose was slick with humidity and adolescence. Her right knee pumped. Though I'd instigated several conversations about her sexual development, she remained prim and painfully modest about her changing body. We'd given her the upstairs guest bathroom to use as her own after she banned first me, then her younger sisters, from seeing her in the nude.

"When Dr. Orlanuk examines me," I told her, "he uses this kind of forceps thing to—"

"Oh, stop it! Just stop. I actually don't want to know. I'll be finding out soon enough on my own."

"Okay," I said, turning on the blinker as we neared the turnoff to Maple Rise. "But it's not that bad, I promise you. Just think how many women Dr. Orlanuk has examined over the course of his professional career. He probably thinks about it the same way a mechanic does looking under the hood of a car. It's nothing to—"

"Mo-om, please." Rachel sighed. She turned to look out the passenger window as we passed Luke's place, and we both fell silent. How much did she know about what had happened between Luke and Paul and me? Up until a year or so ago he'd been a part of our family—an infrequent visitor, true, but nonetheless beloved by my three daughters with far more abandon than they'd ever displayed to any of their often-seen uncles. It seemed to me that their nascent femininity was drawn to his hardened separateness, that lone wolf wariness that has made so many women want to tame him, comfort him, draw him inside the circle of domestic life. To be fair, he'd been unfailingly attentive to each of my daughters, recognizing their differences in a way that touched my heart as little else about him could. He was forthright and inquisitive with Rachel. Gentle and protective of Beanie. A willing playmate for Lia. My cynical side said—of course—they're girls, after all, and he knows exactly how to appeal to them.

Another part of me knew that he must have loved them then and missed them now. I felt a guilty surge of triumph at the thought. All the things Luke didn't have, that I did. Paul. My three lovely daughters. Our home. A job that was giving me a new and growing sense of self and well-being. And, I admit it, all these successes were made sweeter to me by the fact that Luke, once so superior and aloof, had seen his own life fail in so many fundamental ways.

If Rachel was thinking about Luke, too, she showed no sign of it as I downshifted on my way up the curving driveway, and his property disappeared behind a wall of green.

I was pleased to see the Zellers' Lexus was already parked in the turn-around next to a white van that I recognized as belonging to Eric Benson, a building inspector who does a lot of work on properties Nana has brokered and who serves with Paul on the town planning board. Richard and Eric emerged from the woods as I parked.

"This won't take a minute," I told Rachel as I climbed out of the car.

"Maddie, how're you doing?" Eric asked, holding out his hand when we all met on the front path. "How's Paul?"

"We're great," I told him. "And you guys?" I turned to Richard, but he was staring past me down the hill.

"Good, fine. Well, actually, Lori is kind of at loose ends these days since the boys left . . . ," he began, but, glancing at Richard and no doubt sensing as I did his irritation at our small talk, cut himself short. "Are you coming through with us?" he asked.

"No, I'm just going to let you in," I told him, digging out the keys from a side pocket of my bag, as we started toward the front door. "I've some errands to run. Leave these on the kitchen counter, if you don't mind, and I'll drop by and close things up a little later. You should find everything in great shape."

"I bet," Eric said, adding kindly: "Goes without saying if Frank and Paul had a hand in the construction."

I saw Richard's attention sharpen. He turned to me and was about to say something, when he was distracted by voices behind us on the drive. I turned with him to see Anne, Katie, and Max standing by the passenger side of my car talking to Rachel. I heard Anne's distinctive laugh.

"Anne, can we please get a move on here, please?" Richard called over to her, though I think he wanted both Eric and me to understand that his ill humor encompassed the two of us, as well. I quickly opened the door and then turned back to Eric.

"Thanks," I said. "Say hi to Lori for me."

Richard was facing backward toward Anne and the car, so he didn't see Eric roll his eyes as he took the keys from me. "Same to Paul," he added, then he went on into the house with Richard at his heels.

I walked back to the car and around to the passenger side. Anne and Katie flanked Max, who was leaning into the car with both arms extended, talking excitedly to Rachel.

"It's a frog," Katie told me in an awed whisper.

"It's a toad, actually," Rachel told her. "Frog's are usually greener and shinier. You see how brown and sort of dry this one is? That's so he blends in with the dead leaves and twigs and things, and people can't find him."

"I found him, though," Max said.

"Hi there," Anne said, turning to me with a smile. Then she did something I was not at all prepared for: she leaned over and kissed me on the cheek. I could feel myself blushing, which I knew was ridiculous. New Yorkers probably embrace each other all the time. I've noticed how touchy-feely Nana is with so many of her clients. We're a lot more standoffish here.

"As you can see, we've forced ourselves upon Rachel," Anne added, moving back. "But I can't believe you're old enough to have a teenaged daughter already, Maddie! And so beautiful! I would have known she was yours in a second, though, she looks just like you."

Rachel smiled shyly up at Anne, and then held her cupped hands out to Max and said: "Here you go. Mr. Toad says he'd prefer to be with you. Now take good care of him and make sure he gets plenty of bugs to eat."

"Why don't you come play with us?" Max asked Rachel, reclaiming his prize, its scrawny legs scrabbling against the front of his T-shirt.

"Another time," I said for Rachel. "I'm sorry, but we've got to run now. We're already late for an appointment in Northridge."

"You're leaving so soon?" Anne asked. "But we just got here, Maddie. I had a million things I wanted to talk to you about. But, of course, what am I thinking? This is probably your one day off to get your own things done. And we've already held you up. Max, Katie—come on—say good-bye to Rachel.

I'm sure we'll see her again. In fact—I don't know how busy you are, Rachel, but would you consider doing some babysitting for us this summer?"

"I'm not a baby," Katie said.

"Sure, I'd like that," Rachel told her. "In the evenings, anyway. I'm working for my aunt during the day."

"Terrific," Anne said, walking with me around to the driver's side. "I hope we haven't made you late for wherever it is you're going. And thanks so much for coming by and opening up for us. I can't tell you how excited we all are about the house—especially now that we've discovered it has toads! I mean, what more could we possibly ask for? Let's talk again on Monday, okay?"

"I'm really sorry to have to run. But I'll be back to lock up—"

"Anne! *Anne*, will you get the hell in here!" Richard Zeller was standing on a small bedroom balcony on the second floor, his hands planted angrily on his heavy hips. Once again, he was dressed as though he'd come from a business meeting—or was going to one—though he'd taken off his suit jacket and rolled up his shirtsleeves. Sweat flattened and darkened the fabric under his arms and his forehead glistened beneath his thinning hair. He seemed to loom above us, oversized and slightly ridiculous, like the giant in "Jack and the Beanstalk." But I sensed even then that he was far from harmless, that his blustery impatience was merely obscuring some darker, heavier discontent. How, I wondered, did someone as considerate and friendly as Anne end up with such a domineering and self-centered man? It was none of my business, I told myself, but I couldn't help feeling that she deserved better.

The Zellers were gone by the time Rachel and I drove back to the house after the appointment with Dr. Orlanuk and shopping at Price Chopper and Wal-Mart. Rachel had insisted that I leave the room when Dr. Orlanuk examined her, but she emerged from the ordeal in her usual good spirits, though refusing to discuss the details. I filled a prescription for some pain relief medication he'd written for her and that, I was given to understand, was the extent to which I'd be permitted to become involved with the situation. Like her father, Rachel greets the world with easygoing humor, but it's a guise, one that's hard to penetrate. Push a little too hard, ask a question too many, and you bump up against the stone wall behind which their true feelings lie. A barricade upon which I've battered and bruised myself too many times. It's a family trait, I think, an Alden thing. Bob and Ethan are like that, too. Hail-fellows-well-met, friendly to all, known by only a few.

I'm the opposite, really. I'm reserved initially when I first meet someone. Wary and self-conscious. I see a lot of myself in Beanie, though not to her extreme. But then, when I begin to feel more confident and appreciated, my feelings start to unfurl like a morning glory on a warm summer day. I long to be known then—and to know. Paul once told me that he thought I was "greedy for intimacy." Does it come from being a lonely only child? From having older, reserved, and emotionally distant parents? Of course, to some degree. But I think it's impossible to know for sure what makes us what we are, what alchemy of pain and joy, loss and longing, turns one person into a caregiver—and another into a liar.

Rachel came in with me to get the keys and I gave her a tour of the sun-filled empty house with its gleaming floors and soaring ceilings. It smelled of sanded wood and fresh paint. Our footsteps echoed up the uncarpeted stairs. We stood together at the balcony looking down on the enormous living room with the fireplace that took up almost an entire wall. I still couldn't conceive of living there, having a big enough sense of self and entitlement to make such a room feel familiar, everyday. But I could imagine Anne here. I could hear her calling down to her children—something silly and endearing.

"I think *she's* beautiful," Rachel said out of the blue. Neither one of us had mentioned Anne directly all afternoon, but it was as if she'd been reading my thoughts.

"I do, too," I said.

4

"I'm showing the Oak Hill property at three to the new people," I told Paul as we pretended to have a sit-down breakfast with the girls. In fact, we were all springing up from the table at different moments—to get the orange juice or milk or another cup of coffee—the usual carnival act the five of us perform every morning. "Then, at six, I'm taking the Pattersons back to that house in Lakeview. I just know they're getting ready to bite. I'm hoping you can pick up the girls again."

"Oak Hill?" Paul asked, lowering the *Rambler*. It was the last of the three spec houses he'd built for Nicky Polanski over the past two years and, since the Maple Rise sale, one of Nana's hottest properties. "You really are getting up there in the world, aren't you?"

"I told you about them—the Naylors. Anne Zeller referred me. Apparently, he owns a media buying company in the city. From what I can tell on the phone, they're really, really loaded. It's an interesting thing, but when I describe houses to my regular kind of buyer the first thing they ask is the price. But the Naylors? Their most pressing concern seems to be how many full bathrooms the house has. A fun fact for all you real estate mavens."

Yes, I was flying high. I was getting up there in the world. In the ten days that had elapsed since the Zeller closing, my professional life had taken off. Sure, it helps that it's early summer, the best possible time to sell. Tourists and weekenders are streaming back into the area. The days are long, sun-filled, not yet too hot or humid. The peonies and lilacs are in full flower, the lawns that deep, spring-fed, beckoning green. The sight of a screened porch, flaking and rust-worn, that in the cold light of winter would certainly give a prospective buyer pause, on an early June morning, with a wisteria vine clinging to its sagging gutters, will suddenly flood that same person with some latent romantic yearning, short-circuiting what had been up until that moment a methodical, no-nonsense search. Whatever the reason, I now have urgent offers from clients who've been dithering for months about buying. I have three sales in negotiation along my usual lines—local, lower-income buyers whose concerns are primarily financing and taxes. And then I have the Naylors.

"You came highly recommended by Anne Zeller," Rudy Naylor told me when he called the week before. "I took her to lunch yesterday and, along with the rest, she told me about that new house you sold them. Sounds like just the kind of thing we're looking for. I can't take that commute to Amagansett another summer. Two hours from the city, that's the limit for me now."

Nana seems delighted. Surprised, but obviously pleased for me. If she considers her work behind the scenes the real reason the Zeller sale ultimately went through so smoothly—and the Naylors rightfully hers—she keeps it to herself.

"You're definitely on a roll," she told me. "I think you should just go with it for now. You can let some of my paperwork slide for the time being. Who knows? If things keep up at this pace, maybe we can talk about putting on another person. An assistant we all can share."

I'm not used to feeling this lucky, to being on a winning streak, or whatever. Paul and I learned early on to be cautious and practical, to keep our expectations in check. So I'm not entirely sure I like this giddy sensation, or the more keyed-up, chattier me it seems to induce. In fact, I've been so self-involved the past week or so, working late, and letting Paul pick up the slack, that I didn't even notice until he told me when I got home around nine the night before that Lia had been running a fever.

"She seemed a little droopy the last couple of days," he told me as he hurried behind me up the stairs. "Then she had a kind of meltdown at dinner, so I checked her temperature. It's one-oh-three."

"Oh, God. You should have called me at the office. I thought she was being kind of ornery. But I guess I just wrote it off to the weather." The heat and humidity had both started to climb into the seventies the day before, making everybody a little cranky. But Lia's usually impervious to external conditions. She'll splash around in the pond until her lips turn purple and she's shaking like a leaf, then kick up a fuss when I try to pull her out. She's the last to be coaxed in from the cold, or out of the sun. I should have known better.

"Mommymommymommy!" Paul had her in our bed, hemmed in by my needlepoint pillows, which she loves. Her fringe of bangs, cut short for the summer, had clumped into damp tendrils. Her eyes were glassy with unhappiness. She flung herself into my arms, crying: "Mommymommymommy!"

"Do you think we should call George?" Paul asked, sitting down beside me on the bed.

"No, let's wait," I told him as she burrowed between my breasts, her arms girdling me like a vise. Lia has always treated my body as if it was hers to do with what she wished, as though it was a thing—a refrigerator or couch, say—separate from me the person. "George'll just say to see how she's doing in the morning anyway. These things are usually worse at night."

"Mommymommymommy!" she sobbed, though I was beginning to realize she wasn't that sick, or was already getting better. I would have worried a lot more if she hadn't displayed these histrionics, if she'd lain mute and miserable in my arms. Lia is our drama queen, and she was playing true to form, milking the moment for all it was worth. I knew what she was angling for, and, more out of guilt than real concern, I intended to give it to her.

"Can't we let her sleep here tonight?" I asked Paul, who disapproves of the girls climbing into bed with us. He tries to pretend that it's because of his convictions about good parenting, though we both know his concerns are more self-serving. My husband may keep a tight rein on his emotions, but he lets his libido run wild and free when it comes to our lovemaking.

"Sure," he said, getting up with a sigh. He wasn't accustomed to putting in so much time with the girls, and I guessed he felt as exhausted as I did. So we slept with Lia between us, propped up on my throw pillows like some potentate flanked by palace guards, and we woke to find her fully recovered and demanding blueberry pancakes for breakfast.

"I'll pick up if you drop off," Paul said as he stood up and began to clear the table.

"Please, please, whoever comes to get us, please be on time this time," Rachel said through a curtain of parted hair that she'd divided into thirds and was starting to braid. "By five o'clock, I'm ready to start drowning some of those kids. Just put them in a sack like a bunch of kittens and lower them—"

"Rach," Beanie stopped her, "don't say that about kittens." Beatrice, shortened to Beanie by Rachel when she was a toddler, is my nature child. She loves all animals, but especially cats. We now officially have three in residence and are, I suspect, the unofficial headquarters for a motley crew of strays that Beanie feeds on the sly out behind the barn.

"I mean it, though," Rachel replied. "Some of these new kids are just impossible. Spoiled like you wouldn't believe. Like that girl Tova who told Aunt Kathy that she was fat and stupid, and that her house was a dump."

"Who is this Tova person?" Paul asked, as he poured the rest of the coffee into his thermos.

"Some snotty little city kid," Rachel said, pinning her braids back so they formed a kind of garland on the top of her head. She looked like Juliet, I thought, in her cotton peasant blouse with its embroidered yoke and belled sleeves.

"We don't talk about other people like that in this family," Paul said, looking directly at Rachel. "I don't care how they act. It's not our place to judge or criticize. You got that?" His reprimands are often like bolts from the blue, frightening in their intensity and unexpectedness. Afterward, I usually realize that he was right to discipline the girls in whatever way he had, that I hadn't been paying close enough attention to what they were saying or doing, or even that I'd given tacit approval to something he considered bad behavior. In general, though, I think of my daughters as good-natured and well-meaning. But, for reasons that I understand and forgive, Paul is continually monitoring them for flaws and prejudices and remains ever vigilant about keeping them on the straight and narrow.

"Yes, Daddy," Rachel said. "I'm sorry about what I said. But I have to tell you that sometimes I have to work really hard to keep my temper with that crew."

"Good practice for the grown-up world," Paul said.

The Naylors swept in and out of Oak Rise in about twenty minutes. Rudy Naylor was in his midsixties, I guessed: short, trim, evenly tanned, with a head of shiny black hair that looked like it had been shellacked on. She was a petite blonde of indeterminable age with a perfect nose and expressionless eyes, pouty lips and porcelain teeth. They seemed unhappy, I thought, or at least preoccupied. The temperature was hitting the low eighties by the time they arrived, and he kept his white BMW idling so that the two tiny pug-faced dogs in the backseat could pant away in air-conditioned comfort. From their brief asides, I got the feeling that they cared more about the dogs than for each other or the elegant showcase house they were wandering through.

"This could be a home office or a media room," I pointed out when we reached the third floor, with its stunning views of the Catskills in the distance. "Or another bedroom, of course."

"Do you think you should go down and check on them?" she asked him, as though I hadn't spoken.

"No, we're nearly done here. I just wish to hell you'd remembered to bring their water bowls. You know they don't like drinking out of plastic cups. And on a day like this . . ."

I had no idea how they really felt about the house when they left, though he shook my hand with what seemed like forceful sincerity.

"Terrific property. Great value. You know what something like this would be going for in the Hamptons?" And then, perhaps realizing that I was not the right person to be confiding in about what a steal the place was, he abruptly opened the car door and muttered: "We'll be in touch."

I ran the showing past Nana, who summed it up succinctly:

"They're seeing other brokers. Getting a sense of who has what. That's fine. From what you've told me, though, Oak Hill is perfect for them. My gut says they'll be back."

A little past four, Marge Patterson called to say that Gary had gotten tied up at work and that they'd have to reschedule. Briefly, I was tempted to call Paul and tell him I'd pick up the girls, and then I thought about all the filing that needed to be done. I was walking down the hall to Nana's office to unload her out-box when the front door opened and Anne Zeller walked in with Max and Katie in tow. She was wearing a flower-splashed sarong cover-up and silver sandals. The kids were in their bathing suits.

"Hey there! I'm so sorry to ambush you like this at work. I know how busy you probably are. But remember a couple of weeks back when we were talking about the area and you mentioned a swimming pond where everybody goes? Well, we spent the whole day dealing with movers and deliveries. And I think we're going to just wither away and die if we don't find some nice cold water to jump into."

"Hello, Anne," said Nana, who'd come out of her office.

"Hello," Anne replied. "I was hoping Maddie could give us directions to that local pond or lake or whatever. I brought along this map Maddie gave me at the closing—it's been a godsend really because I'm hopeless about directions. I was thinking maybe she could show me how to get there."

"Of course, Maddie would be happy to help," Nana told her. "And we both wanted to thank you for sending the Naylors our way. Referrals of that kind are the backbone of our business."

"Who wouldn't recommend Maddie?" Anne said. "She's just the best." It sounded like a perfectly cordial exchange. And yet, I sensed they didn't much like each other. There'd been an awkward moment at the closing when Anne made it clear that she felt that Nana, who'd come along to give me moral support, was talking too much and wasting everybody's time. Nana does tend to go on, but then frankly sometimes so does Anne, so perhaps that's part of the problem.

On the other hand, I can understand Nana's misgivings: Anne opted to work with me instead of her. Who wouldn't be a bit hurt about that? Especially because, on the face of it, Anne is much more Nana's kind of person than mine. Or their backgrounds are similar, at any rate. But there's clearly something about Nana that seems to put Anne off. Or is it something about me she simply likes more? Perhaps it's because we're both mothers, whose concerns a childless professional like Nana has very little sympathy for.

"My six o'clock had to reschedule," I told Nana. "And the pond's really not something you can find easily on the map. How about if I take off a little early and drive Anne up there?"

"Absolutely," Nana said. "Good to see you again, Anne. When you and Richard get settled in, Dan and I want to have you over for dinner."

"Oh, that would be so nice," Anne said, and then, turning to me, she asked: "Should we follow you, or what? And how about your kids? Would they like to come along, too? Max and Katie just fell in love with Rachel."

So I called Paul and told him I'd get the girls after all, and Anne followed me in her car, a silver Volvo SUV that I'd never seen before, as I picked up my daughters from Kathy's and then took the back way to Indian Pond. It's up a winding dirt road that is badly rutted in places and with a steep gradient on some of the final curves at the top of the mountain, but whenever I checked in my rearview, Anne was right behind me. My girls seemed excited by the unexpected turn of events, as we rarely get a swim in on weekdays, and we arrived in a festive mood at the little sandy beach that the town maintains. The place was deserted, except for an extended family of geese that raised a honking racket when Max chased them into the water. In the summertime, I keep a tote bag full of bathing suits and towels in the back of the car for just this sort of occasion, and my daughters and I changed in the little bungalow in the woods built expressly for this purpose, but often used at night for other, less innocent, activities.

Myths and rumors abound about Indian Pond. Spring-fed, about five acres altogether, it's surrounded by birches, maples, evergreens, and glacial outcroppings. There's some historical evidence that the Mahicans, who had lived in the area for hundreds of years before the first white trappers and missionaries arrived, had a settlement here, or at least hunted and fished in the vicinity. But the story about the Indian maiden who drowned herself after being abandoned by her white lover is surely a fabrication, though good fodder for campfire stories. And yet, I'm not sure why, there does seem to be something a little haunted about the place. Perhaps, for me, it has to do with all the memories of summers past. This is where I learned to swim, where I broke my collarbone roughhousing with my boy cousins, where I smoked my first cigarette with Terry MacElderry and got sick in the marshy underbrush. This is where I stood shivering while a half mile away a tornado cut a path of pure destruction through the woods and into town. And, of course, this is where I used to come with Paul. Though I've hiked up here in the fall and cross-country skied in the winter, it's really a summer place. Its essence is sun-dappled and transitory. This is where my parents and grand-parents, all gone now, picnicked and swam and dove off the rocks. And it seems to me that sometimes I can almost hear their largely forgotten voices echoing across the water.

"God, that was just wonderful!" Anne said, spreading out her towel be-side me on the sand. I mostly go in the pond for short dips because I chill so easily, and I was even quicker than usual that day, overly conscious of my thighs. I'd been watching Anne, who was in great shape, do laps, and the children, led by Rachel, play Marco Polo in the shallows. They seemed a par-ticularly good combination of ages and needs. Max clearly admired Rachel, obeying her every command with glee, which made Lia, often truculent, fall into line. And Beanie, usually standoffish with strangers, entered right into the game, perhaps flattered by Katie's obvious attempts to win her approval.

"Richard's talking about putting in a pool," Anne went on as she ran her fingers through her short damp hair. It was darker wet, accentuating the planes of her face. Her cheekbones were high and rounded and her eyes had an upward-slanting, almost exotic cast. "But I'm going to talk him out of it. This is what swimming's all about, do you know what I mean?"

"Yes," I said, pulling the towel around my legs. I felt suddenly tongue-tied. Up until then, my relationship with Anne had been professional and clearly defined. Though we'd discussed many different things besides Maple Rise, the sale of the house had been the reason we talked on the phone every day, and often several times. I'd felt secure in that role, useful, almost on par with Anne in the sense that we were on opposite sides of an equation: broker and buyer. Now, where were we? Money, education, lifestyles—so many things separated us that I wouldn't know where or how to begin to bridge the divide. And it wasn't just our societal differences. Sitting beside her on the beach, I realized that I wasn't able to match her level of energy, her volatile spirit. Her effervescence made me feel dull. It had been a long day for me, and I hadn't slept well the night before with Lia in our bed. In truth, I was too tired to try to find new common ground with Anne. I felt that we'd reached the end of something.

"By the way, I showed the Naylors that place up on the hill behind yours today," I told her. "I don't think they're going to go for it—but, just in case they do, I hope you don't mind them being so close."

"Why should I?" Anne asked.

"Well, I don't know. I just assume you want to come up here to escape. Forget about work. Don't you do business with Rudy Naylor in the city?"

"Not anymore. That's what I've been waiting to tell you!" she said, turning to me on her towel. "I've got the best news. I've been dying to talk to you about this, actually, but I didn't finally decide until last Friday. F and M lost a big account, Haverford Athletics, as a matter of fact. I think I mentioned to you that things seemed to me to be going downhill fast with them. In any case, the agency brass asked if anyone was interested in a sabbatical. Probably just for the summer, until they get some new business. And I decided to take them up on it. I mean, why not? Richard's got more work than he can handle. In fact, he's adding people as we speak. Plus, I could really use a break. Time with the kids. Pull the new house together. I don't think anybody realizes how hard it is sometimes—"

When her voice faltered, I looked over at her. Anne's eyes were bright with tears. I felt a rush of sympathy and concern.

"What is it?" I asked, touching her arm. She shook her head mutely, laying her hand on mine, then took a deep breath and exhaled.

"How hard it is. With the kids. Wanting to be there for them, but having to drag myself off into the business world every day. Richard doesn't really understand. But the truth is, Maddie: it's been hard, hard, hard! I just feel so torn at times, so unhappy, do you know what I mean? Of course you do—I don't need to tell you. Sometimes I think I would have been a lot happier just being a plain old-fashioned housewife. So I guess I get to find out now if that's true or not. Isn't this just great?"

"Yes," I told her, though I wasn't sure she really thought so herself. Underneath her seeming enthusiasm, I sensed that she was still trying to sell herself on the idea. And a part of me wondered if she'd really thought through what she was giving up: the freedom a life outside the home gives you, that enlarged sense of self. But then I was new to work and Anne had been at it for a long time and in a much more demanding and competitive arena. Still, I sensed that her decision to take time off was more complicated than she was letting on. I also saw that it served to level the playing field between us again. In a way, Anne was choosing my old existence over hers. She was opting out. Her world would be what mine had been for so many years: bounded by the needs of others. For the first time since I met her, I thought I finally had a sense of what her life would be like day to day.

"There was something else I wanted to talk to you about," Anne said, cradling her knees as she turned to me with a smile. "The man who has that crazy place at the bottom of our drive?"

"Yes?" I said, when she didn't go on, though her head remained tilted in a question. "What about him?"

"Well, what's his story again? I mean, is he an artist of some kind? He makes those things he has out on the lawn, right? I've slowed down a few times when we drove past, hoping he'd come over and at least say hello—but I can tell he's ignoring me for some reason."

"The best thing to do is just leave him alone, Anne," I told her. "He's a very private person. A recluse now, really. But, if you don't bother him, you won't even know he's there. He's really—" I stopped myself, though I wanted to say more. I heard the tension in my voice and felt it in my body.

I realized how much I wanted to keep Luke locked away in the past—where I kept him in my own mind—safely out of reach of all those I held dear. It made me anxious thinking of him in the present—and particularly unsettling to consider how close he was living to Anne and her kids.

"But didn't you tell us he came from some wealthy family?" Anne continued. "I know you said that they settled this whole area."

"A couple of hundred years ago, yes," I replied. A cloud was cutting off the sunlight, and I felt cold suddenly, uncomfortable in my damp bathing suit. But the chill went deeper than that. A gust of wind rippled across the pond, and I felt a shiver of foreboding. "They're all gone now. Except Luke. And, believe me, he's nothing but a burned-out case. Not someone you'd want to get to know. I promise."

She turned away from me again and looked back out across the water. The children were still splashing and laughing, but she didn't seem to notice. Her thoughts seemed to be on something else entirely.

Part Two

5

I suppose every place on earth has its own version of royalty. For us, it was the Barnett family. They had the necessary money, property, background, and good looks to make them thoroughly enviable. And they were visited by enough unhappiness to have their special status burnished by our pity and curiosity and endless speculation. Though I never once got to see Mrs. Barnett in the flesh, I felt I knew enough about her from overhearing my parents' conversations and piecing together what I could from my mother's phone calls with friends and relatives to formulate my own mental picture of her.

"Stark naked on the front lawn."

"No, I hear it's drugs this time."

"Third miscarriage, I believe. But are you surprised? The abuse that woman puts her body through."

"No wonder they send that boy away to boarding school."

"Howell's up to his old tricks. He stopped by the store with some blonde in the car." This last was a contribution from my father, the store in question being Heinrich Hardware, which my father inherited from my mother's father and where, for most of my early teenage years, I spent my summers and several afternoons a week stocking the shelves and helping to run the cash register. In the mid-1980s in our rural backwater, this was more my father's attempt to keep me out of trouble than to provide me with actual gainful employment.

"John," my mother said, looking across the kitchen to where I sat at the table, supposedly doing my homework. But I'd seen the woman in Mr. Barnett's Porsche myself that afternoon as I was rearranging our display of batteries and flashlights in the front of the store, so there was no point in trying to shelter me from the knowledge that Howell Barnett was, to coin a favorite phrase of my mother's, a womanizer. Or that Mrs. Barnett was an addict and a drunk. For me, in those slow, slumbering years when I was still under my parents' cautious sway, these vices were pure abstractions to me anyway, as glamorous and unreal as those of movie stars. Born when my parents were both in their midforties and had long since given up on having a child, I was the shy, pudgy miracle that they dedicated their lives to pampering and protecting. I knew, of course, that Mr. Barnett was bad, but that only served to make him more interesting to me. His expansive personality, the fug of smoke and whiskey that clung to him like cologne, and the way he so clearly got under my father's skin turned him into an object of fascination.

"I'm looking for a corkscrew, sweetheart," Mr. Barnett told me, his right fist tapping on the countertop like a gavel, while his left hand jingled the change in the pants pockets of his beautifully tailored, dark blue pin-striped suit. Along with everything else, he was a partner in a well-connected Albany law firm, one that specialized in government contracts, in wheel greasing, in settling unpleasantnesses out of court. He projected the nonchalance of the entitled, the goodwill of the easily liked. Under it all was an unbridled and reckless masculinity, the kind that made some women blush just because he looked at them. No, because he looked at me—fourteen and overweight, full of gauzy fantasies and inarticulate longings.

"Hey there, Howell," my father said, hurrying down the cluttered aisle from the back storeroom. "What can we do you for?" Uncomfortable with just about everybody but his immediate family, my father tended to make up for it by being folksy and overly friendly with his customers. I knew that if he'd had his way, he'd speak only to my mother and me and even then in gruff monosyllables.

"As I was telling this lovely young lady," Howell said, his smile still on me, "I'm looking for a corkscrew."

"Well, this happens to be a hardware store, Howell."

"I'm aware of that actually. But I thought by chance you might carry them. I personally consider a corkscrew one of the more essential pieces of hardware in life." I heard someone giggling at this, realized it was me, and turned to stare furiously out the window. There was the blonde, the visor on the passenger side of the car lowered, reapplying lipstick.

"Sorry. You'll have to look elsewhere. Northridge Wine and Liquor should stock them. Although I imagine you must have several"—my father's gaze followed mine—"at home."

There was no love lost between Howell Barnett and my father, though I think it was pretty much one-sided. I doubt Mr. Barnett registered John Fedderson as being much of an entity separate from his hardware store, while my father fulminated against what he imagined were Mr. Barnett's politics, his coziness with the lazy, liberal Cuomo administration, and his patently loose morals and spendthrift ways. He was the kicking object for a large number of my father's frustrations, so when Howell Barnett died suddenly two weeks after that appearance in our store, suffering a massive coronary while driving home at night on the interstate, I believe my father felt as bereft and cheated as any of what turned out to be Mr. Barnett's many creditors.

Apparently he owed everybody money, with the exception, of course, of my father, who demanded cash on the counter. From what we heard he'd left his affairs in a shambles, dying intestate, leaving his family to deal with a number of shaky investment schemes that seemed just this side of legal. The whole house of cards collapsed with the 1987 stock market crash, sweeping Mrs. Barnett and the Barnetts' only child, Luke, then sixteen, into bankruptcy. With the help of longtime old-money connections, they managed to hold on to the beautiful center-hall Colonial that had been in the Barnett family for over 250 years, and more than two hundred acres of rolling, cultivated farmland and hilly woods, but that was about it. Luke, who'd been at Phillips Exeter when his father died, came home for the funeral and then, about six months later, when it became clear that his mother wasn't functioning and that his expenses could no longer be met, came back for good. He'd been a shadowy figure in my mind up until then, a slim, silent passenger in the backseat of one of his father's luxury automobiles who seemed as disinterested in us as we were intrigued by him.

His unfortunate circumstances automatically conferred upon him a kind of heroic status, though he seemed intent on trying to blend in at the local high school, which he entered halfway through his junior year, when I was just a freshman. He wore the equivalent of our school uniform: jeans, faded flannel shirt, work boots. But he eschewed the backward-facing Red Sox cap and let his fair hair grow unfashionably long for that period. I have a vivid memory of seeing him, warming up for a track meet that spring, whippet-thin, flipping his hair back off his face.

The truth was that I thought about him almost obsessively when he first joined the high school. He was handsome, mysterious, tragic, and so far out of reach. His aloofness made me feel inferior. I never considered the fact that he might have been shy, confused, even ashamed. It's taken me far too many years to be able to think of him objectively, apart from my own intense and complicated feelings. At that point, all I was sure about was that he would never be mine. So I told myself that I didn't want him. I suppose if I had been able to more honestly assess the inner workings of my heart, I would have detected some of my father's defensive posturings toward Luke's father, Howell; that need to wrap oneself in a protective layer of dislike.

So I decided that there was something a little feminine about him, with his finely chiseled features and delicate hands. I concluded that he was actually too handsome for his own good: those startling blue eyes, the ridiculously long lashes, that wide, ironic grin. In fact, he was really not at all my type. I prided myself that I was just about the only girl in the school who didn't make a fool of herself over Luke Barnett, who didn't squeal with delight when he'd cross the finish line in first place, race after race. Though as a tough, competitive runner, he helped lead our usually hapless team into the interleague semifinals that season.

That was the same year my plump obscurity metamorphosed into a generous reapportioning of flesh, a sudden rise of curves, a flow of limbs and hair and obliviousness that made me, for a year or two at least, a beauty. Or so I was told, because I could never really see it myself, except in the frank leering of boys or the sideways measuring looks from girls. I think sometimes that it was Howell Barnett who first caught a glimpse of it and who—with an ambiguous smile that remains in my memory—helped loose some pent-up urge within me to shrug off my parents' confining expectations, to push free, to emerge as something wholly other than anyone, least of all myself, expected.

Everyone we knew back then seemed to be struggling financially. The dairy industry, once the backbone of our local economy, had turned to larger, more mechanized farm machinery, not adaptable to our hilly terrain, and the bulk of that business was slowly moving northward to the big cooperatives upstate. One spring, a freak blizzard in early May froze the delicate blossoms in fragrant bloom, wiping out an entire apple and pear crop and forcing Powell's Orchard, a third-generation concern and the largest in the county, to shut down. Like any impending death, no one wanted to face it, or to call it by its real name. And because the attrition was gradual, it was possible to pretend that the slow periods in the store were seasonal, that the FOR SALE signs dotting our back roads had sprouted up as arbitrarily as mushrooms in the thick summer heat and would disappear just as suddenly with the first real frost.

"Dandridge Alden's last check bounced," my mother, who handled the store's accounts from our kitchen table, told my father one night over dinner. It was early September, the year after Howell Barnett died, and I was too immersed in my own preoccupations to understand the gravity of her statement. At that point the Alden Dairy still had a herd of several hundred Holsteins and a primarily local distribution. A glass quart bottle of their 100% homogenized milk with its cartoon logo of a smiling green cow sat on the dining room table at that very moment beside the paper-napkin rack.

"Not like him," my father said, looking over at my mom and frowning. "He's always been such a stickler."

"I'll call them tomorrow and straighten things out. But I thought you should know. They'll be putting in their winter feed order soon."

"Right."

"You don't want to lose him to the True Value like you did with the Thornsteins."

"And I don't want to lose the shirt off my back handing out credit right and left either!"

"Well, it may be one or—"

They both appeared to realize at the same moment that I was there, listening, my gaze moving back and forth between them as they conducted one of their increasingly frequent arguments. I could remember years during my childhood when their voices never seemed to rise above a murmur. Now I was being treated to these sudden blowups several times a month, and, frankly, found this hothouse atmosphere a lot more interesting.

"County fair starts Saturday," my father said, taking me in with his welcoming gaze. So much else about him appeared tired and gray to me, prematurely aged, but his eyes belied his seeming passivity. My mother and I, at least up until then, were God's proof to him that the world indeed had some good in it. And though he was generally terse and unbending, I never once doubted his deep, almost religious love for us. He was a man, hating all forms of confrontation, about to be forced into the fight of his life. I'm not sure how thoroughly he grasped what was happening, how the darkening heavens crested above us like a tidal wave. "Want to help me canvass with our circulars?"

He put this to me as though he were offering me a treat, and for many years it had seemed that way to me as I proudly accompanied him from booth to booth, passing out Heinrich Hardware promotional flyers. Now, though, it wasn't just that I'd reached that age when the thought of tagging along beside him across the very public fairgrounds made me queasy with embarrassment. That summer, I'd started spending more and more time with Ruthie Genzlinger, whose older brother Kenny had just received his driver's license and who could occasionally be pressured into driving us down to Northridge, where the high schoolers congregated in the parking lot behind Letham's Pharmacy. Though I'd been falling in love on a regular basis since I was ten or so, my passion for Kenny occupied me in an entirely new and obsessive way. His wavy black hair, the slightly close-set dark eyes, his eager bark of a laugh, even his horsey teeth with the buckling incisors— every piece of him was precious to me, jewels that I hoarded and sorted through again and again behind the locked door of my imagination.

"I already promised Ruthie I'd go with her." I'd been yearning for the moment when I could sit in the cab of the Genzlingers' wheezing pickup with just the gearbox separating me from my own true love. To be denied this seemed heartless and cruel. Something of my desperation must have come through in my voice.

"Can't you hook up with Ruthie after you've given your father a hand?" my mother asked.

"I don't want to force anybody," he said, getting up from the table. I saw how the cords on the back of his neck stuck out when he leaned over the sink. I sensed even then how difficult my growing up and away from him was going to be. My parents' mistake was in wanting nothing more from me other than being alive. Being theirs. I was taller than either one of them by that point. This precious gift, left on the doorstep of their middle age, taking on size and shape, becoming human, secretive and judgmental. I think they were both silently afraid that if they made too many demands or imposed discipline too strictly, I might very well be whisked away again. My birth had made them believe in the unfathomable workings of fate, if nothing else, and it resulted in them being overly diffident and accepting. I loved them, yes, but that wellspring was already tainted by a confusing sense of my own power over them.

"No, I'll help," I conceded. "But I did promise Ruthie. So I'll meet up with Dad there, if that's okay."

There were more rides that year. More booths selling grinders and funnel cakes, corn dogs and cotton candy. There was a three-story Ferris wheel and a crazy-eight roller coaster. The atmosphere was different, too, more carnival than fair. Though fewer than in previous years, there were still stalls of animals, and the large 4-H exhibit tent, but the bleachers in the judging arena were nearly empty, and the farmer leading his prize pig around the rink appeared to be embarrassed and maybe a little angry by the lack of attention. He was red-faced, muttering under his breath at the large, slow-moving sow.

"Guy looks just like his porker," Kenny said. Ruthie had gone off to buy us a roll of tickets, and, as I leaned against the fence next to Kenny watching the proceedings, I was reveling in my moments alone with him. I laughed at his comment, delighted that he had deigned to address me, though I hadn't put much thought into what he'd actually said. Encouraged, I suppose, by my reaction, he cried, "Oink, oink, oink!"

I looked up at him, the hands cupping his mouth, the large wrists shooting free of the too-short sleeves of his jean jacket, the close-set eyes squinting in the sunlight, and I felt my adoration, like a trick of the heat on macadam, puddle and waver.

"Oink, oink, oink!"

"What are you doing?" I heard someone say behind us, and I turned around to see who it was. I knew Paul Alden, of course. He was in Kenny's class, two years ahead of me in school. They were both seniors, therefore rarified creatures, whose daily lives and deeper aspirations I could only guess at. Like every class, the seniors had their own finely calibrated pecking order, and though I believed fiercely in Kenny's perfection, I was aware that Paul ranked far above him in social status. Paul was a natural athlete, one of the school's few real stars, and a double threat: a hard-charging fullback in the fall and a slugging left fielder in the spring. He was part of the big, rowdy Alden family. The Alden family, who always seemed to travel in a pack, surrounded by a posse of acolytes and girlfriends, lesser beings who fed off their good-natured hosts. Kenny, on the other hand, was pretty much a loner. He spent his afternoons rebuilding car engines in the Genzlingers' collapsing horse barn.

"Hey. We were just joking around," Kenny said, stepping back from the fence and facing Paul. If I was startled that he'd included me in his questionable behavior, I was proud that he seemed willing to defend himself against Paul, who had at least twenty pounds on him. There was something else in his stance that I didn't understand until later on.

"Okay," Paul said, looking past Kenny to me.

"Hey there," Ruthie said, flushing with pleasure when she saw who had joined us. "I got thirty tickets. Why don't you come along, Paul?"

"Sorry. I got to go help out with the hayride. My dad's running it this year."

"Oh, great!" Ruthie said, walking beside Paul as we all moved off toward the crowded north end of the fairgrounds, with its flashing colored lights and the jangly music of the merry-go-round. "We'll come by there later."

I'm not sure at what point we stopped being a threesome, when it was that Ruthie drifted away and I found myself being strapped into a seat on the Ferris wheel, thigh to thigh with Kenny Genzlinger. We rose up into the bright fall afternoon, above the barbecue smoke and the clanging of bells, the bouquets of helium balloons and menageries of cheap stuffed animals, higher and higher into the rocking, deepening blue until, alone at the top, Kenny kissed me, his breath full of onions and his tongue a slippery frog that made me gag.

"Ruthie says she thinks you like me."

"I never told her that."

"Well, I like you, Maddie. I think you have the most beautiful hair I've ever seen."

Ah, Kenny! If only he knew how often in my daydreams about him I'd put those very words in his mouth. But now they meant nothing to me. My love for him had turned to a lump in my throat. I'd claimed my prize, but it was like winning some huge stuffed panda with plastic button eyes. I felt weighed down by disappointment and shame. He made a grab for my hand as we disembarked, but I shook it free.

"My dad," I said. "I should find him. I told you I promised him . . ."

"Meet us at the hayride at six!" he called after me as I disappeared into the crowd.

I found my father talking to a John Deere sales representative, who was pointing out the finer features of one of the ten or so tractors they had arranged around their booth, one of the largest at the fair, hung with red, white, and blue bunting and snapping with American flags. We had eight acres climbing up the hill behind our house. A few generations back, they had been farmed. Two fields were still cleared and open, though covered in meadowsweet and goldenrod, their boundaries marked by jagged stone walls. We had a busy coop of chickens and a family of nasty geese, but I know it was my father's secret dream to get that land back under the plow. Farming was in the blood of many of the men I grew up with, the same way the sea calls to fishermen, I suppose.

"Here's my girl," Dad said as I came up, clasping his hands behind him and rocking backward on his heels. We rarely touched and never kissed, but I knew how to read his pleasure in seeing me, in my keeping a promise, however belatedly. "Mr. Schnarr here was just showing me their new PowerTrack model."

"Give it some thought, John," the man said, stepping back and sideways so that my father wouldn't notice the way his gaze slid down my body.

"Sure thing, but it probably won't be this year," Dad said, as we turned away. "Having a good time? Do you want something to eat?"

"Ruthie and I had a grinder. Where are the flyers, Dad?"

"Oh, I passed some out. Different kind of crowd this year, though. Not really our customer base, anymore, I'd say."

We walked side by side down the midway, jostled by the growing crowds that were lining up at the food booths for an early dinner. The air was thick with the smell of deep-fat fryers and burning onions, and a sickly sweet crosscurrent of honey-roasted nuts. The sky was turning pink above the whirling rush and whoop of the rides. The path was sodden, flecked with discarded ticket stubs and other trash. I hadn't wanted to be seen with my father earlier that day. Now I longed to tuck my fingers into the crook of his elbow the way my mother did when they walked into church. I was suddenly afraid of losing him. My heart had shrunk back down to a normal size over the course of the afternoon, and I'd come to realize that he was all I really understood about love.

The midway ended at an open field where stacks of hay bales formed a low platform, the staging area for the hayride. I could see the crowded wagon moving across the far edge of the field, being pulled by two plodding drays. My father joined the group of men who were gathered by an empty second wagon: Paul's father, Dandridge Alden; and Paul's brothers, Ethan and Bob; and two other men I didn't know. Except for Bob, who was a class below me in school, they were all smoking in a tense, concentrated way.

"When?" my father asked as I came up behind him.

". . . we had her on the respirator . . . ," Ethan was telling one of the other men.

"My boy's in the EMS now," Mr. Alden told my father. "They got the call around three or so, right, son?"

"Yessir," Ethan replied. "The kid called it in. Luke. Thought she was dead this time, I think. Sat up front with me in the cab. A real cool customer."

"Well, he's been through a lot," my father said.

"You can say that again," Mr. Alden replied, grinding his cigarette out under his boot. "Ethan gave him a lift back here. I asked him if he wanted to stay with us tonight, but he said he was fine."

"They pumped her stomach," Ethan was saying. "I heard it wasn't the first time."

"Don't repeat rumors, son," Mr. Alden told Ethan.

Our little group fell silent as the wagon approached. It was one of the Aldens' old rigs, a rickety affair swaying now under the weight of hay bales and paying customers. Ruthie was standing up in the back, chatting eagerly away at Paul, who sat slouched on the buckboard, the reins loose in his hands. Luke was next to him, an upright figure who, by his very stillness, stood out against the tumult and clamor of the fairgrounds, the lights brightening behind them as the evening came on. I believe it was the first time I saw them together, though I learned later on that they had been close for several months by this time. I've always had a hard time understanding what drew them together in the first place. They seemed so very different, even then.

6

"We're all going back to my house to watch the game, do you want to come?" Paul asked, leaning over and glancing from Kenny behind the wheel to where I sat curled up against the passenger door in the front seat of the pickup. Kenny and I had begun to vaguely "see" each other, the way Paul and Ruthie were doing, though I'd long since recovered my perspective on the gawky, beak-nosed boy beside me. Kenny, on the other hand, was "totally gone" on me, according to Ruthie. He treated me with an almost laughable respect and seriousness, holding open doors for me, presenting me with a tacky velvet-covered heart-shaped Whitman's Sampler, pushing the heat up full blast on the dashboard, as if I were some fragile, hothouse orchid. He obviously had no prior experience at dating and, I feared, was getting his tips on how to handle matters from his grandfather, Hans Genzlinger, the only other adult male in his household. Fortunately for me, old Mr. Genzlinger's romantic bag of tricks was about half a century out of date. Kenny never again tried to kiss me, the way he had on the Ferris wheel, and was generally too ill at ease in my company to engage in much conversation. So we did what Kenny was most comfortable doing; we drove around in his pickup, listening to Top 40 music on the radio.

"Sure. Thanks. I mean, is that okay with you?" Kenny asked, turning to me. I saw Paul smile at Kenny's tone. I knew Ruthie well enough at this point to guess that she was dishing her own brother to Paul, making fun of his puppylike adoration for me. It made me feel angry and protective. It was Ruthie, after all, who'd put poor Kenny in this pathetic position. If she hadn't told him about what I considered my secret crush, he'd be back fiddling around under car hoods, where, at this point in his life anyway, he belonged.

"Only if you want to, Kenny," I replied.

We followed Paul back to his house, his old VW wagon packed with his usual entourage of friends and hangers-on, including Ruthie and Luke. Everyone knew that Mrs. Barnett had been transferred to a mental institution in Albany, where she'd be staying for several weeks, and that Luke had turned down the Aldens' invitation to move in with them for the duration. But I'd learned from Ruthie that Luke was still spending a lot of time at the house, occasionally sleeping over in the unfinished attic, where, in a youthful male chaos so extreme Mrs. Alden had long since refused to clean it, the three Alden boys resided.

"He might as *well* be living there," Ruthie confided in one of the many heart-to-hearts she insisted on having with me. But the sorrier I felt for Kenny, the less I found myself being able to abide his sister, especially her need to share with me every little thing that transpired between her and Paul. I knew all about the three times they'd made out in the back of his VW, and though he'd made no attempt to go any further than that, Ruthie was already considering the pros and cons of various contraceptives. From what I could judge of their relationship, Paul seemed more to be putting up with, than pursuing, Ruthie. It was she who was attaching herself to him, waiting for him after football practice, setting up situations where they would meet—like that afternoon in the parking lot behind Letham's. She needed Kenny to drive her to these assignations, and because this generally allowed Kenny a chance to be with me, he was always willing. But I discouraged Kenny from getting pulled into Paul's orbit. We always parked on our own, away from the crowd that gravitated around Paul. I didn't think Paul was aware of any of this. The laughing, joking center of things, he seemed too active and involved to pay much attention to what was going on around him. But I know that Luke noticed; I was beginning to realize that there was very little that he missed.

"You're not much of a sports fan, are you?" He must have followed me out to the Aldens' kitchen. Everyone else was sitting around the living room, glued to the playoffs on television. Even Kenny hadn't been aware that I'd slipped away. I'd felt restless and unhappy, distracted by Ruthie, who was making a big production out of tickling and teasing Paul. He didn't seem to mind, but then, his attention was so transfixed by what was happening on the screen I'm not sure he even noticed. Paul, like all the Aldens, was a sports fanatic. He could rattle off baseball averages the way a preacher recites Scripture. Wade Boggs was his God, the Red Sox his religion, and every World Series in those years a terrible testing of his faith.

"Oh, well, I try to follow along," I said, alarmed to be alone and singled out in this way by Luke. Though we'd both taken part in larger, desultory general discussions, these were the first words we'd ever spoken just to each other. I felt him scrutinizing me, his long-lashed gaze taking me in with unfeigned curiosity.

"No, it's not just today," he said, shaking his head. "I've seen you sometimes on the sidelines. Your mind is somewhere else. What are you thinking about so hard, Maddie Fedderson?" He sounded a little like his father then. There was that element of provocation in his tone, though he lacked Mr. Barnett's affectionate bantering manner. It was more like he was drilling me, as though he expected—no, demanded—an answer. What I saw was his arrogance and his sense of superiority. I had no feeling, then or ever, really, for the hell he must have been going through, for how vulnerable and alone he must have felt. He was as sensitive as I was, I suppose, as inward and needy. And he was as careful as I to try to conceal these weaknesses. Maybe we were just too much alike.

"Why would you care?" I asked, surprised that what I had intended to be a playful rejoinder had come out sounding so harsh.

"Care? I'm not sure that's the right word. But I am puzzled. That's it, really. You're a puzzle. What the hell are you doing with poor Kenny? Do you enjoy leading someone like that around by his nose?"

"What makes you think you have any right to criticize—" I began, but he cut me off:

"Oh, I don't"—he held up both hands in surrender—"I don't have any rights. I'm well aware of that. But someone has to tell you that you're far too pretty—which I'm sure you already know—to be wasting your time on a boy like that. Face up to who you are. And what about him? Don't you see that you're making him into the school joke? It's like you're trying to help a bird with a broken wing. Leave him alone, Maddie. Let him flap away."

"You don't know anything about it," I told him, but he did. He knew everything. He'd gotten it all in one take. But what I couldn't understand was why he was bothering, what he wanted from me. Already, there was this sense of unease, of friction, between us. We didn't like each other. We were not attracted to each other. Even when he said he thought I was pretty, it wasn't a compliment. It was a jibe. It was just one more thing to throw in my face. I felt then, as I have so many times since, that he grasped the worst about me. He looked through the soft, compliant guise I presented to the world and saw my neediness, my loneliness, my hunger to belong.

"Maybe you're right," he said, cocking his head and smiling at me, as if the exchange had been nothing more than a little harmless kidding. His smile curved downward, self-deprecating and at the same time very knowing. I was flustered and angry, convinced that he was pleased with himself for provoking me in this way. We heard a roar from the living room—followed by a series of moans. By the time we got back out there, the game was over, and there was a general exodus under way.

"Paul said he'd drive us up to Albany to the movies," Ruthie said, coming up to me and Kenny, who was shrugging on his jean jacket in the front hall. Paul was behind her, standing by the open door as people started to leave. "But I know Ma won't let me go unless you come, too. She's still pissed off about the other night."

"I'm almost out of gas."

"Come with us in the VW," Paul said. "Everyone else is leaving."

I don't remember much about the first part of the evening except my growing irritation with Ruthie. She burbled away beside Paul in the front seat in a breathy, keyed-up voice she'd started to affect, fussing with the radio dial to find "Cold Hearted" or "Don't Wanna Lose You," her two current favorites, and turning around every minute or so to try to enlist me and Kenny in her nonstop antics.

"Isn't this fun? Isn't this great, just the four of us like this? Don't you love this beat-up old van, Maddie? It's like driving around in the Summer of Love, don't you think? And see what I mean about the back, right? Can't you imagine driving across the country in something like this? I'd love to do that someday. Wouldn't you love to do that, Maddie?"

"Sure," I said, staring in front of me into the highway traffic. It had just begun to snow, a freakish flurry, far too early in the season. Big sloppy flakes slapped against the windshield. I hadn't told my parents where we were going. All they knew was that I was with Ruthie for the evening. They trusted me, far too much for my own good. Their belief in my essential goodness weighed on me. I felt guilty and also frightened by what I now saw to be inevitable. Yes, of course, I had to let Kenny go. I had outgrown him and somehow grown up in a single afternoon. I didn't know what was wrong with me, but suddenly everything around me seemed impossibly sad. I glanced up and met Paul's gaze in the rearview mirror. It lasted just a moment, but it meant everything. Then we both looked away.

Ruthie was all over Paul at the movies; he just kept patting her arm, trying to get her to see that he was intent on what was up on the screen. We saw *Batman*. Or was it the latest Indiana Jones? It became something of a joke between us over the years that neither one of us could remember for sure. We stopped at a diner on the Taconic on the way home and had something to eat. But all the details are blurred now in my memory. By the time we got back to the Aldens', snowfall blanketed the fields and hills and bowed the branches of the evergreens. The house and barns and outbuildings were oddly dark.

"Power's out," Paul said, pulling up next to Kenny's pickup. "A tree must have come down on a wire somewhere. Kenny, you better drive Ruthie back. You're almost out of gas and the Feddersons' is all the way on the other side of town."

"I think I could make it," Kenny said.

"But if you don't? This isn't a good night to be stuck on the side of the road. I don't mind driving Maddie."

I remember the sound of the windshield wipers, the lights of Paul's van tunneling into oncoming snow. I don't think we actually spoke until Paul pulled up at the bottom of the driveway and braked, putting the car in Park.

"Probably not safe for me to try that hill in all this. These tires are pretty bald."

"That's okay. I can walk it from here."

"Maddie. Listen. I'm sorry . . ."

"Why?"

"Because I've been acting like an idiot. With Ruthie. I didn't know what else to do."

"I'm not sure I know what you mean."

"Yes, I think you do."

We turned to each other. He leaned over and ran his index finger down the side of my face in a gentle, almost brotherly way. It was hard to read his expression, cast as it was in deep relief by the headlights, but I could see that he wasn't smiling.

"But Ruthie is so crazy about you."

"You don't really care," he said, letting me know that he wasn't about to let me get away with any nonsense. That he knew I wasn't like Ruthie. I should say what I meant, because it mattered to him.

"I'm sorry about Kenny," I said.

"Yes, I can tell. You're a real softie, aren't you?"

"I thought he was . . . something he wasn't."

"Sure. I can see that. You're so young. Still wet behind the ears." He reached over and brushed my hair away from my face and lifted my chin. "I hope you're not going to make the same mistake about me. Think I'm someone I'm not."

"What more could anyone want you to be?"

He laughed. Then he realized I meant it. "You could, Maddie . . . ," he said as he leaned toward me in the dark.

Did Luke already know how Paul felt about me? Was that why he had come down so hard on me about Kenny? I couldn't tell. His mother was back at home now, though he never talked about her. In any case, he didn't act the least bit surprised when I was suddenly there, in the center of Paul's world. But then, Luke didn't seem to react to much of anything. He was thoroughly self-contained. Detached, but still intensely observant. I could feel him watching me, weighing how I was doing with Paul. I'm not sure what he thought about me in the beginning, though I felt he was still holding my relationship with Kenny over my head. He poked fun at both the Genzlingers whenever he had the opportunity.

"There she goes," I heard him say to Paul one afternoon the week before the Thanksgiving holiday, when we were all walking toward the school parking lot, Ruthie twenty yards or so ahead of us. "Little Miss Oink Oink."

"Hey, now, come on," Paul told him, glancing over at me. Despite Luke's privileged upbringing, Paul was far the more polite and considerate of the two. Luke had a biting, sarcastic streak that scared me. He often made comments that provoked laughter—but they were almost always at someone else's expense. I knew perfectly well that everyone, except for Paul, could fall victim to Luke's acid tongue. But most of his friends didn't mind. It was almost a compliment, it seemed, if Luke noticed you enough to bother to say something derogatory about you. It was the same, if not worse, for the girls, though he usually made those comments behind their backs.

"No, really, I'm thinking of getting some of that for myself," Luke said, turning to Ivan Metcalf, one of the boys who hung out with us. "I hear it doesn't take a lot of effort."

Ivan laughed. "Maybe for you it doesn't."

And it didn't. Despite his growing reputation for dating three or four girls at once, and for heavy, sometimes overly aggressive making out, Luke was never without female companionship. And he was indiscriminate in his choices. One night he showed up with a waitress from Friendly's, a doughy-looking redhead who must have been in her late twenties. And there was a longhaired brunette named Penny who lived outside of Albany, someone he knew from his prep school days. He took up with Ruthie around Christmas that year. Suddenly, she was once again riding around in the van, sitting in the back on Luke's lap and carrying on in the same way she had with Paul. Ruthie had pointedly ignored me after Paul dropped her, but now she acted as though the two of us were best friends again and as if it was Luke she had had her eye on from the beginning.

"Paul's sweet, isn't he?" she said one afternoon in the girls' locker room after gym. "But Luke is so cool—I don't know—Paul seems like a boy in comparison."

"Yes, but . . . " I hesitated. Luke had been mimicking Ruthie just the day before, tossing his hair around the way she did hers and cooing: "Don't you just love everything in the whole wide world, Lukie? Aren't we just having the very, very best time we could ever, ever have?"

"What?"

"He can be mean, too, you know."

"Of course I know that! That's what I'm saying, that's what makes him so different. He's really been through some tough times, don't you see? He has a right to have a pretty hardened attitude, as far as I'm concerned."

But it seemed to me that people were always finding excuses for Luke's bad behavior. At Paul's urging he'd joined the baseball team that spring, and he'd been caught smoking the very first week of the season. The coach had let him off with just a warning. Anyone else who broke training like that would have been kicked right off the team.

"He's got a mess on his hands at home," Paul told me. "Between his mom and their finances. They're having to sell some of their property to settle debts. That's hard on him, Maddie, letting that land go. I understand that. I worry about our farm sometimes the way things are now." Yes, but it seemed to me that Paul carried his fears inside him like a man, and Luke turned his outward, throwing them back at the rest of us, dispensing blame as if it was his birthright. Not surprisingly, he discarded Ruthie without explanation.

"I don't know what I did wrong," she told me through her tears. "He looks through me now like I don't exist. And just a week ago we were doing it. I went on the pill for him. What more could he ask? He's just so restless and edgy. I didn't know what else to do. The only time he seems happy is when we're, you know—" Ruthie began to blubber. "And the thing is, the horrible thing is—I miss that so much! I miss him so much. He made me feel so—"

"Ruthie, come on—"

It infuriated me that Luke could be so callous to someone as essentially harmless as Ruthie, and that she, in the end, would willingly take all the blame for it. Why was Luke above the laws of common decency? What made him an exception? The Barnetts were like the rest of us now, struggling to hold on to homes and businesses, to stay above the rising tide of debt that was swamping so many in the county. No, it wasn't his family background anymore, or the money, it was something innate in Luke—a powerful charisma, I suppose—that left me untouched but pulled almost everyone else I knew under his spell. Though Luke made the others laugh with his clever jokes and cutting asides, I didn't think he was funny. I sensed the bitterness simmering just under his laid-back attitude, the need to hurt masquerading as harmless sarcasm. And Luke knew I was immune to his charms. Just as he, I became convinced, did not think me worthy of Paul, the only person Luke seemed to genuinely like. No, more than that, revere. He was the only one who could rein Luke in, the only one he really listened to.

"Where'd you get that?"

"Where do you think?"

It was a Saturday night in early May and we were driving up to Albany to pick up Penny and go to a concert at the Egg. Luke, Ivan, and his girlfriend Dana were passing a joint around in the back of the VW.

"You're a total asshole, do you know that?" Paul told him. "Either it or you is out of my car in ten seconds."

"Do you at least want a hit first?"

"Just get rid of it, okay?"

Not that Paul was so righteous. He was the first to party when he wasn't in training. And the Alden house had a certain open-door reputation when it came to beer drinking. But Paul had a true athlete's belief in following the game plan, obeying the rules, and he went through a lot of grief that spring trying to get Luke to feel the same way. We all knew Luke wouldn't survive on the ball team if he were caught smoking cigarettes again. And marijuana? He could very well be kicked out of high school for that. But I frequently thought I'd catch a whiff of something—or was I just hoping to?—on his clothes or in his hair. I suppose in my own way, I watched him as carefully as he did me.

Our straightforward love for Paul forced us to keep our more complicated feelings about each other hidden. I never dared tell Paul how I sometimes resented Luke. Nor, I suspected, did he say anything questionable to Paul about me. We kept our distance. And our silence. I think that almost from the beginning, we realized that we'd have to find a way of sharing Paul—if either one of us was going to hold on to him.

7

I was inexperienced, yes, but I believe that in some essential way Paul was the more innocent. In the beginning, he was fired up about his feelings for me. He'd always been so easygoing and sure of himself, and I think I came along and just knocked him sideways, stunning him with emotions he'd never experienced before. I'm sure that hormones fueled a lot of his confusion. But unlike Luke, his views about sex seemed conflicted and constraining. The Aldens were devout Roman Catholics, a minority in our predominantly Congregationalist area, and were raised to believe in their own moral and spiritual superiority.

"I better get you home," he said one night that first July we were together. He'd graduated the month before and had started working full-time at Alden Dairy, though only until he could save enough money to take the training course necessary to get certified as an electrician. It wasn't easy for Paul to finally come clean about the fact that he didn't intend to join the family business. He'd been born and raised on the farm, spent his boyhood watching his father's hard-pitched battles to keep the place running, and decided that he didn't want that kind of uncertainty in his own life. He was determined to have a trade, something independent of land and cattle, a livelihood that he could control and refine with hard work and his own two hands. Dandridge had never really counted on Ethan, his fun-loving eldest son, to settle down enough to take over for him. But he'd long believed that Paul—strong, capable, honest, obedient—would be the one to carry on the Alden Dairy tradition. I think in many ways his bitter disappointment about Paul's decision was what started the dairy's final slide into insolvency.

"That's Venus over there," I told him, pointing above the tree linc. We were lying on a blanket on the little beach up by Indian Pond, though we'd told my parents we were going bowling with a group of friends, or to the movies with another couple, or to any number of places we never went to with people we never saw. Even Luke, who'd been invited to intern at his father's old law firm in Albany that summer, seemed incidental to the two of us, the only reality that mattered. "You can tell it's a planet because it doesn't twinkle."

"I need to get you home, Maddie," he told me again, sitting up to lean on his elbow and looking down at me. I knew—and I didn't know—what he really needed. We'd been kissing for a long time, and then he'd pulled away from me. I think I was well aware of what I was doing. Of course I was, though it was his pleasure I was interested in rather than my own. What thrilled me was the effect I had on him. The fact that I could simply reach up and pull his face down toward mine . . .

I never considered blaming him or regretting that, in the end, he didn't take me home. I wasn't brought up on a steady diet of guilt the way Paul had been. I'd been coddled all my life, allowed to grow almost to full adulthood without having to learn the meaning of self-sacrifice or discipline. I simply took what I wanted, and gave the same way. But I also think that Paul valued the whole thing far more than I believed it was worth. Afterward, he was as remorseful as I'd ever seen him up until that point. As a rule, it's the girl who's supposed to cry. But Paul wept for us. I remember feeling that I'd been undone, but not in an unpleasant way—more like a present with paper and ribbons scattered all around. So, I thought, I've given myself to Paul. That was all. It had been thoroughly detached from my other, much deeper feelings for him.

Whereas for Paul, it was as real and serious as anything he'd ever done. He'd sinned, and there was only one way in his eyes to make it right. He committed himself to me that night, though he decided not to burden me with the gravity of his intentions until he thought I was ready to accept them. In the meantime, I was to be protected and cherished. He didn't understand that I was complicit in our lovemaking, that in many ways it was me who seduced him. He could not see what Luke saw at a glance: I was willing to do just about anything to be accepted and loved.

I worked for my father that summer, too, though it was as slow as any of the midwinter months. The only steady and significant custom came from Westhover, the contracting firm that was building the new condominium complex outside Northridge. Though my father had initially demanded and received payment up front, he'd extended credit when the company promised him that he would be awarded an exclusive contract as middleman and supplier. It was unlike him to be so careless and trusting; he must have really needed to believe that the offer was legitimate. In fact, the larger hardware and lumberyard in Northridge had run a credit check and knew the organization was shaky. It was about halfway through the summer when my father learned the company was filing for Chapter 11.

"Well, guess who else isn't getting paid?" Paul said when I told him our bad news.

"What do you mean?"

"Dad let two of the regulars go and he's got Ethan, Bob, and me working for nothing. No, not nothing: he claims he's giving us food and board for free. It's no better than being a slave."

"Why didn't you tell me?"

"I promised Dad I wouldn't. We all did. He's a little nuts right now in case you haven't noticed." But I hadn't noticed. I didn't yet understand how much of what transpired among members of that family was hard to detect by outsiders, even those of us who would eventually become in-laws. They communicated on some primordial, nonverbal level, and despite their differing temperaments, they rarely argued. Theirs was an old-fashioned patriarchy, and I was impressed with the respect and obedience Dandridge demanded and received from his children. But for all their seeming openness and bluff goodwill to everyone they knew, the Aldens were a tribe unto themselves, especially when things were going against them. Then the doors slammed shut. It might have been due in some part to their being Catholic, to the sense of separateness that instilled in them, but I think, in the end, that what they believed in most deeply was the idea of family. Their loyalties were never divided. It must have been difficult for Paul to tell me what he did; it was a kind of betrayal.

"What are you going to do?"

"I don't know. I'm obviously not getting my certification anytime soon. I've been looking into other kinds of work. I actually talked to Westhover a few weeks ago, but they said they already had more help than they needed. What a laugh, huh?"

Heinrich Hardware held on for another few years, fueled by a second mortgage on our house and my parents' bitterness over the Westhover debacle. It turned out that my mother had pushed my father to accept the developer's offer, and that he'd finally gone against his own strict business principles to accommodate her wishes. I think they found it easier to blame each other than to face up to the fact that, like so many other small businesses dependent on the local economy, the hardware store was heading in only one direction anyway. But I don't think they could conceive of that; the store had always been there, a three-story white-clapboarded building in the middle of town. In the summer, the long front porch was chockablock with Weber grills and American flags. In the winter, it was stacked with sleds, bags of salt, bundled kindling. This was where you came for your grass seed, house paint, lightbulbs, sandpaper, glue strips, pine bark mulch, suet, kerosene. Real things, useful items. Surely, it wasn't possible that the shelves, filled for so long with so many articles, could lie bare? Or that the floorboards, worn down by so many generations, could now stand empty? For my parents, it must have been like trying to imagine the world without themselves, because the store had been at the center of their lives and their marriage for more than two decades before I came along.

Paul continued to work at Alden Dairy while casting around for something else, anything else, to do. I knew he felt trapped, and that he believed his father was trying to force him into joining the business.

"He's hoping to starve me into it. He thinks I don't have any options." And, as far as I could see, Paul really didn't. The bad economic times nationwide were starting to hit home: the farms that hadn't already gone under just scraping along, Untermeyer Paper, Westhover Associates, and a dozen other firms in bankruptcy, followed by cutbacks, layoffs, unemployment. Nobody was hiring.

I didn't see Luke much during that period, though I knew Paul got together with him once or twice a week. He'd continued on at his father's law firm through the fall with the vague hope, so Paul told me, that the firm might help pay his college tuition. Abruptly, just before Christmas, he was let go. Paul claimed he didn't know why, but I suspected that it had something to do with the fact that Luke seemed stoned a lot of the time. I don't think Paul realized that Luke had a drug problem at that point. He'd have a joint himself from time to time, and didn't see any harm in it. But, for Paul, it was a sometime, after-work kind of thing. For Luke, I was beginning to think it was more a necessity, a way of dealing with the world. It blended so easily with his laid-back, heavy-lidded personality, the knowing nod, the half smile. If you didn't observe him closely, the way I did, you wouldn't necessarily know.

Paul talked about Luke more often during the early winter months. Luke had an idea. For a business. Something to do with his property. Development.

"Honestly, Paul, is he nuts? Nobody's building now."

"It's not just building. It's bigger than that—he's talking about housing units, commercial possibilities, even a golf course. And he's got some people interested in backing him. He's got it all worked out. Really, Maddie, he's got a good head for business."

"If you say so," I said, though I didn't believe him. But I let him talk. He seemed almost happy again, buoyed by Luke's fantasies. There was no risk involved. It was all win-win. They'd use other people's money and their own hard work.

"We? You've been saying 'we' all night, do you realize that?"

"Well, yes. I'm going to help him, Maddie. I'd be crazy to miss out on a deal like this."

From all appearances, he seemed to be right. According to Paul, the pitch that Luke and he made to their prospective financial backers had gone incredibly well. A contract was drawn up and signed. The initial investment capital came through. Suddenly, Paul had spending money. Though I pushed Paul a few times for details about who these "backers" might actually be, he hadn't been forthcoming about the financial underpinnings of his business. But I thought I knew what was going on. I suspected that they were really just a couple of Howell's old cronies, generously trying to give Luke a leg up in the world.

Should I have been more curious? More demanding? I don't know. I was still in high school. A different universe, you could say, but it wasn't just that. A lot of Paul's talk did sound high-blown and vague to me, but I didn't really want to know the details. I'd had enough of the constant ache and weariness of being poor. My parents were bowed down with debt, as beholden to it as serfs serving a cruel landowner. They argued openly and constantly, as if they'd forgotten any other mode of communication. I was sick to death of their bickering about interest payments, their niggling over grocery items, and I began to stop thinking of them as two people struggling to find a solution. They became the problem. Their sourness was self-defeating, their bitterness a smell that permeated the kitchen and drifted up the stairs.

Paul, on the other hand, was never without a thick roll of dollars now. He'd purchased a new Jeep. He and Luke always seemed to be busy, working late into the night out at the site, or driving up to Albany for meetings with their "venture capitalists," as Luke called them. At the end of the summer, after repeated requests on my part, Paul finally took me out to the construction area in the northwestern corner of the Barnett land. Luke and he had been talking about their development ideas for so long that I had to hide my disappointment when I saw what was actually there: a cleared quarter acre or so of woodland and mounds of dirt surrounding a large, roughly rectangular area covered with tarpaulins held down by cinder blocks. Wind worried the edges of the tarps, making them flutter and flap like birds trying to take flight.

"No, don't get out," Paul said when I reached for the door handle.

"But—why? I want a closer look."

"No way. There are nails and loose boards all over the place. It's not safe."

"Oh, okay. So, tell me where everything's going to be. What are we looking at here?"

"It's the foundation, Maddie."

"For what, though? Sometimes, this all seems—I don't know—so vague. Where are the shops going to be? And the golf course?"

"Hey, come on. I told you there wasn't much to really look at yet but you've been badgering me to see it anyway. And now that you're here—Jesus, Maddie—give me a break!"

"I'm sorry."

"No, no, no," he said, shaking his head as he turned to me. "No, I'm sorry. I don't mean to jump all over you. It's just that—this kind of thing takes time. Money. Work. It's not going to happen overnight, but it is going to happen. It's all going to come together. We're going to get there, okay? Believe me?"

I stared out over the clearing. We were in the middle of nowhere, miles from a decent two-lane county highway. The ragged wilderness of wood and underbrush encroached upon us from every side. How well I knew this land, heavy with rock debris and riddled with veins of glittering, worthless mica. A half dozen crows sailed down and hopscotched from dirt mound to cinder block, pecking at the tarpaulin, cawing sarcastically.

"Of course," I said, ashamed that a part of me continued to doubt him. I knew I had to fight my practical, earthbound nature. Nothing great was ever accomplished without a leap of faith, I told myself. I couldn't keep dragging Paul down. I had to take hold of his vision, close my eyes—and let go.

Though Paul and I had often talked about getting married someday, it had always been in a dreamy, make-believe kind of way. Then Paul had some kind of a blowup with his father and moved abruptly out of the house. Luke invited him to stay at the empty cottage on the Barnett estate free of charge, and Paul took up residence there—though I could tell that he was far from settled emotionally. Paul refused to talk about the fight with his father, but I knew it had hurt him in ways that I could do little to alleviate. Whatever had caused the final rupture with Dandridge was fundamentally male in nature, I decided, and no doubt complicated by bad times and disappointments on both sides of the argument. After that, though, Paul was suddenly impatient to take definite steps about our future together. We told my parents that we intended to get married as soon as I graduated from high school in another two years.

My parents were thrilled, of course, though the now formalized nature of my relationship with Paul freed my father to offer him endless business advice. It seemed to me that, as the hardware store continued to languish, my father took a more and more proprietary interest in Barnett-Alden Enterprises. Unlike Paul's own father, my dad was almost pathetically eager to be a part of the new venture.

"You still haven't filed with the town planning board, have you?" he said one night when Paul had come to our place for dinner. Since moving into the Barnetts' cottage, he'd been eating with us a couple of times a week. My mother fussed over these meals in a way she never did when it was just the three of us, and she blossomed conversationally in his presence, usually taking his side against what she also deemed my father's nit-picking tendencies.

"I imagine Paul knows what he's doing," she said, untying her apron to sit down with the rest of us at the table. "And he's getting first-rate financial advice from that outfit in Albany. Isn't that right, Paul?" I surmised that Luke's "venture capitalists" had organized themselves in my mother's imagination into a kind of financial services juggernaut. This was typical of her unquestioning confidence and pride in her future son-in-law. Though they made no bones about their dislike for Luke, both my parents doted on Paul. They were as proud of him as they would have been their own son.

But I was beginning to see a side of Paul they didn't. Without the structure of his immediate family, I sensed he felt vulnerable and a little out of control. He wasn't used to living alone, or even being by himself for very long, so I spent as much time as my parents allowed over at the cottage. It was a brown-stained cedar shake Cape, long vacant, tucked behind a towering stand of hemlocks near the gated stone entrance to the Barnett estate. In more prosperous times, it had been the farmhand's house, and the remnants of an extensive vegetable garden, a barn, and outbuildings attested to past cultivation and productivity. It was still fully furnished, the pantry shelves lined with yellowed newspapers laid down on June 11, 1977, though now pillaged and soiled by the endless generations of mice that had infested the whole structure.

Paul did what he could to clean up the downstairs, though he abandoned the upper floor and attic to the bats that had long ago staked their own claim. He slept on an army blanket on the ravaged couch in the living room, and we spent most of our time there in the kitchen. Luke dropped in on a regular basis. The three of us would sit around the chipped oak-veneer table in the kitchen, playing poker and talking. I'd put out a bowl of pretzels or potato chips, just like any other hostess. Luke was now smoking marijuana openly and every once in a while Paul would join him.

"Deer season opens this week," Paul said one night, passing the joint back to Luke. "My dad and my brothers and I used to always go away for a weekend up to my uncle's place north of Troy. He's got about fifty acres of woodland that's kind of like deer heaven. Ever go hunting, Luke?"

"No."

"We should go out this weekend," Paul went on. "Just the two of us. Hey, we could go back in your woods here. I could show you how—"

"No. Sorry. I don't like guns."

"But, why not? What's the matter with them? Hunting too good-ole-boy for you, that it?" I'd been noticing that Paul sometimes got uncharacteristically mean when he was stoned, his tone alternately bullying and suspicious.

"No, my dad used to hunt. But he got rid of his guns after my mother tried to use one on herself about ten years back. All she managed to do was blow out the glass in an heirloom mirror in the upstairs hall. It was just a bid for attention."

Perhaps Luke had always talked this openly to Paul about his family; Paul seemed to be unfazed by the frequently shocking tidbits Luke let drop. To me, however, raised in repressed awe of the Barnetts' wealth and scandalous behavior, these revelations flung open a window to a world that had always secretly fascinated me. I listened raptly to Luke's offhanded asides about the money Howell lavished and lost on his antique car collection. The weeklong drunks that Luke's parents used to indulge in, behind locked doors in the master bedroom, their dinners brought up to them on trays, as if they were invalids. The parade of maids and cooks who lied and cheated and then walked away with whatever wasn't nailed down.

I took in Luke's stories without comment, vaguely aware that I could break the spell of intimacy if I insinuated myself too directly into his musings. I tried never to appear too shocked or overly interested, and I felt I was rewarded by Luke's openness and sometimes outright anger about his upbringing. Paul seemed not to hear the reticence or pain behind Luke's words the way I did; I think he was too caught up in his own problems. We played cards and talked. Paul and Luke passed another joint back and forth.

"You know, I really miss it," Paul said suddenly. His elbows were on the table and he dropped his head into his hands. "I miss them. Everything. Jesus, I'm fucked up. What the hell's in this shit?"

"Nothing."

"What's in this? What're you doing to me?"

"Nothing, man," Luke said. "Everything's cool."

"Don't talk fucking dope talk to me!" Paul slammed both hands on the table. "Don't think I don't know what you're trying to do."

Luke stared at him, then nodded slowly.

"I guess I better be going," he said, pushing back his chair.

"So go then," Paul muttered, lowering his head again.

"Let me turn the porch light on," I said, following Luke out of the room.

"You going to be okay alone with him?" Luke asked, turning to me as he opened the back door. The air was cold and heady after the close dankness of the kitchen.

"Sure. You know he didn't mean what he said. Whatever it was he was trying to say."

Luke laughed in the dark and I could see his breath puffing in the dampness. I turned on the light.

"I know, Maddie. Don't worry about me." I watched him walk down the overgrown path and cut through the wild, untended vegetable garden, then disappear into the wooded rise that led up to his house. I felt a sudden urge to call after him. To thank him. To tell him I was sorry. I'd been wrong about many things. But I let him go. I heard the snap and crunch of his boots in the underbrush long after I'd lost sight of him. It was the first time I realized that Luke offered Paul and me a kind of ballast, a balancing and leveling off of our still immature and sometimes volatile love. It was the first time I sensed the possibility of a real friendship between us. Two days later all that hope and goodwill came crashing down, like a mirror shattering, like the illusion all of this had been anyway.

"Lukie! I need you! I know you're down there. I heard you come in. I've got ears like a cat, you know. Now get up here, baby!"

I stood frozen just inside the Barnetts' front door, the disembodied voice of Luke's mother drifting querulously down the stairs from somewhere up above. Though I'd visited Paul numerous times, this was the first time I'd been inside the estate's main house. I still wasn't certain why I was there. I'd been studying for my history final in the kitchen down at the cottage, waiting for Paul to come back from his meeting with Luke and the backers in Albany, when the phone rang.

"Maddie," Paul whispered my name.

"Where are you? What's wrong?"

"Go up to the big house. Wait for me there."

"What's going on?"

"Just go. Now."

Though it was not yet five o'clock, the November afternoon was already dimming as I cut through the woods and then up the long maple-lined driveway. The stately white house at the top of the rise looked out vacantly over the dry fountain and empty, leaf-strewn basin, the two diamond-shaped perennial beds gone to riotous seed, and the untrimmed forsythia bushes enveloping the portico. The front gray-veined marble steps, hauled by mule from the quarries of western Massachusetts in the mid-1700s, had survived a fire that had totally demolished the original structure, two murderous Indian raids, three devastating wars, and the mercurial and often self-destructive spirit of seven generations of Barnetts. The property's current state of disrepair—the green-streaked brass-domed cupola, the upper fan window with its two missing panes, the marble urns that were clotted with weeds at the base of the front steps—only seemed to add luster to the mansion's tragic air.

"That is you, isn't it, baby?"

I looked up the wide stairs that divided in two at the landing and turned up on either side of the main staircase in shorter flights to the second floor. An Oriental runner covered the steps and the spacious landing that seemed to also serve as a portrait gallery. Late-afternoon sunlight from the upper fan window slanted across two dozen or so paintings and photographs, arranged with care despite the film of dust that appeared to have settled on every available surface.

The downstairs rooms, shadowy in the late-afternoon dusk, contained a clutter of antique chairs and settees, built-in bookcases filled with dark leather-bound volumes, porcelains and other bric-a-brac arranged on delicate end tables and behind glassed-in cases. A tinny, ethereal *ding! ding! ding!* suddenly broke the silence, emanating from the miniature workings of an elegant clock on the mantelpiece. It was twenty past five by my watch; three o'clock in whatever lost world the clock inhabited. I saw my reflection in the tarnished mirror above the mantel: my round face, pale and luminous as the moon, mottled in the disintegrating surface of the glass. Then I heard the sound of sirens.

The Barnett estate is situated on River Road, a long, lonely two-lane highway that is the main east-west thoroughfare through town. Though that section of the roadway is straight and flat, for some reason it seems to attract more than its share of automobile accidents, primarily teenagers who've been drinking or who take advantage of the road's even course to drag race. The sirens wailed along that road, growing closer, and then I could see the red lights of three police cruisers flashing through the trees.

"Who's there? Who's coming? What's going on?" Mrs. Barnett whispered from above. She was closer than before, perhaps even standing in one of the dark corners of the landing, but I still couldn't make out more than a vaguely defined shadow.

"It's just Maddie Fedderson," I called up the stairs. "I'm a friend of Luke's and Paul's. I was down at the house where Paul is staying, and they called and told me to come up and wait for them here."

"What's happening? Is there a fire? What do you want?" I knew panic when I heard it, but I didn't know what to tell her, or how to calm her down. Then, the wail of the sirens changed direction, and I realized that the cruisers had turned in at the Barnetts' stone entrance and were racing up the driveway toward the house.

I heard a sudden scuffling as Luke's mother ran up the short second flight and down a hallway. A door slammed shut. Her terror, irrational though it might have been, infected me. All at once, I was overcome by the certainty that something terrible was happening. No, had already happened. The sirens wailed. The flashing red lights approached. Strobed through the hallway. And then swept on, into the woods, up the sloping hillside, sirens weeping, north and westward, toward the construction site where Paul had invested his hopes and dreams, where I had made my leap of faith, upward and on to the end of my world as I knew it.

Part Three

8

After that day at the pond, Anne began to wage a forthright campaign to win my friendship. She wasn't subtle in her approach. She would call me at the office and at home, always apologizing for taking up my time, asking questions about where to find a dry cleaner's or how best to deal with a wasp infestation. Then, after some aimless chatter, she'd suggest we take the kids berry picking the next afternoon, or back up to the pond for a swim. I was flattered, of course, but I tried not to take her interest too much to heart. Once she got settled and met other weekenders, I told myself, she'd drift away.

"She's lonely," Paul declared one night after Anne phoned. The area had lost electrical power during a thunderstorm, and she called me to make sure it wasn't just Maple Rise that had gone down. We were already in bed when she called, and I apologized to Paul after she kept me on the phone for several minutes. Though he hadn't yet met her, I'd told him enough about her so that he thought he understood her situation, and he came to her defense: "Listen, she's up here all alone all week in that huge house with a couple of kids and she's probably a little scared. She doesn't know who else to turn to yet. She's lucky to have you, Maddie."

Paul agreed with my assessment that we probably wouldn't stay this close for very long. For one thing, the Naylors had made a good offer on Oak Rise, and between them and the two other Polanski listings that Nana had sold recently, the Zellers were soon to be surrounded by wealthy New York second-homers like themselves. But Paul encouraged me to be a good neighbor in the meantime. I think he approved of the fact that Anne appeared to be genuinely interested in what Red River had to offer as a community—shopping at the local farm stands, swimming up at Indian Pond, taking Max and Katie to the Children's Hour at the town library.

"I've lived in the city for almost twenty years, and I can't begin to tell you how great it is to wake up in the morning and hear birds singing!" she told me on the phone one morning several weeks after the Zellers had moved in. "It's amazing. This is it—do you know what I mean? This is the real thing. I'm actually thinking of starting a vegetable garden. Tell me everything you know about growing tomatoes!"

"Well, it's too late in the season to start from seed," I replied, while running a spell check on an e-mail I'd been preparing for a new client. As Anne usually did most of the talking, I'd found that I could work and chat with her on the phone at the same time. "You'll need to buy some plants. I recommend you get cherries, as they ripen faster. Taylor Farms usually has the best."

"Let's all meet there after you're done today, okay? And then you guys can come back over here for dinner, because Paul will be working late, right? As a matter of fact, we've got this outdoor gas grill I haven't even turned on yet. Well, of course you know! You sold it to me."

Though we'd visited various places together with our kids, I'd managed to sidestep Anne's several invitations to the girls and myself to come back with them to Maple Rise. Then, the day before, I'd mentioned to her that Paul, who was starting a new multimillion-dollar McMansion in Covington, would be tied up at work most nights, now that the sun wasn't setting until nine or so. I'd told her about this because I was so proud that he'd landed such a lucrative job, but now I could have kicked myself. All afternoon I felt apprehensive about the coming evening. I was happy to offer companionship and advice to Anne, but I wasn't going to be able to reciprocate in kind when it came to entertaining.

We live in an eighteenth-century farmhouse that's bursting at the seams with just the five of us. The place was a wreck when Paul and I bought it. For the first three years, we lived on the ground floor, slowly renovating room after room. It still needs a lot of work but, as the family's grown and Paul and I have both gotten so busy, we've let things slide. The kitchen especially could use a total makeover. Day to day, it doesn't bother me. But I had no intention of letting Anne see my battered wood-veneer kitchen cabinets or the chipped Formica countertops. I'm generous and accommodating to a fault. But I won't tolerate anyone's pity.

I picked up the girls from Kathy's and met Anne and her kids at Taylor

Farms around five thirty. I helped her select eight Sweet 100s and a couple of Golden Pear and Spanish plum tomato plants, all now leggy from being in their pots for too long. We picked out seeds for lettuce, arugula, radishes, cucumbers, and bush beans—things that would get off to a fast start in our short growing season.

"Oh, can we get some of these, too?" she cried, reaching for the prettily designed packet of morning glory seeds. "My grandmother used to have them climbing up her back porch when I was a girl. I just loved the way they twined and twisted. They're like something out of a fairy tale—do you know what I mean?"

She was wearing chinos and a pale blue silk work shirt, her shock of white hair now offset by a rich tan. With her milky pink pedicure and Prada backpack, her adorable blond children in tow, she looked like something out of a Ralph Lauren ad: casually chic and absolutely sure of herself. And she was almost ridiculously grateful to me for my straightforward guidance and advice. As we walked together down the crowded aisles, she would nudge me with her elbow, or touch my arm, as if to reassure herself that I was real, that I was actually there, helping her. Her obvious pleasure in us all being together made me feel sad. Of course, she didn't know that I'd already decided this would probably be our last excursion.

"Let's get some corn for dinner. What do you think?" she asked. "And some of those big tomatoes and that buffalo mozzarella. God, everything looks so good! Should we do steaks, Maddie? Or hamburgers and hot dogs? Though I have to tell you that I'm a little nervous about turning on that grill. I assume you know about that sort of thing?"

"Don't worry, we cook out all the time," Rachel told her as we started to unload the shopping cart. "And we have a gas Weber. There's no real mystery to it."

"So you say," Anne replied, laughing. "You have no idea what a total loss I am in the kitchen. It's pretty much foreign territory to me, I'm afraid."

The first thing I noticed when we drove up the driveway to Maple Rise was that the lawn needed mowing. Badly. We'd had a lot of rain over the past two weeks and the grass had shot up nearly a foot since the last time I was there. It gave the expensive, architecturally dramatic house an oddly scruffy appearance, like an elegantly dressed man with a five-o'clock shadow and beer on his breath. I suggested that Rachel organize the younger kids to help bring in the groceries while Anne and I transported the plants to her garden plot. I'm not sure what I'd expected. Knowing what I did about Anne, especially her limited experience in rural living, I should have realized that her desire for a garden would not be supported by any practical measures to make it a reality.

"I was thinking right about here," she said, stopping a third of the way down the hill in the knee-deep grass about a hundred feet west of the house. "What do you think?"

"Here?" I repeated, leaning over to set my cardboard tray of seedlings on the grass. I straightened up slowly. "And you were thinking we'd put these plants in today, Anne?"

"Is it too hot? Are you tired? Of course, we can wait."

"No, it's not that. But I have to tell you that you have a lot of work ahead of you before you'll be able to plant anything—let alone have a prayer that it grows. You'll need to have the soil tilled, the rocks removed, and a layer of topsoil and compost worked in, though raised beds might be more efficient. Also, you have to have a fence around the garden, or the deer and rabbits will be using it for a salad bar."

"Well, you must think I'm a total idiot, Maddie," she said with a laugh and then, laughing harder, she flopped back into the grass. "I'm the fool on the hill, aren't I? Oh, my God! You should have seen the look on your face when I told you where I wanted to put the tomatoes! I'm sorry, but it is sort of funny, don't you think?"

"Yes," I said, sitting down next to her. "You really don't know a damn thing about any of this, do you? And what the hell happened to your lawn? You can't let it go like this, you know, or you'll need to bring in a tractor to mow it."

"Yes, I've been meaning to call these people someone recommended to Richard, but we've just been so busy. I'll call tomorrow. It will be top on the list."

I thought of the several long, late afternoons we'd dawdled away together with our children when, it seemed to me, Anne had all the time in the world. But I kept these thoughts to myself. And later, when we walked back up to the house and I saw that there were still moving boxes lying unopened in the front hall, I kept my surprise in check. Anne didn't apologize for the lack of progress she seemed to be making, nor did she try to explain away the fact that from all appearances, she, Katie, and Max were dining off paper plates and plastic cutlery. The refrigerator, which I opened to put away the watermelon we'd brought for dessert, was a wasteland of sodas and Chardonnay, salsa, and white foam fast-food boxes.

I took over. With Rachel's help, the steak got seasoned, the corn husked, water (once a kettle was unearthed from one of the boxes) put on to boil, the tomatoes washed and, along with the mozzarella, sliced, the table set with Anne's paper and plastic collection, and finally the gas grill activated.

"You're amazing—do you know that?" Anne said, leaning against the deck rail with her glass of wine in one hand and the one she'd poured for me in the other. "When did you learn to do all this stuff? Cooking and gardening, raising a family and running a business, too?"

"Come on, I hardly run the business!" I laughed. I felt myself beginning to blush. She knew perfectly well my position at the agency. "I've only had my license for a year or so."

"Exactly! That's just my point," she said. "Look what you've accomplished in that short period of time. No, I mean it, Maddie. You're very special, and the incredible thing about it is that you don't seem to have any idea that you are. You're so unassuming. It's . . . well, it's lovely, really."

"Anne, honestly . . . " I forked a steak for doneness, keeping my head down, hoping she wouldn't notice that both my face and neck were now flushed. Yes, she was flattering me. I realized that. She was making much too much out of my minor achievements. But for whatever reason, she wanted to see me in that light; she had decided that I was this capable and accomplished person. It felt both disconcerting and emboldening. And what was the point of trying to correct Anne's impression? Wouldn't she just insist on seeing it as further evidence of my modesty? I suppose it's possible to justify just about anything in the end.

It was a lighthearted, lively dinner; a party atmosphere prevailed. We sat out on the deck around a large teak picnic table, eating corn with our fingers. Anne seemed to encourage her kids to converse with her as equals, though perhaps it was more that she didn't mind coming down to their level. The three of them, in any case, were chatterboxes, regaling us with stories about their misadventures as transplanted city dwellers.

"So then Max decided we should have the picnic in this really pretty field . . . ," Anne was saying when Katie interrupted her.

"It had a fence. We climbed over."

"Yes, we should have known better—right, Katie-pie? A fence should have been a sort of clue or something that they were trying to keep people out."

"No," Max said. "They were keeping bulls in! Big fat black bulls!"

"Oh, Lord," Anne said and began to laugh. "They came snorting and galloping down that hill! And we—we just ran for it! I scooped Katie up in my arms and screamed at Max and we took off, leaving our lovely new picnic basket right there in the middle of the field. I hope those bulls enjoyed our expensive pâté."

They were all laughing at this point, remembering their close escape. I thought how carefree the three of them looked, seemingly untouched by the kind of parent-child crosscurrents that are constantly swirling around the girls and me.

"But wasn't there barbed wire?" Beanie asked. "They usually put barbed wire up when there're bulls. Or an electrified fence."

"Oh?" Anne said, wiping her eyes on a paper napkin. "Maybe there was. I guess we didn't notice. We just wanted to sit in the field with all those pretty wildflowers. Silly us! So who wants some watermelon?"

"Rachel, why don't you and the girls clear?" I suggested.

"Sure, Mom," she said, getting up and starting to stack the plates.

"And you guys help, too," Anne suggested. Like the Pied Piper, Rachel led the children into the house.

Anne and I sat in silence for a moment, listening to our kids moving back and forth behind us in the kitchen. A drawer opening, Rachel saying something. Fireflies drifted over the uncut field, blinking lazily in the humid night updrafts. Above the tree line the first stars burned blurrily through the haze. Somewhere, from down below, I heard a high, persistent whine.

"What's that?" I asked Anne.

"What?"

"That sound. Like a buzz saw or something. Don't you hear it?" But even as I was asking her, I realized that the noise was coming from the direction of Luke's place. He must be working in his basement workshop, the windows open, soldering one of his pieces. I was surprised the noise carried so clearly through the trees and up the hill.

"Yes, that's your friend. Luke Barnett, right? I hear him just about every night down there. He seems very driven."

"I hope the sound doesn't bother you," I replied, wishing I hadn't said anything. I still felt uneasy discussing Luke with Anne. He represented so much about the past that I would prefer to be forgotten. The more I got to know and like Anne and, yes, feel flattered by the way she seemed to view me, the more I felt the threat of Luke's proximity growing. "And he's not a friend. He's really a total loner these days."

"That sounds so intriguing!" she said, tipping back in her chair as she drained the last of her white wine. "The misunderstood artist, working away till all hours in his lonely garret."

"Basement," I corrected her. "He works in his basement. And I wouldn't romanticize him. He's not a particularly pleasant person, really."

"Okay, okay! I've been duly warned!" She laughed, sitting forward again. But I didn't relax until, as though what we'd been discussing was entirely unimportant, she abruptly changed the subject. "Oh, Maddie, damn it. I'm sorry about that stupid vegetable garden! You went to all that trouble for me. I really do feel like an idiot. Maybe I can find someone to plow and put in a fence the way you suggested. Who should I ask? Do you know of anybody?"

I did, of course. I knew of half a dozen guys who made their living doing lawn work and land design for wealthy second-homers. I grew up with most of them. They're all locals, like me. Friends, husbands of friends, brothers-in-law.

"Let me think about it," I said. But I'd already leapt ahead in my mind, the way we all do at times, embracing what seemed to me suddenly an ideal solution to a problem I didn't understand then was insolvable. Because I decided that Anne didn't need or want me to reciprocate her hospitality in my house. She needed me to help her, right there, in hers.

"Do you think Bob would have time to rototill a garden plot for Anne Zeller?" I asked Paul as we were getting ready for bed that night. "She wants to put in some vegetables."

"Wow. She really is getting into this, isn't she?" Paul replied, pulling off his T-shirt. He has a farmer's tan, stopping abruptly halfway up his biceps, following the curve of his neckline and forming a vee over his chest. Though he's put on twenty pounds or so over the years since high school, he still carries himself with the purposeful grace of a natural athlete. "Sure. I don't see why not. He could always use the extra money."

"Oh, no," I said, tossing all but one of the throw pillows into the corner. Paul had patted my backside as I climbed up the stairs in front of him before. It was one of his signals. "I don't want us to charge her for it. I'd like us to do this as a favor."

"*Us?*" Paul asked, balling up his T-shirt and throwing it into the hamper. "Bob is not *us*, Maddie. He's already working his tail off and has shit to show for it. Anne Zeller is *your* friend. You can pay him for whatever he does for her, otherwise I'm not asking him. And I don't want you asking him on your own, either, understand?" Though I'm used to Paul's sudden flareups, they're very rarely directed at me. And I felt unfairly charged. Hadn't he been encouraging me to lend Anne a helping hand? Wasn't this just the neighborly thing to do? He was working too hard, I knew, and was having some trouble with the large crew he'd assembled for the new construction job. But it didn't seem right to let him take his frustrations out on me.

"Honestly, Paul, what's the big deal?" I said, jerking back the sheets. "I don't mind paying, of course. But you don't have to jump all over me about it."

"Right," he said. "You're right. I don't know, Mad. I just don't want you ever getting confused about who we really are, okay? We're not in the Zellers' league, or anywhere near it. I guess I don't understand why you couldn't just recommend Bob—and have her pay him directly. Why make it a favor? Oh, fuck it. Don't listen to me. The truth is, I'm bone-tired."

I turned off the bedside light and we turned to each other. Paul, dear Paul. He doesn't miss much. Somehow, in his burst of anger, he'd exposed what I'd intended to keep hidden. He saw it, he questioned it, and then he backed away from it. We know each other so well. Too well, really. We share each other's weaknesses and strengths. It feels sometimes that I can almost read his mind. But I can't, really, can I? I'll never know for certain what fears wake him at night and cause him to roll over on his back and stare at the ceiling for hours. When we make love—as we did then, with bruising passion—I can almost believe that the millimeters of skin and the filaments of thought that separate us are permeable. That we've broken through. That we're one. But we're not. We never will be. Because I was able to lie to myself, and he didn't know.

9

All Bob's ever wanted to be in life is a farmer. He's most at ease on a tractor, most himself in his worn flannel work shirt and jeans, a dark blue Agway feed cap shadowing his eyes. Sometimes I think he loves his goats and cows as much as he loves Kathy and the kids. Or perhaps it's just easier for him to express his affection for them. When I hear him whispering sweet nothings to one of his yearlings, I sense a wellspring of patience and concern not evident in his taciturn dealings with humans.

"Yep, sure," he replied to my request that he put in the Zeller garden the following Saturday morning. He didn't ask why I was the one setting up the job or, after we'd settled on what I considered a more than reasonable price and told him I'd drop off the check with Kathy, why I was the one paying for it. Perhaps he thought it had something to do with my brokering the house sale, but, more than likely, he'd just decided it was a matter that didn't concern him. Like the rest of his family, Bob's very big on minding his own business. He expects the same in return, so I had to restrain myself from going over the details of what was needed more than once.

"You'll want to have split rails for about a thirty-by-twenty plot. And a gate, of course. And a truckload of topsoil or compost. Plus enough one-by-two coated wire to fence it all in."

"We're talking about a vegetable garden, right?" he asked. "I know what they look like."

When Bob and Paul and the rest of their siblings were growing up, the Alden farm was a going concern. Though a DAIRY OF DISTINCTION sign still hangs near the empty milking shed, the farm Bob took over from his father a few years before old man Alden died was already on its last legs. The large cooperatives upstate had been squeezing out the smaller local dairies and, after a few money-losing years, Bob finally threw in the towel and sold most of the herd. Since then, he's scratched out a living growing feed corn and raising cattle for slaughter. In the summer, he rents out the long hill and haying fields for a three-day folk festival and contra dance. Kathy's day-care business helps pay some of the bills, and Bob picks up odd jobs here and there, like the one I was giving him. But it seems a shame to me that he can't make a living out of doing what he loves. The only time I hear him string more than one or two sentences together is when he's talking about the farm—and plans he has to get it back on its feet. His latest scheme is the goat-cheese-making operation that he's plowing every extra dollar back into.

"Stuff sells in the gourmet markets for four, five dollars for six ounces. Think of that! The herd is building itself at this point—I got eight newbies this spring—so's all I'm going to need is another milking machine and the right refrigeration system, and I'm ready to go commercial." Paul listens to his plans for hours on end, though Bob tends—like the true farmer he is—to go over the same ground again and again.

Despite the fact that I think Paul's a lot brighter than Bob and far more social and ambitious, the two of them have always been very close. I used to believe that Paul felt primarily protective toward his baby brother, and I re-call that he was very concerned when Bob decided to take over the farm. He still worries about him, I know, especially about how he's going to find a way to put his four kids through college—the Holy Grail of fatherhood, as far as my husband is concerned. But I also sense that Paul gets something from Bob he doesn't really find anywhere else these days—a connection to the Alden past, perhaps, the tradition that Bob is carrying on in his own hapless way. It's probably not as straightforward as that. Sibling relationships—all that love and jealousy, hero-worship and rivalry—are a tangle of needs and wants I'll never be able to sort out. But I won't ever forget that it was Bob who didn't waver in his support of Paul when he most needed it, didn't ask a single question when everyone else was demanding explanations and an-swers. That was years ago, of course, but those bad times cut deep into Paul's being, and, like bark that's hardened around chiseled initials, I believe those scars will always be there.

I wasn't surprised when Paul volunteered to help Bob that Saturday morning. I sensed he was feeling bad about how he'd reacted to me the other night and was trying to make up for it. I think he might have been a little worried, too, when he learned that I was planning to take Lia and Beanie to sign up for their swimming lessons that morning, leaving Bob to fend for himself against the Zellers. Paul will never admit to me directly that he feels most of his clients need to be "handled," and that many weekenders wouldn't know what to make of Bob's monosyllabic, if not downright dismissive, approach to strangers. I'm well aware that my husband's gotten ahead in construction where many others have failed because he's not above making nice when the situation demands it. I've learned a lot from listening to him on the phone, talking down an outraged client or belligerent coworker. And when he heard that Anne had asked Rachel to babysit Katie and Max that morning so that she could "finally get a few things done," his decision was sealed.

"I'll drive Rachel over there when I meet Bob. Why don't you and the girls swing by when you're through? Maybe we can all drive up to Clearwater, have some lunch, and rent a couple of canoes."

"I'd love that," I told him. It felt like years since we'd done anything so carefree and spontaneous as a family. "You don't have to go over to Covington?"

"Oh, screw it for one Saturday," he said as he and Rachel headed out the door.

As it happened, Lia, Beanie, and I turned into the Zeller driveway two and a half hours later right behind Anne's Volvo. Rachel was beside her in the front seat, the two kids in the back, and a large trellis, handmade from willow wands, jutted out of the trunk. I pulled up beside her in the turnaround.

"What do you think?" she asked, after we'd unbuckled our offspring from their car seats and gathered around the open back of Anne's car. "Isn't it a beauty? I saw something like it in a book I have on French country vegetable gardens called *Potagers*. They all seem to have these kinds of whimsical decorative items in the middle of them, with peas or whatever climbing up them. Anyway, Rachel helped me pick it out at Taylor's. Have you seen what they're doing down there? It's just incredible! Your husband is amazing."

"No, we just got here," I said, noticing that both Rachel and Katie were wearing straw hats with elaborate arrangements of cloth flowers decorating the rims, and that Katie was holding fast to my oldest daughter's right hand. "Cute sun bonnets."

"Oh, yes, I forgot! Where did we put them, Rachel? We got so many things." Anne pulled out a couple of plastic bags that had been stuffed in around the trellis and had soon unearthed four more hats. "Your husband told us that if we're going to be working outside in this heat we'd need to have some sun protection. So we got these in that sweet little clothing store in Northridge. The new one on High Street, you know the one I mean? Aren't these great? Here, Lia, Beanie—everybody gets one!"

The hats were made of finely woven straw, soft and supple as felt, with silk flowers, enameled berry beads, and long satin fringed ties. Someone had removed the price tags, but I knew they had to be expensive. I felt momentarily uneasy accepting them from Anne, until I remembered how pleased and surprised she'd been when I insisted we were putting the garden in as a favor.

"Oh, it's nothing. Bob does this kind of thing all the time. Think of it as a housewarming present, if you like."

"Well, Maddie, honestly. What can I say? I never meant for you to do any of this on your own. It's totally unnecessary. But, okay, for heaven's sakes, I don't want to appear ungracious, do you know what I mean? Thank you. I'm touched. Really."

As I helped Lia put her hat on, her round gray eyes gazed up at me through the shadow cast by the brim. Lia hates any sort of headgear, but she stood patiently still while I tied the bow under her chin. I sensed she was torn between wanting to rip the thing off and longing to be a part of whatever the older kids were doing. Even Max was sporting a straw boater. I realized that I felt torn, too, as Lia and I followed the others down the hill. Were the hats Anne's way of thanking me for the garden? Did I owe her again now? How much? How to pay? Did our friendship really have this kind of debit/credit balance, or was I just being overly scrupulous because the Zellers had so much more money than we did? I disliked my tendency to constantly analyze my relationship with Anne. She would probably be shocked to learn how much time I spent worrying about these niggling details.

As we approached the fenced-in area, I saw that Richard Zeller, dressed in shorts, a polo tee, and leather sandals, was talking to Paul beside the newly installed garden gate while Bob silently raked a layer of manure over the topsoil.

"Jesus, what is this?" Richard asked. "A tea party? Where the hell have you been? I thought you were just running into town for the papers. You've been gone half the day!"

"I decided to ask the Aldens for lunch," Anne said, walking right up to Richard and giving him a kiss on the lips. "So I needed to buy a few things in Northridge, okay with you?"

"The Aldens?" Richard asked, taking us in over Anne's shoulder. Beanie and Lia were still in their bathing suits, and I was wearing cutoffs and a halter top. The hats probably accentuated our motley appearance.

"Paul and Maddie and their girls. The Aldens, dummy," she said, nudging him with her shoulder in a way that had grown familiar to me. Anne had a catlike quality in her need to rub up against those whose attention she sought.

"Oh, but we can't—" I began to protest.

"Yes, you sure can!" she insisted. "In fact, you have to. Rachel and I bought enough sandwiches to feed an army. And we hope you'll stay, too," Anne called over the fence to Bob. It was apparent to me that she'd forgotten his name, if she'd ever really registered it. But Bob heard her, stopped raking, and leaned over to pick up a stone.

"Nope," he said, tossing the stone into the back corner of the garden onto the pile that he'd dug up. There was a silence while we all waited for him to say something else, add an excuse, perhaps, or his regrets. But he returned to his raking without saying another word.

"Thanks," Paul said instead. "That's very kind of you. We'll be happy to stay."

"Hey, listen," Richard said, turning back to Paul. "I bet you could help me out with this. I've been trying to get some straight answers on the best places to fly-fish around here. Last weekend I tried that stretch near Route Eight I'd heard so much about, but it was a total washout. What, is it like a state secret where to go? I used to surf cast out on Montauk and it was like some kind of cabal—all those local guys talking in code about where the striped bass are biting. I hate that kind of crap. Do you fish at all?"

"Don't have the time," Paul said. "But I have a friend who swears by that stretch south of the overpass in Northridge. Do you know where I mean?"

"Yeah, but it's a zoo down there. Pickup trucks parked for half a mile along the roadside. There's got to be some quiet hot spots. I had this picture in my head when I bought this place—me casting out across some sweet little lake or other. I've got to show you my equipment. I just bought the most incredible new lures over the Internet, hand-tied by this blind guy down in Islamorada. And I've got that new Abel Super Five reel. Do you know the one I mean? It's a beauty."

"Like I said, I don't have the time—"

"Come on in and take a look," Richard said. "I'm keeping my rods downstairs for now—though we'll probably be turning that area into a play space for the kids. I've got quite a collection. And you've really got to see this Abel Super Five—*Trout and Stream* said it could just about change your life."

"You okay here, Bob?" Paul asked.

"Yep," Bob said, without turning around. We all followed Richard up to the house, entering through the sliding double glass doors below the deck that led into the enormous unfinished basement. I caught a glimpse of twenty or so rods stacked along the back wall and shelves full of fishing equipment before I climbed up the stairs to the first floor behind Anne and the kids. As I was reaching the top step, I heard Richard saying to Paul, "This is the wine cellar, for the time being anyway. You know Dan Osserman by any chance?"

"My wife works for Nana Osserman."

"Oh, right. Well, Dan has the most incredible wine setup you'll ever see. Temperature controlled, the whole business, plus about half an acre of the most amazing stuff. I'd love to put in something like that someday."

We ate in the Zellers' dining room around the oversized bird's-eye maple table, the kids and Anne and me grouped at one end, Paul and Richard sitting across from each other at the other.

"It's not the money, it's just not having the time to keep an eye on everything," Richard was saying between bites of his sandwich. "I'm spending half my life in airports these days. The airline industry in this country is a total mess, let me tell you. You fly much, Paul?"

"No, I really don't have—"

"Well, it's a disaster. Price gouging. Security bullshit. And first class these days? What a joke! I'm seriously thinking about taking some flying lessons. Get a little Cessna maybe. Combine business with some fun. I've a good friend who . . ."

I should have been paying more attention. I should have kept half an ear out to track the tenor of Richard and Paul's discussion, but in truth it was really more of a monologue on Richard's part. Him buying this. Thinking of doing that. Hoping to put in a pool. A tennis court. And I was carrying on my own conversation with Anne at the same time I was trying to find something that Lia, my picky eater, would deign to consume for lunch. I finally scraped off the inside of a turkey sandwich, spread a little butter on the denuded roll, and cut it up into bite-size pieces for her.

"It's amazing they survive, isn't it?" Anne said while we both watched Lia start to chew tentatively, then hack up the sodden cube of bread into my hand as if it had been poisoned. "And somehow thrive. Max went through a period when he refused to eat anything that was green. So, of course, most vegetables were out, along with grapes, watermelon—not even a speck of green, and no green touching nongreen! A slice of pickle could ruin a perfectly good hamburger for him. I finally won him back over with Lucky Charms cereal—that truly disgusting . . . "

"Well, maybe you know someone, Paul," I heard Richard saying. "The house still needs a lot of work. I've got a long list of improvements I'd like to get going on. And I'm willing to pay whatever's necessary. But the problem is finding someone you can trust. You would not believe some of the horror stories I've been hearing. And today with that . . . " I didn't catch the rest of Richard's sentence, because I talked right over it:

"Paul's in construction," I called down the table. "In fact, I guess you don't realize it, but—"

"I'm booked straight through to the end of the year." My husband, who rarely raises his voice even when he's angry, almost shouted this. Our three girls looked up, alarmed. I was on instant alert. How had I let this happen? Why hadn't I noticed? Paul, usually so careful about keeping his feelings submerged, looked flushed and sweaty, shoulders hunched, ready to blow. What had Richard said? Something about trust. But what else? Paul's used to clients making thoughtless, often demeaning remarks. He prides himself on letting that sort of thing roll off his back.

"Sorry, but, actually, I should be getting back to work now," he added, awkwardly pushing back his chair and standing up. For the first time since coming inside, I noticed that his shirtfront was dusted with dirt and his cap had matted his hair in an unflattering way against the top of his head. I felt embarrassed for him; he looked so unhappy and out of place in the sunlit, high-ceilinged room he'd spent so many months helping to build.

"But I thought we—"

"I've really got to work, Maddie. Sorry," he said, picking up his plate and carrying it out to the kitchen.

"But you and the girls can stay, right?" Anne asked, getting up as well. "I was planning on you helping us finally get those tomato plants in the ground. And finding the perfect place for that trellis, okay?"

We all walked Paul out to his truck, Richard chatting amicably away, obviously unaware that he'd aroused my husband's ire. When Paul got in and slammed the door, Richard leaned his elbow on the open window.

"Maybe you can fill me in on something. That junkyard down there at the end of my drive? What's the story? Can't this town do something about it?"

Paul took a long moment to look down the hill toward Luke's place, now entirely hidden by underbrush and fully leafed-out trees. He turned on the ignition.

"Well, actually, we've tried," he said, putting the truck into gear. "Law says everyone has a right to live the way they want."

"Sure, but, honestly, this is kind of like living next to a dump, Paul," Richard went on. "I bet it's a fire hazard. Maybe a health hazard, as well."

"Kind of doubt that," Paul said mildly enough, though I could only guess what it was costing him to keep his equanimity. "Listen, I'm not partial to those damned icicle lights you see hanging off people's eaves year-round these days. But what can I do?"

"Tear the fucking things down in the middle of the night," Richard said with a laugh, slapping the side of the truck. Then he reached into his pants pocket. "What's the damage for the garden, Paul? I assume you guys prefer cash, right?"

"I believe it's all been taken care of," Paul said, refusing to meet my gaze as he backed the truck around and headed down the driveway.

Dinner was subdued. The girls seemed tired out, probably from working in the garden in all that heat. After a while, the straw hats had grown itchy and uncomfortable and, one by one, we'd been forced to take them off. Even a late-afternoon trip up to the pond hadn't done much to revive my daughters' flagging energies. Or, maybe they'd picked up on the tension that pulsed between Paul and me. He'd stopped somewhere to have a beer with his crew, coming home just as we were sitting down at the table. Paul's not much of a drinker these days; it makes him tired and morose. I think alcohol also serves to loosen the tight rein he keeps on himself—and he dislikes feeling that his control is slipping.

In the summertime, the girls prefer to sleep outside in a tent we pitch for them in the wildflower field. It's their way of getting away, I suppose, without having to leave home. And Paul and I encourage it because we get to make love as often as we like. But that night, after the girls had changed into their pajamas and Paul had walked them out to their sleeping bags and tucked them in, I waited for him in the kitchen, dreading what was coming.

"Hey," he said, the screen door slamming behind him.

"They have a flashlight out there?" I asked, stalling for time.

"Yeah. They're fine, Maddie."

"Paul."

"Listen."

"I'm sorry. Really."

"No, listen to me. This is—" Paul folded his arms on his chest. He's a big man, powerfully built, eighty or so pounds heavier than me. But his physical strength has never scared me. It's his unbending, unyielding, almost unfathomably dense moral core that I find terrifying. He's not preachy or judgmental, but his righteousness is like a ramrod. "This isn't easy for me to say. But what are you thinking? He's such a prick! So entitled and full of himself. I can't believe you actually believe we could be their friends."

"No," I said. "Not him. Not with Richard. I agree with you—he's not our kind of person. But Anne is. She's fun and funny and we—we just really hit it off. And the kids all like each other. You saw how well they got along today, didn't you? How much the Zeller kids adore Rachel?" I could hear the pleading in my voice, and I resented it. Why should I be forced to justify any of this to Paul?

"So, it's just her then? Anne and the kids? Husbands not included? I don't have to go fly-fishing with that son of a bitch?"

"You really don't like him, do you."

"You didn't hear what he said about Bob, did you? At lunch? He said he thought Bob looked like a crook."

"Oh, Paul, I'm sorry. I didn't—"

"He obviously had no idea the guy was my brother. Or who knows?

Maybe he did. But just because Bob refused to kiss his wife's ass—the way I did. Goddamn it, Maddie, sometimes I—"

I made a move toward him, but he waved me off.

"And I'll tell you what else. I can't honestly get a read on her. She seems a little—I don't know—out of control or something. She talks a mile a minute. And I didn't like the way you acted with her today."

"What way? What do you mean?"

"Christ," Paul said, turning away from me and toward the sink. He took a glass out of the drainer, filled it with water from the tap, and took a gulp.

"What the hell do you mean?" I asked again.

"Okay. I mean that you were mimicking her gestures, the way she talks. I've been noticing that you've been using new words and phrases. I don't think you're aware of it, but suddenly you've been saying 'do you know what I mean?' all the time. Then today, listening to her, to the two of you, I realized where you'd been picking it up. From Anne."

"So what?" I was hurt and shocked. I was also horribly embarrassed. Had Anne noticed that I'd begun to imitate her? Had Richard? I could feel my sense of self start to slow, like a top beginning to wobble. Who was I? I hated having to think that I wasn't who I thought I was. That every time I was sure I was getting somewhere, finally finding my footing and striding forward, I'd get kicked back down again. And to have Paul be the one who did the kicking! I was furious with myself. No—I was furious with him.

Paul could be so cautious at times, so plodding. So what if I tried out a new phrase or two? Why should it bother him? But I knew why, didn't I? He needed his world to be absolutely black and white. Good guys here, bad guys over there. Everything set and fixed in its place. He had trained himself to think this way. He long ago decided that his life was something he was going to have to build by himself, one plank at a time, consulting the blueprint in his head, knowing exactly what it should look like in the end. But I was discovering that I no longer wanted to limit myself the way Paul did. I liked the idea of being open to new possibilities. New opportunities. While Paul kept moving along in the same old direction, at the same speed. Afraid to deviate. Unwilling to change. I wanted to shake him up, the way he had me. I wanted to hurt him.

"I think you're just upset that I've made this connection, that I can actually be close to someone like her. You say you hate it when people around here talk about 'us' and 'them' when it comes to the weekenders. But when you get right down to it, I think you really believe we should stay separate."

"No, I don't," he said, putting down his glass and turning to face me. He looked tired and sad. Fighting like this took too much out of us. I could feel him struggling to explain himself, to find the right words. "I just don't want you to get hurt. I don't know what this woman wants from you."

"That's exactly my point!" I said, upset by how badly he'd blundered, how little he understood what I was feeling. "You can't believe that someone like Anne would want someone like me—simply to be her friend."

I went to bed in Rachel's room that night. I lay there sleepless for a long time, replaying the argument in my head, until the words started to lose their heat. The whole outburst began to seem ridiculous, overblown. The bottom line was that Paul didn't like Richard Zeller, and who could blame him? I would have been furious, too, if I'd heard him make that remark about Bob. So Paul had allowed his negative feelings toward Richard to spill over to Anne as well. He didn't know her the way I did. He'd only met her for the first time that day, in Richard's presence, and I was beginning to notice that she wasn't at her best then. I sensed that Richard made Anne edgier, more "on," than when it was just the kids and us. I could see Paul's point: she had seemed a little manic and flakey. But that was due to Richard. The man really was pretty odious. I agreed with Paul on that, as I did on most things.

By four thirty, when Paul climbed into bed beside me, I'd fallen asleep and momentarily forgotten what had happened between us. I automatically nestled up against him. Then, when the argument began to come back to me, it seemed ridiculous to pull away. Our disagreements never last long. Most, like this one, tend to blow over without any lasting damage. But that's how love works, I think, how we all manage to keep soldiering on together. At some subconscious, microcosmic level, we're busy shifting, realigning, rearranging our differences. Breaking everything down, leveling things off, smoothing it all over. So that when we wake up in the morning, it's difficult to recall with any clarity what had seemed so important and divisive the night before.

10

"Mom, you got a minute?" Rachel asked a few nights later. We'd finished supper and Rachel had, somewhat surprisingly, volunteered to take Lia and Beanie upstairs to brush their teeth and get them into their pj's. I was catching up on the household accounts, bills and envelopes spread out in front of me across the kitchen table. Paul wouldn't be home until after dark. Now, around eight o'clock on a warm June night, that was at least another hour off.

"Sure," I said, putting down my pen and closing the checkbook. Rachel remained slouched against the door frame, her arms folded across her chest. She's so like her father at times: the same round, hopeful face, that gray, discerning gaze. And I often feel that, like Paul, she can read me far better than I can her. This past spring, I began to sense that she was distracted a lot of the time, that something had changed in the rhythm of her days, the number and timing of the endless phone calls to and from her friends. And then I saw her one afternoon in Northridge, walking along the street with Aaron Neissen, a senior, two years ahead of her in the large regional high school she attends, and one of the shining lights of the basketball team. He's tall, lanky, a little geeky-looking, but with a rich bass rumble of a voice and a smile that lights up his still-evolving face.

She was tight-lipped and dismissive when I asked her about him. But I remembered what it was like at her age. Her very refusal to share him with me convinced me that he was important to her. Her secret. The beginning of her own separate existence. I've kept my prying to a minimum and have been rewarded with brief updates: he's been accepted at Dartmouth on an academic scholarship; he's spending the summer as a counselor in Maine, where he's worked for the past three years; when the phone rings past ten o'clock, it's Aaron calling, and she likes to be the one who answers.

"What's up, honey?" I asked when she didn't budge from her spot in the doorway.

"I've made a decision about something," she said, hugging her chest. "You and Dad have been telling me that I should start thinking on my own. Working through what I want, what I believe is right."

"Yes," I said, trying not to show my growing apprehension. It was unlike Rachel to stand on ceremony—literally—the way she was doing. "Do you want to tell me what this is all about?"

"Okay. Well, I think you know that I haven't exactly been having the best time working at Aunt Kathy's this summer, right? I mean, it's boring doing the same stupid craft things every morning, then trying to keep the peace in the afternoons when the kids begin to run wild. The problem is, Mom, there's really not enough to do to keep everyone occupied all day. They should put in a pool or something."

"You know they don't have the money for that."

"Yeah, well, I'm sorry, but it's gotten to the point where I really dread going over there. And I know Beanie's unhappy, too. That Tova picks on her all the time. And the thing is, I'd find a way of putting up with it if there was nothing else to do. But last Saturday, Mrs. Zeller offered to pay me twelve dollars an hour to babysit Max and Katie during the day. Do you know what that means? I could be making a hundred dollars a day! That's what Aunt Kathy's giving me for a whole week—and Mrs. Zeller said it would be fine with her if Beanie and Lia came along, too."

"Came along where?" I asked, a little upset that Anne hadn't broached the subject first to me.

"To the Zellers'. Or the pond. She said she'd drive us wherever I wanted to take them. She just really needs some totally free, uninterrupted time to unpack everything, get the house in shape. She told me to think about it. She said that she's never known anyone who could handle Katie and Max the way I do. But she didn't want to pressure me, you know? Then, if I decided to do it, she said she'd ask you if it was okay. And I've made up my mind. I really like Max and Katie. I want to do it, plus I think Lia and Beanie would be a whole lot happier with me and the Zeller kids than at Aunt Kathy's. So. That's my decision."

"I see," I said, recognizing in her nervousness what was left unsaid: how to explain all of this to Kathy. How to break away without hurting her aunt and uncle. What to tell Paul. The Aldens could be so prickly and full of pride. No way that Rachel should even hint that the farm itself, or Kathy's less-than-creative approach to child care, were factors in her thinking.

"I understand," I told her. "The money is fantastic. It would be a little crazy to turn it down. And, of course, you don't want to put Aunt Kathy in the position of trying to match that kind of pay. On the other hand, you don't want to leave her high and dry. Do you know of anybody who might want to help out there?"

"Yes!" Rachel said, finally leaving her post and sitting down across from me. "I called Susie. She's willing to take over. You think this is okay, then, Mom? Is it like, going back on my word or anything? Is Dad going to be mad, do you think?"

"I don't know," I told her. "Let me talk to him about it. But as you said, you've made up your mind. It's your decision. And you're right, we've been encouraging you to think for yourself." Though I couldn't help but wonder how much of Rachel's eagerness to work for Anne was predicated on my friendship with her. Rachel had been witness to its development. The way Anne had showered me with her compliments and praise. Disarmed me with her eagerness for my company, with her overt affection for my children. Not that her wooing of us felt orchestrated or manipulative. I had drifted willingly under her spell. After all, she was exciting and exotic. She was everything that I had, up until this time, always envied. But, perhaps even more important, she obviously viewed me and my family as worthy, indeed exceptional, as well. I think both Rachel and I looked into the approving mirror that Anne held out to us and were seduced by what we saw. It was not Anne so much as our own reflections that attracted us: the beautiful, brighter creatures that, by virtue of Anne's interest and insistence, we saw that we could be.

I believe I took the right approach with Paul. I laid the situation out in strictly financial terms. How could Rachel go on working for Kathy when she had such a better offer? I implied, too, that working for the Zellers would be more of a challenge for her, more difficult and demanding. She'd been helping out at Kathy's on and off for several years now, wasn't it time for her to take on something new and different? If he saw through me and my arguments, he didn't say so. We'd been avoiding even minor disagreements since our blowup the other night. I think we both recognized that the

Zellers—individually and as a couple—represented a serious, unresolved conflict between us. Paul probably realized that if he raised objections about Rachel working for them, we'd soon be wading back into those treacherous waters.

"Twelve an hour? That's more than I'm paying my Sheetrock guy! I guess she does have to go for it, right? You're sure she's okay with this? I mean, this is a real job. She won't have Kathy around to make sure everything runs smoothly."

"She's babysat before," I pointed out. "But you're right. This is different. It's a lot more responsibility. But I think it will be good for her, don't you?"

Typically, Kathy didn't show much of a reaction when I told her that Rachel had been offered an amazing opportunity, one both Paul and I agreed she shouldn't pass up. I was nervous about having to break the news and probably told her more than was necessary. About Anne. The house. How it had been my first big sale. How great Anne and her kids were. Not like so many weekenders.

"Sure, the Zellers. Bob told me about them. Well, you know I can't pay that kind of money. It was sweet of Rachel to line someone else up."

"And Anne said that Rachel could bring Beanie and Lia, too. Max and Katie Zeller get along so well with my girls."

"Oh," Kathy said. "I see. That's great. I took on too many kids this summer for sure. This will help lighten the load."

I thought it had gone well, and told Paul so that night.

"Yeah, Bob gave me a call on the cell this afternoon. Wanted to touch base and make sure everything was okay."

"Meaning what? Did I somehow give Kathy the impression that it wasn't? She said she was relieved, for heaven's sakes. Fewer kids to worry about."

"Right," Paul said. "That's what Bob said, too. Apparently Kathy was a little surprised when you pulled Lia and Beanie out as well. I guess I didn't realize that was part of the deal."

"I'm sure I told you. I thought it was so generous of Anne to make that offer. Frankly, I'm a lot happier knowing Rachel will be watching them, rather than having them running around—" I stopped myself before I said anything disparaging about Kathy's day camp. Lately, I'd been doing more of that, I realized, being selective about what I said to Paul, especially when it came to the Zellers. This was for Paul's sake, I told myself; I was trying to be sensitive to his feelings. But I also knew that I didn't want to hear anything negative about Anne from him.

So Paul began to drop the girls off at the Zellers' every morning on his way to Covington, and, generally, I picked them up. On the following Thursday evening, when I stopped by after work, Anne invited us to stay for supper. She seemed agitated and even chattier than usual and she finally got around to telling me that Richard was insisting that they host a huge party on the Fourth of July, now just a few weeks off, and essentially throw open their doors to the whole town.

"He has no idea how much work this is for me," Anne said. "I mean, I'm still unpacking things, still waiting for the downstairs carpets to go in. He's used to just snapping his fingers at work and getting whatever he wants. He went around last weekend, dropping in on complete strangers who just happen to live near us and inviting them to this. He keeps saying that it doesn't matter how much it costs—but that's not the point, is it? I mean, hiring a caterer, lining up a waitstaff, all of this takes time—and it's exhausting."

Anne did look tired that night and preoccupied in a way that I'd never seen before. Rachel had taken the younger kids downstairs to play air hockey while Anne and I cleared the table and had coffee.

"I'm sure Rachel will be happy to help," I told her.

"It's not that, Maddie. I just don't want to have to entertain a lot of people I don't know and don't want to know. Richard likes to be surrounded by a cast of thousands. I'm sure you've noticed how much he glories in playing the lord of the manor. He's even arranged for fireworks that night. Isn't that just so typical? He loves these elaborate displays. He needs to call attention to himself all the time, to feel important, do you know what I mean? I prefer everything on a smaller, more intimate scale. I don't want more than this right now. All I need is one close, true friend—like you—while Richard insists on the adoration of the sycophantic masses."

Though Anne now had Rachel working for her on a daily basis, I couldn't help but notice that the house looked like Anne and the kids were still just camping out in it. We visited often enough for me to realize that Anne wasn't making much progress organizing their lives there. Boxes remained piled up, left untouched where the movers had dumped them, in the room next to the master bedroom that was supposed to become Richard's home office. There were unopened boxes downstairs in the children's room, as well, and Max and Katie were still sleeping in sleeping bags despite Anne's claim that she'd ordered new beds for them weeks before.

"What does Mrs. Zeller do all day when you take care of the kids?" I asked Rachel as we drove home that night.

"I'm not really sure. But she seems to sleep a lot."

What Anne said about me being a close, true friend emboldened me to call her later that night, after the girls had gone out to the tent and Paul was taking a shower. I phoned her from the kitchen, the pleasantly domestic hum of the refrigerator in the background.

"You kind of worried me tonight," I told her. "You looked tired. And Rachel mentioned that you sometimes sleep during the day. I don't mean to pry, but I'm concerned, Anne. Is there anything I can do?"

She didn't say anything for several seconds, though it seemed like much longer than that to me. Anne's usually so quick to respond, I knew I'd hit a nerve. I could hear her breathing into the receiver, and I imagined that she was weighing something in her mind. From Anne's point of view, I suppose, our relationship up until then had been upbeat and fairly superficial, our children getting on well, the two of us finding enough common ground to enjoy each other's company and conversation. There'd been no real down-side, no dark side, no test of understanding and compassion.

"I'm an insomniac," she said finally. "I've been that way off and on since I was a little girl. And since moving up here, it's been mostly on. I'll wake up at two or three in the morning and start to turn everything over in my mind. And all the little worries start to snowball into—well, I'm sure you've had that happen to you. But for me, it's every night."

"I'm so sorry, Anne. Can't you take something?"

"I'm taking it. Believe me, I've tried everything. Nothing really works for more than a night or two. But that's why I have to nap during the day. That's one reason I wanted Rachel so badly. Why this party seems like such an ordeal. I'm still pretty wiped out, but I'm feeling a lot less guilty know-ing Max and Katie are being taken care of. Actually, now, for the first time, I really don't mind it so much. Being here—being awake in the middle of the night, in the thick of the summer, with the crickets singing away and the moonlight coming through the trees—it's really kind of amazing. And you know, last night, I couldn't help myself: I went outside and I rolled all the way down the hill at three o'clock in the morning! I felt so free, truly alive, do you know what I mean?"

I could hear the crickets, too. And outside the kitchen window, a wax- ing moon cast the field and the tent where the girls were sleeping in an otherworldly light—like a snowscape or the surface of the moon. I don't know if, ragged from lack of sleep, I would have been able to see all of this with Anne's sense of wonder. I had my own worries, but I knew I wasn't troubled in the deeper way that she seemed to be. And if I was, I doubted I would have had the fortitude to handle it the way Anne was doing. On her own, in a strange town, entranced by, rather than afraid of, the night. Of course, I would never leave young children alone in a house to roam around outside, to roll down a hill, for heaven's sake! I was too practical for that, too cautious. At the same time, I realized that I wasn't put off by Anne's behavior. I was drawn to it. She said she felt free. Truly alive! Did I? Was I? Maybe Paul was right. But if there was something out of control about Anne, it didn't seem dangerous to me. Instead, it was mesmerizing: a bright flame that beckoned.

Fourth of July in Red River is a pretty modest affair. There's a parade of homemade floats with patriotic themes, usually comprised of a dozen or so kids on bikes decorated with flags, Owen Phelps in his antique Ford truck draped in bunting, followed by the town's two fire engines and the ambu- lance we share with Covington. There's an address by some local notable, an army reservist or a state representative, at the flagpole in front of the town hall, and then foot races and a picnic behind the old high school. But if you want to see fireworks, you have to drive down to Northridge or up to Har- ringdale, and even then, you usually get stuck in all the traffic on Route 206 and the kids get cranky and fall asleep in the car before the first explosive shoots off.

This year, though, all anyone could talk about in the week leading up to Independence Day was the Zeller open house. Anne was right: Richard seemed intent on inviting everyone in the vicinity. He put notices up at the general store, the post office, on various prominent lampposts, even over at the dump. The posters looked professionally designed and featured a red, white, and blue burst of fireworks. Rachel, who was eagerly helping Anne out with the party arrangements, gave us nightly updates about the plans. A

Cajun band was going to play downstairs in the unfinished basement, where a dance floor had been erected especially for the occasion. Green Goddess, the catering outfit in Northridge who handled the bigger weddings and fund-raisers in the area, had created an old-fashioned July Fourth menu of finger food with a gourmet twist: deviled eggs with pickled jalapeno peppers; miniature grilled hamburgers with fois gras; blueberry and strawberry tartlets.

"Sounds a little too fancy for my taste," Paul said a couple of nights before the big event. "I think I'll just stay here and watch the Macy's thing on TV."

"But you've got to come, Daddy!" Rachel said. "Everyone's going to be there. And Mr. Zeller had the fireworks specially ordered. They're supposed to go on for like ten minutes or something. It's going to be great."

But Paul continued to grouse to me about it until he found out that Bob, Kathy, and the kids were going.

"I couldn't believe it—after the way Zeller treated him!" Paul told me. "But Bob says Kathy wants to see what the house looks like on the inside. And he says he has nothing against free food and some decent fireworks. I guess he's right. Why not take advantage of the son of a bitch's hospitality?"

Cars were parked up and down the driveway by the time we arrived. The house was ablaze with lights. I could already see a crowd silhouetted on the deck and more people on the sloping lawn, which was ringed with citronella torches. I spotted Bob's pickup truck as we made our way up the driveway. Inside, the house was mobbed. I knew almost everybody there, at least by sight, and many were people I had grown up with, gone to school with, and were now our neighbors, fellow volunteers at the fire department picnic, PTA comrades, the local crowd. Others, like the Ossermans and the Naylors, were part of the new elite, weekenders who straddled at least two worlds and lived among us, but not with us. Richard was holding forth in the kitchen, surrounded by a group of men who were older, tanned, dressed in faded polo shirts and chinos—clearly part of the second-home contingent.

"So, I say to the guy, listen, you ever actually seen an XKG before, let alone fooled around under its hood? 'Cause I'm not turning this baby over to some virgin . . . Hey, Paul! Get over here. What'll you have to drink?" Richard put his arm around Paul's shoulder when he approached and, in the same expansive tone, went on: "You know everybody here? This is Fred Dwyer, Dan Osserman . . ."

Beanie and Lia went downstairs to find Rachel, who was in charge of games and supper for the children. I made my way through the crowded rooms, keeping an eye out for Anne and stopping to chat with people along the way.

"I was surprised when she called," I overheard Nana saying to a woman I didn't know. "She's been so standoffish—oh, hi, Maddie. Do you know Sheila Lombardi? She runs the Century Twenty-one office in Northridge. This is Maddie Alden, my superstar sales associate of the summer."

"Nana's the best," I said.

"Who were you with before this?" Sheila asked. It wasn't just her expensive haircut and jewelry, it was something in her balletic stance and slightly aggressive tone that convinced me Sheila was another ex-urbanite.

"I started out as Nana's assistant," I told her. "I grew up in Red River."

"Which has been a godsend," Nana added. "Maddie knows every little nook and cranny in the county. It was Maddie, actually, who caught wind of the fact that the man who used to own all this property—the fifty or so acres that Frank and Nicky helped me develop into these amazing places—was ready to sell. She has marvelous instincts."

"Really," Sheila said, looking me over with new interest.

"Don't you even think about it, Sheila."

I kept looking for Anne, and, though I heard her laughter at one point, I didn't see her in the crowd. I talked to the Naylors, who had brought their silly little dogs. I ran into Kathy and her youngest, Danny, who were waiting to use the downstairs guest bathroom.

"God, what a place!" she whispered. "It must have cost a fortune! And all that food! I think half of it is going to go to waste. But I guess for people like this money doesn't mean a thing." Her tone carried a combination of resentment and envy that I often hear around town, and used to feel a lot more myself. But that's changing for me. I'm no longer so intimidated by the Ossermans and Naylors of this world. Even Richard Zeller, for all his bombast and bluster, was slowly beginning to seem less fearsome to me.

I wandered out onto the deck, a fresh glass of wine in my hand. Below me, children ran down the hill, weaving around the torches, screaming with excitement. I could make out my daughters in the crowd, as well as

Katie and Max, their pale faces and limbs almost phosphorescent against the dense encroachment of lawn, trees, night. The fireworks started with a resounding thud, then exploded above the tree line in a fiery cascade of oranges and blues.

"There you are," Paul said, materializing next to me in the dark. "Some party."

"Aren't you glad you came?" I asked him. He didn't say anything, but he took my hand and squeezed it. We watched the rest of the fireworks like that, hand in hand, and it seemed at that moment that we had never been closer. That our dreams had never been more possible. We were making headway, at last, against the stiff current that had worked against us for so long. And it seemed to me that the party was the fruition of all Paul had hoped Red River could be: the new and old divisions blurring, the town coming together at last. I heard people crying "Ooooooh" with each new explosion and I looked down to see our children, spread-eagled on the hill, enraptured by the sight.

I didn't see Anne until just as we were leaving.

"Great party," Paul told her as she came up to us with a flashlight on the turnaround. I assumed she was helping to guide guests to their cars. The night had turned overcast and ominously humid; we'd probably have a thunderstorm later on.

"Thanks," she said. "We couldn't have pulled it off without Rachel. She's been so wonderful, I can't begin to tell you."

"She told me she's staying to help clean up," Paul said. "Give me a call later and I'll come pick her up."

"Or Richard will drive her home. I just don't know how long some of these people plan on staying." She walked down the hill with us, her flashlight flitting back and forth from the graveled drive in front of us to the trees. "Oh, look, Beanie: I think I saw a fairy over there."

"No way," my shy realist replied. "You know I don't believe in them."

"It's not a matter of belief, Beanie," Anne told her as we reached our car. "It's a matter of keeping your eyes open." Anne waited until we were all in the car, then waved as we pulled off. I noticed that she was continuing on down the drive behind us, though she'd turned her flashlight off now. I wondered briefly where she was going.

The girls fell asleep as soon as we started moving. Other cars were pulling out with us. We drove slowly down the steep incline. I looked in the rearview mirror but saw no sign of Anne. We braked behind a Hummer at the end of the driveway, and as we waited to turn, I saw something flash through the trees below. It was coming from Luke's basement windows: a spray of sparks from somewhere deep inside. Luke hadn't come to the party, of course. He'd cut himself off long ago from everybody, not just us. Paul told me he'd heard that Luke would drive all the way into Albany to do his shopping so that he wouldn't run into anyone he knew. Though we hadn't spoken to him for more than a year, I was certain that nothing had changed with him. He fed on bitterness, burrowing into the past. While we were moving ahead, I told myself. Yes, we were finally getting somewhere. Though my pride in our progress was tinged with sadness; you rarely get to move ahead without leaving something behind.

I'm not sure if Paul noticed the cascade of sparks as we drove by, but they seemed to me a silent echo of the bright display that had filled the night sky a half an hour earlier. Like everyone else, I'd been entranced by the spectacle. But toward the end, without warning, I'd had a flash of insight, one that had momentarily drained the night of its goodwill and promise. As the fireworks bloomed above us, lighting up the sky, I suddenly saw illuminated on the hills beyond—in an eerie negative of night replaced by day—the enormous new houses that Paul had helped build for Nicky Polanski, the mansions that I had been selling for Nana. And in that moment of unwanted revelation, I remembered the fields of corn, a wandering brook, the hillside with slowly moving cattle, a stand of sugar maples red against the limitless sky, the forests and meadows of my girlhood. All gone now and never to be recovered.

Part Four

11

I never did find out for sure who told. Or why. Paul was convinced it was someone connected with the people Luke was dealing with in Albany. Someone with a grudge, or who wanted a bigger cut of the cash that seemed to be floating down from the heavens like manna. Or maybe there really had been an undercover effort, as the state investigator told me, a well-coordinated operation that netted, after all was said and done, a grand total of two boys, barely out of high school, who thought they'd lucked into a way of making a good living in bad times. For Luke, I knew that part of the thrill was the idea that they were beating the system, circumventing authority. I think he probably loved the sense of risk inherent in the whole enterprise, as well as the subterfuge. What a joke! Sure, they were in the formative stages of Luke's big development project. They were busy developing 325 marijuana plants in an underground dirt pit, using grow lights powered by secondhand generators, the whole jerry-rigged operation covered over with plywood and tarpaulins.

"The investigation was conducted by the Drug Enforcement Administration in Albany; the New York State Police Community Narcotics Enforcement Unit; the county district attorney, Stanford MacIntosh; the County Drug Task Force; and the county sheriff's office," the assistant DA reported during the press conference.

"Agents obtained and executed search warrants on the Barnetts' main dwelling, the building on the property occupied by codefendant Paul Alden, as well as an extensive search of the Barnett property, where the growing and processing facility was discovered. Both men are being charged with conspiracy to manufacture, distribute, and possess with intent to manufacture and distribute marijuana, and conspiracy to commit money laundering. Some of the sales took place within school zones, which means a mandatory minimum sentence of two years. We will be seeking a far harsher penalty. The district attorney wants to send a message through this arrest and ongoing investigation to anyone dealing in illegal substances in this county: get out now, because we don't do drugs here."

It didn't help that the district attorney was up for reelection and running in a crowded and hotly contested race. Looking back on it, I wouldn't have been surprised to learn that the "We Don't Do Drugs Here" bumper stickers that began cropping up in the weeks that followed were underwritten by his campaign. Or that the barrage of editorials that ran in the local newspapers supporting the incumbent's "get out now" message were more a rallying cry for a candidate than a denouncement of two young men, both first-time offenders. I can see that now. The larger picture. Public opinion. Political pressures. At the time, however, I did not have the luxury of hindsight. Or the comfort of perspective. I was spinning in the vortex, with nothing to hold on to.

"I tried to warn him," my mother said the morning after the raid and arrests, a morning when the news was sweeping like wildfire across the county. "I tried to tell him that Luke Barnett was no damned good." My mother did not swear, so I knew how upset she must have been. But I don't think she fully grasped the ramifications of what had happened yet; I know that I hadn't. It was such a blow—so unexpected and horrendous—that I think we were both just stunned. We kept going back over the facts as we knew them, sorting through the rubble for meaning, the way people sift through the ashes of a burned-down house searching for cherished belongings.

"You knew nothing about this," my father said, standing at the kitchen sink and looking out over the bright, late-autumn day. "You were duped by him into believing this story about developing the land. You never even saw this—this marijuana nursery, this processing plant! My God, to think that he sat here night after night, lying through his teeth to me."

"I did see it, Daddy," I said. "I made Paul drive me up there one day. He kept talking about the construction site and I wanted to see it. But there was nothing there, really, just a big empty space covered over with tarps. He wouldn't let me get out."

"Good. Fine. You're to tell the police that. You're to be absolutely honest. You have nothing to hide. Nothing in the world to be ashamed of." My father and mother both came with me down to Northridge for my meeting with the authorities. My mother waited outside while my father accompanied me into the small room where a police detective, the state investigator, and a representative from the DA's office took turns questioning me. If I was told their names, I forgot them immediately; I wasn't able to make any sense of what was happening. I felt concussed, out of sync with reality, confused by many of their questions: "You spent a lot of time at the Barnett property. You were at the house Paul Alden was occupying for nearly five hours the night before the arrests were made. We found marijuana being processed in the upstairs bedrooms there. What can you tell us about this?"

Or . . .

"You say that you did visit the growing site with Paul Alden in early September. And yet Mr. Alden claims that you were never there. And that you knew nothing about their illegal activities. How do you account for this discrepancy?"

Or . . .

"What were you doing at the Barnett residence when the police arrived with a search warrant? You said at the time that you had been at the house where Paul Alden was living and that he had called to tell you to leave that residence and go to the main house. Why would he do that? What did he ask you to do when you got to the main house?"

And . . .

"We understand that you and Paul Alden are engaged to be married. Obviously, this means you must have a close and trusting relationship. Do you honestly expect us to believe that you knew nothing, absolutely nothing, about the extensive and extremely lucrative criminal activities that he was undertaking with Luke Barnett? That you did not know, did not even guess, that he was helping to grow, process, and distribute marijuana?"

Of all the questions, that last was the only one that made any impact. It tore through my numbness and sank down to the very roots of my worst fear. Duped. It was my father's word. Tricked. Made a fool of. Betrayed. How could I not know? Why had Paul lied to me, over and over again! I had entrusted him with my future, all my hopes and dreams. I had given him my heart, and now it felt as though he had tossed it on the table, in front of these men. How could I not know?

My father stayed on and spoke to the officials when they were done with me. I went to sit in the hallway next to my mother. We were both utterly bewildered by what felt like a loss worse than any death I could imagine; it was the only time I can remember us ever holding hands.

On the way home in the car, my father told me:

"You will do everything you can to cooperate with this investigation, Maddie."

"But I don't know anything. You heard what I told them."

"I think they believe you, but I'm not positive. I'm going to ask Harry to go with you next time." Harry was my father's first cousin, older than him by at least a decade, and a practicing lawyer in Berkshire County.

"Next time? I have to go back?"

"Yes. I don't know if you really understand how serious this is. These people are going to nail Paul and Luke to the wall. They are going to crucify them. And you are going to help them every step of the way, do you hear me?"

It took me months, years really, to understand how deeply my father was hurt by what Paul had done. He was never able to forgive Paul for allowing him to believe in Barnett-Alden Enterprises, for priding himself that he had a role in what he saw as its early success. I think he felt sullied and humiliated by Paul's deception at a time when he most needed to feel otherwise. I also believe he had truly loved Paul; that he felt he had finally found the son he'd probably always longed for. To lose him in such a devastating and public way fundamentally altered my father's character. That love turned into a nagging, obsessive hatred that would work away at him for the rest of his life.

Dandridge remortgaged the farm to pay Paul's bail and to cover what was bound to be a heavy load in terms of legal expenses. Dandridge stood by his son in court and in every other way in public. The whole Alden family closed ranks around Paul. He was one of them, and they took care of their own. I would learn later, however, how Dandridge worked Paul over in private. Day after day, telling him he was a loser, a liar, a failure, a shame to the family. It was revenge, pure and simple, for Paul turning his back on the farm, for thinking he had a smarter plan, that he was better than his father. But Paul was so wounded already I doubt he really felt his father's blows. He believed it was what he deserved, anyway. Perhaps he even welcomed it.

Paul tried to call me twice that first week.

"You will never speak to my daughter again," my father told him.

"Never call here again," he told him the second time. "You are dead to us."

Harry Fedderson met my father and me at the Northridge police station for my second interview early the following week. This time, they asked my father to wait in the hallway.

"We hope you'll be more candid with us this time," the state investigator began, while the police detective activated a tape recorder. "The fate of your fiancé might very well rest in your hands, in what you can—"

"Paul Alden is no longer her fiancé," Harry interjected. He was an ashen-faced, dour man, but I believe he took his responsibility as my legal representative very much to heart. He understood my father's concerns about Paul's actions tainting me and the family. We were there to cooperate, he stated, to do all that was asked of us, but I was not to be implicated. I hadn't broken any law. No Fedderson had *ever* broken the law. In fact, over the past one hundred years or so, there happened to be at least four Feddersons who had actually *practiced* the law, besides Harry himself.

"We will bear that in mind, Mr. Fedderson," the state investigator responded. "In the meantime, Maddie, we have to assume that you want to get at the truth as much as any of us. You are in a unique position in that—and we will assume for the time being that what you have been telling us is accurate—though you didn't know what Paul Alden was actually doing, you were there while much of this was going on around you. You are a witness to conversations between Paul Alden and Luke Barnett. You knew their work habits and schedules, where they said they might be traveling, who they claimed to be seeing."

"Yes. But I don't know what to believe anymore."

"Exactly. And that's not for you to worry about, okay? It's our job to sift through all the information, to sort out fact from fiction. For instance, did they ever mention who exactly they saw in Albany?"

"By name? No. Luke called them his venture capitalists."

"Yeah. And did they go up to Albany together?"

"I think so. Sometimes, anyway."

"How often?"

"Maybe once a month that they told me about. Or twice at the most."

"And where in the city? Around the Capital District? The university?"

"I don't know. They didn't say. I always thought they were purposefully vague about Albany. I thought it was because Luke's father's old law partners were helping Luke out."

"No. In fact, Earle, Haverford, and Barnett has been cooperating fully with the investigation. Do you know why he was fired by that firm?"

"No . . ."

"He was caught selling marijuana to a paralegal there. He said it was the first and only time he'd ever done such a thing. They let him off, though they now regret that they didn't turn him over to the authorities then and there. Have you ever smoked marijuana?" The sudden change of subject and tone threw me off for a second.

"No . . ."

"You don't sound so sure. Why is it that—"

"She answered your question," Harry interrupted. "For the record, she said that she has not. Can we move on?"

"Have you ever seen Paul Alden or Luke Barnett smoking marijuana, or doing other kinds of drugs?"

"Well, yes. A few times. . . ."

It went on like that for another hour and a half. We backed and filled over the past year, tediously going over the chain of events as I remembered them: Paul's worries about finding work . . . Luke's development idea . . . the financial backing from Albany . . . the sudden influx of cash . . . the trips to Albany . . . the new Jeep . . . my visit to the site . . . the argument a night or two before the raid when Paul cried, "Don't talk fucking dope talk to me! Don't think I don't know what you're trying to do" . . . his call that day telling me to go up to the house . . .

"Thank you," the police detective said. He stopped the tape recorder. "We're going to break for lunch now. Be back here by two o'clock, please."

The meal was a stilted, unhappy affair. The three of us went to Salter's, at that point Northridge's fanciest restaurant. We each silently paged through the lengthy, ornate menu, ordered expensive sandwich platters, and ended up eating practically nothing. I knew instinctively that Harry, who in the past had shown a courtly sort of interest in my existence, was repulsed by what he now thought he knew about the drugs and the delinquents with whom I'd somehow entangled myself. Harry was a practical, no-nonsense kind of man. I'm sure he believed that where there's smoke there's fire, and I could almost feel him sniffing the air around me for a whiff of marijuana.

"Do you have any sense of what's going to happen?" my father asked Harry. We'd ended up back at the police station a good half hour before it was necessary, and were huddled together outside the brick building in the dull gray chill. "They can't possibly charge her with anything, can they?"

"They can do whatever they want," Harry replied.

"I'm cold," I said. "Please, I'd like to go inside."

My father was invited to participate in the discussion that afternoon, though it was really more of a monologue by the state investigator, a Lieutenant Riccio. Over the course of my debriefing, he'd been the one who had asked the most pointed and informed questions. He seemed to have the best grasp of the story line, the characters and settings, the overarching dynamic of our little tragedy. He was a balding, stout man, gentle-voiced, polite. The police detective had badgered me from time to time. The man from the DA's office had been frequently sarcastic. Lieutenant Riccio had approached me with the mild concern of a caring teacher, inquiring about a sudden slip in grades. He made me feel as though he understood exactly what had happened, that he believed and trusted me. I found myself longing to confide in him, to tell him much more than he seemed to want to know, and for this reason I knew him to be the most dangerous person in the room.

"This is such an unfortunate situation, Maddie. I hope you know that we all see that. I have this feeling, and this so often happens in cases of this kind, that good people are going to be badly hurt by what we—the group of us that constitute this drug task force—uncover. What you have to understand is that Paul, Luke, and their little business enterprise are actually part of a much bigger and more serious picture. This investigation started in Albany, you see; it began as an operation to break up a very powerful and professional drug organization that we believe is operating in at least five different counties at this point, maybe more. I will tell you, Maddie, that thus far we have been unable to penetrate the heart of that organization. Our leads take us out peripherally to people like Luke and Paul. Don't get me wrong: what those two have done is criminal. They will both be punished, serve time in jail, be put on probation for years to come. But we also know that they didn't work alone—"

"Maddie knew nothing about any of this!" my father cut in angrily. Lieutenant Riccio, whose gaze had been drifting back and forth from the darkening window to me, now turned to stare at my father. It was a cold, judgmental look, and I realized then that it was Riccio who was in charge of the investigation, that he had been from the beginning.

"I'm afraid I'm going to have to ask you to leave," he said. "In fact, Joe, Scott, why don't you take Mr. Fedderson outside? I'd like a chance to talk with Maddie and her lawyer alone. Okay?"

It was an order. All three men pushed back their chairs and left the room.

"I'll get to the point. Obviously, Luke and Paul didn't work alone. We believe they were financed by the drug organization that I mentioned, and that they were allowed to use an already well-established network to distribute the marijuana that they grew and processed. They are deeply, integrally connected with this organization. We know that. It is self-evident. Though they both deny it. Which is a pity. Especially for Paul."

Riccio stood up suddenly and walked around the table to stand behind Harry and me. I guessed he was looking out the window as he continued.

"I believe I'm a good judge of character. It's something you develop after years of doing this kind of work. I believe that Paul is basically a straight shooter. What you told me earlier, Maddie, about him being desperate to find a decent job? I believe that. What he did was take a shortcut—hoping to make a lot of money fast. I don't think he thought through the situation— that what he was doing was illegal. I don't think he could allow himself to face that, do you understand? He wanted the money too much. And why? He told me why, Maddie. He wanted to put enough aside to get married, to start a construction business, to begin a family."

I felt tears stinging along my eyelids. Riccio's words were like a comforting embrace. He was telling me exactly what I needed to hear. He was giving me back my life. Paul hadn't meant to hurt or humiliate me. He'd taken a terrible and foolish risk because he loved me; he had done it for us. Harry must have sensed something of what I was feeling. I give him credit that he saw before I did where all this was going. He realized that I was part of the bigger picture, too.

"What do you want her to do?" Harry asked as Riccio came back around to his side of the table. He didn't sit down. He just stood there, looking at me, his head tilted appraisingly. I think he was trying to see into me, to understand what I was made of.

"Talk to Paul," he said to me, ignoring Harry's question. "Let him talk to you. Have him tell you what he told me. He needs you right now. He's very much alone and in a lot of pain. Talk to him, Maddie. Let him see that he's only hurting himself by not telling me what he knows. I only need a name or two. Not that much. I won't make this offer to Luke, do you understand? As I said, I'm a good judge of character. I can believe what Paul tells me. Not Luke. Think about that a little bit, Maddie. This was all Luke's big idea, wasn't it? The plants were grown and processed on Luke's property. Luke's in serious, serious trouble. But I think there's a way of making things easier for Paul if he helps us out."

"We don't care about that," Harry said. "What about Maddie? If she does this, will you leave her alone from now on? Will you guarantee us that her name will be kept officially out of the investigation, the trial, anything and all to do with this case?"

Riccio looked from Harry to me. He nodded and gave me a sad smile.

"Of course," he said. "I think Maddie and I understand each other."

12

Everybody knew. I believe it was all anybody really talked about, though never in my presence. I felt both radioactive and invisible; some people avoided me, others looked right through me. A hush fell when I passed certain groups in the hallway at school. Conversations broke off abruptly when I walked into the Red River general store. Word spread. The story, covered extensively by the *Northridge Times-Dispatch,* was picked up by a Boston paper and carried on the AP wire. "New Cash Crop Found in Rural Farming Community: Marijuana." The news articles were heavy on background, especially Luke's, and light on any developments in the case itself. Luke and Paul were out on bail; the investigation was ongoing. My name was never mentioned in any of the items. But I think most people assumed I had to be involved in some way. Over the last six months or so, I'd been seen everywhere with Paul and Luke—and hardly ever with anybody else.

My father and Harry had argued about how I should get in touch with Paul.

"Have her just pick up the damned phone and call," Harry had advised after we left the police station and were walking back to the parking lot. "The sooner she gets the conversation over with, the sooner she can move on. Don't let this fester, John. You need to cut this person out of her life with a knife, do you understand?"

"Oh, I understand," he said. "I also know that Paul would see through her in a minute if she contacted him after all this. He'll know she's been set up. Don't you worry, Harry, we'll take care of this our way." But Harry grasped what my father couldn't. My father assumed the world shared his fury and shame. At that point, I'm sure it didn't even cross his mind that I might feel differently. After we got home and he filled my mother in on what Riccio had recommended, he told me, "This is what I think: Paul's going to try and get in touch with you again. Let him make the first move. It will be easier for you to be yourself with him that way—and to convince him to talk to the lieutenant. That's all you've got to do, Maddie, then you're clear of this thing, okay?"

He believed he was reassuring me, promising me Paul would be out of my life. I thought it odd that no one seemed to realize that there was only one way I would be able to convince Paul to name names. No, I think Riccio knew, or he would never have suggested this route in the first place. Nothing happened for almost another week, then, just when I was beginning to despair, it came via a most unlikely messenger.

"Hey, Maddie." It was the same old pickup truck only hiked up another two feet and refitted with enormous new mufflers. Since graduating last year, Kenny had obviously been busy doing what he loved most. School was out for the afternoon and I was in front of the main entrance waiting for the bus. As usual these days, I was alone.

"What are you doing here?" I asked Kenny. "Picking up Ruthie?"

"No. I thought you knew. She's been out sick. I was just around, seeing somebody. You want a ride home? I'm heading that way."

There was something sweetly comforting about riding along in the front seat next to Kenny; it was like regressing to the lost innocence of what seemed a lifetime but was really less than two years ago. How far I'd traveled, back and forth along these same roads, since that first kiss on the Ferris wheel! Kenny and I had never had much to say to each other. I assumed he'd turn on the radio soon, or else we'd drive along in our old companionable silence.

"I'm sorry about what happened, Maddie," he said soon after we made the turn south onto Route 206. "I bet it's been hard on you."

"Oh," I said. I could handle being misunderstood by my parents. I could take being ignored by my schoolmates. Stared at by people in town. But Kenny's kindness hit me hard. I looked out the passenger window, away from him, blinking back tears. "Yes. Thanks. Thank you."

"These things get all blown out of proportion, I think. Everybody can make a mistake. That's my feeling about the situation, anyway. I've never been that tight with Paul, you know, but I can tell you that he's basically a good guy. He's always been okay to me—I mean, in spite of everything."

These were the most words I'd ever heard Kenny utter at one time. I was touched by what he was trying to say, but I also wondered about what seemed to me like nervous chattiness on his part.

"And Luke. I don't know him that well, either, really. But, you know, he's been a good friend of Ruthie's. And he seems like an okay guy—not the way everybody's painting him out to be. He's been very quiet and grateful since he came to stay with us."

"Luke's living with your family?"

"Well, it's just Ruthie and me right now. My mom's up in Albany with Grand. They got him on life support, you know. When Ruthie heard that Luke's mom was in the hospital again, she made us drive right over there and bring him home to our place. Good thing, too."

"How long has he been living with you?" I asked. I'd been so isolated by my own pain I hadn't really registered the fact that Ruthie wasn't in school. Nor had I heard about Mrs. Barnett being institutionalized again, though I was hardly surprised. I remembered her terrified "Lukie, is that you?" and then her skittering away up the stairs when the police cruisers approached. For the first time, I wondered how Luke had managed his bail, who was supporting him legally and otherwise. It was so like Ruthie to forgive Luke all his past transgressions and take him under her wing. She was the kind of person who was incapable of withholding help to anyone who needed it—even if she knew that it would only end up hurting her in the long run. And she loved the drama and excitement of other people's troubles, from the splashy breakups of Hollywood celebrities to the drunken brawls of the couple down the road.

"A week about," Kenny said, turning onto Old Northridge Road.

"I thought you were driving me home."

"I was hoping you'd come back to our place," he said, glancing sideways at me. He looked anxious and unhappy all of a sudden, his dark brow furrowed. "There's someone who wants to talk to you."

"Kenny, please, no! I can't see Luke." I meant that almost literally. I couldn't really conceive of him anymore. He was no longer a person to me. Riccio may have given me back Paul, but he'd taken away any human feelings I might have had for Luke. Riccio had more or less said what I believed in my heart: this was all Luke's idea. His fault. His responsibility. He'd manipulated Paul into helping him, and now Luke was allowing an essentially innocent man to face the consequences of his own grandiose and disastrous schemes. Luke Barnett was a black hole, sucking all the light and joy out of my life.

"It's not Luke. It's Paul. He has to see you, and your dad won't let him. So Ruthie thought up this idea, you know?" He kept glancing over at me. "I was supposed to break the news gently. Talk you into it. Because we used to be friends?"

"We're still friends," I told him. "Don't worry. You did the right thing." I saw it all now, especially Ruthie's role in devising this solution. I'm sure she saw Paul and me as star-crossed lovers, Romeo and Juliet, in need of a quiet chapel to plan our elopement. I knew that as far as she was concerned, our predicament was tragic and thrilling, and she loved being in the middle of all the intrigue. Oh, what I would have given at that point to have Ruthie's capacity to spin the sad facts of our situation into one of her romantic fantasies!

The Genzlinger place was made up of three mismatched structures: a prefab A-frame where the family lived, a double-wide trailer that had been home to Kenny's grandfather until his recent stroke, and an enormous shingled barn, the only structure left over from the original farm that had once stood on the property, where Kenny worked on his cars. The quarter acre of land separating these buildings was patchy and rutted, both turnaround and parking area for the dozen or so cars and trucks that Kenny was in various stages of rebuilding. I thought the A-frame looked abandoned. The windows were curtainless. A garbage can sat on its side—its lid having rolled a few yards away—at the bottom of the short flight of steps that led up to the side door. Then I saw Ruthie at the window, the door opening, Paul coming out, and then turning around to say something to Ruthie and wave her back inside the house. He came down the steps with an almost painful deliberation, his hands thrust into the back pockets of his jeans. All the Alden boys walked that way, in a kind of he-man saunter that looked cocksure to those who didn't know any better.

"I'll take you home when you're ready," Kenny told me, getting out of the car. He left his door open. Paul got in and slammed the door shut. We sat there, both staring straight ahead at the automobile graveyard before us. The situation felt hauntingly reminiscent of the night Paul drove me home in the snowstorm and we sat in his VW at the bottom of my driveway. The night when, in talking about Kenny, he said to me: "I hope you're not going to make the same mistake about me. Think I'm someone I'm not."

I didn't know that I was crying until I felt the tears rolling down my cheeks. I tried to wipe them away before Paul saw them.

"All I've been thinking about is how much I've hurt you," Paul began. His voice was shaky, and it took him several seconds before he could continue. "I don't know if I can explain any of this to you in a way that will make sense, but I'd like to try. Will you let me try?"

I nodded enough times for him to see, without turning my head. I knew that if I looked at him I would fall apart, and I couldn't let myself do that. I had rehearsed what I was going to say to him, and I needed to stay in control of myself.

"Luke didn't tell me in the beginning exactly what he had in mind," Paul began. "He talked a lot about using what we had—our birthright, our land—to build our future. He had this idea, he said, for developing the Barnett estate. Yes, it was vague. I remember you saying to me that it all sounded so vague. And it stayed that way until . . . well, until it wasn't anymore. There are things I can't tell you because I don't want you to know more about any of this than you need to. But I will tell you one thing, Maddie: you can't know, you'll never know, how much I hated keeping you in the dark about everything. But I couldn't let you get involved. I didn't want you to be in the middle of any of this. Do you understand that?"

"I think so." It was the first thing I'd said aloud, and my voice sounded girlish and small. "What did you think when you found out what Luke was actually doing?"

"At first, I thought he was crazy. The whole thing was illegal. Risky. Just plain nuts. There was a week or so when I wanted out. Luke said fine, but that he was going to go ahead anyway. He didn't need me; he had his Albany people. And then, I don't know, I just sort of let myself go along with it for a while. Things were so bad at home. I was working for nothing at the dairy, and there was no other work out there. Nothing. And Luke said something that struck me as true: we were just farming, really, and then selling what we grew. It was the natural order of things. We were growing something that people really wanted, and would pay good money to buy. Then we actually started to make some money. It happened so fast. It was so easy!" Paul shook his head as he stared out past the half-dismantled cars and trucks.

"You lied to me. You lied to my parents. You—"

"I lied to myself, Maddie. I kept finding reasons why it was okay, why it all made sense. Why it was just the beginning. A way to make a start. I was putting some money away. Luke and I—you know we still kept talking about his original idea. Trying to do something with the land. Maybe put up some houses on spec. I began to think that it was all doable. We just needed to get a little money together. Get past this first phase. That's how I thought about it. I want you to know that I was determined to be out of it—done with the marijuana—before we got married. That was my deadline. By then, I figured I'd have enough money put away. . . ."

"What happened?" I asked. "What was going on when you called me at the cottage?"

"We heard something—from one of Luke's contacts."

"Were you in Albany?"

"What does it matter, Maddie? I just knew I had to get you out of there."

"Because why? Because you had drugs there, too, right? Upstairs?"

"I'm sorry. How did you find out?"

"The police," I said. There was no point in not telling him at least part of the truth. "I've talked to them twice. They made me go over and over everything. I think they finally had to face the fact that I couldn't help them much."

"I'm so sorry. God, I'm just . . . "

"My parents, well, you know they'll never get over this. My dad is like . . . insane, I think."

"And my dad has me by the balls," Paul said. "In a really weird way, I realize that—deep down—he's not all that upset about it somehow. He's got me where he wants me now. You know that fight I had with him this summer? When I moved out? I don't know how he knew, but somehow he found out what Luke and I were up to. I wouldn't put it past him if he drove up to check out the site himself, you know? He was so pissed when I decided not to stay with the dairy. He told me I was a lowlife, a loser. And now he tells me that every day just to make sure I haven't forgotten."

"And Luke? Kenny told me he's living here now."

"Yeah. Well." Paul shook his head. "He's in pretty bad shape. I guess I never really realized how much dope he was smoking, but it was obviously a lot more than he should have. He says he's an addict. That it runs in the family. Ruthie's driving him up to Harringdale for NA meetings. He has an uncle in Saratoga who says he'll be willing to help him out if he can pull himself together. This has hit him really hard. I should have seen what was going on with him. I should have realized he was losing it."

"So you don't blame him for any of this?" I asked, turning to him finally. "Can't you see how he's manipulated you? From the very beginning! How he's used you and—"

"No, Maddie," he said, reaching for my hand, but I pulled it away. "I take full responsibility for my actions. I knew what I was doing. I knew why I was doing it. I blame myself for not stopping Luke when I should have. For letting him get in way over his head."

"I don't believe this! I can't believe what I'm hearing! This was Luke's idea. Luke's land. His contacts. His total and absolute screwup. And *you* want to take responsibility for it?"

"Yes," Paul said. "I do. Luke and I went into this together, but I realize now that I was the one who went into it with my eyes wide open. I think Luke was too out of it most of the time to really understand what was going on. I should have known that this was all just a crazy pipe dream—literally. It was all just stoned bullshit. What idiot wouldn't get that, Maddie? I'll tell you who: someone who wanted way too much to believe it could actually work out. Someone who didn't want to see what was right in front of his fucking face: a friend who was spinning out of control."

"And taking you with him!"

"I let him, Maddie. I allowed it to happen. And I wasn't stoned the whole time, was I? That's the difference. That's where the blame lies. Luke was not responsible for his actions. I was. Can't you see that?"

"What's going to happen?" I asked.

"I'm going to jail. I'm not sure for how long."

"Riccio told me you have some say in the matter. You have a choice."

"No, I can't do that."

"You can't? You can't give the man a name or two in order to get a reduced sentence?"

"That's not what this is about," Paul told me. "It's not about the names. It's about turning on my best friend. They know they've got Luke, and they won't let him go. They're not going to cut him any slack. But they see me as a gray area, someone whose involvement they can paint a couple of different ways if they need to. I'm not a fool, Maddie. Talk about being manipulated! That's what they're trying to do with me. I'm sorry they're trying to use you, too. I'm so sorry you're involved in any of this. I think you better go. I think your dad is right. I should be dead to you."

"It doesn't work that way," I told him. "You don't stop loving someone because he made a mistake."

"I think you do," Paul replied, reaching for my hand again, and this time I let him hold it. "I think you do, if that mistake is so bad it could ruin your life."

"That's why I'm saying: you have a choice."

"What? Between more time in prison and betraying Luke?"

"No. The choice is between Luke and me," I told him. "I'm willing to wait for you. I'm willing to support you in any way you need. Because I love you, Paul. But I have to know you love me, too, more than anything else. That you want to be with me, marry me, start a family with me, as soon as we can. You have to prove to me that our life together is more important than anyone else's. That's what I'm asking. I'm willing to give you everything. But you need to do this one thing for me. For us."

They both pleaded guilty, though Paul's charges were reduced to drug possession and conspiracy to commit money laundering. At the sentencing hearing, District Attorney Stanford MacIntosh spoke approvingly of Paul's "sense of guilt and spirit of cooperation." He was sentenced to eighteen months' incarceration in the County House of Corrections, to be followed by five years' supervised release. They were a lot tougher on Luke, just as Riccio had predicted they would be. Even with family connections that still crisscrossed the power grid of state politics, he was given one of the stiffest sentences ever handed down to an eighteen-year-old in county history: eight years' imprisonment in the state penitentiary, followed by five years' supervised release, along with, in legal language, forfeiture of assets representing total estimated proceeds of the marijuana conspiracy. What that meant, in fact, was a further whittling down of the Barnetts' already greatly diminished fortunes. I don't think that it helped matters for Luke that Paul's information did not bring the big break in the larger case that Riccio had been hoping for. Who knows? If they'd been able to penetrate the Albany ring, and finally make some key arrests, they might have gone easier on Luke in the long run. But that didn't happen.

I still have a photo that I cut out of a *Times-Dispatch* article from the day of the sentencing. It's of Paul and Luke on the steps of the courthouse. They're both in handcuffs. The shot was taken just as they were being separated halfway down the steps to be led off to different police vehicles—and then on to their differing fates. Paul's face is turned away. But Luke seems to be looking directly into the camera. For many years, it was the only photo I had of Luke. I used to take it out, unfolding it carefully as its creases stiffened and yellowed, and gaze at it for minutes at a time. I've always known that Luke's look of scornful defiance, seemingly caught by chance by some news photographer, was actually planned and calculated. He's staring straight at me.

13

I became adept at lying. In front of my parents, I was subdued, sometimes withdrawn—the embodiment of someone who has been deeply hurt and disappointed. They were so solicitous of me, tiptoeing around subjects that might touch, even tangentially, on Paul, the trial, anything to do with a scandal that was still the main staple of local gossip. They encouraged me to join the student orchestra. They were delighted when I told them I was thinking of tutoring a freshman girl in music. I'd been playing the piano since third grade and had become proficient, if not inspired, at the keyboard. My father sent away for catalogs to Mannes and Juilliard and carefully studied the sections on scholarships and financial aid.

"You could do it," he told me. "You've got talent. Discipline. There's no reason not to start thinking about it, Maddie. Your future is wide open. The sky's the limit, as far as I'm concerned."

"It's not very practical, Daddy," I told him. "Being a musician. And I'm really not that good. I've got a heavy touch, according to Mr. Lockhardt."

"That's ridiculous," my mother said. "What does he know? A part-time piano teacher in a little town like this all his life! I agree with your father. And I believe you're a lot better than you give yourself credit for. You've just got to start setting your sights a little higher."

I know that their sudden interest in my future was in many ways fueled by their feelings of guilt about my recent past. Shouldn't they have been able to protect me against what had happened with Paul? I'd been young and impressionable, easy to influence. Shouldn't they have been able to see through his big talk and bluster? I was aware that, supposedly out of my earshot, they debated these questions, analyzing their mistakes, indulging in endless speculative hindsight. But, at this point, I know they also felt that we had all dodged the bullet. Paul was gone, punished. And I was safe. Unscathed. Theirs again.

Their belief in and love for this person I pretended to be touched me deeply. As I played to their sympathies and fabricated rehearsals and tutoring sessions, as I became more and more skillful at hiding my true feelings and motivations, my affection for my parents only grew. I looked upon them with a new tenderness and concern, our roles reversed. Their childlike trust in me made me feel old beyond my years—and filled me with sorrow.

In the beginning, it was mostly Kenny who drove me up to see Paul. The County House of Corrections was in north Harringdale, a run-down neighborhood of a once thriving manufacturing town that had been down on its luck now for more decades than it had flourished. Kenny would pick up Ruthie and me after school and, like our earliest days together, we'd make the forty-minute trip north with the radio blaring and Ruthie skipping up and down the AM dial. With Luke lodged in the state penitentiary, Ruthie turned all her needy attentions on me. Her brush with the notoriety surrounding the arrest and trial had freed her to be even more emotional and histrionic. I think she felt she herself was in the spotlight, or at least warmed by the scandal's reflected glow.

In spite of Ruthie's self-important airs, I was thankful for her help and protection—and by extension, Kenny's. I still don't know if she browbeat Kenny into all those hours of chauffeuring, or if he did it willingly. He was a mute but reassuring presence on these excursions. He didn't seem to mind waiting in the car or walking around the parking area, smoking and checking out the other vehicles, while Ruthie and I visited inside. Eager to take up what she saw as a noble cause, Ruthie had started volunteering at the jail, reading to illiterate and aging inmates.

When I think back on those days it seems always to be winter, bitter cold, the fields of feed corn showing an uneven stubble under frozen-over snow, a hawk circling above a deserted farm. The little towns we passed through with their white clapboard and pink brick houses were bundled up, silent in a somnolent landscape.

"How are you?"

"I'm fine. How are you? What have you been doing? How are your folks?"

"Good. Nothing. They're good. How are you?"

But he didn't need to tell me. I already knew. His self-disgust was palpable; you couldn't miss seeing it. But you could see something else, too: I had become everything he wanted to go on living for.

"You look so pretty. I like your hair like that."

"It's the same as always, really."

"No, something's different. It's a little longer, right? God, what I would give . . ."

He'd spoken to his father. Swallowed his anger and pride. Made his amends. He'd return to the dairy. He had no choice, really. Who else would take him on? Nothing mattered to him now except our future. He worried endlessly about my situation at home, the fact that my parents still didn't know we intended to marry. Wouldn't it be better if I told them the truth? His own father had come around; he was certain my dad would, too

But I knew my father would never change his mind. I was sure of this. He was not a passionate man, and yet he'd allowed himself to be seduced by Paul. My strict father had been taken in by Paul's exuberance and optimism. He'd believed in him. Maybe, if he hadn't cared so much, things would have worked out differently. But he couldn't forgive Paul—or himself—for being deceived. And Paul was almost too eager to reassure me that our future was secure, though his plans lacked the enthusiasm he'd shown when he was going into business with Luke.

"I've been talking to Bob and Ethan about the dairy. We're all going to give it another shot. Really work together this time. Bob's been talking to that organic farming cooperative in Lakeview. Now, of course, we're going to have to talk Dad into making some changes. . . ."

But there was no joy in his voice. No real passion. He'd given all that up. It was one day at a time now. It was as if he'd sworn off any sort of larger ambitions. No more dreams. He was afraid to let himself think big. He was learning to contain his true feelings. Keep a rein on himself. My heart broke every time I saw him, because he was so fundamentally changed. Humble. Grateful to me. No, it was more than gratitude. It was the beginning of his need to idolize me. To put me up on that damned pedestal, where I felt even more remote and alone. I was all too well aware that I'd helped create the man he had become. He was doing this for me. For us, as I'd made him promise. But I was beginning to realize that bargains are never really equal or fair.

One day in late March, as Ruthie and I were leaving the prison, we ran into Paul's younger brother, Bob. Of course, I saw him at school, but he tended to keep his distance there. I was a little surprised when he stopped and grinned at me in that lopsided way of his.

"Hey, Maddie," he said. "Ruthie. So Kenny's been driving you up, huh? I just saw him in the parking lot."

"Yes."

"Listen. I got my license now and Paul's Jeep. You can come with me sometimes, if you like."

The timing couldn't have been better. Ruthie had recently met Lester Hall, the marine she would eventually marry. And as her interest in him flared, it started to flicker for the work she was doing at the prison. She still stood by me, I'll give her that, but her attention was elsewhere now. So I began to make the trip with Bob and sometimes Ethan, too. Though Paul's parents had forbidden his sisters to visit, once Louise also snuck along. It was the first time I'd been with any of them without Paul around. Slowly, I began to get to know them as individuals, as well as how they fit into the overall family structure, which was still something of a mystery to me. Both brothers shared Paul's fair-haired, round-faced good looks, though Ethan was already putting on weight and Bob was a short and wiry version of the standard large-boned Alden issue. They shared some of Paul's traits, as well: they had the same rolling gait and wide-open smile. But Bob was laconic, soft-spoken, shy; Ethan was far more talkative and expansive. The two brothers were unfailingly polite, even gallant, in their own ways. I suppose Paul had filled them in on my difficulties at home, and I was treated like some kind of valuable and potentially breakable cargo.

"We'll be waiting for you outside, Maddie," Ethan said one afternoon after we'd all hung out with Paul for half an hour or so. "Watch your backside, bro."

By then, the worst of that winter was behind us, and when I left the jail twenty minutes later, flanked by Ethan and Bob, the sunlight dazzled across the surface of the wet parking lot. I closed my eyes briefly against its glare, and when I opened them again I saw a familiar figure leaning against a police cruiser at the bottom of the ramp, talking to someone. It was Harry. It turned out that he'd made a private arrangement with the sheriff, who was a college buddy of Harry's younger brother, to keep an eye out for who visited

Paul Alden. I'm not certain why it mattered so much to him. Perhaps he was just getting back at my father and me for involving him in any of this in the first place. Or else he was one of those men who cared more about the idea of family, the sanctity of the Fedderson name, than in the individuals who formed it. Because he'd never been particularly close to my father, it seemed to me, or interested in our family's existence until that point. On the drive back to Red River in his car, he told me he was doing it for my own good.

"And how would you know what that is?" I asked him. I'd never been fresh with him before, but then Harry had taken it upon himself to meddle in something that could only bring heartache to everyone concerned.

"I can tell you what it *isn't,* young lady," he replied. "It isn't hanging around with drug dealers and other scum. It isn't dragging your good name through the streets like some rag. It isn't shaming your parents and your family, especially after we stood beside you, after we jeopardized our own reputations in the community to help you."

"Oh, I see, so this is all about you then," I told him. I was so young and righteous. Angry and stupid. If only I'd held my tongue. If only I could have thought ahead. I didn't understand how easy it is to make enemies. And, once made, how impossible it is to undo the damage.

"No, I'm telling you. You're not," my father said. "I forbid it." It was evening now. Harry had gone. Many words had been exchanged. Tears shed. My mother, exhausted and terrified, was clattering around in the kitchen behind us, trying desperately to normalize the situation by making supper.

"You can't, Daddy. We love each other. I'm my own person. You can't stop me."

"I can. You're underage. You have no money. I refuse to support you if you insist on throwing your life away like this."

"I have no life without Paul. We're meant to be together. Don't you remember how that feels? Don't you—"

"Don't you *ever* equate your mother's and my marriage with whatever you think you share with that person! It makes me sick. You have no idea what you're saying, Maddie. You're just too young to understand what love really means. Don't you see how naive you're being? How selfish? And after everything we've done for you—"

So it went. In tighter and tighter circles. For another hour at least. I understood that my deception had only made matters worse. I sensed that my parents were thinking back over the past few months—and all the seeming harmony and closeness of that time was burning through and disintegrating in their minds like film from an old home movie caught in the projector light. They were shocked by all the lying I had done. What kind of person had I become? How could I hurt them like this? My mother put something on the table that nobody even looked at. My father, finally beginning to realize that he might actually lose this battle, began to spew out his bitterness and rage. I wish he'd hit me instead. Words are so much worse than blows. They never really heal.

"Don't imagine you can come crawling back to us once you take up with him," he said. "You leave this house now, and that's it. You'll never be welcome here again."

"No, John, listen, Maddie, please—" my mother said. Though practical and disciplined for the most part, she tended to lose her head in a crisis. And I don't think either one of us had really understood until then just how thoroughly my father was consumed by his hatred for Paul. Even in the best of times, my father nursed grudges the way some men do alcohol. He'd despised Howell Barnett just on basic principles. And now it seemed that the world had actively turned against my father, slowly robbing him of his livelihood, stripping him of his self-respect. He desperately needed someone to blame for his downfall, and he'd found him.

"That's your choice," I said. "And this is mine." I think I can recall everything about that moment: the close cooking smells in the kitchen, the dull sheen of the linoleum as I crossed the floor, the feel of the cut-glass knob in my hand. I remember a sense of *déjà vu*, of time shuddering back and forth like in an earthquake. Had I done this before? No, it was that I would do it again, over and over again, as I thought back on it in the years to come, leaving and not coming back, my mother weeping and my father dry-eyed, leaving for the first time, the doorknob turning in my hand, and leaving forever.

Part Five

14

I'd finished work early and was helping Anne and the kids in the vegetable garden, when I looked up and saw the police car making its way slowly up the Zellers' driveway. It was the second week of July, and we were in the middle of a heat wave. At nearly six o'clock on that Friday evening, the thermometer was still hovering in the low eighties. The garden was thriving in all the heat and humidity: arugula, Boston lettuce, and the mesclun mix grew in thick ranks, the cherry tomatoes were tiny fists of bright hard green, the purple and white bush bean flowers heavy with promise, and the morning-glory vines, their sky blue parasols tightly furled in the late-day shade, scaled the trellis that Anne had set up at the juncture of the four raised beds.

The front window of the cruiser was down, and I recognized the beefy arm that was draped nonchalantly over its frame. It belonged to Tom Langlois, Red River's chief of police. He'd been three years ahead of Paul in school, a member of one of the extended families of French Canadians who migrated south at the beginning of the last century, lured by the rolling farmland and a relatively gentler climate. Tom was third-generation law enforcement; he'd joined the department shortly after coming back from the first Gulf War, and had taken over as chief a few years back.

"Damn," Anne said when I pointed the cruiser out to her. "I didn't hear the security alarm, did you? I hate this system. A mouse sneezes and it goes off. It's been triggered for one silly reason or another four times since we moved in." We started up the hill together, leaving Rachel in charge of the children.

"Legally, or whatever, the cops have to come by and check things out if we don't respond right away," Anne said. "But after the third call they get to charge us twenty-five dollars a visit. So, of course, *they* don't mind." She wiped her hands on the back of her khaki shorts. We were both sweating.

I felt damp and uncomfortable, my fingers grimed with dirt, but somehow Anne, slim and tanned in shorts and a sleeveless T-shirt, managed to project a casual elegance. Tom's dark glasses were mirrored, but I could tell his gaze was on her as he climbed out of the cruiser and started toward us across the turnaround. He still carried himself with military pride, though his body had long since given way to fat, his stomach bulging out over his low-slung belt and holstered revolver.

"Mrs. Zeller," Tom said, nodding at Anne. "I'm really sorry to bother you about this. Hey there, Maddie."

"I'd say it's our problem, not yours," Anne replied as she walked right past Tom to lead the way up the front path to the house. It always surprises me how chilly and dismissive she can be to people she doesn't want to know, but I was also aware her attitude wouldn't bother Tom. He's like Paul in the way he's learned how to handle the wealthy weekenders, though some people believe he leans too far over backward in their direction. I'd always thought that he just enjoys the feeling of power his office bestows on him, that he likes to think of himself as being on an equal footing with the millionaire lawyers and brokers who banter with him about knocking off points from their speeding tickets.

"Well, frankly, I think this whole business is ridiculous," Tom said. "I thought you folks were extremely generous to invite everyone up here the way you did. My wife and I had a great time, I can tell you. But, that said, it's still my duty to pass these things along."

Anne stopped at the front door and turned around.

"This isn't about the alarm?"

"No, ma'am," he said, balancing one booted heel on the top step. "We got a complaint about the party, I'm afraid. One of your neighbors called me up about all the cars parking on his land. Apparently, somebody damaged some of his personal property."

"What neighbor? I thought we invited everybody nearby."

"Well, you may have invited him, but he didn't come. He lives down at the end of your road. It's that little brown shingled cottage set back under the trees." Tom pointed down the driveway, but the Zellers' long teak porches and the summer vegetation blocked Luke's house from view.

"Oh, really?" Anne said. "I guess I remember hearing that someone used to be there, but I thought it was abandoned now." I looked at her, surprised. I was sure she knew who lived there; we'd talked about Luke several times already that summer.

"No, ma'am." Tom chuckled, shaking his head to show that he agreed entirely with her assessment of Luke's living conditions. "It's owned by Luke Barnett. He lives and works there, making what he calls his art pieces."

"What happened? Did someone knock one of them over or something?" Anne laughed. I could tell that she'd overcome her initial hostility toward Tom; he was so clearly trying to court her good opinion. But I couldn't understand what kind of a game she was playing with him—and me. Why pretend she didn't know about Luke?

"Yep. Ran right over it!" Tom said, laughing with her, obviously captivated. I hated him at that moment, the way he so quickly sacrificed Luke, whom he had grown up with and known all his life, to gain a little recognition from a relative stranger like Anne.

"I'm sorry it upset him," Anne said. "Is there anything we should do? Maybe go down there and apologize?"

"Well, personally, I'd forget about it," Tom told her. "I think he just needed to vent. He's a little on the loony side. Goes off on these tirades. Most of us have been on the receiving end of his anger at one time or another, isn't that so, Maddie?"

I didn't know what to say. I was confused by Anne's white lie—as well as her obvious assumption that I wouldn't call her on it in front of Chief Langlois. And how could Luke have been so foolish to complain about something so unimportant? He'd exposed himself to ridicule now—as well as unwanted scrutiny.

"I think I've mentioned him to you, Anne. He is a little eccentric," I replied evenly, though I felt an urgent need to defuse the situation.

Richard Zeller did it for me, honking the horn of his silver Lexus as he raced up the driveway toward us. Anne had complained to me a number of times about her husband's fast, aggressive driving, but it seemed to me just part and parcel of his whole domineering personality. I could hear Max and Katie yelling and running up the hill to meet him. As usual, away on business all week, he was being greeted by his children on this Friday night as though he was a returning god. It helped that, like any self-respecting deity, he tended to arrive bearing gifts from his travels: a Pittsburgh Pirates cap for Max, or a San Diego Zoo T-shirt for Katie.

But it wasn't just his largesse that made his children jump all over him as he climbed out of the car. Though absent a lot of the time, when he was home, Richard focused a lot of his attention on his kids. Unlike Anne, he didn't treat them as equals, and he disciplined them with no-nonsense brevity, as though they were underlings on his payroll. But they seemed to thrive on it, perhaps ready for a tougher kind of love after a week of Anne's free-rein approach to parenting.

"We should be going," I told Anne as Richard picked up Katie and Max in either arm and lumbered up the path toward us. My children followed in their wake.

"Oh, Christ, don't tell me—" Richard said when he saw the chief of police.

"No, it's not the alarm this time," Anne cut him off. "And, hold on a second, Maddie. I need to write a check for Rachel for the week. I'll be right back."

"What's up, Tom?" Richard asked, setting his children down with a grunt of relief. I guess I shouldn't have been surprised that he remembered the chief's name. Richard is very good at making people he considers important feel that way. I, on the other hand, often feel more or less invisible in his presence. The babysitter's mother. Someone Anne knows.

"I hate to even bring it up, but . . . " With the same shaking of the head, Tom repeated to Richard what he'd just told Anne.

"What a load of crap!" Richard responded when the chief finished. "As far as I'm concerned, it's too bad someone didn't take the opportunity to flatten the whole damned mess. The place is like a pigsty, don't you agree? I mean, we've got these four really beautiful homes up here now, pumping Christ knows how much tax revenue back to you folks in town, and we've got to look down on that pathetic garbage dump. There's got to be something you people can do to force this crazy shithead to clean things up."

"Well, I know it's been tried," Tom replied. "And I sure wish I could be of some help. But I'm strictly on the serve-and-protect end of things, I'm afraid. This is really a problem you should take up with the selectmen, Mr. Zeller, if you feel so strongly about it."

"Hey, come on, it's Richard to you, Tom," he said, throwing his right arm around the chief's shoulder and walking him back toward the cruiser. Anne came out at that point with her check for Rachel, so I could only catch snatches of what Richard was saying to Tom: ". . . fed up with the attitude . . . whatever you can do to get the ball rolling."

My daughters had heard the entire exchange between Chief Langlois and Richard, so I wasn't surprised when Rachel asked me in the car as we made the curve around Luke's place:

"Is Luke in some sort of trouble?"

"I don't think so," I told her. "You heard what happened, right? I mean, he has a legal right to complain about something like that, don't you think?" As we braked to make the left onto River Road, the late sunlight glinted off some of the objects in Luke's front yard. I'd spent so many months trying to ignore them, trying to force Luke and all of his concomitant problems out of my mind, but now I turned and let my gaze travel over the metal bolts and hubcaps welded into an enormous sea turtle, a rhinoceros, a scarecrow, the mufflers fashioned into a gigantic bouquet of sunflowers, the pair of chairs soldered together from old tractor parts—and the dozens of other wacky, sardonic creations—many of which had been rusting away undisturbed for years. *Oh, Luke,* I thought, *what have you done? Why have you started this now?*

"I guess so," Rachel said, turning to look out the passenger window. The long hay field on our right was lush with humidity, swallows circling and swooping above it, the tree line beyond melting hazily into the purply backdrop of hills. Rachel had been working full-time for the Zellers for nearly a month now, and though she was clearly thrilled with all the money she was making and obviously doted on Katie and Max, I sensed the experience was not altogether a happy one for her. But I couldn't figure out what was wrong. The house was finally in great shape, thanks in large part I'm sure to Rachel's organizational abilities and hard work. Anne and she appeared to be hitting it off; in fact, every once in a while I found myself envying all the fun they seemed to have. I knew that part of my concern stemmed from my sense that Rachel was drifting ever further from me. There were places in her heart that I could no longer reach, moods she fell into that I couldn't account for at all.

"Do you ever see Luke when you're over there, Rach?"

"No. Not really."

"What does that mean? Either you see him or you don't. I believe I asked a pretty straightforward question."

"Sure. What other kind do you ask, Mom? And I'm saying that I've been kind of busy trying to take care of four kids—plus about a million other things. I don't have time to notice much, okay? Besides which, I don't think I'd even recognize him now. I hardly remember what he looks like."

Her anger startled me: where in the world had that outburst come from? Was it just part of her general moodiness, or was something else going on? I glanced over at her but she was staring fixedly out the side window.

"I remember," Beanie announced from the backseat. Though she was only three and a half when Luke stopped speaking to us, I believed her. Gentle, dreamy Beanie has a mind as swift and accurate as a calculator.

"I 'member, too," Lia declared, not wanting to be left out of whatever we were discussing. This was actually the first time I'd talked to my daughters about Luke since that final blowup. Paul and I had decided when it happened that it was all too complicated and sad to try to explain to them. So, frankly, we'd taken the coward's way out: if we stopped talking about him, perhaps we could all eventually grow to believe that he didn't matter to us. That he never had. But now I was forced to face the futility of what we'd attempted.

We had dinner, as we usually did in the summer when the weather was fine, out on the temporary screened-in porch off the kitchen that Paul assembled early every May and took down each fall. This is where we'd long planned to build an extension, a family room cum sunporch, screened on one end, that would run down the entire length of the house. He'd constructed a little deck a few summers back, but then got too overwhelmed by regular work to do more than throw together removable screened panels and corrugated plastic roofing. We'd started a savings account for home improvement years ago, but now Paul was beginning to talk about that small accumulation as Rachel's college fund. And most of the money I was earning had helped pay down a home equity line of credit we'd taken out after Lia was born and Paul wasn't able to work for a long stretch. Though we'd be almost entirely debt-free in a week or two when I got my commission check from the Naylor sale, I knew Paul wasn't ready yet to start investing in renovations. He was almost ridiculously proud of my success, but he didn't trust that it would last. Nor, for that matter, did I. I'd been lucky, that was all. And both of us knew how quickly luck could change.

"The police were at the Zellers' today," Rachel told her father shortly after we sat down in front of our bowls of tossed pasta and chicken salad. Considering her reluctance to discuss the matter with me in the car, I was surprised she'd brought it up so freely with Paul. But then she remained more open with him than me, more needy of his attention.

"What?" Paul asked. "Are they collecting for the steak roast already? Those guys are totally shameless." Paul was a longtime member of the volunteer fire department, which was in constant, often acrimonious competition with the paid police force for fund-raising dollars, especially those coming from the roomy pocketbooks of second-home owners.

"It was just Tom, actually," I said, looking across the table at Rachel and wondering what she was hoping to accomplish. I'd intended to tell Paul about the visit when we were alone later on, when I could put my own spin on what had happened. Rachel must know that any discussion of Luke with her father was bound to be difficult.

"He was there to tell the Zellers that Luke had called him about their party," Rachel continued. "He'd complained to the police because someone had run over one of his sculptures. Mr. Zeller says that he's crazy. That Luke's place is like a garbage dump. That the town has to do something about him."

Paul looked at me. He put down his fork.

"Sounds exactly like something Mr. Zeller would say."

"But he can't really force anybody to do anything, can he?"

"It's already been tried. If Ingrid Soneson and the Red River Historical Society can't get Luke to clean up his act, I seriously doubt Mr. Zeller has much of a chance. There's nothing to worry about, okay?"

"I just wish . . ." Rachel speared a pasta shell and then dropped her fork into her bowl.

"What, Rach?" I asked, but it was her father Rachel turned to when she blurted out with surprising vehemence:

"I don't understand why we can't be friends with him anymore, okay? I mean, I know something happened between you guys. I know all that, and I don't care about it. Because he was our friend, too, you know! It's not fair. It's just not fair! I don't think it's right that he has to be all alone—" Rachel, like her father, rarely lets her emotions get the better of her. She's usually so careful to keep her feelings under control that when they start to spill out, she's easily overcome by them. Now, her face streaming with tears, she slammed out the side screen door and stamped off across the lawn. I began to get up from the bench to follow, but Paul dropped his napkin beside his bowl and said:

"No, no. I want to go."

Beanie and Lia and I finished our meal in subdued silence. Beanie, as usual, seemed lost in her own world, but I knew she must be thinking about Luke; he was her first real friend outside the family. Lia was too young to understand much more than the fact that calm, loving Rachel, whom she adored, was mad at Paul and me. As mother and day-to-day disciplinarian, I was frequently resented and challenged. But Paul's authority was sacrosanct, so Rachel's outburst had, along with resurrecting memories of Luke, overturned the natural order of her younger sisters' existence. Strawberry pop-ups eased their worries a little, but they lingered at the table long after they were done, watching and waiting for Paul and Rachel to, hopefully, make their peace and return.

I sat with them, listening to the rising chorus of cicadas and the distant hum of the highway traffic, always heavier on Friday nights in the summer because of the influx of weekenders and tourists. This is the time of year when you frequently can't find a parking spot in Northridge and you need to make reservations at almost any decent restaurant in the area. It really does sometimes feel as though we're being invaded by aliens, creatures from a far more privileged and aggressive planet who honk their horns and think nothing of swearing in front of our children. These are the people who make up my client base now, and I do believe I'm beginning to know how to handle them better. I'm growing the same kind of armor that Paul has, impervious to insults and snubs. But the conversation I'd overheard between Richard Zeller and Tom Langlois that afternoon had pierced whatever illusion I'd been fostering that the community was coming together. The fault lines were still there. And I knew they lay dangerously close to everything that mattered to me.

By the time Paul and Rachel returned, Paul with his arm around her shoulder, Beanie and Lia were falling asleep at the table. We decided to forgo toothbrushing and pj's for one night, and I carried Beanie and Rachel took Lia out to the tent, and tucked them into their sleeping bags, leaving the electric lantern on low by the screened flap. Rachel walked back with me to the porch, where Paul was sitting down to finish his dinner.

"You two okay?" I asked as we joined him at the table.

"Yep. We're good," Paul said between bites.

"Dad told me what happened. About the property and the sale. How Luke didn't really understand the situation. I just think you could have been a lot clearer with him, you know? And me, too, for that matter."

So, Paul had made me the fall guy. I could tell by the way he was concentrating on the food in front of him that he knew perfectly well what he had done. But how would I have explained things to her? I wondered. I knew how easy it would have been for me to cast doubt on Paul's own role in the mess, to suggest that he, as Luke's best friend, could have done a lot more to avoid what had happened. The story could be told so many different ways. And, in fact, the story began so many years ago that, unless we started from the beginning and told Rachel the whole thing, she'd only always be holding on to pieces of the truth, the way she was now.

"Please remember that I was just starting out, okay?" I told her. "I didn't know how important some of this stuff could be."

"Well, in any case, we've got a plan," Paul said. "We're going to go over to Luke's tomorrow. Buy one of his things. See if we can get a detente going."

"Oh, for heaven's sake—" I started to say, then I saw the look on Paul's face. He and Rachel had worked this out between them; my objections at this point would only make matters worse. "Okay, whatever," I said. "If you think that will help things."

Later, undressing, I said to Paul:

"Sometimes I wonder if we shouldn't talk to Rachel—about everything." We'd been over this ground before. Many times, but not for several years now.

"Water under the bridge."

"But what if she finds out on her own somehow?"

"She won't. Nobody cares about it anymore, if they even remember."

I thought otherwise, but I also realized that there was no point in pursuing the subject with him. Paul liked to think of himself as an accentuate-the-positive kind of guy. Eliminate the negative. It's the Alden way to bury the bad. Cover it over. Keep going. And never speak about what is dead to them. I've always thought of this as another sign of Paul's inner strength. But sometimes I worry that, on my part, it's more an indication of weakness, or cowardice. I just pretend, really—as much to myself as anyone—to have moved on.

"So, are we going to say anything to Luke about Richard—and his threats?"

"Yeah, I'm going to try anyway. Let me do it, though. It can only work coming from me, don't you think?"

"You're sure I should even come? Maybe it would be easier if it was just you and the girls."

"No, I need you there," he told me, rolling onto his side. "I need you here."

I lay awake for a long time afterward, thinking about how much I dreaded facing Luke again. I could never tell Paul this, but the last thing I wanted was Luke back in our lives. I hated the thought of him becoming friendly again with my daughters. Or, much worse, with Paul. My husband might be convinced that people could forgive and forget, but I wasn't. And Luke had the power to open the floodgates to the past, a corrosive force that sometimes seemed more real to me than the present. I knew that I couldn't stand in the way of any of this, especially now. I tried to tell myself that my objections were irrational, unfounded. The stuff of my girlhood. But, even then, I think I knew better.

15

"What is this?" Barry Hightower asked, running his right index finger along the clapboard. He was tall and powerfully built with a wide, generous smile and a highly cultivated baritone. "Aluminum siding?"

I flipped through the computer printout on my clipboard. The multiple listing on Sawyer's Mills Road, near the top of Younger Mountain, was something of a last-ditch effort on my part to find what had initially sounded like an easy enough proposition—"some quiet little farmhouse we can have some fun fixing up"—for Barry and Ted. But we'd been at it now for the last three Saturdays in a row, and I'd yet to show them anything that seemed even remotely close to what they were looking for.

"We're a little concerned that you're just not getting it," Ted told me earlier that afternoon after I drove them over to see the log cabin on Hampton Lake. Nana had suggested I put it on the itinerary, as "overlooking water" had been on their initial wish list. They hadn't even gotten out of the car.

I found the exterior construction entry on my sheet and called after Barry, who was walking around to the back of the house:

"Yes, it's aluminum."

Barry just shook his head and kept walking. With a sinking feeling, I followed behind him next to Ted Lundgren, a gentle-faced, pudgy man with a receding hairline and wire-rim glasses that gave him a diffident, academic air. In fact, I knew from Luanne Naylor, who'd recommended me to Ted and who served with him on the board of trustees of the Wellman Dance Theater Company, that Ted was a tough-as-nails, respected, and highly remunerated entertainment lawyer. Though I knew nothing about modern dance, I was not surprised to learn that Barry had been a compelling presence on the stage for over a decade, a principal at Alvin Ailey before joining Wellman. It was Ted who told me that Barry was suffering from adult-onset diabetes and was being forced to leave the company at the end of the fall season. The house in the country was Ted's retirement gift to Barry, I suspected, and a well-timed project to keep his restlessly energetic lover happy and occupied.

"Is that part of the property?" Ted asked as we came up to stand next to Barry on the rise behind the house, which sloped down to a field and small pond that was clotted with purple loosestrife. A low line of hills marked the hazy horizon.

"Yes," I said, looking down at my notes. "And there's a seasonal brook back in the woods, defining the southern boundary of the land. It's about twenty-three acres altogether, which I know is more than you—"

"It's spectacular," Barry said, turning to Ted. "Don't you think?"

"It's a stunning view," Ted replied. "But the house?" We all turned around to look up at the dilapidated Cape and the ill-advised modern addition, with its enormous picture window that destroyed the gentle symmetry of the older dwelling behind it.

"Yes, I know. But did you see the gingerbread on the front porch?" Barry said. He turned back to take in the pond and mountain view again. "And then, of course, there's this."

I knew enough at this point to say as little as possible, to let Barry do the talking, the convincing. We walked back around to the front and went inside. The older part of the house needed a thorough renovation and the kitchen was a disaster area: chipped Formica countertops, torn linoleum floors, and a four-burner electric stove that looked like something had exploded inside the oven. But the foot-wide pine floorboards were solid underfoot and the doweled staircase was beautifully constructed. The place had been in one family for a long time, then handed down to heirs who only used it occasionally in the summer and more often as a hunting lodge in the fall, which explained the ugly add-on. The long room was hung with pelts and stuffed animal heads.

"Well, this has got to go," Barry said, stepping gingerly into the room. "Immediately."

"What's that?" Ted asked, moving over to the window and pointing to the west, to the patches of red showing through a stand of hemlocks.

"That's the barn. Apparently it's still in pretty good shape. I was going to show it to you on our way out. This used to be a farm, you know. Years ago."

"Let's put on a show!" Barry said, laughing as he came up to stand next to Ted. They looked out the window together for several moments without saying anything aloud, though I sensed an intense mental exchange going on.

"It's going to be a hell of a lot of work," Ted said finally.

"I know. It's what I need. But I don't want to spend your money with reckless abandon. Is it going to be too much?"

"That's not the question."

"Okay. I love it. I think it's what I want."

We went outside again and walked around to the barn, which still smelled of hay and manure. An old-fashioned baler and a tractor were parked in adjoining stalls. Though dust motes danced through the rays of sunlight let in by missing shingles on the roof, the soaring, dim space had a cared-for, tidied-up air. It seemed to me that the soul of the farm, the life of the family that had worked these hilly fields for so many generations, resided here, not in the house. The property had been on the market for over a year, and I knew that what was left of the family just wanted it off their hands.

After making a thorough inventory of the barn, Barry decided he wanted to see the brook and the woods. I led the way, tramping in front of them through the second-growth forest and underbrush, the brambles scratching against my skin and whipping back behind me at the two men. The ground was soggy, more woody wetland than real forest. The afternoon had turned overcast and humid, and gnats swarmed in a nimbus around our heads as we made our way out of the woods and back up to the pond. But Barry's enthusiasm for the property, the view, all the possibilities he saw in the place was infectious. Ted, usually terse and skeptical, was obviously buoyed by his partner's excitement.

"We'll clear this out," Barry said, looking out over the weed-choked pond. "And enlarge it. I can see building a little pool house down here. Something simple but with a stone patio, perhaps, where we can sit out and have cocktails on summer evenings."

"And where we could maybe put up extra guests," Ted added, "when we have big weekends."

We walked back up to the house, stopping to admire the overgrown apple orchard, the lilac bushes barricading the cellar door. I could tell that they didn't want to leave. We went through the house again, this time venturing up into the musty unfinished attic and down into the dank basement. In truth, the whole place needed a daunting amount of work to make it even habitable, let alone the showcase I knew the two men intended it to be. But they were already seeing it as it would be when it was transformed, and I was beginning to feel confident that, barring any truly serious structural problems, they were going to put a bid down on the property.

I was supposed to meet Paul and the girls at Luke's at three o'clock, but when I glanced at my watch as we climbed back up the cellar stairs to the kitchen, it was already ten past the hour. As quickly as I could without seeming too obvious about it, I drove Barry and Ted back to Nana's, arranged a meeting between them and Eric Benson, the building inspector, the whole time talking up the farm and congratulating them on spotting and appreciating such an overlooked gem. But they still wanted to linger and talk. About the beauty of the countryside. The history of the town. The people in the area they already knew, such as the Naylors. By the time I finally turned into Luke's overgrown dirt driveway, it was well past four o'clock and there was no sign of Paul's pickup or my family.

I put the car in park but kept the engine running, the air conditioner on. My first instinct was to pull right out again. I hadn't wanted to come in the first place and I knew that, however Luke might have greeted Paul and the girls, I wasn't welcome. I think that Luke holds me responsible for everything that's gone wrong in his life, and I him. Our animus goes back so far and down so deep; it's like one of those fires burning in the farthest reaches of an abandoned mine, feeding on itself, noxious and unstoppable. His place oppresses me, too; it always has. The hemlocks, dense and towering years ago when Paul briefly lived here, now blocked out the sky entirely, casting the house in deep shadow and making the land around it bald and barren. I know Rachel believes Luke's art pieces are funny and inventive, and Paul views them as clever, satiric. But, to me, Luke's sculptures seem to sprout out of the ground like goblins—bizarre heads twisted at odd angles, grotesque limbs clawing at the sky. I've done what I could to keep my feelings about them to myself. But, God, I think they're ugly. Accusatory. Mean.

When he knocked on the front passenger window, I jumped. He leaned down, looking in, unsmiling. The shock of seeing him jolted me. He was both unchanged and hardly recognizable: paler than I remembered, gaunter, with deep creases bracketing his mouth. His lips, though, were still girlish and full, and the dark-fringed eyes that distant, unreadable blue. His hair seemed lighter, a few streaks of gray mixing in with the sandy blond; it was beginning to recede at the temples. He still wore it long, tucked carelessly back behind his ears; I believe he knew that it had always been one of the things that women found attractive about him. I pressed the button and lowered the window.

"They left about ten minutes ago," he said, resting his elbows on the open window. The voice was the same soft tenor, carefully modulated, almost expressionless.

"I got tied up with a client."

"I'm sure you did. Little Maddie, busy as a bee." The sarcasm was like a slap, though why should I be surprised? I hadn't really believed that he would change. Now I knew it for sure. But I felt that I had undergone a metamorphosis since the last time I'd seen him, and I believed that he was no longer a threat. That he'd lost his power to hurt me.

"Yes, I have been busy. I've been having a great summer."

"Well, good for you," he said, cocking his head to one side as he took me in. It was an old trick of his, that bland, seemingly harmless scrutiny. And yet I knew him well enough to be aware that he was simply sizing me up, searching for the weak spot. "And you look good. Very prosperous and professional. I see you escorting your clients around town. Paul says that you're a great success."

"I'm doing well, Luke. We're doing well. We hope you are, too."

"That's very magnanimous of you, Maddie. And, thank you, yes, I am doing fine. I've got my health and my art, my ten little acres and house here, as you know. Not everybody longs to live in one of your enormous mausoleums. We don't all aspire to your idea of greatness. Some of us just want to be left alone to live quietly and modestly."

"I didn't come here to pick up where we left off," I told him. "We just wanted to warn you that—"

"No." He cut me off. "Your chance to warn me is long gone. You got what you wanted. And—who knows?—maybe we both got what we deserved. But, please, give me a little credit. Don't come around here pretending you're worried about my welfare, okay? I know what you're trying to say. I know what you want me to do. Watch my step. Stay out of the way. Roll over and play dead while a bunch of fucking idiots who don't give a—"

"It was an accident!" I said. "They're your neighbors, for heaven's sakes. They were having a party. You were invited. Everybody was. We were all having a good time. They're perfectly nice people. You don't even know them. And you don't want to, do you?" *Stop!* I told myself. *Take a breath. Get a grip.* I was stunned by the speed and intensity of my anger, and I hated that I'd let Luke see it. How easily he could still get to me! I knew he probably enjoyed seeing my flushed face and creased forehead, the way my hands gripped the steering wheel. I told myself: *don't say another word.* But I did. "No, of course you don't want to know them. It might just get in the way of your being able to hate them—along with everybody else."

He looked at me impassively, his elbows still resting on the window frame. A strand of hair had come loose and fallen across his cheek; he brushed it back behind his right ear. I noticed how rough his hands were, the nails rimed with dirt, like a farmer's or a mechanic's. Richard was right: the place looked like a pigsty. Rusting mufflers were stacked on the front porch, alongside other bits and pieces of scrap metal. Plastic bags filled with—what? trash? scavenged treasure that only Luke would want?— roosted around the front steps. A bathroom sink leaned against the side of the house, overflowing with needle droppings, flanked by a collection of mismatched hubcaps. Yellowing pillowcases had been hung in the downstairs windows; makeshift curtains, I supposed, though sunlight couldn't possibly penetrate that woodsy gloom. They must be his attempt to keep prying eyes away. I looked back at him. He'd been looking away, too, staring up into the wooded rise. He must have sensed my gaze, because he glanced back at me and shook his head.

"You just don't get it, do you?" he said, stepping away from the car. "You never did. But, I'll tell you what: let's not put Paul in the middle of this damned situation again. You have something you want to tell me in the future, Maddie, have the guts to come over here and say it yourself."

He turned and walked back to the house.

Well, he didn't get it either, I thought bitterly as I backed the car down the drive. Hadn't I come—as had Paul and the girls—with the best of intentions? Out of friendship? Concern? It wasn't my fault that Luke had willfully misread this. That he needed to keep despising me when I was only doing what I could to help him. I knew he kept a running mental tally of enemies. As the years went by, as he cut himself off from more and more people, the list had grown. He saw injustices everywhere. He had the time and the soli-tude to nurse these grudges, these causes, all the wrongs of the world. I real-ized that most people in town saw him as a total eccentric, perhaps even a little mentally unstable. I wished that I could feel the same way. That I could write him off, dismiss him as a misfit. But I knew too much about him. A part of me had to admit that he was one of the few people I knew who truly lived by his convictions, who refused to compromise. At the same time, it seemed to me that he was fighting battles no one cared about anymore. The rest of us had moved on.

But he was right about one thing: I was deeply concerned that his ac-tions were going to cause problems with the Zellers—and bring a load of trouble down on all of us.

I saw it as soon as I turned up our driveway: the enormous sunflower, about Beanie's height, welded together from mufflers and hubcaps. At one point, its petals had been spray-painted a bright metallic yellow, but the paint was now pitted and rusting. Paul had set it up on the front lawn, where the girls usually built their snowmen. It could be seen from every window in the front of the house and from the road as people drove past. Paul knew perfectly well what I thought about Luke's work. I suspected Paul, by po-sitioning the sculpture front and center on our lawn, was laying down the law. Of course, he would have weighed my feelings and decided that my own misgivings were insignificant compared to the loyalty and support we needed to show Luke. This hideous flaking monstrous flower was Paul's sig-nal to the town that we were friends of Luke Barnett's—and proud of it.

"Where've you been?" Paul emerged from the garage as I got out of the car.

"I got to Luke's right after you left. Sorry I was so late, but I'm pretty sure I've got another sale."

"That's great," he said, giving me a one-armed bear hug and then turn-ing me around so that we were facing the sculpture. I'm sure he'd seen me looking at it from the garage, so I didn't pretend to act surprised.

"What do you think?" he asked when I didn't say anything right away.

"I'm grateful that you didn't go with the flying sea turtle, okay?"

"You see Luke, or what?"

"Yes," I said. "I take it you told him about Richard Zeller?"

"Yeah. But I really hated to bring it up and waited until the very end," he told me as we walked through the garage into the kitchen. "He seemed so happy to see the girls. I guess I somehow forgot how great he's always been with them. We just fell into our old easygoing way with him right off the bat. You should have seen how Beanie opened up to him; she was chattering away like a little magpie. And Lia! She was suddenly so shy! So girlish; it was cute. And you know how Luke gets. He called her Princess Lia and insisted on getting down on one knee and kissing her hand. It was great to see him, don't you think?"

"And Rachel? How did they get on?"

"When we first got there and he gave her a hug, she began to cry. It made me realize how much Luke has always meant to her, to all of them. He's like this lost symbol of their childhood—like a teddy bear or something—only real and really loving. It was amazing to me, but he got her to tell him things that were total news to me. Like this boy she's been seeing? You know she's planning a trip up to Maine at the end of August to visit him? Did you know that?"

"No," I said, though I wasn't surprised. Nor was I surprised that Rachel would so willingly confide in Luke. I knew she respected him. Perhaps even idolized him a little. From the kitchen window I could see my daughters playing badminton in the backyard with a high school girlfriend of Rachel's who lives down the road. I could tell they were in high spirits, no doubt buoyed by seeing Luke again and bringing home the sunflower.

"He took us down to his shop in the basement and showed us what he was working on. I told him that he really had to start clearing some of the stuff out down there. The place is a firetrap, and you know he's using these welding torches. Sparks flying all over the place. The department would come down on him like a ton of bricks if they saw the place. How did it go with you two?" Paul asked, opening up the refrigerator and squatting down to see what we had in the way of soft drinks.

"Not so great. I think he kind of blames me for the Zeller thing. I can see why, though, of course. I'm pretty much in the line of fire. What did he say when you brought it up?"

Paul stood up again and closed the door without taking anything. He turned around to face me, frowning. He'd put on a little weight over the last couple of months. His stomach strained against his T-shirt and his strong jawline sagged a little with what might someday become jowls. But I loved him more than I ever had; more than I ever imagined I could love anything or anyone. And I longed to be able to give him what he wanted. To share what he felt for Luke; what he believed our daughters felt for him. But Luke has been a long-running argument between the two of us, and though we'd managed to put it behind us for a year or so, I knew now that none of that had changed. Paul shifted his weight and crossed his arms on his chest, as if he knew what I was thinking about his appearance, about everything.

"We'd hoisted the sculpture into the pickup. We were facing up the hill, toward the Zellers' place. I just said he shouldn't let people like that get to him. He turned and stared at me. He said, 'So that's what this is all about.' He was sweet saying good-bye to the girls, but all the fun was gone, you know? I felt bad about it. I should have known he'd see right through me."

"No, he thought it was my idea. And, who knows? Maybe it did some good. Maybe, after he lets things sink in a little, he'll see that you're right. Was he happy at least that you bought something?"

"Yeah, but that was before. Damn. I don't know, maybe I shouldn't have hauled everybody over there. I did it for Rachel, really. No, who am I kidding? I did it for myself. I'm just a big sloppy sentimental idiot, aren't I? I'm just a sap."

"Yes, you are. I've always thought it was one of your finer qualities."

16

Every year, on the third Saturday in July, the entire Alden family gathers at the farm for a cookout. These get-togethers have been taking place for as long as I've known Paul, and from what I understand, for several generations before any of us were born. It's one of those traditions that's etched in stone, planned for months in advance, and is automatically on the calendar, like Christmas or Easter. If you're an Alden, or married to one, and are more or less alive, you come. Nelwyn, Dennis, and their teenage boy fly in from Indiana; Ethan, Barb, and the kids drive over from Boston. Louise, her husband, Mike, and their three young kids, who live a few miles south of Northridge, usually pick up Clara Alden at the retirement home on their way.

Though Paul, Beanie, and Lia had gone over to the farm earlier in the day to help Bob set up the grills, Rachel and I didn't get there until the picnic was well under way. I'd had two showings that morning and Rachel was doing something for Anne. It wasn't until I pulled into the Zellers' turnaround to pick her up that I discovered what it was. Rachel and Anne came down the front path toward me with their arms full of what looked like a closet's worth of clothes, most still swathed in plastic dry-cleaning bags. Rachel, who'd left the house that morning dressed in white cutoffs and a T-shirt, was now wearing a silky, low-cut dress, printed in a red-and-black geometric pattern. The bright colors didn't really flatter her and the dress looked far too tight, clinging to her youthful hips and riding up her thighs. She still had on her flip-flops, which made her overall appearance look a little dumpy and definitely top-heavy.

"Well, what have we here?" I said, lowering the window.

"Can you believe it?" Rachel said with an eager smile. "Mrs. Zeller is giving all these things away! To me, Mom! What do you think? This is like an original Diane von Furstenberg." She spun around in front of the car, obviously delighted with her new acquisition.

"We can't possibly accept all this," I said to Anne, as I climbed out of the car. The clothes appeared to be mostly silk or linen: elegant, striking, urban designs. "It's an entire wardrobe! Why in the world are you getting rid of all these beautiful things? They must be worth a small fortune."

"Oh, come on, of course you can take them," Anne said, opening the back car door and tossing the clothes into the backseat as though they were so many bags of groceries. "I brought them up from the city to sort through and give away. They're mostly just business clothes that I'm tired of. You can't get away with wearing the same outfit at work for more than a year or two, do you know what I mean? And, honestly, a lot of these things really belong in a museum. But Rachel seemed to want them."

"Really, Rachel, I don't think—" I began, but Rachel just walked around the front of the car to the passenger side, opened the back door, and laid her clothes down on top of the ones Anne had tossed in. She slammed the door and turned to stare at me across the roof of the car.

"Mrs. Zeller isn't actually giving them away, Mom," Rachel said. "It's payment for extra things I've been doing for her."

"That's right," Anne said, nudging me with her elbow the way she does when she's trying to get me to see her point of view. "They're hardly freebies! Rachel has been a total godsend to me this summer. Without her, we'd all still be living out of boxes. And what's the point of dropping this stuff off at the Goodwill or somewhere? Besides, don't you think she looks fabulous?"

That's where I knew better than to argue. Rachel could be so touchy about her looks—and, in fact, her appearance can still change pretty radically from day to day. Overnight, acne will break out across her chin or cheeks, temporarily marring her round-faced prettiness. For a day or two before her period, she often looks bloated. Then, without warning, her natural loveliness will shine through again and I'll find myself staring down men who eye her hungrily on the street. But I know she's still far from confident about her looks, so I try to keep my criticisms about her choices of clothes and hairstyles to a minimum.

"She always looks fabulous to me," I said, hoping to at least win a smile from my oldest daughter, but she climbed into the front passenger seat and folded her arms across her exposed cleavage without another word.

"Thanks, Anne," I said as I slid back into the car. "You've really been more than generous."

Rachel and I drove down the driveway in a strained silence.

"What is it?" I asked finally as I made the turn onto River Road. "You're like a little gloom cloud sitting there."

"You don't like my dress."

"That's not true. It's very stylish. But it's also, well, very adult-looking. Sophisticated. I'm not sure it's right for you—I mean, at least not at this point in your life. And I guess that I don't think it's particularly appropriate for the Alden family picnic."

"And who gets to say what *is* appropriate, Mom? You? What's wrong with trying out a new look? With wanting to be different?"

"Nothing's wrong with it, Rach. But I think it's important to pick the right moment. That's the kind of dress you'd want to wear out on a fancy date with Aaron, do you know what I mean? It's just not suitable for running around and playing with your cousins at a cookout."

"We don't exactly run around anymore, in case you haven't noticed," Rachel said with a sigh. "God, it's like you still think of me as some stupid little kid! Like I don't know what's going on in the world. You don't think twice about giving me all these responsibilities. But the moment I try to do anything new and even slightly radical, you just go ballistic!"

"I really don't think that's fair," I told her. "But I'm not going to argue with you about this any longer. Wear what you want."

It seemed to me that Rachel and I were having more and more of these blowups; they'd come roaring out of nowhere and we'd be on each other without warning. Sometimes we argue about real things—like Anne's clothes—but more often than not I'm uncertain what we're actually fighting about. It usually feels deeper and more complicated than whatever issue sets us off. And though we're both pretty quick to patch things up and move on, nothing ever seems to get resolved.

By the time we arrived at the farm, everyone was already gathered around the long picnic tables that had been pushed together and covered in red-checked plastic. Paul was down at the far end, deep in conversation with Ethan and Bob; he barely glanced over at Rachel and me as we filled our plates at the serving table. Rachel took a seat with the group of cousins who were her own age, and I slid in next to Barb, Ethan's wife, whom I've always liked.

"Rachel's gotten so pretty and grown-up," Barb told me, glancing over at the older cousins and perhaps comparing Rachel to her own gawky, dark-haired daughter, who, at fourteen, still shows little sign of sexual development.

"It seemed to happen overnight," I said, lying a little to be kind.

"Maybe it's that dress, but she suddenly looks so mature!"

"Well, please don't tell her you approve, okay? We had a knock-down, drag-out fight on our way over here. It's a hand-me-down from the woman she's working for this summer."

"So, she's not helping Kathy out this year?" Barb asked.

"She did for a while, then she got this great job as a nanny. I sold the house to the family that hired her. The Zellers. It was my first really big sale." Unlike the other women in the family, Barb was encouraging and helpful when I first decided to go to work and is always interested in how I'm progressing. An assistant principal of the largest public high school in Brookline, she loves her own demanding professional life. And I think she looks down a bit on Kathy, Louise, and Nelwyn, who, except for some assistant teaching and volunteer work, really don't do much of anything outside their homes.

"Good for you. And what a great time to get into real estate. I can't believe all the building around here. Makes me wonder if Bob's ever going to throw in the towel. Think what he could get for this place!"

"They'd have to carry Bob out feetfirst," I told her.

"Yeah." Barb shook her head and kept her voice down. "He told us all about the goat-cheese plans. Showed us the shed and the little herd and all. I know there's a big surge in organic farming and these kinds of specialty products. I just wish I had a little more confidence in his business abilities. Maybe I'm being, I don't know, my usual negative self when it comes to this place. But doesn't it seem even more ramshackle than usual? The toilet in the downstairs bathroom has been running since we got here."

You stop noticing the details when you see a place every day, but I hadn't been out to the farm for over a month and I, too, thought it had started to look . . . worse than ramshackle—more or less given-up-on. Bob still hadn't gotten around to taking the winter plastic and weather stripping off the upper windows. A whole section of the front porch railing had apparently come loose and was propped up into position with cinder blocks. The constant traffic of kids in and out of the house had left a smeary buildup of scuff marks and fingerprints on the doorframes and woodwork. Now, with so many mismatched chairs out on the lawn and cars parked up the drive, it looked more like an unpromising tag sale than a family celebration.

The light started to soften. Louise and Kathy took their babies inside for a nap. The older cousins led the younger ones away on a treasure hunt, something Rachel had started a few summers ago and which had evolved into another part of the tradition. Clara was helped up to the porch and into one of the more comfortable wicker rockers, and the adults gathered in a group at Paul's end of the table. Most of us were working on cups of decaf. Ethan and Bob had topped off their beers. Dennis lit a cigarette.

"Noticed driving in that the Barnett place is getting all chopped up and developed," Ethan said.

"Yep," Paul said. "I'm sure I told you about that. I did a lot of the work on it."

"You're doing okay now, aren't you, boy?" Ethan replied. It was like something Dandridge would have said, only with humor and appreciation rather than envy. Ethan had failed early in the eyes of his father, and retreated quickly from that particular battlefield. If he remains affable but utterly without ambition, I think it's largely because those first scars never fully healed.

"It's Polanski who's *really* doing okay," Paul said. "But we're not complaining. Especially Maddie. Her job is going just great."

"Kathy was telling me about how you've become this real estate hotshot," Nelwyn said. She's almost ten years older than me, and, perhaps because we see each other only once or twice a year, we've never managed to become that close. She inherited Clara's judgmental ways and is not afraid of sharing her opinions with those she thinks might benefit from them.

"It's been terrific," I said, mimicking Nana's upbeat tone, the way I often do when I'm feeling insecure on the job. "I get to meet all the new people moving into the area before anybody else does. It's a great way to make friends."

"You really need new friends at this point in your life?" Nelwyn replied. I was stung by her tone, but I was also pretty sure what was behind it: Kathy must have been complaining to her about me.

"Honey?" Dennis asked, exhaling. He's a truck driver, and he makes an excellent living doing long hauls, but he has a mouth on him that makes most of us jumpy when he's around the children. "You got something up your ass?"

"I was just saying," Nelwyn went on, "that it's easy to forget who your real friends are when you're so busy making new ones."

Later, as I was getting ready for bed, I heard Paul laugh out loud to himself in the bathroom. He's always in a good mood after being with his family. He just rolled his eyes when I told him about Anne's largesse and shook his head as he watched Rachel carrying her loads of loot in from my car. Maybe it was because he'd had a few beers, but he didn't seem to register what she was wearing.

"What is it?" I called in to him.

"What Dennis said to Nelwyn. You got to love the guy! She's always been so damned good at minding other people's business."

"You don't think she's right?" I asked. "I mean, that I'm too busy working to keep up with everyone the way I should?"

"Listen, you do the best you can," Paul said, walking into the bedroom in his jockey shorts. "I know the hours you're putting in. And I'm proud of you. Frankly, I think maybe the others are a little jealous."

Of course, I told myself, Paul was right: Nelwyn was just envious. And Kathy? If she had a problem with me, shouldn't she come right out and tell me herself rather than let someone else do her dirty work for her? Nelwyn's nastiness rankled for a day or two, but it was soon overtaken by the demands of my twelve-hour workdays, as well as my ongoing worries about Rachel. She'd started wearing Anne's clothes on a daily basis. She'd pair a navy blue blazer of Anne's, which was too snug across her back and chest, with her own cutoff jeans and sandals; or one of Anne's tailored skirts, cut on the bias and straining across her broader beam, with a peasant blouse or halter top. Usually so sensitive and cautious about her appearance, Rachel seemed oblivious to the fact that she now often looked awkward or just downright odd.

It was Anne's influence, of course. *Don't you think she looks fabulous?* Anne had asked me the afternoon she gave Rachel her castoffs. But if I knew better, I was pretty sure Anne did as well. I suspected she sensed how much my daughter coveted all those expensive designer things—so much so, in fact, that Rachel couldn't see how wearing them actually undermined her own fresh-faced beauty. I understood Rachel's impulse to want to *be someone different*. Anne made me feel that way, too. I was learning how to handle it, I told myself. I could manage the sometimes powerful sway she exerted over me. I believed I finally had Anne in a pretty good perspective. My concern was for Rachel.

Then, a week or so after the Alden picnic, I was driving down River Road to a client showing in Northridge and I saw Anne talking to Luke in his driveway. She'd gotten out of her car and was leaning back against the hood of her silver Volvo wagon, hands on her hips, nodding her head in response to whatever Luke was saying. He was less than a foot away, arms folded across his chest, head tilted in that speculative gaze I knew so well. Even from that distance, I could tell he was smiling.

I was so shocked I almost braked. I'd warned Anne away from Luke—how many times that summer? That she would so blatantly disregard my advice seemed like a kind of betrayal. It was a double betrayal, really. Because I could only imagine what Luke might be saying to Anne about me! I felt like I'd been punched in the gut, breathless and sick to my stomach. But I didn't stop. I kept driving. I knew I didn't have to worry about them seeing me pass by; they were too wrapped up in each other to notice.

17

Three days later, Anne's silver Volvo pulled into the parking lot just as I was closing the office door. It was six o'clock, the end of a busy day and one that represented a breakthrough for me. For two weeks, we'd been interviewing various candidates for the assistant job, and that afternoon Nana had formally offered it to Alice Tolland, a reserved, studiously serious woman in her midtwenties. She'd grown up in Harringdale, moved away to Boston for college and an early marriage, then recently returned to the area when the marriage went sour. She'd be working mainly for Nana, as I had originally done, helping out Heather and Linda, and answering the phones.

"And you'll be giving Maddie a hand, too," Nana had told her, as she walked her through the office. "Tomorrow, maybe you can help her set up her new work station next to Linda. This will be your desk, where Maddie used to sit."

The car stopped in the driveway below me. I hadn't seen Anne since the afternoon I spotted her talking to Luke, and I was still hurt and upset by the incident. I was trying to decide what I should say to her about it when all the windows came down at once and I saw that she had everybody with her in the car: Rachel in front, Max and Katie in their car seats in the back, Beanie and Lia sitting cross-legged in the rear area, wedged in among grocery bags, folding chairs, and inner tubes. I felt a wave of panic when I saw them. We never let them ride in the car without being firmly strapped into their car seats. It's not just illegal, it's dangerous.

"I drove about five miles an hour," Anne told me, seeing my expression. "We wanted to surprise you! I was shopping in Northridge and stopped in at that incredible new gourmet grocery on Federal Street. They have these fantastic picnic hampers all ready to go. So, we've come to kidnap you and whisk you off to the lake for a supper where—finally—you will not have to lift a single finger!"

"Oh, Anne, you shouldn't have . . . ," I began, biting back what I was really tempted to say. She could be so impulsive, so irresponsible! She hadn't listened to me about Luke. And now she thought nothing of putting my children in danger. Then I looked down at the car full of grinning faces and felt myself relenting a little. I finished locking up and walked down the steps.

"But I wanted to!" she said. "This is my way of thanking you for all the wonderful meals you've been making for us. Beanie, Lia, I'm going to pop the back now so you can drive up there with your mom."

"I think I'll go with them, too," Rachel said, releasing her seat belt.

"Okay, fine," Anne said, turning to her. "Thanks for all your help, Rach."

The girls scrambled out of Anne's car. Rachel buckled her sisters into their seats, then climbed in the front beside me. As we pulled out onto River Road behind Anne, I turned to Rachel and said, "I can't believe you let your sisters ride in the back like that!"

"Honestly, Mom? I didn't have much of a choice. She came back from wherever—shopping, she said—all excited about making this a big surprise for you! I told her we should call you, that it would be a lot better if you came over and picked up the girls in your car, but she insisted that would ruin things. So you go ahead and tell me what I was supposed to do, okay?"

I glanced over at Rachel. She was staring straight ahead again, her mouth set in an angry line. She was right to be upset; I was blaming her for something Anne had done. At the same time, her attitude was so hostile and unbending, I just couldn't find it in me to apologize.

The picnic hamper, an enormous woven basket lined with a bright paisley tablecloth and four matching napkins, was packed with delicacies obviously selected with a cultivated adult palate in mind: pâté de foie gras with truffles; gherkins; spicy oil-cured black olives; a thick wheel of triple crème brie; two long, stiff baguettes. Anne had also purchased a bottle of wine, which still had the price tag on it—$49.95!—but had forgotten to pick up anything for the kids to drink. Rachel doled out plastic cups and marched the children up to the bungalow, with its rudimentary unisex bathroom, and they filled up with water from the sink.

We spread out the cloth and arranged the expensive picnic items on top of it. Rachel made cheese sandwiches for Beanie and Lia, which they nibbled on politely but soon discarded. Max and Katie, obviously more accustomed to this kind of fare, made periodic raids on the gherkins and olives, and chewed good-naturedly on the tough baguettes. Dessert was usually their main course, anyway, I'd noticed, and in this case they were smart to wait. At the bottom of the hamper was a box of walnut brownies, iced with dark chocolate, a bag of pecan shortbread cookies, and a decorative tin filled with cocoa-dusted truffles.

"Let me have your glass," Anne said, gaily raising the wine bottle. The children had wandered off to play on the rocks to the right of the swimming area, where Rachel was sitting, intent on something she was writing. I assumed it was a letter to Aaron, who, as a counselor in a wilderness camp, couldn't get or receive e-mail. In addition to having frequent and extended telephone conversations, the two teenagers had been keeping up a busy correspondence the old-fashioned way.

"It's still half full," I told her, holding the plastic cup up so that she could see its contents. I don't drink very often, and when I do, it's usually just a shared beer with Paul or a glass of white wine at a party. Anne's wine was too strong for me, a potent ruby red more appropriate for a rich winter dinner than summer picnic fare. She leaned over and filled my cup to the brim anyway, spilling a few drops on the paisley cloth as she did so.

"Oh, come on, Maddie, let's celebrate a little!"

"What's the occasion?" I replied, debating whether to ask her about Luke. Tell her I'd seen them together and wondered what was going on. But she seemed in such a jubilant and forthcoming mood; I didn't want to be the one to put a damper on it.

"Life. Summer. I don't know, the mystery of the spheres," she said, refilling her own glass and leaning the bottle against the side of the hamper. "No, wait. I know: to friendship!" She extended her cup to mine and we touched the rims together.

"I'll drink to that," I said.

"It must be kind of wonderful, growing up in a town like this," she said. "And knowing everybody all your life. My father worked for the military, and we were always moving around." Anne had never talked about her childhood to me before, and I was intrigued.

"What did he do?"

"Oh, he was a systems analyst," she said, looking down into her glass.

"He still is. Though he's in Washington now, at the Pentagon. Something very hush-hush and high up. He remarried after my mother died. I don't really talk to him anymore. Well, to be honest, I never really *did* talk to him, do you know what I mean? I listened."

"Do you have brothers and sisters?"

"Hmmm?" She sipped her wine and looked out vaguely over the glassy water. I heard voices across the lake, and I saw that the children had taken the footpath around the perimeter and were directly across from us. Rachel was with them. I waved, and they all waved back.

"Speaking of friends," she said, "I met our neighbor finally. Luke . . . Barnett?"

"Oh?" I said. I was relieved now that I hadn't confronted her about it. She had been planning to tell me herself, of course. It had been silly of me to get so worked up.

"So he and Paul—and you, too—were all friends growing up?"

"He told you that?" I asked, turning to look at her more closely. She was still gazing across the lake, not really focusing on anything; I'm not sure she even realized that the children were over there. What else had Luke said? Though I'd seen the two of them together, I still had a hard time imagining what they'd have to say to each other. They seemed to me to occupy such vastly different realms that it was hard to conceive of them actually existing in the same dimension. And the thought of them talking about Paul, me, and our past made me feel anxious and unsettled all over again. "What else did he say?"

"Not much," she replied. Something broke whatever spell had held her, and she looked at me and smiled. "You were right. He is a little eccentric. When I drove up, he came out to meet me carrying a gun."

"Oh, Lord!"

"It was just a BB gun!" She laughed, sipping her wine. "I know what you said, but I still felt I had to apologize for what happened after our party. Life is too short for bad feelings like that. It was such a stupid misunderstanding, and I hated driving past his place knowing he was sitting there despising us. It seemed like such a waste of energy. Well, I have to say he was hardly what I was expecting. I mean, he's obviously very intelligent, very much his own person. He really is a sort of free spirit, isn't he? In a funny way, I think I envy him."

"I think of *you* as a free spirit, Anne," I told her. It was true, of course, though I probably wouldn't have said anything if the wine hadn't started to loosen my reserve. I sat back on my elbows, looking up at the canopy of leaves.

"You do?" she said with a laugh. "Well, I'll tell you—this summer, finally, I feel like I'm getting my priorities straight. I know this will probably sound a little trite, but, after years and years of letting petty things get in the way, I believe I'm beginning to see my life clearly. I guess it's because I've finally given myself the time and space to get a little perspective. It's wonderful," she said, pouring herself some more wine. "It's also kind of scary."

"Why scary?" I asked. I wasn't totally sure what she was saying, but I thought I understood in a general kind of way. I, too, had been feeling that I was getting a better sense of who I was that summer. Who I could be.

"Because," she said, "I'm finally able to accept that my marriage is a disaster."

"Oh, Anne," I said, sitting up. I felt light-headed from the wine. The afternoon suddenly seemed hyper-real, the tree line across the lake razor-sharp, the rippling reflection of sky and clouds on the water like the simplified masses of a paint-by-number canvas. I felt angry with myself for getting muzzy, just when Anne was opening up to me. My only real confidant in life is Paul. Conversations with my woman friends, including my sisters-in-law, rarely touch on anything too intimate. Perhaps it's the reclusiveness of rural living, but we tend to keep our deepest thoughts and feelings to ourselves. Though I wish it could be otherwise. I find myself longing to get behind all that superficial neighborly goodwill—like Kathy's forced sunniness—but it's actually as impenetrable as stone.

"Don't look so upset! It's okay, really. It's actually something that I've been avoiding facing for a long, long time. Here, let's empty this."

"I'm already a little woozy . . . ," I began, but she refilled my cup, and then hers.

"The thing is," she said, leaning on her right elbow and hip and turning toward me, "Richard is totally controlling. He always has been. That's actually what attracted me to him in the first place. When we met, I was having some problems, and I found that quality comforting. This big, strong man wanted to take care of me, do you know what I mean? I could finally let go of some of my worries, all this baggage I was carrying around, and have him shoulder some of it. And that's been our dynamic. Richard is the great, all-powerful Oz; and I'm Dorothy, the meek and humble. Plus, he'll never let me forget that I used to be . . . that I had some emotional problems."

"What kind of—"

"In fact, I'm really beginning to think that he wants me to *stay* troubled. It lets him remain in control, do you know what I mean? But, moving up here has been such a liberating experience for me, Maddie! I feel so much better. Clearer. Stronger. I knew I was doing the right thing when I took that sabbatical. In the back of my mind, I think I knew perfectly well what I was doing. You know what it is? This summer—it's really a kind of trial separation from Richard. I'm breaking away."

"I'm sorry," I said. I was raised to think of a failed marriage as a tragedy. At the same time, I wasn't surprised—more relieved, in fact—to hear Anne's complaints about her husband. Early on, I'd pegged Richard as overbearing and domineering. A bully, really. I've seen the way he watches Anne, following her movements with a calculating gaze. When he speaks to her, I've never found anything loving or supportive in his words. And I've also sensed that he doesn't much approve of me. I think he hopes Anne would choose friends from their own social milieu. I also think that he doesn't particularly like the fact that his children are spending a lot of time with mine. I'm sure some of my dislike is due to these suspicions; but I also think that Anne deserves better. She's really such a positive person, so full of enthusiasms and spirit. I think Richard holds her back, purposely puts her down, forces her to remain earthbound.

"And in bed?" Anne went on. "It's getting harder and harder to fake it. Sometimes when his tongue is in my mouth—God, I want to just gag—do you know what I mean?" Anne looked at me. She laughed. "Oh, Maddie, I'm sorry, I've upset you!"

"No," I lied. I never talk to anybody about sex, except Paul. I never have. I don't think I'm puritanical exactly, it's just not something I'm used to discussing casually. But I was flattered that Anne confided in me. I felt that she'd cleared the way for a new level of intimacy between us. I believed that she really needed me as a friend she could really talk to and trust. I knew things about her now that even her own husband didn't.

"Why do I think that you and Paul don't have any problems in bed?"

"Problems?" I hesitated. I knew what she was asking, and I also understood the impulse behind it. When I was a little girl, Dorie Nelson and I became "blood sisters." We'd pricked our fingers, squeezed out a droplet of blood, and then touched our fingertips together. Anne had made her move; it was my turn now. And this was what I wanted, wasn't it? This level of trust and sharing—knowing and being known? But it was harder than I thought, though all she was asking for was a confirmation, a nod. I started to pick up the empty plates and cups. I folded a napkin. I felt sleepy from the wine, my limbs heavy, as though I was moving underwater. I heard our children approaching, their voices echoing across the still surface of the lake. The light was diffused, opalescent, suspended between afternoon and evening. Finally, with a vague feeling of betrayal, I said:

"Well, yes, you're right. We really make the bed rock."

"Here it is!" Max cried. He'd run over to where they all had been playing before and was waving a piece of paper in his hand.

"Really?" Rachel said, following the other kids as they raced over to join Max. "Let me see. Yes, I think you're right. Look at this. I'm sure you're right. Now, what we need to do is sit down and figure this out. Letter by letter. Who has the note?"

"What are you doing?" Anne asked.

"Mom, you've got to see this!" Max cried, running back to us. "We found a note from the fairies on the other side of the lake! Look, see, it's written in fairy language! And—and—and—" He was literally breathless with excitement.

"I told him where the fairies keep their secret alphabet book," Rachel said. "I mean, I thought everybody knew that they always hide their most precious things in really mossy places, right?"

"And the mossiest place is by that rock!" Max said. "And that's where I found this! Look at this!"

"My goodness," Anne said, smiling. "It's a very strange but beautiful alphabet." I looked over her shoulder and recognized Rachel's elegant, slightly slanting script.

"Do you really think it's real?" Beanie asked.

"I think the only way to find out," Rachel told her rapt audience, "is to see if this note makes sense when we translate it. So let's sit down and . . ."

Anne and I finished putting away the picnic things and packed up the cars while the younger children sat in a tight circle around Rachel, helping her translate the twelve-word note. By the time we were done, Rachel had written it out. The message read: "Build us a fairy garden under the trellis and see what happens."

Later, on our way home, Beanie announced from the backseat: "You wrote the alphabet, Rach. I saw you when we were playing."

"No, it's the fairies!" Lia protested.

"You wrote it, didn't you?" Beanie said. "It's like a joke. Or a game."

"It's whatever you want it to be, Bean," Rachel said. Night fell quickly as we came down the mountain. A car came toward us, and, as it passed, I looked over at my eldest daughter. For an instant her face, illuminated by the headlights, seemed almost incandescent. I suppose every succeeding generation is a mystery to the one that comes before it. We give our children life, we teach them everything we know. Then, all at once, they seem to understand so much more than we ever did or ever will. And, somehow, without our help at all, they grow taller and stronger and kinder, blossoming into creatures from some other, wiser planet. With an alphabet all their own.

"You've been drinking," Paul said when he got home around nine thirty. I'd just finished walking the girls out to the tent and, seeing his headlights on the drive, had come around the garage and met him as he got out of his truck.

"How can you tell?" I asked him, standing on tiptoe to be kissed again.

"Your breath," he said, pulling me to him. "Wine? Red wine?" He smelled of sweat, fresh paint, and some deep-seated, waxy, essentially masculine aroma that was his alone. I could feel him against me. I ran my hands over his biceps, along his neck, and down the top of his back, massaging the muscles just above his shoulder blades that are always tense after the long commute. He'd been working too hard, putting in twelve-hour days at the Covington site, pushing everyone—himself most of all—to complete major construction by the beginning of September. The owners were planning to host a huge family wedding there on Labor Day weekend and promised the crew bonuses if they met the deadline.

"Did you at least stop off for dinner somewhere?" I asked him. He shuffled me around in a clumsy kind of dance until I was up against the side of the pickup truck. He lifted me onto the running board. We were nearly the same height then, and I could feel the full weight of his body against mine.

"I don't remember," he said, leaning over to kiss my neck. "I don't care. Where have you been?"

"We had a picnic up at the pond with Anne and—"

"No," he said. "I mean where have you been? Why haven't we . . ."

I knew what he meant, and I didn't know the answer. Was it because we'd both been working so hard? He came home late; I tended to get up early. But we'd always had a way of making time before. Somehow, over the last few weeks, we just hadn't found the right opportunity. Was that it? Or was it something more? We hadn't really talked much since the family cookout two weeks back. It was deep summer now; a lush, almost tropical heat lay over the fields, the night was alive with the constant susurrus of cicadas and tree frogs. Suddenly, from the woods behind us came the strangled shriek of the barn owl. Though it had been hunting on our property on and off all summer, its voice still unnerved me every time I heard it. I knew it was just a birdcall, but it sounded so human: heart-rending and inconsolable, like a mother who's lost a child.

"Hey, okay . . . ," Paul said when I pulled him closer. I'm very rarely the sexual aggressor; Paul usually calls the shots. I'm not sure what made me feel so brazen, but it had something to do with the heavy night heat, the owl's cry, the blur of stars above us. And, yes, with Anne. With what she'd confided to me about her marriage; what I'd conceded to her in return. I knew I should tell Paul about the way things seemed to be shifting around me—and within me. But how could I explain that I was elated by Anne's friendship, that I felt buoyant and special in a way I never had before? That I knew my success was somehow tied to this new person she allowed me to be? Up until now, Paul had been my only champion. My other. The one who completed me. But my thoughts were rarely free of Anne's lingering presence these days, the sound of her quick, low voice whispering in my ear. She allowed me to see possibilities in myself and my life—what had once been empty spaces were now filled with my own blind yearning. I knew I was opening myself up to the unknown in a way I never dared to before. I should have been afraid, but instead I felt exhilarated.

I was wearing a sundress, a floral-printed sheath that was silky and flimsy and tied in the back. I slid my underpants down. I heard the shocked intake of my husband's breath. I was wet and ready. I was somebody else.

"Jesus," he said afterward, holding me in his arms. "I'm not complaining, but what's gotten into you?"

"I don't know," I told him. "The wine, I guess." A part of me knew that I was wrong not to tell him. That, at the very least, he deserved my honesty. But I also believed that it could only hurt him, and that he would see that I was allowing Anne to come between us. Which was something I had long ago made him promise we would never let anybody do again.

18

"Searching . . . Searching . . . Searching . . ." the message crawled across the face of my cell phone. We have very patchy service in our area, and I suspected that the worsening weather wasn't helping the reception any. It had been in the nineties all week, the longest hot spell of the summer, and so humid that our towels could hang on the clothesline all day and still feel damp. An earthy smell kept drifting up from the basement and insinuating itself into our bedsheets and towels. That morning, kissing the top of Beanie's head when I dropped everyone off at Anne's, I caught a whiff of it in her hair. I didn't really mind the oppressive heat. What I dreaded was the thunderstorm that inevitably led to a break in the weather and which I'd been watching build on the western horizon for the last hour or so.

I slipped the cell into the front pocket of my shoulder bag and went back inside the pretty Acorn modular I was showing the Walshes. I could hear their raised voices upstairs. I couldn't make out what they were saying exactly, but the flow of their words had the staccato cadences of another argument. They were a couple in their late sixties, both recently retired teachers, who were in the midst of selling their Manhattan co-op in order to realize their long-cherished dream of a house in the country. But what they'd looked forward to as a joyful life transition was turning out to be an unexpected trial. They assured me that they usually agreed on everything. But they'd had almost polar opposite reactions to the dozen or so houses I'd shown them over the last couple of weeks.

"Since when have you liked wallpaper, for heaven's sakes?" I heard her ask as they came back down the stairs.

"I've never disliked it per se. When it's done right, the way that bedroom is, I think it can add a lot of charm."

"God, I think it looks so schmaltzy! This whole place feels faux to me.

It's pretending to be a sweet little cottage in a wildflower field but it's really just some builder's idea of one. Don't you see: everything looks like it's been designed by committee!"

"If you mean that it looks well-thought-out, then, yes, I agree. Hey there, Maddie," he said, seeing me by the door. "We're going to need a little more time, I'm afraid."

"That's fine. Wander around all you want. I'll wait outside for you on the porch, okay?"

"Which is a perfect example of what I'm saying," she told him. "That wraparound porch with its perfect white railings? It looks like something out of the *Andy Griffith Show*. Straight out of some Hollywood back lot. . . ."

"Well, I don't know what the hell it is you're looking for anymore . . . ," I heard him say as the screen door closed behind me. I decided to walk down the steps and out into the field of black-eyed Susans and yellow tickseed that was starting to brown from nearly two weeks without rain. Dark clouds billowed above the hills, rapidly devouring the robin's-egg-blue swath of sky above. Two shafts of sunlight slanted dramatically through the massing spectacle. I flipped open my cell phone and redialed Rachel's number. Then I tried Anne's:

"Searching . . ."

Thunder rumbled in the distance, increasing my feeling of anxiety. My palms felt slick. I couldn't seem to catch my breath. Where the hell were my daughters? Why couldn't I get through? How much longer could I put up with the Walshes and their ridiculous nit-picking? I felt an irrational anger toward them that I knew was really a symptom of panic on my part. I had an almost debilitating fear of thunderstorms, a fear that was rooted in being witness to the tornado that touched down in Red River when I was a girl.

It had been a Sunday afternoon in August, and I'd been swimming with my cousins up at Indian Pond when my uncle Petie, my mother's younger brother, whistled us all out of the water. He'd heard some thunder, he said, and besides, we'd been in the pond for over an hour. We sat on our towels on the beach and ate slices of watermelon that he cut for us with his Swiss Army knife. My uncle fascinated me. He had lost a hand in a stock car racing accident when he was a teenager, but was able to perform magic with his knobby stump. His three boys were around my age, though he and Aunt Adele were a decade younger than my parents. The whole family seemed carefree and adventurous in a way that my reserved, well-regulated home life was not. I spent as much time with them as my parents allowed and was brokenhearted when they moved to California a few years later.

I remember Aunt Adele saying that she didn't much like the look of the sky. We all went up and huddled under the lean-to. When the wind started to strengthen, Uncle Petie put his arm around my shoulders and pulled me to his side. Aunt Adele had wrapped the boys up in the beach blanket, but I was still in my wet towel and I was shivering. *It's going to be okay. Everybody just hold on to each other tight*, Uncle Petie said as the wind roared around us. A tree splintered and fell nearby and leaves tumbled through the air around us as though it was late autumn. Strange waves lapped against our tender little beach and sand swirled like snow onto the parking lot. A fiberglass canoe, flung upward by a powerful gust, sailed across the launching area like some enormous waterfowl and slammed into a tree trunk. I remember hearing Uncle Petie saying *Jesus Christ, Jesus Christ*. And then, suddenly, the worst of the wind and the noise was over. It wasn't until we all got back in the car and started down the road to town that we discovered the full extent of the devastation.

"I guess we're ready to go," Dan Walsh called down to me from the porch. "Wow. Was that lightning?"

"Yes. A storm's coming," I said. "I think if we head back now, we might be able to beat it. I just need to lock up. Where's Beryl?"

"She's using the downstairs bathroom. She'll be right out. You know, I really like this house. It's the perfect size, and the setting is so nice. Looks like it would be really easy to keep up. And I think that's important when you've lived in an apartment your whole adult life, don't you? The price is in our range, too. I wish Beryl felt more the way I do, but I'm hoping she might come around. I think what I'm going to do is work on her this week when we're back in the city, and next weekend we'll come back for another—"

"Is she about ready?" I asked. "I'd really like to get going before—"

Thunder cracked across the blacked-out sky. The field had taken on an electric brightness against the backdrop of the gathering storm. I hurried up the steps, fishing in my bag for the keys. I could feel my fingers trembling as I pulled them free. It was about five miles back to Red River Realty, along winding narrow roads. I never drive in thunderstorms. I just freeze at the wheel. If, for whatever reason, I'm alone or with the girls when one hits, I pull off to the side of the road until it passes. But now a competing fear—one no doubt just as irrational—kept me from admitting my weakness to the Walshes and suggesting we wait things out in the house: I was certain that my daughters were in harm's way. I don't know why. Rachel's so smart and practical. If they were up at the pond, she'd know what to do if the storm went in that direction. Lord knows, because of my own anxieties, I've drilled it into her enough times. *One little roll of thunder, you understand me? And I want you out of that water.*

Once we were in the car, the Walshes settled down quietly in the back. I think they must have picked up on how nervous I was. Sitting forward in the driver's seat, gripping the wheel, I tried to focus my eyes and thoughts on the road in front of me. I hadn't noticed driving in, but the dirt road had a deep gully running along the right side, forcing me to drive on the left and directly into any oncoming traffic. I could feel the storm looming behind us, though some patches of daylight still glimmered through the trees ahead. If only I could go a little faster I might still be able to outrun things, I thought, but the treacherous turns and washed-out shoulder kept me down to about twenty miles an hour. In my mind's eye, I kept picturing Indian Pond, the tree limbs thrashing, the surface of the water rippling in the wind.

Once again, I tried to remember what Rachel had told me that morning about her plans for the day. Because of the heat, she was spending a lot of time with the children up at the pond. From what I gathered, Anne dropped them all off in the morning and then picked them up at the end of the afternoon. It occurred to me that, in this scenario, I didn't know how they managed their lunch. Did Anne make sandwiches for them? Somehow, I couldn't imagine her at the long granite counter in that beautiful but underutilized kitchen, laying out bread slices. No, Rachel probably packed the picnic, I realized. And gathered the towels and blankets. The changes of clothes for Katie and Max. The blow-up water toys, shovels, and balls. It was Rachel I trusted to take care of everything. Rachel who allowed me the peace of mind to work these often twelve-hour days without worrying about who was watching over my children. But it was Paul who noticed how this new responsibility was affecting her.

"Does Rachel seem a little, I don't know, kind of distant to you?" he'd asked me a couple of mornings back.

"Not any more than usual," I said. We were in our bathroom. I'd just gotten out of the shower and was toweling off. "I mean, you know how she is with me. I'm not exactly the first person she confides in." Paul stepped behind me into the shower. I waited for him to turn on the water, but he didn't. I turned around to look at him. He was just standing there, looking down at the tiles. "Why do you ask?"

"I don't know, really. I can't put my finger on it. But it seems to me that she's been withdrawn lately. Since about the time we went to see Luke, I guess. It's not anything I can point to specifically. I just don't feel—I don't feel our old closeness. It's like she's holding something back from me. Does that make any sense to you?"

"Oh, yes," I said. "I've tried to tell you: that's how she's been with me for the last couple of years. But I think it's normal. In fact, I think it's good. She's separating from us, starting her own life. I have to force myself not to breathe down her neck, to give her the privacy she needs."

"So you don't think this has anything to do with Luke?" Paul asked. "I still feel like I screwed all that up big-time, that I let everybody down." We hadn't heard or seen anything from Luke since the afternoon Paul and the girls went over to his place and brought home the sunflower. Though I assured him that Anne had gone down to apologize and that the whole thing seemed to have blown over, Paul was convinced that, along with everything else, Luke now resented our meddling in his problems with the Zellers.

"I think it's a lot more likely that Aaron's on her mind," I told him. "I remember how it was when I was her age. You were all I could think about! And my poor parents. They had no idea. I don't ever want Rachel to think that she has to lie to us about her feelings. I suppose you could say I'm taking a 'don't ask, don't tell' approach to the whole thing."

"I guess you're right," he said. "I just hope we're not missing anything important by being hands-off. It's really hard for me, though; it's like I'm already having to let her go. And I miss her—even though she's still here."

"It's a stage," I told him, turning to the mirror and starting to comb out my hair. "We just have to be patient." I could hear the water splash on behind me.

"So I was all you could think about, huh?" Paul said, leaning out of the shower and pinching my backside. "Why don't you step back in here, little lady, and tell me about some of those thoughts?"

That pleasant memory was shattered by a sudden lightning flash and crack of thunder—the noise so close and loud I automatically slammed on the brakes.

"Should we turn back maybe?" Beryl asked, leaning forward. "Or pull off to the—"

"Oh, no, this is nothing, really," I said, though my throat was dry. When I stepped on the gas pedal again, I could feel that my whole leg was shaking. "You'll get used to these when you live up here for a while."

When I'm driving clients from house to house, I usually like to get them talking about the pros and cons of the place they've just seen, or start preparing them for what's next on the itinerary. Up until this point, the Walshes and I had kept up a lively and mostly nonstop conversation on the road. But now, as the storm crackled around us, a heavy silence filled the car. I knew I should be doing something to relieve the tension, but I was too nervous and preoccupied to care.

How could I have been so negligent? In truth, I simply didn't trust Anne to have noticed the worsening weather and go up to the pond to collect our kids. My reservations about her parenting skills had been growing slowly over the course of the summer. I found out that she let Katie and Max eat ice cream for breakfast, telling me with a laugh: "Oh, don't look so shocked, Maddie, it's chock-full of calcium, isn't it?" I discovered that when Richard was away they all slept together, sprawled across the king-size mattress in the master bedroom, the kids staying up and watching late-night television with Anne. I could think of numerous other examples, large and small. But, perhaps, most sobering of all was the fact that I'd never, in all the carefree weeks I'd spent with Anne, heard her say *no* to her children. It was always *yes*, and *why not*, and *last one in is a rotten egg!* I finally had to face the fact that I didn't trust her with my children. I'm not even sure that I trusted her with her own.

By the time I dropped the Walshes off in the parking lot, the heavens had opened. I waited a minute or two, hoping the rain would let up, because I could barely see beyond my hood. Then, unable to contain my impatience any longer, I eased my way out of the parking lot and made the right onto Route 198, wipers at the fastest speed. It's usually a ten-minute ride to our house; that afternoon, driving primarily by memory and intuition through a tunnel of water and wind, it took me at least twice that time. The house was dark when I pulled up in front of the garage, so I knew my daughters weren't there. If they were home, at the very least the kitchen overheads would be shining onto the breezeway. I ran up the driveway and into the kitchen, pooling rainwater in my wake, grabbed the wall phone, and tried Rachel again. Then Anne, whose phone rang four times before a recording of Katie's and Max's voices announced: "We've been kidnapped by pirates, but if you want to leave a message . . ." I quickly checked the answering machine on the phone in our upstairs bedroom; the red light was blinking, but the two work-related calls were for Paul.

I ran back out to the car, my anger and anxiety building. Surely by this point Anne should know how worried I would be. Why wasn't she trying to reach me? Where were the children? I saw the revolving red lights of a police car ahead of me in the darkness. *Oh God, please,* I prayed, *don't let it be them!* I slowed to a crawl, coming up beside the cruiser. Al Simonetti, wearing a bright yellow hooded slicker and carrying an electric torch, waved me to a stop. I lowered the window on the passenger side of the car and he leaned in:

"Lightning knocked down a power line ahead. We got it cordoned off, but take it slow."

By the time I made the turn up Indian Mountain Road the rain seemed to have eased up a little, but the badly maintained track that wound up the mountain to the pond was teeming with treacherous runoff. Now I had to worry about the car sliding into a gully or getting stuck in the mud. I edged forward, taking the curves slowly. Then the rain picked up again, so hard and blinding that I was forced to stop; I couldn't see a foot ahead of me. I turned on the hazards, pulled up on the emergency brake, got out and started to run.

I hadn't gotten very far before I heard voices. Children's voices. Singing. In a round. "It's raining. It's pouring. The old man is snoring . . ." They were stumbling down the road toward me, Max and Beanie first, holding hands, followed by Rachel, who was carrying Lia in her arms, while Katie marched along beside her clutching a corner of the bedraggled towel that Rachel had wrapped around her waist. Max and Katie wore nothing but bathing suits and flip-flops. My girls at least were wearing their cover-ups and Keds, though everything was soaked through. Their legs were splattered with mud.

"It's Mom!" Beanie cried, seeing me first. In another moment, I was clutching wet limbs and dripping hair to me, breathing in the sweet perfume of my daughter's body.

"It's raining, it's pouring!" Max cried, jumping in place. "I win! I never stopped! I'm the winner!"

"We're having a singing contest," Beanie told me, as I brushed the wet hair out of her eyes and kissed her forehead. "We've been singing all the way down the road."

"That's great," I said, standing up and turning to Rachel. I longed to tell her that I was terrified, grateful, sorry, ashamed. Instead, I reached out my arms and said: "Let me take Lia for you."

There was no safe place to turn around, so I was forced to back the car down the road. The children, wrapped in the spare towels and blankets I carried in the trunk, were in high spirits, all squashed together in the back. Rachel, her hair turbaned in a towel, sat next to me in the front seat, helping me navigate our difficult backward passage. By the time we made the turn onto Route 198 the rain was nothing but a light smattering on the windshield. I think Rachel sensed how upset I was, but we both have a tendency to tread lightly when heavy emotions are involved.

"You know, I tried to call you," she said. "But I couldn't get a signal."

"I tried to call you, too," I told her. "Quite a few times. You must have been walking for—what? Half an hour?"

"About that. I decided we should go when the lightning got really bad. I left everything there on the beach. I'm afraid Mrs. Zeller's picnic hamper is pretty well ruined."

"Did you try to call her?" I asked.

"Yeah," Rachel said. "Like I said, the signal's—"

"Where is she, Rachel?"

"I don't know, Mom. I really don't. The last couple of weeks she's been late a lot of times picking us up. Once, we didn't actually get back until just before you. Like around seven or so."

"I wish you'd told me," I said, trying to sound calm. "I could have said something to her."

"She told me not to," Rachel said. "She said not to worry you, because you were so busy at your job. She's always really sorry. And thoughtful. She's been giving me an extra ten dollars each time to make up for everything."

19

I dropped the children off back at our house and told Rachel to give everyone a hot shower, including Max and Katie.

"Wouldn't it just make more sense to drive them right home?" Rachel asked.

"No, I think this is better," I said. "I'm going to run over there and talk to Anne."

"Oh, Mom, please—"

"Don't worry. I won't tell her what you told me. I just need to find out what's going on. If I'm late getting back, go ahead and give everybody supper."

The temperature had dropped precipitously since the front had come through, and the air had a charged metallic smell, like spent gunpowder. The sky was clear again, and the low-lying sun shimmered across the rain-soaked fields and woods, setting the trees aglitter and turning the roadway into a river of light. As I made the turn onto Maple Rise, I noticed that Luke had put up a new piece to replace the sunflower Paul had bought from him. It was more abstract than his usual fare, a curving shaft of tempered metal, about five feet high. It felt odd to be approaching the Zellers in such an emotional state. I usually feel so privileged to be making the climb up the curving hillside and tend to compose my best self for Anne: the loving mother, the good listener, the sympathetic friend. Now I was too upset to care how I came across.

I parked the car in the turnaround behind Anne's Volvo and walked down the rain-slicked pathway to the front door. I don't think I'd ever used the bell before; I'm usually expected and just walk right in. Now, though, I felt the need to formalize my anger. I pressed on the buzzer. I waited. I leaned toward the door to listen for Anne's footsteps. Silence. I buzzed again.

Nothing. That was the moment it occurred to me that something might be wrong. That Anne could have had an accident, fallen down the unfinished basement steps or taken too many sleeping pills trying to get some relief from her insomnia. There's always a part of me that worries about her. I don't have her emotional problems. I don't understand what it feels like to carry such a burden, though I've seen her at both extremes—feverishly exhilarated and anxiously deflated. I've been a good, practical help to Anne, I know. But her deeper troubles remain beyond my grasp. I tried the bell again, but I was already pushing open the front door as I did so.

"Anne?"

Late-afternoon sunlight filled the soaring space: the entrance hall, living room, and the long gallery leading to the master bedroom suite. From the foyer, I could see straight through into the spacious dining area and the cutout windows that opened to the kitchen. The rooms were finally fully furnished. Rachel had helped with some of the ordering and had brought home a few of the glossy catalogs as souvenirs, I suppose, of her summer sojourn in what must sometimes seem to her a foreign country. She'd been shocked by the prices for what looked to her like stripped-down and not particularly comfortable furnishings. Except for the whisper of the central air system, the house was silent. The rotating ceiling fan in the kitchen gently riffled some papers on the countertop. Other than that the rooms seemed preternaturally still.

"Anne? Are you here?"

I stepped down into the sunken living room and walked across to the dining area, glancing down the corridor on my way. The door to the master suite was closed, the hallway ending in shadows. I continued into the kitchen, opening the door to the deck to make sure that Anne wasn't reading or sleeping on one of the chaise lounges. The outside air was damp and chilly, the trees and the sloping field beaded with water and dripping. I closed the door. In the silence, I heard a sound. Someone. I crossed the kitchen to the hallway.

"Anne? It's Maddie—is every—"

"Maddie."

Luke was walking slowly toward me down the corridor.

"What are you doing here? What's happened? Where's Anne?"

"It's okay," he said. "Everything's fine." But I could tell from his tone of voice that it wasn't. He looked disoriented. Disturbed. I feared the worse. He had found Anne—where? In the garage with the car running? In the bathroom, bloody water overflowing? Some instinct had drawn him here, or else she had cried out. *Help me. Help me.* Afterward, I would think back on my initial impression of what had brought them together, and would wonder if I hadn't actually hit on something pretty close to the truth.

"Where's Anne?"

"She's coming," he said gently, taking me by the elbow and leading me back into the living room, as though I was a child who needed comforting. But his tone only frightened me further. What was he doing here? Luke Barnett, in his worn jeans and fraying T-shirt, inviting me to sit down on the Zellers' pristine white leather couch? I felt as though I was in one of those nightmares where, standing in a familiar room and engaged in what seems like a perfectly normal situation, I find myself conversing with someone I know to be long dead. The whole scenario seemed surreal, off-kilter. Luke turned as Anne emerged from the bedroom and went to meet her at the steps that led down to the living room. He took her hand.

I try to remember how I saw them then, that first time. How they struck me as a couple, because it changed so much about how I thought of them as individuals. For one thing, they both looked exhausted and somehow radiant at the same time. They didn't have to say anything. I understood immediately that they had become lovers. It was crazy. I knew that. Their circumstances were so utterly different; their daily lives might as well be taking place on different planets. And yet, despite my vast reservations, I also saw how right they looked together. How, physically, they seemed to be made for each other—both slight, tense, restlessly attractive—and how, together, they appeared to complete each other. Calm each other. A part of me saw all this, but I still had angry questions for Anne.

"Do you have any idea where your children are?"

"Katie and Max?" Anne asked, looking baffled. "Why, they're with Rachel, aren't they?"

"Yes? Up at the pond? In the middle of the worst thunderstorm of the summer? Christ, Anne, they could have all been killed up there! While you two were—"

"Is everyone okay?" Luke cut me off. I noticed how he'd put his arm around Anne's waist, pulling her to him protectively.

"Now they are. When I couldn't get through here, I drove up there my-self. I found them on the road, they'd walked at least half a mile in the rain. They were soaked right through. I left them at our house with Rachel."

"Thank God," Anne said, as she stepped down into the room and slid into an armchair. Luke sat next to her on the ottoman.

"Do you really care?" I asked, and saw with some satisfaction how Anne bowed her head, how Luke nodded, appraising me.

"You must be furious with us," Luke said. "You came here to confront Anne, didn't you? And you discover us together. This isn't the way we wanted you to find out, Maddie. We wanted this to be a—well, a joyful moment, not one filled with anger. We've been in our own world, really. We didn't hear the storm, okay? Tell us what happened."

I think what surprised me most was Luke's measured, solicitous tone. It seemed utterly lacking in the bitter sarcasm I'd become so accustomed to hearing from him. As far as I was concerned, he had never really bothered to hide his dislike for me. Though for several years he managed to temper it in front of Paul and my daughters, I'd always sensed it was still there, just below the surface. And the last time we saw each other, we couldn't have parted on worse terms. *You have something you want to tell me in the future, Maddie, have the guts to come over here and say it yourself.* But he seemed to have forgotten all that now. What I didn't understand then was that he was already starting to view me as an extension of Anne's life. He'd discovered I was her friend, her confidante. I learned later that she told him I was the only other person besides Luke himself who knew about the collapsing state of her marriage. So he thought of me as an ally. An advocate. And much more. He saw me as belonging to the magical circle of life that surrounded Anne. I would come to realize that he held Max and Katie, whom he knew only by sight, in the same loving regard. He also saw me as part of their future, as someone who, along with Paul and my daughters, would be built into the architecture of their happiness.

At that point, though, as I described the storm that had raged through the area, I felt only a deep uneasiness. Despite Luke's impoverished circum-stances, he could still have almost any woman he made an effort to seduce. Women seemed to be drawn to his reckless disregard for their feelings, his willingness to let them batter their lives and families against his impenetra-ble solitude. He'd never had a relationship that lasted more than a year, and if anything went on even that long it usually only meant that the woman was unwilling to let go. The worst of these, or certainly I think the one most injured by it all, had been Kathy's older sister Leslie, who met Luke at Kathy and Bob's wedding and had abandoned her own life for what turned out to be nine months of misery. I remember Ruthie telling me years ago that she thought he was simply incapable of love. She was engaged to Lester Hall at that point, seemingly happy to be planning a traditional wedding with bridesmaids in matching gowns and a raised dancing platform at the reception, when she confessed to me that she still thought about Luke all the time.

"He gets into your bloodstream," she told me. "Like a disease. But he's only a carrier, you know? He's never touched by any of the symptoms—the fever, chills, heartache, and everything. It's like he's empty on the inside. Though he's so intense and seductive it's hard to believe he doesn't really feel anything. But he doesn't. I think that he's just kind of immune."

And Anne? She seemed so vulnerable to me. She was just beginning to pull herself free from Richard's domineering orbit. She needed time, space, the self-determination to find a new footing in her life. But I already sensed that whatever she and Luke had found together, it wasn't going to help make her more independent. No, it was as though they were collapsing into each other. I could almost feel the pull of their mutual attraction.

"God, we didn't hear any thunder, any of this," she was saying, leaning over to rest her elbow on Luke's shoulder. She tucked a strand of his hair that had fallen forward back behind his ear. "We've just lost all track of time. All track of everything. Maddie, it's been—oh, I know I should have told you. We wanted to tell you, really. I mean, we were so excited when we realized that we shared you. As a friend. Someone who could understand. But we—this thing has floored us both, really, do you know what I mean? I can't explain it."

I was irritated that they imagined they could co-opt me so easily. That they just assumed I would take their part. Their passion had made them utterly self-centered, blind to any possible misgivings I might have about their being together. I was raised in a conservative family; like Paul, I believed that marriage was sacrosanct. And yet they sat there together, the aura of recent sex almost palpable in the room, expecting me just to throw up my hands and join in their celebration.

"So this has been going for—what?—over three weeks? It started before you told me about the troubles you and Richard were having, didn't it?" What hurt me most was the memory of how she'd made me think we were sharing intimacies—and the whole time she was keeping the real story, the deepest secret, to herself. I couldn't help but wonder, too, if it wasn't actually the start of her affair with Luke that had forced her to see that her marriage was failing. Was Anne the kind of woman who couldn't conceive of giving up on even the most destructive relationship unless there was a new one in the offing? I realized I was viewing her in the worst possible light. But I felt she had manipulated me, and that she had taken advantage of our friendship.

"I know I should have told you," Anne said. "But it's been such an amazing time for us. Just the two of us. It happened so quickly. Neither of us was ready, or knew what to do. But from that first afternoon—when we first talked—it was just kind of inevitable. It was right. I know it was unfeeling of me, but I didn't want that part of things to end. I wasn't ready to share what we had yet, Maddie. Even with you."

I understood that; it was how I felt when Paul and I were first together. We were a power of two, alone in the world. I sometimes think that it was the strength of that realization that helped us hold things together through the bad times. It was always there to fall back on; that memory of our beginnings, that sense that our love made each of us better people, and that what we had was somehow destined to be.

"She's leaving Richard," Luke announced, taking her hand. "The marriage is over. It's just a matter of working things out about the kids, the house."

I felt a weight lift at his words. This was what I needed to hear: divorce, custody, plans, legitimization.

"So Richard knows?"

"Not yet," Anne said. "He's on a business trip. This is not something I can very well tell him over the phone. But, yes, I'm sure he already knows. Not about Luke. Just the impossibility of the two of us staying together."

"Do the children know?" I asked. I thought about Paul's concern that Rachel seemed distant to him, moodier than usual. He'd been worried that it had something to do with Luke, and now suddenly I did, too. Rachel's so observant, sensitive to other people's lives and feelings. She told me that

Anne had often been late recently picking the children up, that she didn't know where she was. But had she perhaps sensed what had been going on? Or worse, had she seen Luke and Anne together? Making love in the master bedroom? "Did Rachel find out somehow?"

"No!" Anne said, both hands closing around Luke's fist. "Believe me, we've been careful. We've never been together when the kids are in the house. Never. Please, Maddie, I'm not that careless. That thoughtless. Nobody knows but you. Just the three of us. And we need to keep it that way for a little while longer. Until I can talk to Richard rationally. I'll need as much money from him as I can possibly get. I'll have to think about how to manage things with Max and Katie. I know I'll have to talk to a lawyer soon, start sorting all of this out. But it's been so hard"—she lifted Luke's hand to her lips—"to think beyond the moment."

"These are all details," Luke said, turning to look at her. "What matters is us, all the rest of it is going to fall into place. Don't worry. Hey, come here."

He pulled her into his arms, and she curled up like a child on his lap while he rocked her back and forth. It was as though they'd forgotten I was there, or that I even existed. Nothing was real to them except themselves. On the surface, it was hard to imagine them as a couple. Anne was utterly impractical, volatile, indulged. Though she was well educated and clearly intelligent, I'd never heard her express any strongly held opinions. She was self-referential, her interests circumscribed by her work, her family, her houses, her possessions. She was a consumer, who would buy and discard things on a whim. Her kitchen closet was filled with empty shopping bags that had piled up in the few months she'd lived here. And Luke was such a loner. An eccentric. He held radical views on the environment, animal rights, living an ecologically sustainable existence, and endless other issues. He recycled everything, washing out and reusing plastic bags and bottles. He was a vegan and a reformed addict who hadn't touched alcohol or drugs in over fifteen years. He seemed to me as unbending and set in his ways as Anne was careless and changeable.

On the other hand, I couldn't deny that on some deeper, more essential level, none of that mattered. As Anne said, *it was right*. It was that feeling of *yes* I had when I first saw them together that afternoon. They had both been so essentially unhappy, plagued by a separateness, a neediness—two unbalanced, unfinished selves who had finally heard an answering cry. Their passion for each other was almost tangible—a kind of music.

As if hearing my thoughts, Anne lifted her head and looked at me.

"You think I can't do it, don't you? That I can't live without all of this?" She looked up into the space that rose above us. Shadows had settled into the corners of the room. "But you're wrong, Maddie. This is nothing. None of this means anything to me. I can't wait to leave it behind."

No, I believed her. I wanted to believe her. Only love can transform us. It is the one true miracle of humankind. I understood its redemptive power. And I knew even then that I could never stand in their way. That I couldn't even warn them that none of this was going to be easy. Because I knew they wouldn't hear me. They'd been given a gift; it came with a price. If I'd reached out to stop them, I think they could have walked right through me.

20

It was a little after seven by the time we left the house, and the sun was already sinking behind the distant purple wash of the Catskills. Long ranks of cirrus clouds were underlit with the fiery colors of autumn: deep oranges, reds, and golds. I thought I caught a hint of fall itself in the air: that achingly nostalgic mix of leaf mold and wood smoke. In another month, my children would be back in school. Cricket song filled the night air as we walked down the front path to the turnaround. Anne was driving to my house to pick up Max and Katie, and I was going to follow her back. After Luke walked Anne to her car, he came over as I was buckling my seat belt.

"Give me a ride down?" he asked.

"Okay," I said. He got in and we followed Anne's red taillights down the driveway. I think he probably sensed that I was unhappy about agreeing to help him and Anne keep their relationship a secret. Even though I'd insisted that they see each other at Luke's place and only when Rachel was babysitting. That under no circumstances were the children to be exposed to their affair until Anne had talked to Richard and the separation was official.

"And no cutting corners," I'd told them. "No phone calls when the children are around. Nothing that would alert them to any of this."

"We're not diseased, for heaven's sakes, Maddie," Anne had protested with a laugh.

"My daughters have led a very sheltered life," I told her. "They're totally innocent, and I intend to keep them that way. I'm especially worried about Rachel. She's at a really sensitive age and I don't want your adult decisions confusing her. Do you understand that? If you can't comply with this, then all bets are off."

"No, we understand," Luke had said. "And we agree with you. The children are our biggest concern."

"I promise you we'll be careful," Luke told me now as I turned onto River Road and then made the immediate left into his driveway.

"I hope so," I said, braking in front of Luke's darkened house.

"What do you mean?" he said, turning to look at me in the dusk. "Hope so?"

"I'm sorry, Luke," I said. "But I've just found out about all this. It's a little bit of a shock, you know?"

"Well, okay, let's talk about that. Turn off the engine for a second."

"I'm sorry, but I'm tired," I told him, which was true. "And I'm worried about the girls. I'm not sure when Paul's coming home. I think I better get going." But the truth was I really didn't want to hear his side of things. I knew Anne well enough to realize, now that I understood the situation, she'd been filling me in on the whole affair. She loved to talk, and this was obviously something she was bursting to share with me. I didn't mind being her confidante; I could handle that. But I knew instinctively that if I heard both sides of the story, I'd have a hard time holding on to my own perspective. I'd be coerced into somehow being the keeper of their flame. This was their decision, their problem, but I already felt implicated in ways that made me feel very uneasy.

"Please," Luke said. "We need to talk about a few things." It was the first time in my life that I could remember him ever asking me for anything. Nor had I ever asked him for even the smallest of favors. We've always been so wary and distrustful of each other, I think we haven't wanted to feel beholden or to give the other one the upper hand. But now Luke was changing the rules, or abandoning them altogether. I turned the engine off.

"Thank you," Luke said. "Do you want to come in?" The house was a dark shadow surrounded by dark shadows, and, for me, enshrouded in memories I'd rather not have to confront.

"No, this is fine," I told him. "So?"

"So I don't think you really understand what's happened," he said, turning to me. His voice has always been oddly high for a man, and melodious, and when he wants it to be, I realized now, it could also be intimate and compelling. "To me. Us. I've never felt this way about anybody before. Does that sound crazy to you? Sentimental?"

"Not if you really mean it," I said. "But, honestly, Luke? You don't have a particularly good track record when it comes to women."

"Yes, I know. I've been a total shit in the past. But I never promised any woman anything before in my life. This is not that, Maddie. This is nothing like that. This is a whole different universe."

"I don't want Anne to get hurt," I told him. "I don't think she's really in the best state of mind right now to get involved with anybody new. Especially something like this that seems so—" I was going to say complicated, but he cut me off.

"Overwhelming, I know. And I agree with what you're saying about Anne. I'm worried about her, too. She's struggling with a lot of problems—I know that. She's told me some things about her past, and a lot about her present situation. I'm well aware that she's been used to a certain kind of lifestyle. And so have the children. We've talked a lot about this. These sorts of practical details. She's actually a lot less worried about it than I am. But she's seen the way I live; she knows my attitude about things. That she's just been filling up her life with useless stuff, because she's been so unhappy. Well, you heard her: she can't wait to get out of it. To be free."

"Free?" I asked, turning to face him. "So you're bringing freedom to poor, enslaved Anne and her kids? Do you have any idea how ridiculously idealistic that sounds? I have a feeling that Richard isn't going to be particularly delighted about any of this—even if, as Anne says, they were going to leave each other anyway. I have a feeling he's not going to like having her pull the plug first. And he'll be furious when he learns who she's leaving him *for*, Luke. I'm sure of this. The man has an enormous ego—and he's a bully. He's going to be a formidable opponent. He'll begrudge her every penny, I bet, not to mention make things extremely difficult in terms of custody. I have a lot of problems with Richard Zeller, believe me, but I do think he dotes on those kids."

"Are you trying to scare me off?" Luke asked, laughing. "Do you really imagine we don't already know all this? Haven't talked about it endlessly? But it's not that I don't appreciate your concern; I do. I can't tell you how happy I am to know Anne has a friend like you, someone who really cares about her, who understands how much support she's going to need, emotionally and otherwise. She's so lovely and giving, but I know how fragile she is underneath it all. I know how hard this is going to be for her, even though she says otherwise. But don't you see? That's what I can offer her that Richard can't. I understand what she's going through, and I can give her the love and attention that he doesn't. Do you know what his solution is to every single one of her problems? The anxiety? Sleeplessness? Agoraphobia? Drugs, drugs, and more drugs. I've already talked her into giving up that damned Ambien. What she needs is someone who's willing to listen, to give her unconditional love every minute of the day. Not just on the fucking weekends. This is exactly where—"

"Luke." I finally had to interrupt his diatribe. I'd never heard him talk with such passion and conviction, and at the same time sound so erratic and rambling. "Listen. I'm sure that what you're feeling now is sincere. I don't doubt that. But how long have you known Anne? Three weeks? And here you talk like you've known her forever, and know what's best for her."

"Actually, that's exactly how I feel," he told me. "Anne and I had an instant and absolute connection with each other. You know, you don't have to believe everything I'm telling you right now. I realize that this has come as a surprise to you, that you need to let it all sink in. Time's on my side here, Maddie. You'll be able to watch me over the months and years to come with Anne. I'll be able to prove to you then—by doing—everything that I'm telling you now. I've never been this sure of anything in my life. We're going to get married as soon as we legally can. It finally occurred to me the other day what 'husband' really means. In the best sense of the word, it's not a noun, it's a verb: to take care of, to nurture and protect. That's what I want to do for Anne. I've wondered for a long time why the hell I was put on this earth. Now I know: I'm here for Anne, in every way that she needs me."

"Luke, that's—"

"There's something else I want you to know. I understand now why you made Paul turn state's evidence back then. I knew you were behind that, of course. He would never admit it to me, but I knew. Detective Riccio probably convinced you that they'd go easy on Paul, if he gave them what they needed."

"Yes, but Paul never actually—"

"It doesn't matter," he said. "I don't need to know what happened; that isn't the point. What I want to tell you is this: I understand now why you did it. And why Paul agreed. It's so simple, but for years I didn't get it. I thought it was really about revenge. Your way of getting back at me for leading Paul down the garden path. But it wasn't that at all, was it? It was about the two of you wanting to be together. Needing to be."

"Yes," I said, because that was what I knew he wanted to hear and what I'd always hoped Paul would believe.

"I don't think Anne knows about my prison time," Luke said then, "unless you told her."

I smelled the sweat on him suddenly, a ripe scent that was no doubt intensified by his afternoon with Anne in bed. And it finally occurred to me what he meant when he said "we need to talk about a few things." It was this. Not my feelings or concerns.

"No, I haven't," I replied. It was not something I would ever willingly share with Anne, or with anyone who didn't already know the story. Even talking about it now, I felt the old rush of panic and shame. After all these years, it remains an open wound for me, painful, untreatable, something I just don't want to touch. It's also a subject that Paul and I very rarely raise, and when we're forced to do so it's usually in an elliptical way. *Sometimes I wonder if we shouldn't talk to Rachel—about everything.* In many ways, our marriage has been built around the mutual need to separate ourselves from those events. To be something other, different and better. And that's exactly what we have become. We are respected members of the Red River community. We're well liked, well known, hardworking. We're civic-minded, willing volunteers. There's not a town committee or organization that either Paul or I haven't served on over the years.

Have most people forgotten? Paul thinks so. I don't know, really. But those whose lives were most affected by it—my parents, Harry, Dandridge Alden—are all gone now. I think the outline of the story itself still lingers, like the ruins of some old stone foundation by the roadside. *Remember that marijuana farm up in the hills somewhere around here?* A month ago in Northridge, the police arrested a man selling crack cocaine and methamphetamines to a group of ninth graders. I suppose that, in some respects, what Luke and Paul did seems almost harmless now in comparison. Except to us. The stigma is always there. Though times have changed, I'm still sure that most people today who don't already know about Paul's past—his clients, coworkers, suppliers—would be truly shocked to learn that he had served time. It doesn't matter for what, or even for how long. It doesn't matter that it all happened almost two decades ago. The fact alone is enough to make people reevaluate what they think about you.

"It's something you really have to tell her," I said. It was terrible of me, but my immediate concern was what Anne was going to feel about Paul and me. My daughters. How the news would change the dynamic of our friendship, the careful balance of equality we've managed to maintain despite our differences. I realized that just as Luke and I had once competed for Paul's love, we were both now vying to hold on to Anne's affection and approval. Telling her the truth about our shared history would threaten this, but I also saw that it had to be done—and soon—before Anne somehow found out on her own.

"I know," Luke said. "I will. I keep planning to, but then it never seems to be the right time. It's not going to be easy. I don't want to . . . I don't want to scare her in any way."

"I understand," I told him. "But Anne really needs to know."

"Right," he said. "You're right." I thought that the conversation was over. We sat together in the car, looking out into the soft darkness, not saying anything. I knew I should be heading home. I wanted to get there before Paul did. I didn't want him to find out about Anne's negligence from anyone but me. I was already thinking about how I would tell him about the larger story, the one that explained why things happened the way they did that afternoon. I'd certainly need to wait until the girls were in bed, outside in their sleeping bags. Perhaps it would be best if we made love first. Afterward, I could turn to him and say: *I have something really kind of weird and wonderful to tell you.* I realized then that I was thinking about all of it in terms of "breaking the news" to Paul, as though it was actually a bad thing.

"I really should get—" I began, just when Luke said:

"I really sort of thought my life was over. I felt like I was slowly going numb, losing all feeling. After things fell apart with you guys, I began to think: what the hell is the point? Who would really care if I didn't wake up some morning? I'm not telling you this to lay anything on you, Maddie. It was all me, my doing. I know that. I was cutting the world off. You know, my mother did the same thing, making her circle of contacts smaller and smaller every year. Until, finally, in the end she was totally alone. Except for me. I did what I could to help her. But I finally realized that she was just too damaged on the inside. Who knows why? I think in many ways she was born that way, with this sort of slow-release time bomb ticking away inside. I was beginning to think that I'd end up the same way. Dying from the inside out."

"Oh, Luke, I wish you'd—"

"No, please," he said. "The only reason I'm telling you any of this is because I feel so differently now. I realize how I was totally wrong about many things. Me. You. And I wasn't doomed at all. Just unlucky. I had to wait way too long to find the answer. To find Anne. And now I'll do anything to keep her. And anything to keep her happy."

"Then you need to start by telling her about this," I told him again. "And if she feels the same way about you, then what happened will be something she'll come to understand."

"*If* she feels the same way? Do you doubt it?"

Luke had opened his heart to me. With a candor and directness I found almost breathtaking, he'd told me things I doubt he'd ever told anybody else before. Except for Anne, perhaps. He'd always been such a mystery to me: this maddening Chinese puzzle of a person. For years I'd worked and worked away at him, frustrated and failing at every turn. I'd given up. Now, in a single evening, he'd abandoned his defenses. He'd invited me in. Perhaps it was the speed of it that made me feel so uncertain. Or what seemed like a complete and utter surrender on his part. But it was all too sudden, too much. I was concerned for him in a way that I'd never allowed myself to be before. He was as vulnerable as Anne, I realized.

"No," I said. All I meant to do was ease his mind. "I don't doubt it."

"Then you need to do me a favor, Maddie. If Anne asks you about me—if she starts wanting to know what things were like when we were all growing up together, please don't get into it with her: what Paul and I went through. Let me be the one to tell her. In my own time. When it feels right. I need you to promise me. Let me be the one."

"Okay," I said, leaning forward to find my key in the ignition. "But I wouldn't wait too long."

21

When I turned into our driveway, Anne was pulling out. She honked her horn. In my headlights, I could see that she was waving to me. Katie and Max, strapped into their car seats in the back, waved, too. They all seemed to be chattering away to each other, unconcerned, carefree. I felt myself relax a little. I clicked the remote and opened up the garage door. Paul's pickup truck was already parked there. So he was home. He would have spoken with Anne. He already knew.

". . . I'm just trying to get the full picture here . . . ," I heard Paul's voice in the kitchen as I closed the door to the garage behind me.

"There's nothing else to explain," Rachel was saying. "Like I said, I couldn't get through on the cell phone and—"

"That's no excuse!" Paul shouted. There was a crashing noise and the sound of glass tinkling. "Oh, shit—"

"I'm back," I said, surveying the damage from the kitchen doorway. They had obviously started to clean up after dinner. Paul was at the sink, his arms wide, and Rachel was standing on the other side of the open dishwasher. Lia was in her high chair and Beanie on her booster seat at the table, plastic bowls of melting ice cream in front of them.

"Okay, nobody move," Paul said. "There's glass all over the floor. Welcome home. You're not going to believe what happened this afternoon. This whole babysitting stint is over." He bent down and began to pick up the shards of a water glass that he must have hit against the countertop.

"Daddy, please, that's totally unfair," Rachel said. "It's not anybody's fault. Just because Mrs. Zeller didn't notice that—"

"A huge electrical storm was raging outside her window? Rachel, please, give me a break. She's not to be trusted. She's— Maddie, do you know that Anne left these kids up at the pond—"

"Yes, Mom knows. She was the one who brought us all home, Daddy."

Paul looked up at me from where he was crouching. He held a long sliver of glass between his right thumb and index finger.

"I got worried when I couldn't get through on my cell. Rachel's right. I think the power outage did something to the signal."

"And so you behaved like a normal person. You dropped everything and drove up there to make sure your children were safe. Thank you, dear. You just proved my point. End of argument, Rachel. I won't have you working for that woman any longer."

"And why do you get to decide for me?" Rachel said. "This is just so typical of how things work around here, you know? You two tell me that I'm old enough to make my own choices, to be my own person. But anytime you feel like it, you think you can just snap your fingers, and I have to do whatever you say!"

"This is not just *any* time," Paul said, as he opened the door under the sink and pulled out the dustpan and brush. "This was an extremely dangerous situation when the adult responsible for your safety was suddenly missing in action."

"Rachel was like an adult," Beanie announced. She hates conflict of any kind, even if it's just between cartoon or fairy-tale characters, and often plays the role of family diplomat and peacemaker. "And we weren't afraid, Daddy."

"That's great, sweetheart," Paul said as he brushed up the splinters of glass around him. He got back on his feet with a heavy sigh. "I don't mean to dictate to you, Rachel. I've been really proud of the way you've handled yourself this summer. I know how hard you've been working. Not just for the Zellers but for me and your mom, too."

"Then let me keep this job," Rachel insisted. "Come on, I can handle it. The money is fantastic; there's no place else I could be earning even half this much. And I really love Katie and Max. We have a great time together, don't we, guys?" Rachel turned to her sisters. Lia, the bottom half of her face covered in chocolate ice cream, cried: "Maxie! I love Maxie!"

"Rachel is the best babysitter," Beanie said, loyally. Sometimes I feel almost jealous of the adoration she so clearly feels for her older sister. It's what I always wanted: someone to look up to in life.

"What do you think, Maddie?" Paul asked me. "She's your friend. You know her a lot better than I do. You know how I feel. I've always thought that she's more than a little—"

He wasn't going to come right out and say what he felt about Anne in front of the girls. And I could tell that his anger was receding. He was ready to be swayed by Rachel. To listen to whatever I had to tell him. Paul very rarely doubts me, or challenges my opinions. He doesn't need to, because we see eye to eye on most issues. In fact, the Zellers are the only thing that has come between us in a long time. But from the moment he met Anne, Paul was put off by her. He saw instantly what it has taken me most of the summer to face: beneath all that composed beauty and natural charm are uncertain depths and unresolved problems. And now there was the added complication of Luke. If Rachel's summer job ended, it would put Luke and Anne's relationship in serious jeopardy. Rachel was the reason they could meet as often as they did. It had been Rachel's babysitting that had afforded them the opportunity and freedom to discover each other, to fall in love, to start planning a new life. And now, more than ever, I knew they desperately needed that time together.

But I also had my daughter's welfare to consider and parental worries that were far more serious and substantive than anything Paul knew about. What was I exposing Rachel to if I let her keep working for Anne? Surely she'd wondered why Anne encouraged her to get the kids out of the house every day. Or what Anne was doing with all that time by herself. I know Rachel helps with the laundry and makes the beds. She understands the intimate workings of the Zellers' domestic life. How much does she really know? Or guess?

"Mrs. Zeller and Mom are like best friends, Daddy," Rachel said in a tone that implied she was simply stating the obvious. "Of course she thinks I should keep helping her."

"Really?" Paul said. "Well, I'd still like to hear it from her. Maddie?"

I told myself that I was doing it for Rachel. This was what she wanted, and she'd answered my concerns by so clearly stating her eagerness to hold on to the job. Would she have been that adamant if she was seriously troubled by anything happening in the Zeller household?

I told myself I was doing it for Paul. To shield him from his own overly protective instincts. If he learned about the affair now, I knew he'd absolutely refuse to let Rachel continue to work for Anne. And where would that leave Luke's chance at happiness?

I told myself that I was doing it for Luke, Anne, her children—everyone but the true beneficiary. Because I couldn't face the fact that I was doing it for myself—and for a friendship that had done so much to enlarge my sense of who I could be. I no longer trusted Anne, but I couldn't give her up. It would feel like letting go of everything I'd worked so hard for. Yes, I understood that this was actually a moment of truth for me, a turning point. But I chose without really thinking. How could I let myself consider the consequences? I know I should have felt torn, guilty, or, at the very least, uncertain. But I didn't. This was what I wanted—and that need overwhelmed everything else.

"I think Rachel's right," I said. "She's certainly shown us how responsible she can be. I think she gets to decide this for herself."

"Okay," Paul said, throwing up his hands in mock exasperation. "Outmaneuvered and outvoted by my women once again!" The tense tableaux relaxed and everyone began moving again. Lia opened her arms to me, her signal to get down. Beanie leaned over to lick her bowl like the cat she often pretends to be. Rachel went back to loading the dishwater. Paul came over and hugged me as I set Lia back on her feet.

"Where've you been?" he asked.

"Well, I went over and had a word with Anne," I told him softly. "Believe me, I was furious, too, when I found them all straggling down the road like that."

"I bet," Paul replied. "Did she have a better excuse for you than the one she gave me? I mean, what's with this falling asleep in the middle of the afternoon?"

"That's what she told you, too, huh?" I replied. At least it fit into the general picture I'd already painted for Paul of Anne's emotional problems. "It's the insomnia, I guess. It must throw your regular sleeping patterns totally out of whack. But she knows how upset we are. I really think she'll try to be more thoughtful in the future."

"Owen phoned me at work today," Paul said, as I rinsed my dinner plate in the sink. Rachel had taken the girls out to the tent and we were alone in the brightly lit kitchen. "He's calling a special meeting to vote on the town hall plan."

Owen Phelps is the longtime head of Red River's select board, upon which Paul is now serving his second term. During that period, one of the most controversial issues has centered around the old meetinghouse that in recent years has housed many of the town offices. In desperate need of repair, the fate of the once gracious Greek Revival structure is a subject of hot debate. Over the past three years, a variety of plans and proposals— from making it the headquarters of the Historical Society, to dividing it into retail and commercial spaces, to razing it entirely—have dominated most town meetings. Now, in a move that Owen believes will solve numerous problems, he's made an exploratory application and been granted an initial go-ahead by the state to file an application for the building to be recognized as a historical landmark. Such status would bring with it the possibility of numerous grants and allowances, making plans for its future less divisive and stressful for everyone concerned.

"Good," I said. "When's it going to be?"

"On the twenty-fifth," Paul said. "I already put it down on the calendar. I think we should both be there." There was something about his tone that made me turn around and look at him.

"I'm happy to go. But are you really worried this thing won't pass? It's a great solution. I just wish someone had thought of it a couple of years ago."

"I'm not worried about the vote," Paul said. "But Owen mentioned that he'd been contacted by Richard Zeller, who apparently is lodging a formal complaint about Luke's property. He says he thinks the town needs only one dump."

"Oh, no." I sat down next to Paul. "What did Owen say?"

"Oh, you know Phelps. He made a joke about it that I won't repeat in polite company. But he thinks Zeller ought to have his say. I'm hoping that he just intends to listen—and then stall him."

The phone rang then. I got up and answered it, correct in my assumption that it was Aaron calling for Rachel.

"She's outside with the girls," I told him. "Hang on and I'll get her for you."

After Rachel had gone upstairs, Paul talked some more about Zeller's complaint, whether or not we should be seriously alarmed—or perhaps warn Luke what was up. But Paul was still hurting from Luke's response to the last time he'd intervened—when he ended up buying that awful sunflower—and decided just to let things take their own course. I listened for the most part, adding my two cents from time to time. Of course, this was the moment to tell Paul that Richard Zeller had every reason to be furious with Luke, and it had nothing to do with the rusting sculptures marring his expensive view. But I didn't. I'd made my decision. The news that Richard was going public with his complaints complicated matters, but it really didn't change anything. Or so I told myself.

By the time Paul and I headed up the stairs a half hour later, I'd forgotten that Rachel was on the phone until I saw that her door was still closed and that the cordless receiver was missing from its cradle on Paul's bedside table. It was nearly ten o'clock now, and they'd been talking far longer than usual. I knocked as I always do before entering Rachel's room. She was lying on her stomach on the bed, facing away from me.

"... no, it's not like that, really. But Katie did ask me if I liked him, and of course I said yes. He's really one of the sweetest—"

"Rachel—"

"Mom!" She spun around, red-faced. "Don't you knock first?"

"I did, sweetie. I guess you didn't hear me. It's getting late."

"Okay," she said, sitting up on the bed and crossing her legs. "We'll say good-bye soon. Could you please close the door now?"

Paul was already in bed, and I was brushing my teeth when I heard Rachel's footsteps on the stairs. I opened the bathroom door.

"Rachel? Got a sec?"

"It's kind of late."

"You'd still be on the phone with Aaron if I hadn't come in."

"Barged in is more like it."

I walked across the landing and leaned over the banister. She was halfway down the stairs, dressed in the flannel pajamas I'd bought for her a few Christmases back. Bright red candy canes danced in the dim light from the bathroom overhead. It seemed as though only moments ago I'd put her down in her crib.

"I did knock, but you were too engrossed in your conversation. What were you talking about for so long?" I knew as soon as I asked that this was exactly the wrong approach. I'd made a point of not prying into Rachel's relationship with Aaron. In the past, she'd been quick to tell me to mind my own business when I made such a slip.

"Just the usual stuff," she told me. "Mostly about my plans to go up there. He thinks I should take the bus to Bangor, and his dad can pick me up." The Neissens have a summer house on the coast of Maine where she and Aaron planned to spend the long Labor Day weekend.

"Is everything else okay?" I asked.

"What do you mean by everything?" I thought I heard her sigh.

"I don't know," I said. "You're just growing up so fast. I don't want you to ever believe that you can't tell me things—whatever you might be feeling."

"Sure, Mom," she said, as she continued down the stairs. "See you in the morning." I knew she was only heading out to the tent to curl up in her sleeping bag between her two younger sisters, but it still felt to me as though she was walking away for good. That, in one way or another, she had been leaving all summer, this part of her and then another, disappearing into a world that I could no longer control. And where I was forbidden to follow.

Part Six

22

After I left home, Ruthie's mom let me stay with them for a couple of months until I got waitressing work in Northridge and a studio apartment in the depressed area behind the old railroad depot downtown. I made it through those grim days only because I knew the situation was temporary.

I moved into the house trailer on the Alden farm the weekend after Paul was released from jail. It was a single-wide Elcona, over twenty years old even then, and had housed extra farmhands during the years when the dairy actually needed more help. Though Clara had made Nelwyn and Louise scrub and air the place out for me, the small wood-veneer-paneled rooms still smelled of mildew and a peculiar kind of vegetal rot. The Formica tabletop in the kitchen area was scarred with cigarette burns and the bathroom showerhead had been decapitated. But it seemed wonderful to me then, and remains so now in all my memories of the place. Love endows the lowliest things with beauty. It was our first home. It's almost impossible to believe that it no longer exists in any place but my heart—and Paul's. Bob had it towed and junked a few years after we left, but I swear that if I could step up into that dim, cramped space today I would still be able to reach—blind—for the oven mitt on its hook by the two-burner stove or a new, dry, bright pink sponge in the tiny cupboard under the sink.

Paul did everything but sleep over with me there, and even then he rarely left until after midnight. But his parents were strict Catholics and his family's social life had long revolved around St. Anne's, the small parish church over in Covington. It was assumed that we would get married there, and I would have been happy to do so. Religion didn't color my attitudes the way it did the Aldens'. It wasn't the first thing I wondered about when I met somebody new, though I know it was that way with Clara. I don't think she could ever have fully embraced a non-Catholic in her family. And I was raised a Congregationalist, which was, in Clara's mind I'm sure, one small step up from being an atheist. It was true that my belief system had very weak roots. I was a joiner by nature, and I was eager to make myself a part of the Alden family. So the idea of converting, planting my faith in more fertile ground, appealed to me: it seemed like a quick and painless way to gain acceptance.

"I'm hosting a tea for Father Timothy on Thursday," Clara announced at dinner the second Friday that Paul was back. By that point, I'd worked myself up to the day shift at Salter's in Northridge, and was able to join the Aldens most nights at the big round table. Paul was back at the dairy, working alongside Ethan. When Bob graduated from high school in another month, he'd be joining his brothers and then, the three of them had decided, they were going to approach Dandridge about making some necessary renovations and investment in new machinery and livestock. It was Bob who had come up with the idea of converting the operation to organic, selling most of the Holsteins and buying up Jerseys, whose milk was yellower and thicker, just right for the heavy cream and yogurt products he saw the dairy shifting into. Bob spent a lot of time up in the trailer with Paul and me outlining and expanding on his ideas, and Paul just let him talk. I knew Paul was for changing and upgrading in general, but I also sensed he was still feeling his way with his family, especially Dandridge. They said very little to each other in front of the rest of us, but you could feel each of them secretly monitoring the other, antennae up and attuned to what was said, what was not.

"I thought Maddie might like to join me," Clara added. "Father Timothy only gets a chance to visit every other week." Catholics were so few and scattered so far afield in the county that the parish had to make do with a traveling pastor, and even then St. Anne's was not big enough to rate more than a weekday stopover.

"She's working afternoons," Paul said, not looking up from his plate.

"I could probably get—" I began, before Paul cut me off.

"We'll talk about it later."

"What's there to talk about, son?" Dandridge asked. "It's time she got going on this if you're planning on a summer wedding."

"I haven't had the chance to work out the details with Maddie yet," Paul said.

"Well, get working then. I don't like all this pussyfooting around. And I don't like her living in that broken-down old rust bucket out there. It's time for you two to clear things up and move in here with us where you belong."

I think Dandridge believed that in the best of all possible worlds, his children would never leave him. At that point, with six bedrooms and the large unfinished attic space where Ethan and Bob were living, it was more than feasible. I knew that Clara was fixing up the two-room annex behind the kitchen with the idea that Paul and I might move in there. It had been a storage area for many years, but had originally been a servant's room of some kind. It had its own small bathroom and entrance with an overgrown rose trellis on either side. The plan was still vague, but Clara had asked my opinion about fabric for curtains she was making for the bedroom windows. It didn't occur to me then, but it says something about Clara that she knew enough not to offer Paul and me one of the large, sunny upstairs bedrooms. She was already aware, I believe, that Dandridge and her middle son required at least one floor between them to be able to sleep in any kind of peace.

"Son of a gun just pushes and pushes," Paul said as we walked back up through the haying pasture to the trailer after dinner. "Every day, it's something else. Yesterday, it was that I was going light on the milking quota. Today, I didn't put a vacuum hose back just the right way. It's always something. I don't talk up the way he likes. I don't look him in the eye. It's like some kind of Chinese water torture. I'm back just three weeks and we're already at each other's throats."

"But it's not just you," I told him. "He's like that with everybody, as far as I can tell. Even your mom. It's just his way, don't you think?" In fact, I believe that a certain cussedness was ingrained in Dandridge's character. He was stubborn and opinionated, querulous and outspoken. But I also saw that he loved Paul, I believe more than any of his other children, maybe almost as much as he loved Clara. But he expressed his feelings for both of them by this constant, childish needling and complaining. Nothing anybody did was ever quite good enough for him, but he came down the hardest on his wife and Paul. It was his way of getting their attention, I think, and perhaps distracting them from taking stock of his own shortcomings. Because, in fact, the business continued to struggle badly.

I was never privy to the true financial situation, though I knew that the dairy had been mortgaged at least once to help pay Paul's legal expenses. The money Nelwyn was earning as a secretary in Northridge went right into groceries, as did my own contribution from waitressing. I believe that at this point, ours was actually the only real cash coming into the household. When Dandridge had taken over the dairy from his own father it had been a thriving concern, one of the biggest operations in the county. Through circumstances beyond his control—the consolidating trends in the dairy business, the downturn in the economy in general—Dandridge had been forced to oversee its slow demise. Two hundred head had been reduced to almost half that; a third of the 175 acres sold off. For a man of such impenetrable ego and pride, this must have caused terrible internal damage. He was always so controlled and controlling, I can only guess at the truth; still, I do believe that he had to have sensed that Paul was driven to throw in his lot with Luke because he saw that the dairy was failing. Surely, somewhere deep down inside himself Dandridge understood his own culpability in what had happened to his favorite son.

"Doesn't mean I have to stand for it," Paul said. "I won't be backed into a corner on this. I already told him plain as can be that we weren't going to have our wedding at St. Anne's. But he refuses to hear it. It's like he's deaf as a post, as well as being dumb as an ox."

"But I'd like to be married there," I said, stopping in the pasture. It was mid-May and the fields were sweet with the smell of wild thyme and frais des bois. In the early night sky, a new moon smiled thinly above us. For me, the world was still an open question, full of possibilities. It was different for Paul, and I was only beginning to learn how much.

"I don't believe anymore," he said simply. "I'm not sure I ever did. But now it's important for me to be clear about it. To say where I stand. It didn't matter before; but I refuse to pretend now, or ask you to either, just to keep up appearances."

"But your mom will be—"

"I'll talk to her. She's dealt with disappointment before this, believe me. But I'm sorry for your sake. It would have made things a lot easier for you with her. And everyone."

So we were married in a secret ceremony by a justice of the peace in Albany. Ethan and his new girlfriend, Barb, whom he'd met at a Red Sox game on a day trip to Boston, were our witnesses. Barb was an upbeat and matter-of-fact girl from Brookline with more spirit than looks at that point, though self-confidence and a kind of athletic poise would give her an attractive sheen as she grew older. She saw the whole thing as great fun, and her enthusiasm for us, for the fact that she'd been included by Ethan, whom she was clearly taken with, infused our wedding day with a gaiety it might otherwise have lacked.

Paul and I spent the night in a Holiday Inn not far from the turnpike, traffic noises roaring through my confused dreams. We sent Ethan back to break the news to the family. By the time we returned around noontime the following day, the battle lines between Paul and his father were already drawn. Paul moved his things out of the house and up to the trailer that afternoon. We still took dinner at the farmhouse, but from that day forward my position as an outsider within the family was solidified. I don't think anyone blamed me for what had happened. I believe they all understood how much I wanted to please them, to be a part of things, but it was impossible. I was shy and unused to such a large, demanding group to begin with. And then I'd somehow allowed Paul to close the door on the one thing that might have drawn me in.

But I was also beginning to realize that the family's seeming closeness was complex and often uncomfortable. There were a lot of issues that were simply not discussed: Paul's prison time, the dairy's worsening finances, Ethan's drinking. Besides a quick hug when Clara first saw me after we came back from Albany, she never said a word about the fact that I'd married her son. But at least she had the good grace to ignore it. Dandridge took every opportunity to rib Paul about living in that "old tin can," or "sending the wife out to bring home the bacon." The tensions only increased with the news that Nelwyn was planning to marry Dennis Ditmars and move with him to Indianapolis, where he was starting a new job with a trucking firm. My sense was that all the dairy's meager profits were being siphoned off to meet the mortgage payments, so this meant that the family's ready cash flow would be reduced to the tiny trickle I brought in through waitressing. I began to take on some double shifts at Salter's, though Paul hated my doing so. I would sometimes be so tired when he picked me up at midnight that I'd fall asleep in the car before we'd pulled out of the parking lot.

It took me a while to realize that my weariness wasn't temporary. That my queasiness in the morning wasn't just a lingering bout of indigestion. I was already six weeks along by the time I got the confirmation that I was pregnant.

"Marty knows a place in Troy," I told Paul that night. "Her sister went there."

"What are you talking about?"

"How are we going to keep it? We don't—"

"That's not even an option."

"We can barely feed ourselves at this point. And I'll be the only one working outside of the dairy. Besides, you said yourself that you're not a Catholic anymore."

"That has nothing to do with how I feel about this. Our child. A part of us. Nothing is more important than that. This is what kept me going. Come over here." I'm sure Paul thought I was crying because I was so relieved that he wanted to keep the baby. But, in fact, I wept that night because I realized how uncertain I was about what was right and wrong. I was ashamed that I had thought and said what I had. I was driven by fear and uncertainty. After everything we'd been through, I still didn't know my own mind.

And Paul was so sure. I was just beginning to see the rock-solid sense of purpose that had taken hold in him. He'd been tempered in a fire of guilt and shame. His beliefs had been reduced down to basic and unshakable principles. I began to understand that I could trust him completely. No, more than that, I could believe in him. He was the church that I finally joined. But, like all faith, this was also the beginning of my dependency on him. He was my compass. I could let my own moral reflexes soften. Why would I need them when I had him? He believed in me, too, though I think his conviction went far deeper. Where I relied on Paul for guidance, he needed me for sustenance. I was his life force, pure and blameless.

Soon after this Paul worked one Saturday afternoon unloading inventory for Salvatore Petrossi at the Northridge Agway he managed. He'd played football in high school with Sal's son Ricky and had always gotten on well with the extended, gregarious Petrossi family. That half Saturday turned into full ones, then weekday evenings when big shipments were scheduled. He was still putting in his hours at the dairy, but the Agway job was what he wanted to talk to me about when we got home. A month before I was due, he was introduced to a brother-in-law of Sal's named Nicholas

Polanski, a building contractor from Danbury who was starting a big construction project up in Rydell. Polanski hired Paul at Sal's recommendation, even though Paul didn't have any real experience.

"So, I'll be the gofer," he told me that night as he rubbed my feet. We'd had dinner at the house, but he hadn't said anything about the new job. "I'll work my tail off and learn what I can. It's fourteen dollars an hour. I'll kick in half of that to the household for the time being, though no matter what I do I know Daddy's going to be mightily pissed. But this is too good a deal to pass up money-wise, and it's just the chance I've been hoping for."

"What's going to happen here?" I asked.

"I don't know. I'm pretty sure Ethan's leaving, too. Barb's uncle has a liquor store over in Newton and has offered him a job. It's like setting the fox loose in the henhouse, I guess, but anything's got to be better than here for him. And Barb's tough. She'll keep him on the straight and narrow."

"But Bob can't handle the dairy on his own, can he?"

"If any of us can make a go of things, it's him," Paul told me. "Because he wants it to work so badly. It's all he thinks about. Gallons per head. Price per gallon. Milk versus cream. Feed corn or hay. Bob could talk about dairying all day if anybody would listen. And I think he's got a lot of good ideas. If Daddy will let him take the lead."

"When are you going to tell him?"

"Construction doesn't start for another three weeks. By then I hope the man will be a grandfather and maybe start taking a gentler view of the world. In any case, I'm planning to wait and give him the bad news along with the good."

I wasn't there to hear what happened, of course. It had been a breech birth with an emergency C-section. I'd woken up groggy and upset that Rachel didn't seem to want to take my nipple. In an instant, my world had narrowed to her dark blue gaze and that sweet slack bow of a mouth.

"Hey there, beautiful," I murmured. We'd named her Rachel Clara, hoping that would help mend the many rifts. It was the visit from Paul's younger sister Louise, then a redheaded, large-boned high school sophomore, that gave me the first clue our news had not been received with unqualified joy. She came bearing a green glass vase filled with wildflowers.

"For you," she said, setting the vase on the windowsill and leaning over to smile at the baby. "From everybody. Oh, isn't she something?"

"Where are they all?" I said, looking to the door. Paul had asked a hospital orderly to bring in half a dozen extra chairs, explaining that he came from a big family.

"Mommy sent me," Louise said, sitting on the edge of the hospital bed. Though she was several years my junior, Louise had always seemed composed and mature to me. She had Clara's measured delivery, along with her martyrish way of sighing every other minute. "The house is kind of in an uproar right now. Daddy's real upset."

"Because she's a girl?" I asked, angrily. That's how quickly all my thoughts had already started to revolve around the new life in my arms.

"Oh, no! It's Paul leaving the dairy. Taking that job in construction. Daddy says that all Paul's doing is kicking him when he's down, and after all we did for him. He threw a chair at him. One of the kitchen ones. Told him if he's going to leave, then he should just clear off altogether. He wants you both out of the trailer. I'm sorry, Maddie."

She wasn't my only visitor that day, although I wish she had been. Paul stopped back in briefly with Ethan to say he'd found a place for us to rent outside town and that they'd be busy moving our things over there. I could smell the beer on them, and I sensed Paul's blurry anger under his attempted good humor. He held Rachel for a moment before he left. I can't recall him ever looking sadder than he did at that moment, staring down into his daughter's questioning gaze.

Around seven, I dozed off with Rachel asleep beside me. When I woke up, my mother was standing by the bed. For a moment I thought I was still dreaming, but then I noticed how much she'd changed from the woman I'd last seen up close over two years before. Over that period, I'd caught glimpses of her and my father—at the Mobil station, or waiting in line at the post office—but I'd always turned away before having to face them. Now I stared. It was as if someone had sifted white flour over her; her hair, her skin, even her lips seemed strangely pale and powdery.

"I heard the news," she said. Of course, I thought she meant the baby and I turned Rachel around so that she could see her better. But she didn't even look at her. "About Dandridge kicking Paul out of the house. They were talking about it at the general store when I went in for the paper. About how he refuses to help out at the farm. After Dandridge mortgaged the place for him and everything. Oh, Maddie! I guess you see now. What your father and I tried and tried to tell you. We talked about it. We think you should come back and live with us. You and the baby."

I looked from my mother to my daughter's sleeping face, the tiny lashes tucked so perfectly into the pale softness under her eye. Oh, this miracle that Paul and I had somehow created from our own two clumsy, needy bodies!

"The baby's name is Rachel, Mom. Take a good look. Because this is the one and only time I'm ever going to let you near her." That's what faith does: it makes you strong and unbending. It fills you with righteousness. It blinds you to compromise, tolerance, or empathy. It rushes through you like adrenaline, as sweet and numbing as wine. It enables you to drive your mother, who only always wanted what was best for you in the world, out into the indifferent light of a hospital corridor. It gives you what feels like peace. For a while.

23

We lived in a cocoon of domesticity, a world of three. Though we were so close it often felt that we were really more like one extended being: lying on the hammock with Paul's arm around me and four-year-old Rachel asleep between us. From the outside on a summer's evening, the house we rented looked almost charming: a white-painted brick Colonial with a shingled roof and center chimney. Before we took up residency, the house and surrounding six acres had been in the Anderson family for generations. After Lily Anderson's death, it had fallen into the hands of a nephew who rented it out—and let it drift into a general decline. When you got up close, you could see that the front steps and shutters were spongy with wood rot and the foundation was crumbling in places. The interior was dark and cramped with low-beamed ceilings and plastered walls, and the floors and stairs creaked. At night the wind whistled around the loose window frames.

But over time its drawbacks began to seem less important than its familiarity. The rent was reasonable. I cleared out the overgrown perennial beds in front of the house and discovered a nicely laid-out border garden. The second summer, we planted vegetables behind the barn and purchased a small molded plastic aboveground pool where Rachel and I could splash around after the chores were done. Paul was getting steady work with Polanski Builders and his pay had been upped to eighteen dollars an hour. There were a lot of building jobs to be had and experienced help was now at a premium. The second-home market was beginning to take off; land values were rising slowly. But the farms were still struggling, and despite Bob's Herculean efforts, Alden Dairy barely limped along. It seemed that Paul had made the smart choice after all. Construction was the place to be.

That's not to say we didn't have our problems. I didn't have the heart to tell Paul about my mother's visit to the hospital when Rachel was born, so he didn't know that relations between us had deteriorated even further. Never giving up hope that he could somehow bring my parents around, Paul convinced Polanski that he should use my dad as his paints and stains vendor. It was a major piece of business and might have helped boost the hardware store back into solvency, but then my father found out how he'd landed the contract and refused to fulfill it. A few months later, we saw the CLOSING SALE—EVERYTHING MUST GO signs in the store's front windows, and learned through Ethan that the bank was forced to foreclose on my childhood home as well. Ethan had gone to the sale and picked up a lot of heavily discounted supplies—as well as an earful of local gossip.

"Her old man's crazy," I overheard Ethan tell Paul that night when they thought I was asleep. As usual when he'd had too much to drink, Ethan's voice carried a lot farther than he knew. "He was ranting on about you, like you were the one who drove him into bankruptcy or something. Clear to anyone who half listened, though, that he wasn't making any sense. They're moving up to that retirement home in South Harringdale. Good thing, too. You need that kind of bad-mouthing like a hole in the head."

With Clara acting as go-between and facilitator, Paul managed to patch things up with his own father. I've no idea what Clara said, what threats she might have used, but the following July we were invited to the family picnic. Though Paul and Dandridge had nothing more than a jury-rigged relationship after that, one that couldn't carry the weight of true feelings or an honest exchange of opinions, we were slowly taken back into the fold. Rachel, who I thought looked pure Alden from the day she was born, was a welcome addition and diversion. In those days, it seemed there was always some family event to attend. Nelwyn and Dennis's wedding, followed three months later by Ethan and Barb's. Then more births and christenings, anniversaries, holidays, the endless march of birthdays. We always had Thanksgiving, Christmas, and Easter dinners over at the farm, the dining room table growing longer every year. Rachel, the first grandchild, somehow legitimized me with the women in the family, and I felt vaguely a part of things in a way I hadn't been able to before.

I know these weren't the happiest of occasions for Paul. He worked hard to keep his temper, while Dandridge did his best to provoke him into losing it. With the upturn in the economy and his sense of self-worth rising along with it, Paul had begun to invest in a small way, establishing an account with Brent Longhauser at the Charles Schwab office in Northridge. God only knows how Dandridge ferreted out this information, but he began to take sadistic pleasure in poking fun at "high-rolling" Paul and his "Wall Street cronies." Though Paul didn't advertise it, neither did he hide the fact that he was impressed by and supported Clinton, despite Paul's dyed-in-the-wool Republican upbringing. Dandridge took this evolution in his son's thinking and attitudes as direct criticism of his own politics. He saw everything Paul did and said strictly in terms of how it correlated with his own ideas. Every difference was another affront.

"So now they're saying your friend Mr. Foster committed suicide," Dandridge told Paul as the women started to clear off the tables after the annual Alden picnic. I was pleased to see that Bob had actually thought to invite Kathy Finn to join us; he'd been seeing her off and on for the last two years and I think we were all hoping that this might be the beginning of something more permanent between them. Kathy was heavyset and rosy-cheeked with wavy dark hair and an easily wounded gaze; I felt she looked to me for support when it came to Bob and the family, and I enjoyed the fact she so obviously courted my good opinion.

"Vincent Foster is actually not my friend, Dad. And why do you sound so dubious? You can't really be buying into that bull that the administration had him knocked off because he knew too much."

"Let me tell you, son, I would not be surprised by anything those people in the White House do. They're a bunch of cold-blooded politicians, pure and simple. And she's the worst of them, as far as I'm concerned. You know she made the Foster fella come up to Washington with her. Everybody knows they were having some kind of—"

"Where do you get this garbage from?" Paul asked, pushing back his chair. "I mean it's one thing to disagree with a man's ideas, it's another to smear his reputation for the hell of it."

"No, you're not listening to me," Dandridge insisted, his voice rising. "I was talking about *her*. Though I wouldn't put anything past him. After that what's-her-name Flowers woman. Oh boy! Let me tell you . . ."

It had gone on like that until, pleading bedtime for Rachel, we were able to slip away. Now, with our daughter dozing between us, we gloried in the quiet calm of the long summer evening as the hammock rocked gently back and forth.

"Did you get a chance to talk to Kathy at all?" I asked him in a low voice. "I think she'd be really good for Bob."

"No, I didn't. She kind of clams up around me. But I'm glad you like her. It would be good for Bob to have somebody over there who's totally on his side. I don't know how he stands it day after day."

"But your dad doesn't go at him the way he does you. Though sometimes I think Bob would prefer it if he got a little bit more attention from him—good or bad. No, unless it's something to do with the business, your dad just ignores him most of the time; that's got to be galling in its own way."

"You don't miss a whole lot, do you, Mad?" he said, and then he reached over and took my hand. Our loosely clasped fingers rested gently on Rachel's stomach. I knew something was coming. Paul rarely compliments me outright like that. He doesn't need to; he knows I know how he feels. No, this was his way of preparing me.

"Sometimes I do," I said.

"You know I've stayed in touch with Luke," he said. He hadn't told me outright and I hadn't asked, but he'd left enough clues around for me over the years. I was the one who paid the household bills, and I checked every item over carefully. I'd never asked him about the long-distance calls to a 315 area code. Nor did I question him too closely about his hunting trips upstate with Ethan. But I'd sensed the truth without being consciously forced to accept the facts. I knew because I understood who Paul was, how he still shouldered responsibility for Luke's mistakes, how his loyalties and loves were the subterranean riverbed that fed his being.

"I guess so," I said, looking up through the dark leafy ceiling above us. I knew he was watching me, trying to read something in the still silhouette of my upturned face.

"He's getting out Friday on early release. I want to go up there and bring him home."

I thought I had a few more years before this happened, but I'd always known that the day would come. I wasn't ready, I never could be, but I felt better prepared to face him than in the past. I was married now, a mother. I had earned a place in the world. I no longer really doubted that I deserved Paul's love. And now Luke would be forced to see how well I'd done with what I'd been given. In our own modest way, we were making a go of things.

I guess that a part of me actually imagined Luke would be envious of the careful little life we were building: our two used cars, the new slipcovers on the living room couch, the MacIntosh computer with its Internet connection that Paul had set up in the guest bedroom. To me, these things signified security, stability—everything one could hope for in this world.

What I'd forgotten was that Luke had always lived outside the parameters of a normal, settled life. He'd never known familial love, or seemed to understand its value. He was an emotional nomad, rootless. When I think back on it, I realize that one of my biggest mistakes has always been to judge Luke through the prism of my own needs and wants. And not to be able to foresee that, like me, he could change over time—or, perhaps more to the point, time could change him.

I'd gone to a lot of trouble over dinner. I'd marinated some expensive strip steaks. Made my pineapple cheesecake, a favorite of Paul's. I'd covered the dinged-up dining room table in a dark blue and pink-flowered cloth and arranged fresh candles and a vase of cosmos and Shasta daisies as a centerpiece. Rachel, who loved to help me around the house, carefully folded the cotton napkins I'd ironed into rectangles and aligned them next to the forks. She was going through her pink stage at that point and demanded to be dressed entirely in that color, which meant her wearing battered ballet slippers that shed sequins all over the house. But I was grateful for her excited, girlish company. We didn't entertain often, as most of our celebrations were with Paul's family at the farm, and I probably would have felt nervous in any case. I so longed to have our household seem effortlessly perfect. And it was going to be Luke who would be sitting down in that small, cluttered parlor, who would be meeting my slightly chubby, eager daughter for the first time, who would be looking me and my life over again with that cool, skeptical gaze.

"They're here!" Rachel cried, jumping off the window seat, where she'd been sitting for the last half hour. I watched the two men climb out of the pickup truck and walk around to the steps leading up to the front walk: my tall, broad-shouldered husband with his easy, loping stride and the slight, pale man who seemed to glide along next to him like a shadow, as if hoping not to be seen. We never use the front entrance, and I was touched that Paul was doing so now. He must have known that this formality would please me; it struck me how much he, too, wanted this dinner to be a success, the start of a new beginning for us all. I'm such a coward. I wasn't ready after all. I slipped away into the kitchen and let Rachel be the one to greet them.

"No? Really?" I heard Luke saying, as I ran my hands up and down my aproned hips. "I could have sworn you were a fairy princess. Yes, you are. I can tell by your silvery wings."

"I don't have wings!" Rachel cried, already captivated. "And I'm not a fairy princess. I'm a fairy queen."

"I do apologize," Luke said, turning to face me as I walked down the hall. "Maddie. Hello. Thank you for having me." Neither one of us knew what to do. I think Luke was leaning forward to kiss my cheek and I was reaching up to give him a hug, but somehow both gestures lost their momentum and we ended up doing the most ridiculous thing: we shook hands. Paul, no doubt sensing our discomfort, proceeded to make matters worse by saying, "How about a beer, Luke?"

"No, thanks."

"Oh, shit!" Paul said, hitting his forehead with the heel of his right hand. "I'm sorry. I totally forgot."

"Hey, it's okay," Luke said with his old down-turning smile. "It's not like I'm going to lose my sobriety because you offered me a drink. I've been straight too long for that now."

"How about some iced tea then?" I asked. "Or lemonade?"

"Water's fine," he said. "I'm off just about everything at this point. Caffeine. Sugar." And, as it turned out, red meat, white meat, dairy products, refined flour, almost the entire contents of the dinner I'd spent so much time preparing. Not that Luke would have been particularly impressed if he had been able to eat any of it. He seemed in another world to me, subdued, tentative, like someone who has suffered a long, life-threatening illness and is only now beginning to come around. He let Paul do most of the talking and listened without any obvious reaction to my husband's animated description of how the area was changing, the new people and businesses moving in, the way land values were beginning to escalate. The only thing that seemed to capture—and hold—his attention was Rachel, who insisted on sitting next to him at the head of the table.

"So what do fairy queens do around here to keep busy?" he asked as I served him a bowl of strawberries and the three of us the cheesecake. Rachel, who in those days was something of a chatterbox around Paul and me, had sat dumb throughout the meal, staring up at Luke like someone bewitched.

"Fairy things," she whispered into her cake.

"What? Like night flying and turning invisible and teaching frogs to dance? That sort of old-fashioned kind of fairy stuff?"

"Yes!" Rachel laughed. "And making fairy gardens. Do you want to see?"

"Try and stop me."

Paul and I cleared the table while the two of them disappeared into the backyard, where Rachel had spent numerous hours that summer constructing a miniature castle out of twigs, moss, pebbles, and flowers. There was a muddy moat and a drawbridge made of bark, a pasture with a long stick fence, and a tiny flagpole that flew the emblem of the kingdom: a small ridged beech leaf.

"He's doing great, don't you think?" Paul asked, hoping, I guess, that wishing could make it so.

"He's lost a lot of weight," I said.

"Actually, eating prison food should have put weight on him. I know. But he seems to be clearheaded. Determined."

"What's he planning to do?" I asked, remembering how hard it had been for Paul to get started again.

"He's going to fix up the house," Paul told me, rinsing a plate. "He wants to get it back to where it was." Mrs. Barnett had died suddenly about two years before this. She'd been institutionalized on and off since Luke was sent away, and had ended up at a state facility that was notoriously badly managed. Some people said that she'd committed suicide, others that she'd simply been given an overdose by mistake. The house, already in disrepair, had begun to fall apart. I'd driven up there earlier in the summer on some odd impulse and saw how the elegant windows had been boarded up. Grass was growing in the mossy patches on the roof.

"Why? It's a mess, Paul. It's going to take real money to get it back into any kind of shape. That, and some practical knowledge about how to go about it. And Luke doesn't have either. That doesn't sound like someone who's particularly clearheaded to me."

He was silent, letting what I said sink in. Then I realized what he wasn't saying.

"No," I told him. "Don't tell me you're going to help him. Please, don't tell me that."

"Well, yes, I'd like to give him a hand. When I have a free moment from time to time. It's not such a big deal, really. I'd like to see him get back on his feet again. Wouldn't you?"

I watched as Luke and Rachel emerged into the porch light from out of the darkness. She was chattering away at him, all inhibitions cast aside. She was holding his hand. And he was listening, nodding his head. But not with the amused, barely suppressed condescension that most adults would have. He seemed to be taking in what she said, about all the fantastical details of her four-year-old world, with the utmost seriousness and respect.

"Of course," I said, because I knew then that I had no choice. I would have to learn who Luke was all over again, understand the ways in which he'd changed. And I'd have to change, too. How else was I going to be able to protect those I loved?

24

"Hey, Kath, who's that usher with the long blond hair?" Leslie Finn, Kathy's older sister, called from across the vestry at St. Anne's. It was Kathy and Bob's wedding day, and Leslie, Nelwyn, Louise, Barb, Rachel, and myself were waiting for the ceremony to get under way. We were dressed in matching apple-green dotted Swiss ankle-length gowns with wide white satin sashes.

Leslie was standing at the emergency exit, the door propped open, smoking a cigarette. Divorced, rehabbed, remarried, and divorced again, she looked every bit the part of her bad-girl reputation. She'd been living in Springfield since her last divorce, where, according to Kathy, she was "working on her sobriety and collecting unemployment." The Finn sisters had been raised in what my mother used to call "a broken home," but where Kathy had emerged seemingly unscathed by the experience, Leslie brandished all the scars of her childhood.

"I'm kind of busy now," Kathy said and sighed, rolling her eyes for my benefit. "Getting ready for my wedding, you know? You'll have to wait and do your man-hunting at the reception."

"Jesus Christ, do you know who that is?" Leslie cried. "That's what's-his-name! Luke Barnett. Is he not the sexiest fucking man alive? Is he married?"

"Leslie, watch your mouth, please," Kathy said. "We've got a little girl present."

"And an old lady," Clara added, as she came up to the two of us. "You look lovely, Kathy." Clara had been going around the room fiddling and fussing over everyone's dresses and now tugged loose my white sash and retied it. She'd been so much more welcoming to Kathy than she'd been to me. I told myself that it was because Kathy had converted, but I couldn't help but be hurt by it anyway. Kathy knew this and did everything she could to make Clara recognize my worth.

"Thanks to Maddie," she said now. "She did my makeup."

"Not that you needed any," Clara replied. "Well, I think it's time we all started to line up. Rachel? Here's your flower basket. Now, remember to walk very slowly down the aisle, just the way we practiced. Count to three before each step. . . ."

It was a long service, and a hot afternoon for early May. I felt my mind drifting as Father Timothy's voice droned on through the mass. As usual, my thoughts snagged on all the sore subjects and problems in my life. The Anderson nephew had decided to sell the house, now that prices were on their way up, and had offered us first refusal on it. We'd been on the verge of approval from First State Bank for a mortgage, when, without explanation, it fell through. We were applying elsewhere now, but we'd wasted a lot of time in the process, and Paul was still baffled and upset by the setback. He was making a decent salary, we had the necessary ten percent to put down: what had gone wrong? Should I tell him that I learned from a friend who worked at the bank that Harry served on the advisory board? But there was probably no way to prove that he'd blocked our loan, so what was the point of stirring up bad feelings?

More and more these days, I found myself pushing the past where I felt it belonged—behind me. I hadn't seen my parents or Harry for six years. The hardware had been taken over by the True Value chain and now, with so much building under way, it seemed to be thriving again. The house where I grew up had been torn down by the new owners and an enormous structure in a quasi-Victorian shingle style, with multiple porches and an actual turret, was being erected in its place. It was disconcerting to drive by and recognize all the trees and the old stone wall running along the seasonal creek, and then have to see a monstrosity rising in the place of my childhood home.

"Louise told me that a dentist and his wife from the city are building it as their weekend getaway," I'd told Paul a few weeks back. "Two people! Rattling around in all those rooms. It's kind of disgusting, don't you think? Just a splashy display of wealth—and bad taste."

"Well, it's wealth and bad taste like that that are helping us put food on the table," Paul reminded me, "and buy a place of our own. These huge places are going up everywhere. Think of it this way: the bigger and more elaborate the house, the more business Polanski gets out of it. Which means the more work for me."

But despite the fact that Paul was steadily employed at Polanski Builders, he never allowed himself to relax, or take our well-being for granted. He seemed so easygoing and confident to the outside world, but I knew he worried a lot in secret. I'd sometimes wake up in the middle of the night and see him lying beside me, eyes open, staring at the ceiling. When I'd ask him what was on his mind he'd say his father, who'd recently suffered a series of small strokes, or Bob's ongoing problems at the dairy, or our being able to make ends meet when we took on the added financial burden of a mortgage. It was always something specific along with, I suspected, a deeper, more amorphous kind of dread. I don't think he'd ever been able to forgive himself for going astray so early on, and in such a public and damning way. I think he was still trying to make up for that early mistake, though perhaps he didn't understand that that's what was driving him so hard. Not wanting to name them, he internalized these feelings, but they were as real and demanding as any sentence handed down. He was still doing time. And a big part of that, of course, was his need to help Luke.

His "free moment from time to time" had quickly escalated into every Saturday afternoon. Paul would get his chores done around the house, pack a lunch, and load his electric tools and building supplies into the back of the pickup. He'd be back home by six or seven in the evening, exhausted but happy. There was no question in my mind that Luke was giving something back to Paul. Perhaps, by accepting Paul's help with the house, Luke was easing my husband's guilt about selling him out to Riccio. But I never sensed it was that simple or direct. They shared a friendship and a host of memories, complicated ties that had survived, and perhaps had been strengthened by, everything that had come between them. I never visited the house myself, and I wasn't able to get much out of Paul about how the work was progressing. I knew it was bound to be an enormous task, but if anyone could help Luke pull it off, it was my determined, indomitable husband. So I was shocked when Paul came home early one afternoon about six months into the renovation and told me that Luke was abandoning the project.

"I don't think his heart's been in it for a while, really," Paul told me. "In fact, he's kind of gone in a whole different direction. Come on out to the truck and take a look."

It was lying facedown in the pickup. At first glance it looked to me like just a pile of junk: a garbage-pail top, some broken pieces of dinner plates, a couple of doorknobs, and two dozen or so cedar shake shingles. But when Paul lifted it carefully out of the back and stood it on end, it became clear that it was meant to be an owl. A very large, ghastly-looking owl with eyes made out of two shot glasses.

"He's been working on these during the week," Paul told me. "Taking bits and pieces from all over the house. He finally walked me out to the barn this afternoon and showed me what he's been up to. He's planning to set up a gallery or something and sell these to the public."

"You didn't actually pay for that thing, did you?"

"Yes, I did. What was I supposed to say? He told me that he doesn't need my help with the house anymore. He seems to really love putting these things together. And he has this whole kind of complicated philosophy about how he's recycling our past—"

"Oh, for heaven's sake. He's nuts. That owl is just a piece of junk— literally. You're not going to get involved with this crazy gallery idea, too, are you?"

"He didn't ask me to. He seems to think he's found the answer to everything. It's all a little abstract, kind of cosmic, really. I couldn't follow a lot of what he was trying to say."

"He's smoking dope again, isn't he?" I demanded. "We can't be involved with him, Paul. You know that. We can't risk—"

"No. I know, believe me. But he's still off drugs and he's not drinking, or doing anything like that. He just seems to have found something he believes in. It's harmless enough, I suppose. Though God knows how he intends to support himself by doing it."

But Luke's needs were modest enough. He lived in what had once been the servants' quarters on the ground floor of the big house, using an old Jotul stove to heat the small back rooms. He seemed to subsist on brown rice, vegetables, and fruit that he purchased at a natural foods co-op market that had opened recently in Northridge. He spent his days scavenging items from what remained of the contents of the mansion—silverware and china that had been in the Barnett family for generations, chandeliers, fireplace utensils, his mother's costume jewelry, old TV parts—and welded them together into bizarre pieces that were both whimsical and grotesque. He started displaying them in the front yard of the farmhand's cottage that bordered River Road, where Paul had briefly lived. If he felt haunted or unhappy by this strange, hermetic existence, he didn't let it show. He wasn't broken or humbled, as I guess I'd hoped he might be, but I did feel he was uncharacteristically resigned. Though there was always that undercurrent of tension between the two of us, when he came to our house to visit he seemed more at ease with himself than I ever remembered him being before. It helped that Rachel was there. She was unabashed in her girlish love for Luke, and I believe he was genuinely touched by this. Once, as we were sitting down to dinner, she'd reached out and taken his hand.

"Would you like to marry me?" she'd asked him.

"I'd love to, Rach," he'd told her. "But I'm afraid that I'm really not the marrying kind."

There were plenty of women, though. I would hear about them through Paul, Kathy, and others around town. Or I would see him with some girl beside him in his father's old gas-guzzling Oldsmobile convertible, one of the last remnants of the good old days, wind whipping his hair back as he drove with one hand on the wheel. But none of these relationships ever lasted very long. I think women would fall for his go-to-hell good looks and think that, with the right amount of love and persuasion, they could bring him around. But they'd learn soon enough that Luke had no intention of changing, no desire to commit to anyone or anything. He was just what he appeared to be: a lone wolf who was probably happiest on his own, soldering together broken pieces of his collapsing legacy into "art works" that nobody in his right mind would want to buy.

"Do you, Robert Matthew Alden . . ." Father Timothy's sudden change of tone brought me back to the present. I was embarrassed that I'd let my thoughts wander so far from the ceremony, and I forced myself to follow the rest of the proceedings attentively. Rachel, mindful of her grandmother's directions, took forever leading us back down the aisle, dropping careful handfuls of rose petals in front of her as she stepped and stopped, stepped and stopped. I could hear her counting aloud, "One, two, three . . . one, two, three." I walked back down with Paul, the two of us holding hands as we all shuffled along behind our dutiful offspring. As it turned out, Leslie and Luke walked down together, as well. Months later, Ethan would comment wryly: "From the beginning, I doubt any of us would say that it was a match made in heaven."

There were about seventy or so guests at the reception in St. Anne's annex. We saved on costs by making the dinner a buffet and doing most of the cooking ourselves. This allowed Bob, who loved bluegrass music, to be able to afford the only thing he'd requested for the wedding: a live band called Hard Times, from outside of Boston. It was a good choice. Like so many emotionally reserved people, the Aldens were enthusiastic and tireless dancers. Since Bob had started dating Kathy, we would often accompany them to contra dancing events up near Albany. It was a fun, invigorating, family-friendly way to pass a Friday evening, and I felt it let Paul relax and get out of himself.

"My, oh, my," Barb said to me as we were carrying trays of lasagna out of the kitchen. I followed the direction of her gaze and saw Luke and Leslie locked in an embrace as the band played an up-tempo version of "Your Love Is Like a Flower." They were moving at about half the speed of everyone else around them, and seemingly oblivious to anyone but themselves. I felt a real jolt watching them, the kind of vicarious thrill you sometimes get seeing movie stars make love on the screen. I could see, for the first time in a long while, what Luke's sexual appeal might be. Although it was Leslie he was holding, I could almost feel the pressure of his hand on the small of *my* back and the warmth of his breath on *my* fingers as he raised her hand to his lips.

"Is that even legal in this state?" Ethan asked, coming up to Barb and me. I think every adult in the reception hall was staring at the slowly gyrating couple in the middle of the dance area. When the song ended, the band broke into whooping laughter as Luke and Leslie kept dancing. I looked away, upset with myself for getting so worked up, and when I glanced back again, they were gone.

But seeing them together like that put me in a peculiar mood: restive and unhappy. I felt frumpy in the green bag of a dress I wore and uncomfortable in the tight heels I'd sprayed white to go with it. I'd willingly volunteered earlier but now I resented the fact that I was forced to help in the kitchen, warming up trays, scraping off pots and pans, listening to the rau-

cous thumping of the banjo and fiddle. Feeling overheated and exhausted, I
stepped outside at one point to get some air, the screen door closing behind
me with a sigh.

"No, I've got to get back. They'll be wanting to serve the cake soon."

"What cake?"

"Oh . . . no . . . yes . . . please . . ."

"I've got my car. Let's just go . . ."

"I can't, baby . . ."

"Yes, you can."

Eventually, with Barb's help, I found the rectangular single-layer wedding cake that Leslie had made. It was in the industrial-sized refrigerator,
and it was beautifully iced with red and pink roses and a large-script "Bob
and Kathy 4 Ever" across the center. I didn't feel particularly sorry that Leslie didn't get to see her younger, happy sister cut the cake she'd obviously
put so much time and effort into. I thought then that she'd behaved in an
unforgivably shameless and selfish way. I didn't understand what loneliness
can do to you, how longing can make you crazy. Leslie didn't leave Luke's
house after that. They lived together in those cramped little rooms for the
next ten months. But I began to feel bad when I heard from Kathy that Leslie had started drinking again. Luke asked her to leave, but she wouldn't or
couldn't. She moved upstairs, sleeping in Mrs. Barnett's old room, until that
autumn turned so cold.

It was Tom Langlois, then a deputy, who found her wandering down
River Road one night trying to keep her balance on the double yellow line.
He knew enough—the whole town did by then—not to take her back to
Luke. He drove her instead over to Alden Dairy. Kathy and Bob got her
back into rehab. But, according to Kathy, she never really got back on her
feet again after that. She moved to Florida, and from what we hear she's
still drinking.

"Not so much now that she can't function," Kathy told me a year or so
ago. "But enough so that she doesn't really have to feel anything anymore."
And Luke? He went on as he had before. He never mentioned Leslie when
he came by to see us. I wonder sometimes if he ever thought about her, if he
ever felt responsible for what had happened. I remember years before when
he had warned me about Kenny: "It's like you're trying to help a bird with
a broken wing. It's a waste of time. Let him flap away." It had seemed to me

such a cold thing to say, even if it was true. It's continued to reverberate with me because I've never really thought of Luke as someone who was troubled by pity, or regret, or any of the lesser sorrows. But then I've come to learn that most of the time you only think you know the truth about other people, even those you believe you know best.

25

Beanie was born a month after my mother died and nearly six months after Dandridge suffered another stroke, a major one this time. He was on life support for a week until Clara, believing that his "soul had gone on to God," took him off. He was only sixty-nine, though he looked much older at the viewing: the leathery face, creased and frowning, seeming to withhold his approval and love even in death.

I thought Beanie looked a lot like my mother with her heart-shaped face and cleft chin. She has her hazel eyes, as well, flecked with little bits of gold. But she has none of my mother's sanctimony or passive aggression. From the beginning, Beanie seemed otherworldly to me, dreamy and gentle. A changeling. Rachel, who was ten years old when her younger sister was born, thought of Beanie as her own, a living doll. She fed her all the stories and fantasies she herself had been raised on and loved. It took us all a while to realize how smart Beanie was. She never crawled. She just stood up one day and waddled across the kitchen. She didn't traffic in nonsense words, either, but went right to "milk," "car," and "cat," without dropping consonants or doubling syllables. She could count to twenty by the time she was two and a half. A lot of this, I think, is due to her amazing memory. When she was three, we found her confidently reading *In the Night Kitchen* aloud to her cousin B.J. She'd simply memorized the thing, page by page.

There seemed to be a lot to deal with that year, between our parents dying and 9/11, though Paul and I felt closer than ever. We'd been trying to have another child for two years before Beanie was conceived. Her arrival felt like a kind of blessing, a cosmic nod that we were on the right road, that we deserved all this hard-earned happiness. Especially since others were less fortunate. Bob finally closed down the dairy, selling off the last hundred or so head without telling anyone, even Kathy, until the outfit buying them rolled up the drive with their cattle haulers.

"Kept looking at them through Daddy's eyes," he told us one night about a month after they were gone. "Kept hearing him telling me all the things I was doing wrong. Dairying's dead around here anyway."

"What are you going to do?" Paul asked. "I bet Polanski could use you. He's got more work now than he knows what to do with. Just give me the word."

"Heck, no. I'm a farmer. I'll be putting in feed corn for the time being. Pumpkins, maybe. I've got some other ideas brewing. You'll see. We'll be fine."

It helped that Louise stepped in and insisted that Clara move down to Northridge to live with her and Mike shortly after the two of them got married. At first, I think we all assumed that Kathy was at the root of Clara's problems. Things deteriorated pretty quickly between the two of them after Kathy moved in and began keeping house. Or not keeping it, actually. The big, rambling place was over two hundred years old, and Clara had devoted her life to its care. She'd been a great believer in the value of white vinegar—as window cleaner, drain freshener, floor wash, spot remover, ironing spray—so that every room, but the kitchen especially, always had a briskly astringent smell. She'd lavished on that house all the physical attention she was never able to bring herself to give her children: dusting, scrubbing, washing, ironing, beating the dust out of the carpets with Ethan's baseball bat. I think this was her way of expressing love, at arm's length and without sentiment: freshly laundered sheets, tucked in tight, the pillowcases starched and ironed.

But Kathy didn't know the first thing about how to take care of a house, let alone a place that big. Her mom had raised her and Leslie in a series of furnished apartments, where the two girls slept on fold-out couches and ate boilable dinners or takeout. I had to show her how to change a vacuum-cleaner bag, how to defrost the freezer. Though I did my best to help her, I had a house of my own to take care of, a family to feed. Inevitably, the farmhouse began to show signs of neglect: a gummy buildup on the linoleum, filmy windows, dust collecting around the newel posts, mildew spreading on the shower curtain liners.

"Clara hardly speaks to me anymore," Kathy confessed to me about two years after she and Bob were married. With Dandridge gone and everyone else married and moved out, it was just the three of them together in that enormous sprawl of a house. We were sitting in the kitchen having coffee, keeping our voices low so that Clara couldn't hear. Claiming that her arthritis was getting the better of her, she'd moved into the small downstairs bedroom behind the kitchen where years ago she'd planned for Paul and me to live. She kept a small portable television going all the time, even while she slept. Now I could see its blue light flickering at the end of the hallway behind Kathy and hear the disembodied laughter of some morning talk-show audience.

"Did you have a fight?" I asked, though I had a hard time imagining that. Clara preferred to grumble and complain under her breath; it was Dandridge who had enjoyed lashing out and courting confrontation.

"No, nothing like that. She just seems to forget I'm here. Bob, too. She lies back there on her bed watching television all day. Though I'm not even sure she's really watching it. She kind of stares right through it into something else. I'm sure she's depressed. That she misses Dandridge and all the others. But she won't even tell me what she wants for dinner, so I'm not going to try and talk to her about anything like that."

"Do the girls know?" I asked, meaning Nelwyn and Louise, the daughters and therefore those whose opinions actually meant something. As in-laws we both knew that we had, at best, supporting roles in the overall family structure.

"I told Bob we had to say something," Kathy told me. "But I don't think he wants to. You know he's feeling like such a failure these days. I think he believes the least we can do is find a way of coping with Clara."

"That's crazy," I told her. "If any of us could get along with her, it would be you. She took a real shine to you, Kath, you know that. No, I think you're right. I've noticed how much vaguer she seems since Dandridge died. Something's definitely wrong. You and Bob have done the best you could. I'll talk to Paul about it."

That night Paul called Louise, and then Nelwyn in Indiana and Ethan, who had recently moved up to Brookline with Barb and the kids, as soon as I talked to him about Clara. They all agreed not to let Bob know that they were intervening: what possible good could that do? Louise and

Mike seemed more than willing to take Clara in. Mike was already pretty well established as an insurance broker and had inherited the ranch-style house from his folks. I knew he was hoping for a big family, and I think he envisioned his mother-in-law helping out with the kids when they came along. Of course, nobody realized how far gone Clara was at that point. I overheard a lot of the planning that was done over the telephone, my heart nearly stopping once when Paul said: "Well, we'd have her come here but . . ."

God, no! I thought, and luckily we didn't have to. But I came to realize over the months that followed how much it ate away at Paul that we hadn't tried to do more to help Clara. I think he felt that if he'd noticed her mental decline before it became so acute, he might have been able somehow to prevent it. He'd weathered Dandridge's death without too much sorrow or regret, though I think it can often be more difficult to deal with the death of someone you didn't get on with than someone you did. They say hate never finds a comfortable resting spot.

"Polanski took me up to that new site outside of Harringdale today," Paul told me a few weeks after Clara was resettled with Louise and Mike. "Land went straight up a mountain. We're talking a thirty-degree gradient. We're going to need to lay in switchbacks the whole way up. It's getting really crazy. I can't believe their town zoning people let that one get by. It would be a total nightmare trying to get a fire truck up there."

We were having a lot of conversations along these lines since Paul began sitting on Red River's planning board that spring. As well as having solid experience in the construction business, Paul served on the volunteer fire department and was good at troubleshooting potential problems the town might have trying to service all the new houses going in. Since 9/11, the local real estate market was booming: prices soaring, new home permits at a record high. It was about that time we heard that a real estate brokerage was opening up in town. The wife of a wealthy retired weekending couple had purchased the old Hildebrand house on Route 198 and had renovated it for office use.

I just assumed that Paul saw only the good in all this development. He was always telling me to look on the bright side of things. Yes, the rural landscape was being transformed by all the expensive and enormous new homes, he would agree, but think what the burgeoning tax revenues meant for the school district and the town budget, which for years had limped along on a deficit. And all the new people, driving in to the general store for their Sunday *Times*, and actually honking when old Theo Magnusen took a minute or so to get his slipping clutch into gear? Paul would say, "Give them time to get acclimated. There's just no point in getting your hackles up. Think of all the places farther upstate that are still losing population. We're lucky. We're in a growth spurt. Things will settle down. These kind of changes always take some getting used to."

I took him at his word. I didn't see what all this was costing him on some deeper, emotionally inaccessible level. I'm not sure if he understood himself how much he suppressed things, always trying to put a good face on a bad situation. We'd been doing it for so many years now that it had simply become our way of coping. He seemed so positive to me, confident about the future. We weren't planning to have another child so soon after Beanie, but when I told him I was pregnant again, he'd seemed happy. I should have remembered how he felt about children: each one was a miracle to him. What could he do but open his arms again, provide unconditional love?

We saw Luke on a pretty regular basis in those days, though his visits were rarely planned. Paul would run into him at the transfer station and invite him back to the house for pancakes. Or we'd drive past and see him brush cutting around his sculptures in front of the cottage and stop to chat. He'd moved out of the big house soon after Leslie had left and settled into the old farmhand's place, setting up a workshop in the basement. With Paul's help he even started a Web page to help sell his sculptures, as well as link them to listings on eBay and other online venues. If Luke sold three or four pieces a year, Paul told me, you'd have to think him lucky. But he scraped along somehow. And I think the two of us had finally reached a point of accommodation. We covered up our mutual dislike for the sake of Paul and the girls. And I had to admit that Luke engaged Beanie as no other adult I knew could. She was skittish and shy with her aunts and uncles, but she'd race out to meet Luke whenever he pulled up in that rust-pitted Oldsmobile.

"I hope it's okay with you that I invited Luke for supper," Paul told me when I was about four months along with Lia. It was a Sunday in late

October and we'd spent the afternoon raking leaves. I was still plagued by morning sickness and usually feeling exhausted by dinnertime. I had laundry to fold and Beanie to feed, but all I wanted to do was go upstairs and lie down.

"Oh, Paul . . ." I sighed.

"Hey, don't worry. I'll grill some hamburgers for us—and some portabellas for him. I can do the whole thing. It's no problem. Rachel can help with Beanie. You go on up and take a nap. We'll call you when we're ready to eat."

I'm not sure what happened. I glanced out the window before I crawled into bed and saw Paul rolling the grill out of the garage with one hand while holding a can of beer in the other. I didn't think I actually fell asleep, though the hour or two that I thought I was lying there seemed to pass quickly. I heard Luke's voice at one point, crying: "Go out long. Way back!" He and Paul both enjoyed teaching Rachel how to play baseball and football, reliving their high school glory days. I woke up in the dark, their voices suddenly loud and insistent below me in the kitchen. I'd been asleep for almost four hours. They were sitting around the table when I came downstairs, dirty plates stacked in the sink. Beanie was in her high chair, her bib smeared with catsup. Rachel was sitting in my chair at the end of the table, her face pale under the bright overhead lights. Paul and Luke were obviously in the middle of an argument. I'd heard a phrase or two of it on the stairs. It was one of the few times I could ever remember hearing them raise their voices at each other:

"It's the most hideous thing I've ever . . ."

". . . started working on it two months ago. Who's to say . . ."

"That's no excuse, damn it . . ."

"Hey there, remember me?" I asked now, walking into the room and coming up behind Paul. I massaged his shoulders, feeling the tension in his muscles.

"I went up to get you," Paul said, "but you were sleeping so peacefully, I didn't have the heart to wake you. There's a burger or two over there somewhere."

"What's up?" I asked, looking over at Luke.

"I just found out that your husband is helping to build that enormous eyesore of a place on Jarvis Mountain. I thought it was a hotel at first. Some kind of resort. Turns out two people are going to live there. Just two! What an incredible waste. It just destroys that lovely uninterrupted stretch of ridge and forest. It's all you see when you drive up North Branch now."

"Oh, it's not that bad. Once they do a little landscaping . . ."

"Come on, Paul! They took down a ton of really great hardwood trees. Oaks and birch, wonderful old sugar maples. Who cares about their damned landscaping plans? They've already raped—"

"Luke . . . ?" I said, nodding my head toward Rachel.

"Sorry," he said, drumming his hand on the tabletop. "I know I get kind of worked up on this subject."

"Well, I do, too," I said. "Paul and I have this argument all the time." I heated up my dinner in the microwave and ate standing up at the counter, I was so hungry. By then it was nine thirty and I made Rachel and Beanie say good night. Rachel gave her dad a hug and then walked around and hugged Luke, too. I held Beanie up to kiss Paul and then took her over to Luke.

"Sleep well, Beanstalk," he told her, giving her a kiss on the forehead.

Things seemed to have quieted down between the two men while I was upstairs, though I could still hear the rise and fall of their voices. But when I came back down a half an hour or so later, it seemed that the conversation had deteriorated once again into an argument, though the tone was more subdued than before, sadder. I stopped at the bottom of the steps and listened.

"But it's an outrage that the town doesn't try to stop it. And I have a hard time accepting that you are a willing participant in all this."

"It's a job. A damned good one. You looked around the table tonight and saw those girls. They're what I have to think about first now. Them, and another baby on the way. I wish I could afford to have your scruples. But I can't."

"You know what it is? I feel like we're cannibalizing our birthright. The one good, beautiful thing we ever had was this land, you know? And now, in order to survive, we're devouring it—or letting strangers have the pleasure. All that'll be left soon are the rusting hay balers and the tires, and crazy me, trying to put the past together again and sell it along the roadside."

"And you think I don't feel the same way? Give me another option and I'd jump on it in a second. But after a certain point you just have to say:

okay, man, this is it. This is the deal. Make the best of it. Live with it. Let the rest of it go."

"Well, I guess that's the real difference between you and me."

I heard their chairs scrape as they pushed back from the table. Luke's voice faded somewhat as he headed for the door. "I'm not going to let it go. I can't."

Part Seven

26

"I just feel like there's no end to him. Every day, I find out something new and amazing. I mean, this whole thing about his dad. The family, going back to the founding fathers or something. And that house? It must have been incredible. He showed me a photograph he has of it. I guess it was taken sometime around the turn of the last century. It's one of those sepia prints with these women—you know how beautiful they looked back then with those long white gauzy dresses and great wide-brimmed hats—all dressed up and playing croquet on the front lawn. The house is kind of spread out like a stage set behind them. All those rooms! Those long French windows! Was it as wonderful as it looked in the picture? It's such a shame it had to be torn down."

I squinted into the strong morning sunlight. Anne and I were sitting on the octagonal section of the deck that wrapped around the southwest corner of her house, looking down on our children playing in the garden. Rachel had them all keyed up about the idea of fairies. After having them discover the letter written in "fairy language" up by the pond earlier in the summer, she'd helped them construct a miniature fairy castle and garden under the trellis. When nobody was looking, she'd sneak down and leave little gifts she'd bought at the general store—Pez dispensers or balsa wood airplanes—for them to find. Beanie and Lia had been raised on this fantastical fare so they took Rachel's inventions pretty much in their stride, but for the Zeller children, especially Max, it had opened up a whole new world of wonder. Anne had told me that the first thing he did every morning was to run down to the garden to see "if the fairies had come."

"Well, it had pretty much fallen apart by then. Literally. The roof had collapsed and there was water damage everywhere. Nana had an architectural firm specializing in old house restoration come in and look it over, but they said it would take millions of dollars to make it habitable again."

"So where had it been exactly?" Anne asked me, turning around. She held her hand up to shade her eyes and looked north into the woods. "Luke took me up there the other night, but he got confused and turned around by the new houses. He thinks it's more or less where the Naylors' place is now."

"You were with him at night? What about the kids, Anne?" I knew that her children were not my concern. I had no right to worry about them. But I couldn't help myself. For the past week, ever since I'd found out about Anne and Luke, I'd worried a lot about what was going on, and, despite the two adults' assurances, about how exposed and vulnerable the children seemed to be. I'd purchased new cell phones and a better wireless plan and had taken to checking in with Rachel at least twice a day. She didn't seem surprised by or to resent my concern, which made me wonder all over again how much she knew about why I suddenly seemed so vigilant. And I'd just found out that any hope for a quick resolution to all the subterfuge had been dashed. Richard had come up from the city the night before and then turned right around earlier that morning to head down to Kennedy Airport and a flight to Europe. He was in the midst of some big new piece of international business, which, according to Anne, had preoccupied him all summer.

"He'll be back this Thursday for a week's vacation. I'll tell him then when we have the time to really talk things through. And when he's in the right mood to listen. You can't believe how he gets when he's in the middle of a business deal. It's like his mind actually morphs into one of those PowerPoint presentations, do you know what I mean? He doesn't even see me then."

Anne seemed happy enough to delay the confrontation, and I guess I couldn't really blame her. I didn't envy her having to force a final face-off with Richard. From what she'd told me, they both knew the divorce was inevitable, but I'm sure that didn't make the hard reality of breaking up a home any easier to handle. In the meantime, Anne was on a high. I'd never seen her so exuberant and carefree. If she was given the opportunity, I sensed she would talk about Luke for hours on end. But my busy work schedule was only getting busier as I tried to juggle new inquiries and showings, walk-throughs and closings. I'd also suffered my first real setback since becoming a broker, something that had confused and upset me so much initially I hadn't even told Paul about it yet or allowed myself to dwell on it for very long. This was actually the first opportunity I'd had to sit down alone with Anne—out of earshot of our offspring—since learning about her and Luke. And now, when she didn't respond to my obvious concern about her children, I wondered briefly if I'd somehow overstepped my bounds. But it remained one of the things I liked most about Anne, that she didn't seem to want to set any limits when it came to intimacy. I got the sense that she felt free to tell me anything—and expected the same in return.

"Anne?" I asked again. "You're leaving the children alone at night to be with Luke?"

"For heaven's sakes, I told you weeks ago that I do that! Before Luke, before you, before moving up here. I can't sleep. I go stir crazy. So I go out. Max and Katie are fine. They're heavy sleepers, and besides, they're totally used to it now. Also, I'm sorry to turn this around on you, but you really don't leave us too much choice. It rained three straight afternoons this week, so Rachel and the kids were around here the whole time. You see, I'm just trying to abide by the rules *you* insisted on, and also get to spend a little time with Luke. But it's never enough! I hate having to leave him. Having to come back up here. I don't feel right anymore unless I'm with him. I feel unbalanced, actually *physically* unwell. It's like he acts on me in an almost chemical way—like an antidepressant, or mood stabilizer. I've never felt like this with anybody before. That *craving* to be in his presence. I can't wait—I really don't know if I can wait—to be with him all the time. The idea of waking up in the morning with him beside me in bed is—"

"Are you going to try to get this house in the settlement?" I asked, cutting her off. "I can't see you living down at Luke's place somehow." I really didn't want to hear all the intimate details of their physical relationship; I would have thought she'd remember how embarrassed I'd become in the past when she tried to talk to me about her sex life. But I guess she couldn't resist; the need to confide—to talk about her lover—was just too powerful.

"I don't know. I don't care," she said. "I know I have to start thinking about all of these things. And I will. Soon. But right now I just so much want to live in the moment, in my own body. I have never felt so alive as a human being, so happy to be who I am, where I am. Maddie, he's just the most sensual man I have ever met in my life. Do you know what he asked me the other night?"

"No, really, Anne—"

"He wanted to know if it was true that a woman could have an orgasm just by having her breasts kissed and caressed. He'd heard somewhere that it was possible, but he'd never tried to find out before if it was one of those urban legends or not. So, of course, we—"

"Anne, please, I really don't want to hear about all this."

"Oh." She turned and looked at me. "Oh! I'm sorry. I keep forgetting how well you two know each other. I bet it's like hearing someone talk about your brother. You must see him so differently than I do. I'd love to know everything *you* know about him. I actually envy the fact that you knew him as a boy. That you got to see him growing up. I can't imagine it somehow—Luke as a child or teenager. You must have this wonderfully clear and complete picture of him. I just can't seem to get him in any kind of perspective, do you know what I mean? There are so many different parts, and I feel like I could spend my whole life with each of them. Putting aside his sexuality, there's the whole artistic thing. Have you seen some of the new pieces he's been doing? They're really amazing. So simple and powerful—like totems, I think. Incredibly erotic. I have a good friend in the city who runs a gallery down in Chelsea, and I've been talking to Luke about putting together a digital portfolio for her. It's crazy that he doesn't have any kind of representation. I just know that with the right gallery behind him, he could really—" She saw something in my expression that made her hesitate. "I'm ranting on, right? Like a maniac. It's just so good to have someone to talk to about all this, Maddie! I'm bursting with love and excitement—and hope—for the first time in years and years."

"I *am* happy for you," I told her. "But I'm worried, too, okay? I really, really want this to work out for the two of you. For Max and Katie, too. But I think that you and Luke need to start dealing with some of these realities, and with Richard. Do you know that he's planning to lodge a formal complaint about Luke's property at the special town meeting on Friday night?"

"No, I—what do you mean? Complain about what? To whom? He doesn't know a thing about us, he can't possibly . . ."

"No, it's about the condition of Luke's place. The art pieces by the roadside, all the materials lying around. He wants Luke to clean things up. He called Owen Phelps, who's head of the board, to say he wants to raise these concerns with the select committee at the meeting."

"Oh, for heaven's sakes," Anne said, looking out over the tree line. "Isn't that just so typical of him? He needs to get his way no matter what. He's been bitching about Luke's place since the moment we bought up here. And he's so single-minded when something like that bothers him, no matter how ridiculous it is. Do you know that he totally badgered some downstairs neighbors of ours in the city about their dog? It used to bark in the morning and wake Richard up earlier than he liked. I mean, by maybe fifteen minutes or so. But he couldn't stand it. He got the co-op board involved, then he actually forced them to take legal action. The people finally moved out, can you believe it? He's just relentless. Well, so what? Let him carry on any way he likes! Let him make an utter fool of himself!"

"But that's what I'm saying, Anne. If he's like that about something so trivial, how is he going to react to the news that you're leaving him?"

"Oh, he's going to go ballistic, of course," Anne said. She got up from the chair and walked over to the deck railing. She turned around to face me, her white hair backlit by the sun. "There's not a whole lot I can do to prepare for that, Maddie, do you know what I mean? All the thinking and planning in the world aren't going to make it any easier. I'll just have to find a way to get through it. But this time, I'll have Luke. This time, I know I'm doing the right thing. So nothing Richard says or does is going to make a damn bit of difference. Let him huff and puff until he blows the house down. The truth is, I'm just not there to frighten anymore. I'm already gone."

Both Paul and I needed to work that afternoon, so I'd been relieved when Anne had called soon after Richard left to ask if Rachel would come over to babysit. Now, though, as I got up to go, I found myself tempted to ask Anne what her plans were exactly. Why did she need someone to help with the kids on a Saturday? But I worried that it would sound too much like I didn't trust her, that I thought she was going to find a way to be with Luke. So I just called down my good-byes to Rachel and the kids; they all waved back. In my rearview mirror I saw that Anne was still standing on the deck where I'd left her, watching me go. She seemed so contained and solitary, her arms crossed on her chest. Maybe all she wanted, I told myself, was to have the time to be alone with her happiness.

As I drove back to the office, it occurred to me that Luke needn't have worried that Anne would ask specific questions about his past, or his troubled history with Paul. Though Anne was well aware that we had all grown up in the same small farming community, she seemed to have a deeply romanticized impression of what that had been like. I wouldn't have been surprised if she half believed that we'd lived the kind of life she'd seen in that sepia photograph of Luke's. Sometimes I felt she was almost willfully blind to the blue-collar realities of my own background and upbringing.

And now? Did she allow herself to look around and really see the impoverished circumstances in which Luke was living? I could only guess that she let herself confuse the glamour of the Barnetts' lost fortune and social status with Luke's current situation, casting him as a kind of tragic hero and rebel artist. I couldn't help but worry that her feelings for him were seriously over-idealized. She seemed to view Luke as almost newly born when they met, the miraculous answer to all her physical and emotional needs.

But wasn't that just what falling in love usually entailed? I asked myself. Don't we always imagine the loved one as the best possible version of who he or she can be? And, in many ways, isn't it just this—the vision of the perfect other—that helps sustain our feelings and commitment when faced with reality?

Both Nana's Mercedes and Linda's Explorer were already parked when I pulled into the lot. It had been a hectic month for all of us and, even with Alice Tolland's help, I was falling behind on my paperwork. I was hoping to spend the hour or two before my first showing that afternoon going over the contract for a closing that was scheduled for the following Monday afternoon. I also wanted to tell Nana what had happened with the Pattersons earlier in the week.

"I was just going to phone *you*," I told Marge Patterson when I heard her voice on the other end of my line. She was a good friend of Paul's younger sister Louise. A year or so ago, when we first started to search, the Pattersons had represented the upper tier, money-wise, of my client roster. And they meant a double commission for me; two sales in one, if all went according to plan. But, despite feeling we were close on several occasions, nothing had worked out as of yet. Earlier in the summer, we'd been in contract on a pretty Colonial in Lakeview, but Gary had finally decided that the commute to his office in Harringdale would be too much of a grind.

"Really?" Marge said. "I thought you said you were going to get back to us last week."

"It took a little longer to pull together the listings than I anticipated. That happens when you've already seen so much of what's out there. And when I know so well what it is you're looking for. We've talked about this; inventory is tight. But I do think I have three places you'll be really interested in. So when—"

"Well, that's why I'm calling you, Maddie. You know, we've been working with you for over a year now. In the beginning, both Gary and I were pretty impressed with your enthusiasm. You seemed so willing to go the extra mile for us."

"Thanks, Marge. You know I love working with you guys," I said, keeping my tone purposefully upbeat, though I was pretty sure I knew what was coming. And I was already smarting from the injustice of it; I'd worked my tail off for them! I hadn't made a peep when their oldest son, Jason, spilled Snapple all over my backseat. I'd been more than accommodating when they'd pulled out of the Lakeview house at the last minute. I'd put up with their nit-picking complaints about a number of listings that seemed to me to fit their needs.

"I think maybe you used to," she told me. "But right now both Gary and I have the feeling that you have bigger fish to fry. Louise and Mike told us about that million-dollar sale you made in Red River. We really can't begin to compete for your attention with—"

"It was more like nine-fifty, and that's just ridiculous! We've put in a lot of time together. I think I have a really good sense of what you guys need, the kind of place that would make you happy. I bet that if Mike and Louise hadn't told you about—"

"It's not just that," she cut in. "Do you really want me to make this harder than it has to be?"

"We've worked together for a year, Marge. Yes, I think I deserve to know what you think the problems are."

"Okay. You don't return my calls. You keep showing us places that are out of our price range. We've mentioned to you three times that we don't want another ranch, and yet you took us back to—"

"You can't have it both ways, you know. Maybe you don't want to face it, but perhaps the truth is you really can't afford anything other than a ranch right now. Maybe you've just set your sights too high. You know how prices have gone through the roof—"

"A Century Twenty-one agent showed us something we really liked last night. First time out. It's perfect for us. And it finally made us realize that the problem isn't us—it's you. It's been over a year, so we've met our legal obligation. I'm tearing up the contract; I assume you'll do the same."

She'd hung up on me before I had a chance to say another word. One of my first clients. Not to mention a friend of the family. Of course, word of this would filter right back to Louise and Mike, then spread outward to the rest of the family. I could already imagine them talking about how I'd let my success go to my head. How I'd overreached. I could hear Nelwyn at the Alden picnic, saying: "It's easy to forget who your real friends are, when you're so busy making new ones." Of course, I felt hurt by the call. It was my first rejection. I'd become so used to the upward trajectory of my work life, the ever-growing numbers on my sales chart. Yes, I knew that things would have to level off. Nana kept warning us about how the market was softening in the city, that we were bound to feel its effects soon. But the funny thing was, none of this really bothered me as much as I assumed it would.

The more I thought about what had happened, the more I realized that I wasn't as humiliated as I might have been even a few months ago. In fact, I actually felt a certain amount of relief. Marge was right. I really had lost interest. She and Gary had been demanding and particular, and yet I felt they were looking for the kind of house I now thought of as utterly conventional; nothing special. I realized that I had stopped working so hard for my lower-income clients, the local families I'd grown up with, who'd formed my initial customer base. It was the Naylors and Zellers, the Barrys and Teds whom I was trying my best to please and impress now. This was where the big money and excitement was, after all, and where I saw my future headed. And, yes, it was more than just about real estate sales. Nelwyn was right: these were the people I wanted for friends. By the time I got around to talking to Nana about the situation later that afternoon, I felt I'd gotten the whole thing in a better perspective. And what she said only confirmed this for me:

"You cut your teeth on them. Think of it that way," Nana said. "This whole area is upgrading so quickly, I'm actually surprised they were able to find anything in that price range. I know a lot of local people are complaining that they're being priced right out of this market. That their kids can't afford to stay here, get a starter house. Well, what can you do? It's all a matter of supply and demand. You know you tried your best, sweetie. You don't need them anymore. And they really weren't my idea of our kind of client anyway, if you want to know the truth."

27

"**W**here's Rachel?" I asked when Paul pulled his pickup in beside my car in the parking lot. Lia and Beanie were riding in the jump space in the rear of the cab and the passenger seat was empty. We'd arranged earlier in the day that Paul would collect the girls from the Zellers' when he was done with work and meet me at my office, where we'd switch over to my car, which could accommodate all of us, for the drive over to Bob's farm. This was the second day of BlueFest, the bluegrass festival that Bob had started organizing the year after he shut down the dairy operation, and, being Saturday, the night with the biggest name acts. The festival's attendance numbers and reputation had been growing steadily each August, and last year, despite a deluge during the second night of the three-day festival, Bob told us that he had finally started to turn a profit. This summer, both the River City Ramblers and the Gil McNally Band were headlining. Bob had confided to Paul last week that advance ticket sales were the strongest yet. And the weather was going to be beautiful.

"Anne asked her to stay on through the evening," Paul said as he climbed out of the cab and turned around to unlock Lia from her car seat. "She offered her more money because of the short notice. I wasn't happy about it, but what could I do?"

"What a shame. Rachel loves BlueFest," I said as I helped strap Beanie into her bumper seat in the back of my car. "Did Anne say if she was going out?"

Of course, my suspicions were aroused. Richard was away on business; why did Anne need Rachel on a Saturday night? When we talked that morning, she'd sounded so desperate to be with Luke. I knew her well enough to guess that she would see keeping Rachel on as an easy solution to my concerns: Katie and Max cared for by my responsible oldest daughter. What more could I ask of her?

"I didn't actually talk to Anne. It was Rachel who came to the door, and she didn't say. Did you talk to Kathy? Is Bob going to have time to meet us for dinner?"

"Damn, I'm sorry," I said, as I started to back around. "I forgot to call. But we'll see them; we always do, don't we? It's a tradition, isn't it?"

"Just like our going as a family," Paul said as I edged out onto Route 198. "For all that means to some of us these days." It was unlike Paul to sulk or complain, so I knew that Rachel's decision not to come with us had really hurt him. Had something more been said between the two of them that he wasn't telling me about? Or was it just that, like me, Paul was seeing Rachel starting to pull away from us? With each argument Rachel and I had, every sharp word, she was drifting a little further beyond my reach, away from the safe haven we'd worked so hard to create for her. Paul and I have never minded going with less to give our children more. I think that good parenting is all about restraint, patience, holding back. But letting go? It seems to go against every instinct of being a parent. And it feels like such a terrible price to have to pay for loving a child.

The traffic began to slow about a quarter mile before the turnoff to the farm, and we could see the campers and RVs, the brightly colored tents and tarps dotting the long hill above the barn and sheds. About half the audience camped out during the festival, many of them families. There was an ongoing joke about all the babies born in May. We had our windows down and, as we inched our way along, we could hear the strengthening sound of music above the underlying murmur of the crowd.

In addition to the main stage, a raised wooden platform in the meadow that Bob now left up all year, there was a tent for bluegrass jams, another for children's entertainment, and a large tarpaulin-topped arena for contra dancing. The long roadway from the parking area and ticketing booth to the main stage was lined with concession stands selling German bratwurst, funnel cakes, cotton candy, pizza slices, curly French fries, old-fashioned lemonade, and frozen desserts. A couple of years back, Bob had invited some local artisans to sell their wares, and that had grown quickly into an outdoor bazaar of jewelry, pottery, tie-dyed T-shirts and skirts, stained-glass panels, wooden utensils and bowls, wind chimes, kites, and musical instruments made by crafts workers from all over southern New England.

Carl Linden, who served on the volunteer fire department with Paul, waved us into the parking area, and as we made our way up to the house, we ran into a lot of people we knew. Paul carried Lia on his shoulders. I held Beanie's hand. I couldn't help but think that we must have looked like a handsome family, walking along like that. That we belonged here, surrounded by neighbors and friends. Just as we were about to turn in at the gate to the house, Paul spotted Jeb Halsman, a fellow selectman, ahead of him in the crowd.

"I've got to talk to him about Friday," he told me. "Go in and see if you can find Kathy. I'll meet you at the food tent, okay? Lia and I will save us all a table."

So it was Beanie and I who went into the house, shaded in the late afternoon by the stand of hemlocks on its western side, to look for Kathy. We entered a cool front hall that felt still and gloomy; all the noise, excitement, and activity was taking place outside. Kathy hated BlueFest. She's never liked crowds, and she resented the swarms of strangers who treated her home like public property. But the worst of it was—and this was a secret she'd never confided to Bob—Kathy couldn't stand bluegrass music. She'd told me this the second season of BlueFest when it finally occurred to me that she kept finding excuses not to attend the actual performances. There was always a baby to feed or a meal to prepare. But she finally told me the truth.

"It gives me such a headache. But I can't tell Bob that now after claiming before we got married that I loved it. I thought maybe I could grow to. But you know, on my wedding night? My head was pounding! I thought maybe it was just nerves, all the excitement. I figured out later that it had been that damned band he wanted so badly. And now this—every summer—but I can't tell him. It makes him so happy. Sometimes I think it's the only thing that makes him happy anymore."

"Kathy? Aunt Kathy?" Beanie and I called now as we walked through the messy downstairs. Kathy had never really gotten the hang of housekeeping, and after a certain point, I guess about the time B.J. was born, she'd basically given up. Having the day-care center didn't help matters. The living room, which in Clara's heyday had been a showplace of chintz-covered order and gleaming mahogany furniture, had essentially been turned into an enormous playpen: couches pushed against the wall, the floor a wasteland of board games, Legos, remote-controlled cars, trucks, and robots. A miniature basketball hoop on its pole stood in one corner. A scuffed plastic hopscotch board had been taped to the floor.

We walked down the hall into the kitchen. Dishes sat stacked in the sink and a carton of milk stood open on the counter surrounded by a little colony of half-filled cereal bowls. The yellow ruffled curtains that Clara had sewn years ago for the windows over the sink were pulled tight; they looked faded and water-spotted.

"Kathy?"

"I'm in the basement," she called back. We went down, me having to duck under the electrical wiring that sagged from overhead and Beanie holding tight, as I'd long ago trained her, to the wooden railing.

"Back here," she said when we reached the bottom. "I'm doing laundry."

"It's so dark. Is the bulb out?" I asked, taking Beanie's hand as we walked around the stairs and down the short hallway lined with metal shelves to the cramped laundry room.

"No, I like it this way. It feels cooler somehow. Hey there, Beanie."

She was sitting on a plastic folding chair in the dark. None of the machines were running, and I didn't see any sign of clothes, dirty or otherwise. I hadn't spoken to Kathy since the picnic in mid-July, and I was astounded by how heavy she'd gotten. She looked pasty and bloated, and she clutched her stomach to her like a pillow. Of course. I should have known. Kathy was pregnant again. This couldn't have been planned. She'd told me outright that Danny had been an accident, one they could hardly afford. I knew, though she'd never come right out and talked to me about it, that she'd suffered through intense mood swings when she'd had the other kids. And the money was still so tight.

"Beanie, honey, go on out to the playroom and make a pretty picture for me and Aunt Kathy, okay?"

"Why, Mom? I thought we were going to go have dinner and hear Johnny Johnnycakes." He was a favorite of Beanie's: a clownish one-man band with a washboard and harmonica contraption who entertained in the children's tent every year.

"I just want to talk to Aunt Kathy alone for a little bit, and then we will." Lia would have objected or demanded more of an explanation, but Beanie probably picked up on the tension. Without another word, she turned and walked back to the open area where Kathy ran the day-care operation.

I squatted down next to Kathy. I took her hand. It was flaccid—and also surprisingly hot and damp, as though she were running a fever. Her face was flushed as well. She wouldn't look at me. I knew there was no point in saying that she should have called, she should have told me. Kathy never asked for attention. I honestly believe that she felt she didn't deserve it. She had come to her marriage so full of love and high hopes. She'd wanted Bob so badly and for such a long time, she told me when they first got engaged, that when he proposed marriage to her she felt that she could never ask for another thing in her whole life. She'd used up all her wishes on the first round, and now the genie was gone, and the spell could not be reversed. When I first knew her she'd been a little bit more forthcoming, but now she very rarely talked about her real feelings.

"How far along are you?" I asked.

"Only five months. I already look like a tub, don't I?"

"How are you feeling?"

"Oh, like hell, but then I always do."

"I'm sorry that I've been so busy. Is there anything I can do? Are you guys going to be okay?"

"Oh, sure. We're good. We're great."

"Were you . . . was this planned?"

"You know what? I've kind of stopped thinking about it that way. Life isn't something you can plan. It happens. You adjust. You learn to be grateful for what you get."

"Yes, but with Danny . . . I mean, you went through a pretty tough time with him. I hate to think of you having to go through that kind of thing again."

"Well, you know what? You don't have to worry about me. I'm fine. We're doing good."

"Okay," I said, letting go of her hand and standing up. "We came to get you for supper. Paul and Lia are saving us all a table."

"No. I can't." She looked up at me, and with my eyes now adjusted to the dimness, I could see that her face was all swollen and splotchy. She'd obviously been crying. Hard.

"Oh, Kath—"

"No! Don't you dare look at me that way! Leave me alone! I told Bob you probably weren't coming this year. He's busy anyway. Dealing with everything."

"Okay," I said. There was a time, and not that long ago, when my concern would have been welcome. I felt helpless. And sorry. I couldn't bear to leave on that note. So, struggling to find something else to say, I told her, "It's great that BlueFest is doing so well. Bob told Paul about the advance ticket sales."

"And what exactly did he say?"

"Just that you were way ahead of last year, and you'd turned a profit then."

"Is that what he's saying?"

"What do you mean?"

"You know what?" Kathy said. "I bet Paul is beginning to wonder what happened to you and Beanie."

It was a beautiful night. Moonless and clear. The stars were brilliant against the black sky. We picked out the summer constellations: the Little Dipper, Cassiopeia, fleet-footed Pegasus, roaring Big Bear. The warm night air smelled of newly mown grass—as well as the freshly rolled kind. Many in the crowd were old hippie types, with graying beards and balding heads, black leather vests and biker tattoos. Luckily, the food tent had been crowded and noisy, and we were forced to share a table with another family, the Ludlows from Framingham, who came every year. We could hear the "Dinner Hour Jamboree" behind us on the main stage: five different banjos going full tilt at "Foggy Mountain Breakdown."

"I do a little banjo picking myself," Al Ludlow had told Paul. "To me, bluegrass is the real country music. It's pure, authentic. I wouldn't miss BlueFest for the world." When Al heard that the farm had been in Paul's family for generations, it seemed that he would never stop talking. His family had sold their farm forty years back, and he'd always regretted it. I chatted in a desultory way with the wife as we fed our kids. But I was grateful that the

Ludlows were there, serving to distract us from the fact that others were not. Paul had merely nodded when I told him quietly that Bob was busy and Kathy not feeling well. He could tell by my expression that something was up. That we'd talk about it later.

"These old farms. They're what New England's all about. It's great to come back here summer after summer. So I guess the festival helps keep things going, right? I hear a lot of farmers are doing this kind of thing now to help make ends meet."

"That's right," Paul said. "My brother was one of the first ones to try it. He struggled with it for a while, but now it's turned into a revenue source."

"You used to be a dairy, too, right? I noticed the old milking sheds."

"We were. Biggest one in the county at one point. Bob's got a plan to move into manufacturing goat cheese next. *Chev-rah*. He's got a lot of irons in the fire."

"We should get going," I told Paul as I began to gather up our used paper plates and napkins. "We don't want to miss Mr. Johnnycakes." In fact, I couldn't listen any longer to my husband's optimistic talk about his brother's plans. How were things really with Bob? Bad, I thought. No, I think I knew. The Ludlows would not be coming back to BlueFest next summer.

Underneath it all, summer is really sort of a sad time, I think. It can never live up to everything you want it to be. And then, too, it comes freighted with so many memories. Seeing one firefly brings back a hundred lost nights of fireflies blinking like thousands of tiny white Christmas tree lights in the darkness. The voice of a child calling—*Hey, everybody, wait up for me!*—was one's own once, or that of a grandmother, long gone now. I watched Lia and Beanie listen with rapt attention to that silly one-man band and felt my heart breaking. It wasn't fair that such belief in an old clown's talent—such admiration for his red sponge nose and orange fright wig—would turn into boredom in another few years. We stayed for the sing-along afterward, then walked back to the food concessions and bought ice cream cones. Marie Bisel was on the main stage. She was singing "Don't Fall in Love with a Rambler" in her haunting contralto, backed by her husband on the mandolin.

"River City isn't on until nine thirty," Paul said. "Let's take a quick look at the contra dancing." Bob always hired a good caller and a first-class fiddler from Buffalo. The tent was crowded and hot—I think everybody had the same idea as we did—but we managed to slip in anyway and were soon digging for the oysters, digging for the clams. Shoo fly, don't bother me. I feel, I feel, I feel like a morning star.

I saw them before I realized who they were. They were dancing alone, off in the corner of the tent, to their own music. The way Luke had done with Leslie years ago. *But this was nothing like that,* Luke had told me. *It's a whole different universe.* And it's true that I felt they really did exist in another dimension, one where the regular rules didn't apply. Though they were being foolish, of course. Anyone could have seen them there, could have started rumors flying. Though no one did. Except me. I would glance over from time to time to see them moving together in the shadows. Until, when I looked again, they were gone.

28

I thought it was clever of Owen Phelps to decide to hold the meeting in the old town hall. For the last fifteen years or so, in order to accommodate our town's growing numbers, we've moved these bigger get-togethers to the old high school gymnasium, where there's a lot more room to spread out. But this meeting was *about* the town hall, after all. We were going to discuss and vote on the possibility of nominating it for inclusion in the National Register of Historic Places, the first step in Owen's long-percolating plan to restore the building to its former glory.

When it was built just before the Civil War, the two-story white-clapboarded structure was probably considered pretty standard for its day, and it still retains a certain utilitarian air that aptly reflects its no-nonsense Yankee roots. Its wide pine floors are dark and scuffed with age, and the twenty-foot second-floor ceilings are a patchwork of stopgap repairs. But the upstairs meeting room is beautifully proportioned, its row of four arched windows telling of a time when public spaces were built with civic pride in mind—and little thought for fuel prices. In fact, during the middle decades of the nineteenth century, smoke from dozens of active charcoal kilns drifted over the hills surrounding the town.

For most of the last century, the rooms downstairs housed the police and town offices. But the upstairs has always had a more social function: lectures, teas, dances, plays, even, briefly, a series of basketball games were held there. Paintings and photos of these and other town events line the walls: graduations, marching bands, church suppers, Fourth of July parades, large groups of somber-looking men in three-piece suits and heavy mustaches, standing at attention for some long-forgotten ceremony. It always strikes me as shortsighted that so few of these carefully framed photographs are labeled, that we'll never know the names of these shyly smiling children in front of the single-room schoolhouse.

Glassed-in cases against the north wall display dust-covered exhibits: the electrical hand generator model created in the mid-1800s by our local inventor; a neatly folded but fraying Union flag; a grouping of badly moth-eaten taxidermy experiments; arrowheads and flints left behind by the Mahican Indians. If our history is to be found in any one place, it is here. Though the room was crowded and stuffy—the town had never found the funds to replace the old ceiling fans with air-conditioning—it felt appropriate to be deciding the building's future in the very place that had been witness to so much of our past. By eight o'clock almost every folding chair was taken, and a number of men, out of politeness or dislike for the hard metal seats, were leaning against the back wall. Paul was there, talking to Carl and Bob, though he'd be joining Owen and the other selectmen at the dais when the meeting was called to order.

I was sitting between Janie Hibbert and Nina Clymer, both longtime residents of the town, friends, fellow mothers. I served with Janie on the school committee. I've helped organize numerous Girl Scout events with Nina.

"Haven't seen you at the pond all summer," Nina was saying to me, "though Rachel and her crew seem to be there every time we are. Who are those cute little blond children she's taking care of?"

"Max and Katie Zeller. The family bought the big place that Paul helped Nicky Polanski put up."

"Oh, right," Nina said, exchanging a quick glance with Janie. "You mean the people who had the fireworks this year. The place above Luke Barnett's, right? Didn't someone tell me that you brokered that?"

"Yes," I said. "And the other big one farther up."

"That's what I heard," Janie said "And I say good for you. That's really sticking it to him."

"No, honestly, I didn't—" I began to say, but Nina waved me off.

"Hey," she said, "I think it's great, too. He's only getting what he deserves. That family always expected special treatment. And that's just how he acted during that whole big flap. Like laws weren't meant for him." They were talking about Luke, of course, and they thought they were doing me a favor by running him down.

"Okay, I'd like to get the ball rolling here," Owen called from the front of the room, banging his little gavel on the tabletop. "I just love doing that! Takes me right back to kindergarten and old Mrs. Ebert. Now, come on, everybody, let's settle down. Find a seat if there're any left back there."

Owen has an easygoing, irreverent manner, and, according to Paul, a very salty humor around the men. He was born and raised in Red River, but had gone up to Williams on a scholarship and then on to Harvard for a law degree. After a successful career in the Hartford area, he retired back in Red River, buying and restoring the old Thornstein house and farm, and taking up the reins of local government. Both Paul and I believe we're all pretty lucky to have him. He likes to affect a kind of hayseed folksiness, but underneath that lies a sharp intellect and an often ruthless determination. In many ways, the meeting tonight was just a lot of window dressing. Owen had already decided that we were going to restore the town hall. In fact, Paul told me that Owen and his ad hoc committee had been holding lengthy discussions with historic preservationists and architects and were homing in on a contractor. But Owen was smart enough to know that the townspeople needed to feel that they had given the project their blessing. Or better yet, that it had actually been their idea from the very beginning.

"Okay, then, shall we move to dispense with the reading of the minutes from the November eighth meeting? Do I have a taker . . . ?"

It went pretty much as Owen had planned it. He had one of his preservation specialists, a Mr. Ingers from Northhampton, address the meeting and read from his report on the significance of the building, how it "epitomized the pre–Civil War Greek Revival tradition, once seen throughout rural New England but now sadly disappearing from our architectural landscape." Then Owen gave a slide show he'd put together of "great moments in the town hall's history," which included a good sampling of historic prints and photos, but as many shots of people presently in the room, even one of a skinny young Bob Alden, getting pinned with a second-prize ribbon for some 4-H project. Owen gave a humorous running commentary to go along with the show. The whole room was laughing by the time the lights were switched on again. The proposition was read and a vote taken immediately after that. It passed unanimously.

"Okay, then, moving right along here," Owen said, looking over his half glasses at his notes. "We have a few more pieces of business to address before we can launch our headlong attack on the Greater Years refreshment table . . ."

I looked around the room for Richard Zeller, and I noticed Paul scanning the audience as well. We'd both admitted on our way over that we worried about what Richard would say—and how the committee might react. Luke didn't have many friends left in Red River these days, as Nina's and Janie's comments attested, and the town's attitude toward the Barnett legacy in general had turned distinctly negative over the years. That the Barnett and Hughes families had originally settled the whole northern half of the county, had worked for generations to clear the forests, help build the first churches, underwrite the militia, pay for the first teachers—all this had been forgotten in light of the family's more recent history. What people remembered was Howell driving drunk through town. The debts he'd left behind. What people talked about was Mrs. Barnett's drug taking, her years in and out of mental institutions. And, of course, they remembered Luke, the golden boy brought down by tragedy who refused everybody's pity. Who had been as arrogant and isolated in poverty as any Barnett had been at his wealthiest and most secure. Who had brought shame to what was left of his family's reputation—and scandal to the town. And who, for a good part of the last decade, had appeared to relish the role of outcast and iconoclast, thumbing his nose at propriety and appearances and becoming a thorn in the side of local government.

"The other day I tried to get Owen's reading on the Luke and Zeller thing," Paul told me in the car. "But all he would say was that he's sick and tired of the whole issue. It's been worrying me, though, that he's letting Zeller go public with it. It might mean Owen's finally ready to take some action."

Of course, I had plenty of reasons of my own to be worried about Luke and Richard Zeller. I knew from Rachel that Richard had been delayed in the city and hadn't been expected at Maple Rise until early in the evening. I was hoping that Anne had decided to tell him right away that she wanted out of the marriage. And that he'd been blindsided by her news. With something so catastrophic to deal with, I hoped he would have forgotten about the town meeting altogether. Distantly, I heard Ellie Warden's reporting on the Labor Day picnic preparations. I'd only been half listening to other people all day, it seemed. I'd been thinking about Anne instead. Trying to imagine her waiting to greet her husband and tell him that their marriage was finally over. I found myself mentally willing her: *Do it now. Tonight. As soon as he walks in the door.*

"Thank you, Ellie," Owen was saying. "Sounds like you ladies have things well in hand for next weekend. Okay then, we have one more item on the agenda. Richard Zeller would like to say a few words. I think a lot of you know him from his open house on July Fourth." Owen looked up and around the room, then waved to someone in the back by the stairs and said, "Why don't you come on up here where folks can hear you, Richard."

We don't usually see many second-home owners at our town meetings. They don't have voting privileges, the meetings are often held on weekday nights, and the issues raised probably seem pretty mundane to most of them. I think, though, that Owen had scheduled this special meeting for a Friday night, hoping he might be able to entice some of the wealthy weekenders to join us. He'd had some flyers about the purpose and importance of the gathering run off and posted around town—at the general store, post office, True Value—places where second-home owners might see them. After all, Owen would be needing their money when he started fund-raising for the renovation campaign. He may even have hoped that by giving Richard Zeller a hearing he'd be able to extract a little quid pro quo from him in the near future.

Richard lumbered up the center aisle, a heavyset man with a business jacket tossed over his shoulder and a well-worn leather satchel slung across that. He wore suspenders in a rich paisley pattern. The cuffs of his pale raspberry pink shirt were rolled halfway up his forearms, a midnight blue tie was loosened at his neck. He looked powerful in every way a man who's not handsome can: both physically imposing and emotionally confident. Owen made a move to get up and give him his seat and access to the microphone, but Richard waved him back down. His voice could be heard in the back of the room without him straining. It was clear that he was accustomed to speaking to large groups, and that he was comfortable on his feet, talking as though to friends. He was good at using his hands to include people in his thinking.

"Thank you for giving me this opportunity. It's good to see you all again, and I'm glad I could make it. Though I just did—the Friday night traffic was awful. My wife and kids and I feel very fortunate to have a home in this beautiful and welcoming community. We've been very happy here. We really enjoyed so many of you coming to our house to see the fireworks. But I'll tell you, a kind of sad thing happened after that. That man who lives down at the end of our driveway complained, actually called up Tom Langlois here"—Richard nodded to the chief, who was sitting in the second row—"and made a stink because someone had bumped into one of the tacky so-called sculptures he insists on displaying on his lawn."

This good-humored, telling-it-like-it-is account roused a chuckle from the crowd.

"Anyway, the thing is, I was thinking about this and it seemed to me that I was the one who should be complaining about the stink *his* place makes. It's one of the first things you see when you come up River Road into town from the west, and it gives a really god-awful first impression of this wonderful community. So, you know, I talked to a number of people around here about the problem. And I understand you've kind of been over this issue before?" He turned around to address this question to the dais. Paul was sitting two down from Owen, hunched down into himself.

"Oh, yes," Owen Phelps said and sighed. "This committee has had reason to discuss Luke Barnett and his property on prior occasions." Several people laughed out loud at this. Oh, yes, we were all in this together, good neighbors having to deal with a bad seed.

"Well, I'll tell you. As far as I'm concerned the place is literally a dump. And it's my guess that it's a fire hazard, too. I think something needs to be done."

"We've tried," Owen told him. "We've already sent Mr. Barnett several letters asking him to clean his place up."

"And when were these papers served?"

"Well, they weren't legal notices. Just informal requests. We sent the last one in December, I believe. But, you know, it's very difficult to enforce this sort of thing without stepping all over Fourth Amendment issues."

"Right. I realize that can be a real problem. But, as I said, I've been thinking about this and I even decided to do a little investigating. Hell, it didn't take much. A Google search was all. I've got to say I was more than a little shocked to discover that I had a convicted drug dealer for a neighbor!" A few people turned to look at each other, puzzled. Those who knew looked down or gazed away. An uneasy stillness had fallen over the room.

Richard pulled some papers out of his satchel and quickly scanned one of them. "That's right, in 1990, Luke Barnett was convicted of conspiracy to manufacture, distribute, and possess with intent to manufacture and distribute marijuana, and conspiracy to commit money laundering. He was sentenced to eight years in a state penitentiary. *A state penitentiary for eight years!* You're all good folks, I know that. But we're dealing here with the kind of person most of you probably just can't believe lives in a town this nice. I think he's a dangerous man. And I can tell you right now I don't like the idea of him living so close to my house and my kids. On top of that, I don't like the fact that he thinks he can live in that pigsty, making the rest of us have to put up with his—well, honestly?—kind of sick way of life."

I couldn't bear to look at Paul. I felt frozen, though my face was flaming red. The whole room seemed paralyzed, uncertain what to feel or think. Of course, many if not most of the people there knew all about Luke's time in prison and Paul's role in the old story that Richard had referred to. But it had become one of those things that time covered over, wearing down the sharp edges, blurring the memory. Subsequent events had diminished the story's power. Life went on. Nothing bad had happened. Parents worried about crack and methamphetamines now. But Richard had succeeded in turning the facts around so that Luke's conviction was no longer relegated to the past. Unknowingly or not, he'd also tapped into the ill will so many people already felt toward Luke and his hermetic existence. *Surely there's more than meets the eye. Why is he living in such squalor? Making that stuff? Refusing to conform? How have we allowed this to happen?* Richard let these thoughts sink in before he continued in a gentler, reasoning tone of voice, "So, let's get together here. As a group, okay? I've a feeling you're all pretty much with me, right? Let's see what we can do to get some traction on this problem. Okay, I've said my piece. Now I'd really appreciate a little feedback."

As if on cue, Tom Langlois stood up and turned to face the room.

"Yes, I think you could say most of us agree with you. And besides the issue of unsightliness, Luke Barnett is using that property as a place of business without—and I've looked into this, too—filing any of the appropriate paperwork. So, for starters, we can go in there. Close down the work area. Seize his machinery."

"Oh, for heaven's sakes, Tom!" Paul said. *No!* I almost cried out loud to him. *Keep your head down. Stay out of this!* "You mean you're going to take his blowtorch away?"

"I mean there are rules about running businesses in this town that we expect everyone to adhere to," Tom said.

"A business? Oh, come on! This is just a trumped-up excuse for you to go in there and—"

"Listen, I'm just trying to do my job. Preserve and protect, okay?"

"And I'm saying you know perfectly well that Luke's harmless. We all do. *Seize his machinery*? What kind of a town are we turning into here?"

"I'm surprised you're so eager to take his side," Richard said. He paused briefly to slip his papers back into his satchel. "From what I understand, you weren't always so supportive."

It took a moment for this comment to sink in. For me. For everyone. Then Paul, shaking his head, rose from his seat. He pushed back his chair.

"Just what are you trying to say?" he asked as he began to move behind the dais toward Richard, but Owen shot up and blocked him from going farther.

"That's it for tonight, folks," he said, holding tight to Paul's right arm. "This meeting is adjourned."

29

The aisles were clogged with people leaving. I could see Paul and Owen at the dais, heads bowed together in an intense exchange, as the rest of the select committee silently worked its way around them. Richard was talking to Tom, his big hand resting on the chief's forearm as he made some point; then they both threw their heads back and laughed. A little bottleneck had formed around them as people waited to talk to Richard.

"It's about time we all did something," Janie was telling Nina. "The place really is an eyesore, isn't it? And Zeller's right about it being the first thing you see coming into town. . . ."

Nina hadn't said anything as I slipped past, not even good night. Was it my imagination, or were my friends and neighbors avoiding my gaze? The past seemed to hang in the air like smoke; it stung my eyes, blurring my vision. I kept my head down as I shuffled behind the others on the stairs, though I wanted to scream: Let me through! I have to get by! I didn't have much time. No, I think I already knew that I didn't have any time at all. I didn't know Luke's number, or even if he had a phone these days. If anyone was going to get to Anne before Richard did, it could only be me.

Outside, the air was damp and chilly. A front had come through the final day of BlueFest, sweeping before it what felt like the last sweet warmth of summer. The night temperatures were starting to dip; Paul was blanketing our tomato plants with plastic sheeting most evenings. Though they'd left the tent up, hoping the weather might still improve, my daughters had moved back inside to sleep. The summer season wasn't over yet officially for another ten days, but it felt like we'd come to the end of something. Way too quickly.

I shivered as I moved with the crowd toward the parking lot, trying to get a signal on my cell phone. I held it over my head. I turned it off and then on again. But Red River had been built in a valley with hills cradling us on every side; the reception was notoriously awful in town. I knew of only one place close by that might be high and clear enough to allow me to get through, though I hated the idea of going there. I hadn't set foot near the hardware store since the break with my parents. I'd cross the street on the way to the general store; I'd even look the other way. Of course, it was inconvenient and silly of me; after all, the store had been part of the True Value chain and managed by other, anonymous hands for over a decade. But, on some childishly superstitious level, it still felt wrong to me to be there, as though I'd be walking on someone's grave. Now, though, I cut back through the crowd and hurried across Main Street. I was jogging, making a right onto Bridge Street, the white-clapboarded presence looming up in front of me with a nightmarish unreality. The whole last hour seemed to have passed like a bad dream, warping time and memory.

The old wooden outside staircase that I remembered had been replaced by a metal one, more a fire escape now than steps. I had to jump up and tug on the raised bottom rung to bring it down. Then I climbed up as best I could, my heels clanging on the metal slats. The top of the third flight ended as abruptly as it had begun. Gone was the ten-foot-long landing where I used to sit during the final summer that I worked for my dad, smoking a forbidden cigarette and daydreaming about Paul.

From here you could see almost the whole town: the two church steeples, the many shingled roofs, the bridge with its flower boxes trailing petunias in the summer, the rust-tinged, mineral-rich river running fast and deep, rushing over the dam by the old mill. From here you could see why this spot would have appealed to those first settlers and missionaries. It was so well protected, situated in a pleasant river valley that promised fertile farming. There was the old railroad line, laid down in the town's mining heyday in the mid-1800s, that used to run up to Albany and now stopped without fanfare in front of the post office. And farther, you could just about make out the skeletal imprints of a large complex of buildings, some of which had been burned, others abandoned: the overgrown remnants of the once extensive Colt & McCafferty iron smelting furnace and works, left in ruins behind the old high school playing fields. And beyond that the slowly flattening hills and fields rolling out to disappear under the steep shadows of the Catskills.

"Anne?"

"Who is this? I can hardly hear you. . . ."

"It's Maddie."

"Where are you? This connection is terrible."

"You haven't told Richard yet, have you?"

"What? No. Richard isn't back yet."

"I know. I just saw him at the town meeting. I'm calling from town, Anne. I need to tell you something."

"You're breaking up again. Why don't you call me on your landline when you get back home?"

"No! Don't hang up. Listen to me. Richard found out something. About Luke. About something that happened when Luke was just a kid really."

"What are you taking about?"

"Luke hasn't said anything to you, has he? About what happened right after high school?"

"No."

So I told her. I rushed through it, I know, but I wanted to get the whole thing out before Richard got home. I needed to get to her first, before Richard's gloating report on how he ripped that crazy Luke Barnett to shreds in front of the whole town and had the select committee eating out of the palm of his hand. Oh, I could just imagine how he would sound telling her. How he'd relive his triumph in front of her and then start to criticize her for being so sloppy about choosing her friends. Did she have any idea that Paul Alden had been involved with this marijuana business, as well? And Maddie, too, no doubt. Alden had totally lost it at the meeting. And he'd done time, too. He was just a small-town criminal, really. Leave it to Anne to pick up with people like that, for heaven's sake! When was she going to learn to exercise some judgment? To show a little discrimination?

"You have to understand how young we all were then," I told her, breathlessly. "Young and kind of desperate. The recession was—"

"I don't understand. Luke? He was in jail? For how long?"

"He didn't have to serve the full sentence. He got out on early release, for good behavior, I think."

"How *long* was the sentence?"

"Eight years."

"Wait. No. I can't believe this. You're—what are you saying? Luke is a criminal? He's a drug dealer? This doesn't make any sense to me. . . ."

"It was almost twenty years ago, Anne. Way, way back in the past. Richard just dug this up to—"

"Hold on. Please. Stop. This is so . . . I don't know what to think. . . ."

"You have to think that it doesn't make any difference! That you know what kind of a man Luke is, deep down. Gentle. Good. That you love—"

"I see Richard's headlights coming up the drive," Anne cut me off. "I've got to go."

Paul was waiting for me behind the wheel when I got back to the pickup. He was lost in thought, staring out the front window. He didn't ask where I'd been, though we were the last car in the parking lot. The town hall was shut up for the night. Main Street was deserted.

"I'm sorry I lost it like that," he said finally, turning to me. "God, I hate losing my temper. I don't know what came over me. One minute I was calmly sitting there telling myself to stay cool, let the bastard have his say, and the next thing I'm like this raving maniac."

"Not raving," I said. "He played dirty and he knew it. He knew exactly what he was doing, and how he might get a rise out of you."

"You think so?" Paul asked. Under the cold light of the high streetlamp his skin looked bleached out. A part of me was shocked to learn how close all this was to the surface with him. How much it still mattered, though he kept trying to tell himself otherwise.

"I know so," I told him. "I told you before he's a bully. He wanted to get you riled. It only helped him make his case."

"And people bought it, too, didn't they? Even Owen, I'm afraid. He says he's been getting pressure from other quarters. And obviously old Tom is just raring to go in there, guns blazing! I'd like to believe that it's just the new people, you know, like the Zellers. But it's not. It's our friends and neighbors, Maddie. It makes me wonder what they think about *me* after all these years. What if I stumbled again somehow? Made a mistake. Spoke up the way Luke did? Or have I done that already by saying what I did tonight? Am I next?"

It was painful for me to hear Paul doubt himself. His convictions run so deep. It showed me that what had happened that night had shaken him to the core. His faith in the town, in people's essential goodness and goodwill, has always been immutable.

"No," I told him. "This isn't about you. And I don't think people really care that much about the drug conviction. That's just an excuse for them to believe they have a reason to feel the way they do. The truth is: they don't like Luke. He's too aloof. Superior. Especially after all he's been through. They don't trust him. They want him to be sorry. They want him knocked down a peg or two."

"And what about you?" Paul said.

In all the years that Luke had come between us, Paul had never come right out and asked me how I felt about him. It was one of the few things we never discussed, I think because it could so easily open up a chasm between us we might not know how to bridge. Why now? He couldn't be testing my loyalties. He knew I would always stand by him. No, I think he must have sensed the shifting dynamics between the three of us: Luke, Paul, and me. He suspected something. But what? I believe a part of him wanted to find out, while another part knew that I must be keeping things from him for a reason. I guessed that he'd been picking up on my half lies and partial truths. He'd been looking the other way, purposefully not asking. Because he knew that I was protecting someone, or something. That's what he was really asking: *what about you*? But I didn't know what to tell him. And I didn't want to add this uncertainty to all the rest of his burdens. Did I really think that Anne would leave Richard now, knowing what I had told her? I'd heard the shock in her voice. And the fear.

"I want what's best for Luke," I told him, though I don't think I knew then—or will ever be sure—what that might have been.

"I know you do," Paul said, turning the key in the ignition. "Of course. What the hell's the matter with me, anyway? It's hardly the end of the world. Owen agreed to let me go over and have a heart-to-heart with Luke. Let him know what's brewing. I think I'll be able to convince him to make some changes. They want him to take some kind of action before the next select committee meeting. That's doable, don't you think?"

"Sure," I told him, as we drove home through the shadow-filled, silent town. It seemed like a surface exchange but it had actually touched upon our deepest selves. Good, strong, optimistic Paul. And eager, accommodating me. I would only always tell him what he wanted to hear. It was our old sweet song, our lifelong refrain. *That's doable, don't you think? Sure.* What else could I say?

Part Eight

30

Our luck didn't hold. Or, perhaps it was more that a lot of things caught up with us all at once. My father died in 2002, right after Thanksgiving. I hadn't seen him in almost ten years. A second cousin called to tell me the day before the funeral service. It was Nancy, one of Harry's nieces, so I can only imagine what she'd heard about me over the years. I think she was around my age; I could hear children fighting in the background:

"I've gone back and forth about getting in touch with you," she said. "Your dad left a list of who he wanted at the service, along with what hymns he wanted and everything."

"I take it I wasn't included."

"But I kept thinking: this is really about those of us who are still here, isn't it? I lost my own father three years ago. That was hard enough—and I got the chance to say good-bye. I decided that it was only right to at least give you the option of coming."

The Feddersons tend to be a stoic and reserved lot. Their Nordic roots, transplanted to the Berkshires go deep—but not far. My father was one of the few who had left the immediate area, and that, along with the well-known facts surrounding my rupture with him, affected his relationship with the rest of the family. But they'd done their duty by him in the end. Paul and I dropped the girls off at the farm and drove over to the service in Great Barrington, which was held in the Lutheran church. It was Paul who had really wanted to go, not me, so I was surprised how touched I felt seeing the first four rows of the church filled with people.

After the service, we stayed and talked to various cousins and second cousins. Paul is so good at this sort of thing; he likes people, and they feel it and respond in kind. By the end of the afternoon, he was exchanging e-mail addresses with half a dozen men. If anyone remembered Paul's past or my break with my parents, they didn't let it show. I don't think they cared anymore. Most of the adults were around Paul's and my age; middle-class, hardworking, well-meaning. Their parents were dying off and with them all the old grudges and grievances. There were other worries now. Mortgages. Home equity loans. Escalating property taxes. All the new houses going in.

"I couldn't afford to buy here now," one of the men said, and a few others nodded.

"Who could? I feel lucky to have inherited our house from Pam's folks. But where are our kids going to live? That's what I worry about."

"It's the same where we are," Paul told them. "I work construction so I see firsthand the money that's getting poured into these places. People putting twenty-five thousand dollars' worth of granite countertops in the kitchen, then having us rip it all out because they decide they don't like the color! Multimillion-dollar mansions overlooking some old cow pond."

"Yeah. It's crazy, isn't it? You know, Paul, you should bring your kids over at Christmastime when we have the big Fedderson family party. I'll make sure you get the e-mail about where and when."

It had snowed while we were indoors. We drove home under a pearly gray sky, the white hills hushed and ghostly in the cold failing light.

"That was nice, don't you think?" Paul asked me. "Aren't you glad we went?"

"Of course," I said. "But it seems like such a waste in a way, doesn't it? All those years of not speaking? It just seems so stupid to me now."

"Do you have any idea how angry you sound?"

"No, I don't. I'm not. I just find it really, really sad that he could sit there by himself day after day, when he had three wonderful granddaughters he never even knew or wanted to know!"

Paul was smart enough to keep quiet after that. I didn't believe that what I felt was anger, because I'd worked so hard over the years to tamp down my bitterness toward my parents. Especially my father. I was determined not to be like him. Dribbling away his days, pawing through old hurts and disappointments, like a miser with his gold. But as the days grew darker and Christmas approached, I found myself dwelling more and more on the past. On my father's failures: to keep the hardware store, to stand by Paul and me when we were down, to get beyond his own limitations and disappointments. To be a better, stronger human being. What a waste! I kept going back to that: he'd missed the opportunity to know us, to share in our happiness and love.

Two nights before Christmas Paul drove us back to Great Barrington, to the home of Tim Reidel, who had married one of my Fedderson cousins. The Colonial-style home was ablaze with Christmas tree lights when we pulled up, the driveway and curb lined with cars. I was still nursing Lia then. She was asleep when we got to the party and I told Paul, Rachel, and Beanie to go ahead without us; I'd nurse her and we'd join them in a little while. I climbed into the backseat, but I just sat there after they left, thinking about my dad. He'd loved Christmas the way I do, and, I imagine, for much the same reasons. He was a homebody, happiest in his own living room, and so many of the Christmas rituals—trees, gifts, wreaths, candles, stockings—seem best enjoyed there.

Then, for a brief moment, I felt that he was with us in the car, in the front seat, turning around to face me at last. And I found myself asking him, *Why were you such a stubborn old fool? What the hell was wrong with you? Why couldn't you manage to love me—at least a little bit more than you hated yourself?* But just as quickly, he was gone. Truly, finally, gone. He wasn't there to hear me anymore. He'd turned a deaf ear at last to all the insults and criticisms I'd been flinging at him over the years. Because that's how I'd been dealing with his absence, I realized now: by debating him endlessly, silently, somewhere deep inside. Yes, he was the one I'd been proving myself to, whose good opinion and approbation I'd been seeking all along. I thought I was all grown-up, moving ahead with my life. But a part of me had stayed a child, crying out for attention: *See how well we're doing without you, Daddy? Look what a beautiful new baby I have in my arms. Yes, we've bought a home, the old Anderson place out on County Route 198.* The truth was: I hadn't stopped begging for his approval since I'd walked out of his house. Just as he'd never stopped withholding it. He'd been my silent adversary. The door I beat my love against; the heart that wouldn't open. And it had been this exhausting, ongoing, one-sided argument that had kept him alive for me all that time.

Christmas passed in shades of gray. I felt bone-tired. I was almost grateful when I caught a stomach flu somewhere and Paul insisted that I spend a few days in bed. He had a touch of something, too, but nothing ever seemed to stop him. Nicky Polanski had him working ten-hour days on the new condo complex at the ski resort above Vandenkill; cookie-cutter time-shares slapped together on the cheap with Sheetrock, Tyvek, and molded plastic fittings. And Polanski really knew how to put the screws on. Paul hadn't taken a real break in over a year.

Rachel was off from school for the holidays, and as I drifted half awake through the afternoon, I could hear her and her friends rattling around downstairs, watching rented videos and making popcorn. The acrid smell of burning butter filled the house; I heard Lia crying and I knew that her diaper probably needed changing. The cries grew louder, more plaintive and demanding. I turned over, trying to find my way back down into sleep.

"Mommy?" It was Rachel, standing in my bedroom doorway. "Mr. Polanski's on the phone. Daddy's in the hospital."

I dove for the extension on our bedside table:

"What happened? How is he?"

"We don't know," Polanski said. His voice had none of the oily flirtatiousness I'm used to from him. "The crew told me he just curled up and started moaning. He's conscious, but in a lot of pain. I'm at the ER in Harringdale. I'll be waiting for you."

I didn't trust myself to drive; Bob took me. Kathy came over and picked up the girls. We followed the same route we used to take when Bob and I visited Paul in prison: back roads through silent little towns, the desolate highway, the wintry rural landscape giving way to the wide, mostly empty thoroughfares of postindustrial New England. Harringdale was starting to make something of a comeback, the old downtown attracting an eclectic range of new businesses—a reference publisher, a candy producer, an insurance brokerage—by offering some hefty tax breaks. A theater company was rumored to be moving into the old Hatfield Athenaeum. But it was the influx of retirees and the concomitant need for more and better health care that had really pulled the failing local economy back up on its feet. The Harringdale Medical Complex had burgeoned over the last five years and was now considered the best-equipped hospital in the region.

Polanski was on his cell phone when we got to the waiting room at the ER. He clicked off as soon as he saw us. He shook hands with Bob and put his arm around my shoulder. He's usually such a tough, demanding, foul-mouthed man; his politeness terrified me.

"It's okay. He's going to be okay. They think it's an ulcer. A bleeding ulcer. He's probably been walking around like a fucking time bomb for Christ knows how long."

I knew Paul took a lot of aspirin, but then he had a lot of aches and pains. He had a physically demanding job, after all, and a couple of old sports injuries that were always kicking up: a trick knee and a torn ligament in his left shoulder that had never healed right. He usually popped a couple of Advils or Bayers when he got home from work at night, and sometimes a few more before he went to bed. I had no idea how dangerous this could be until the doctor told us.

"Long-term use of nonsteroidal anti-inflammatory drugs is the second most common cause of ulcers, and that rate is only increasing. Most people get away with it. You're one of the unlucky ones. We've done an endoscopy. That's effective in controlling bleeding in most cases. And we've shot some epinephrine into you just to hedge our bets. But I'm sure glad we got you when we did. And I don't intend to let you go for a while."

I liked and trusted the doctor. I don't think what happened was his fault. But the first endoscopy didn't stem the bleeding after all and somehow, during the second, there was a perforation of the intestinal wall. It was a risk; it said so in the fine print of the document Paul signed and I witnessed. Whoever or whatever was to blame, suddenly two days into the new year Paul was undergoing major abdominal surgery.

"Six months until he's really back on his feet," the doctor told us after the operation, addressing most of what he had to say to me. "And even then he's going to have to take it slow. No lifting! I'll be seeing him for a follow-up in a couple of weeks."

We got Paul onto disability, but it was less than a quarter of what he was bringing in through Polanski Builders. Far worse than that, though, was the fact that we didn't have major medical; it was just so expensive for a family of five! And we'd justified our stupidity by telling each other we'd only really need it when we got older. The hospital bill came to over eighty thousand dollars. We took out a home equity line of credit, but the monthly interest-only payments hit us like body blows every month; and we couldn't even think about dealing with the principal yet. Not surprisingly, Paul was not an ideal patient. He detested the soft, low-residue diet Dr. Reitz put him on. He hated feeling useless and "all cooped up." It didn't help that, along with everything else, it was winter and he was housebound. He seemed to always be in my way: opening the refrigerator when I was standing right behind him with two dripping ice-cube trays; cluttering the dining room table with the thousand-piece jigsaw puzzle he barely even looked at; sprawling on the couch, newspapers all over the carpet, while I tried to vacuum. We bickered a lot. I think we were both terrified that this was just the beginning of a more serious backsliding. I would wake up in the middle of the night and think about our debt load; it towered in front of me like a mountain. Insurmountable. And then I'd turn and see Paul awake beside me, staring at the ceiling.

"I saw a notice in the Starbucks in Northridge that they're hiring," I told him one night. "They've got health benefits and a kind of profit-sharing thing."

"So?"

"Well, you're well enough now to take care of Lia—and run the house. I think I should look into getting a job. I could always go back to waitressing."

"I'll be working again in another couple of months. I think we can hold on until then."

"We're going to strangle each other if we go on much longer like this. And we've got that loan to pay down. I don't like getting so far behind. I hate the feeling that everything we've worked for is just slipping away."

"It won't. It can't. I'll never let it."

"I know, but I'd just feel better if—"

"Listen, Mad, I don't see the sense in you driving back and forth to Northridge every day for some minimum-wage, entry-level job. We'll get through this. I was thinking that I could start to sort through some of the stuff in the attic and maybe post some things on eBay. At least that will get me out of your hair."

But the overall sense of oppression didn't lift. March roared in like the proverbial lion, the wind rattling the windows and the snow blowing sideways, forming three-foot drifts up our driveway. Ever since Paul's operation, Bob had been coming over to plow us out. We never asked, he just did it without saying a word. And Kathy had been great, too, dropping by with homemade rice pudding and nutless brownies—the kind of things she knew Paul could eat. I was feeling too low to show much gratitude, I know. But we would have done the same for them; it's what family does. At the end of that long, dark month, I was surprised to see a big green truck turning into our driveway with the signature gold "Polanski Builders" lettering running along the side. I was almost alarmed when Nicky Polanski himself jumped out of the cab. He never shows the least bit of interest in his employees' personal lives. In fact, I believe he wishes they didn't have any; I know from things Paul has said that Polanski hates dealing with personnel issues. Paul must have seen him, too; he came downstairs to greet him at the front door.

"Son of a bitch," Polanski said, looking Paul over. "How're you feeling?"

"Good. Come on in. Want some coffee or whatever?"

"No, thanks," Polanski said. He wouldn't let me take his coat. "I'm not going to stay. I just wanted to see how you were. I need you back, Paul. That fucking Janowski is poaching our guys and we got a backlog you wouldn't believe."

"I really can't do much for another three, four months, Nicky. I'm sorry."

Polanski looked down at his shoes.

"Yeah, well. A foreman doesn't do much besides yell as far as I can tell. I don't know why the fuck I have to pay somebody good money to sit around and mouth off all day, but there it is. I need you."

So Paul went back to work, promoted out of the day-to-day heavy lifting, though hardly away from all the stress. He had crews reporting to him now, supplies to order and oversee, schedules to meet, owners and architects to deal with. Paul learned that one of the reasons Polanski was so busy was the partnership he'd recently formed with the new Realtor in Red River, a Nana Osserman, and the well-known local architect Frank Miles. They were putting up two luxury spec houses near the old Tucker Hill quarry.

"I think this Osserman woman is really the brains behind the whole deal," Paul told me one night. I was worried that he was already working too hard. He looked pale to me, but his eyes were alive again. I also sensed that he'd stepped right up into his new position and that Polanski was impressed with his performance. "She's a real operator. Talks a mile a minute. Walks around the site like a drill sergeant."

And, as it turned out, she was looking for some help, too. Her agency was booming. And she needed someone to handle the phones. Typing. Filing.

Simple office work. And, as she and the other two Realtors at the agency were relatively new to the area, she wanted to try to find someone who knew something about the county. The roads. The houses. Families who might be thinking of selling. Farmers ready to throw in the towel. Someone with local knowledge.

31

"... And the truth is, I never intended to get into this. I've been in television all my life. God, I lived and breathed programming, ratings, sweeps months, demographics for as long as I can remember. And honestly? I didn't want to retire. I'd still be there today—happily—but Dan was given a gentle nudge at Dewey Ballantine. He's a bit older than me, too. And he had a prostate scare. And then 9/11 hit. Well, it all seemed to make sense that we switch gears. Downshift. Except, of course, I couldn't! I'm a doer. It's just in my nature. So when friends began to ask if I knew of a good real estate broker in the area—and I had to tell them no because we had the most god-awful experience when we bought—well, I thought: why not? And, the truth is, I really love it! Also, knock on wood, I've been incredibly lucky in terms of timing. I mean, since 9/11, the market up here has just totally taken off. But, you would know that. Nicky tells me that your husband works for him."

"Yes. He's Mr. Polanski's foreman at the Tucker Hill site," I said, remembering to smile as I did so, though I didn't get the feeling that Nana Osserman was actually paying much attention to my people skills. She'd looked me up and down when I first walked into her office at Red River Realty: the gray wool blend Talbot's jacket, white cotton turtleneck, black pants, black heels, shoulder-length hair brushed back off the face in a black velvet headband. I could almost see the little checkmarks of approval in her gaze: practical, neat, nonthreatening. I thought that she, on the other hand, looked totally out of place in the middle of Red River. She was wearing a severely tailored Chanel-style suit in a green weave with bright pink braiding and a gold chain-link necklace that must have weighed about ten pounds. Her hair was an auburn coiffed helmet, her face a mask of makeup and, I guessed, cosmetic surgery. Her hands and neck gave away what her wrinkle-free face would not: she was probably somewhere in her late sixties. However, I would quickly come to learn that Nana was just what she said she was: a doer, a dynamo, an ageless, aggressive, unabashedly self-promoting force of nature. And, yes, I was put off by her at first. That loud, carrying voice. The long lacquered nails, like talons. She was actually petite, shorter than me, but she seemed larger than life. She filled the room. I couldn't take my eyes off her.

"What I need is someone to free us up from all the damned office nonsense: phone, mail, word processing. That sort of thing. Heather, Linda, and I are just on the go all day long, in and out of the office. We need someone back here, holding down the fort."

"What sort of software would I need to know?" I asked, as Paul had advised me to do. It was my biggest concern, but he had assured me that he'd be able to purchase and download over the Internet whatever system the office used and that I could practice on his computer at home.

"Oh, God, I have no idea," Nana said, wrinkling her nose. "Linda can fill you in on that. I still have to ask her or Heather to print out my e-mail and the Hot List every morning. That's the kind of thing you'll be doing for me from now on. How does all this sound to you, sweetie? Do you think you might be interested?"

I was waiting for her to ask to see my résumé. Paul had spent hours helping me create it. Or quiz me about my office skills and experience. To counter the obvious fact that I didn't have any, I'd prepared a little speech about my organizational abilities and willingness to learn.

"Oh, yes. Very much. You know our house is just eight minutes down the road from here."

"Ah, so you timed it? Very practical. Terrific. Yes, I think Nicky told me that you've lived around here most of your life. So you know the county pretty well. That's really fabulous. The three of us are still driving around with maps open in our laps half the time, getting lost on all these rutted back dirt roads. And you know people? You would hear if someone is interested in selling or buying? Or, God forbid, if somebody dies."

"Yes, Mrs. Osserman. I think I can say that I know pretty much everything that happens around here."

"It's Nana, sweetie. I'm Nana to you. To just about everybody."

I'm not saying it was easy, especially in the beginning. I was nervous and shy, easily hurt. I'd never worked in an office before, let alone one so fast-paced and hectic. And I was worried, initially, that Heather and Linda didn't really like me. That Nana felt she'd been too hasty taking me on. She must have assumed that all the endless problems I was coping with for the first time—changing copier ink cartridges, unjamming the fax machine, handling three or four phone calls at once—were essentially routine for me. I kept waiting for one of the women to realize how insecure I actually was; how I covered what seemed to me endless blunders with little excuses. But nobody seemed to notice how much I was, literally, learning on the job. They barely said hello to me in the mornings before they were immersed in their calls, tapping on their keyboards, running out the door, tossing client agreements, contracts, and ad listings on my desk to proofread or file, type up or print out.

The first morning I was there, Linda took me through the Promatch tutorial. Paul went over it again with me a couple of times later that night and during the week at home, and showed me how to find my way around Yahoo, Google, MapQuest, and other Internet tools he thought might be useful. It made it easier for me that Linda worked from her apartment in Manhattan two days a week and, even when she came in was, like Nana and Heather, actually out of the office for so much of the time. This allowed me to call Paul on his cell and ask him to help me troubleshoot a printing problem, or teach me how to send a file as an e-mail attachment. He's always loved computers and had long tried to interest me in them. Now that I needed to know, I was a quick learner. I actually surprised myself by how much I was able to pick up even in those first few bewilderingly busy weeks. And not just about the job.

"I can't deal with this right now, Mom," I heard Heather tell her mother one afternoon. I'd taken several messages already that day from the quavery-voiced Mrs. Duffy when Heather was on other calls. "I'll phone Reena and try to sort this out tonight, okay? I'm sure she didn't mean to shortchange you. Yes, I know, but we're only talking about a dollar or two, right? Yes. Yes, I know, every penny . . ."

It didn't take me long to realize how much time Heather, a divorced single mom who'd relocated a few years ago from Cambridge, spent dealing with her own mother's problems, both real and imagined. In pretty short order, because I was frequently the only one around for her to vent at, I, too, got to know Mrs. Duffy and her many trials and tribulations. I also became friendly with Linda Cassini's teenaged daughter, Jeri, who, when I first started working for Red River Realty, was waiting to hear back from the many colleges she'd applied to. She usually called in around four thirty, when she got home from school and had sorted through the mail.

"Sorry, she's out, Jeri. Did you try her cell?"

"Yeah, she's not picking up. Not that she'll really want to hear my news."

"Oh? Smith?"

"No, Vassar. My mother's fucking alma mater!"

"Well, come on. You were accepted at Bard and Purchase, right?"

"Yeah, but they were my safties. They don't count. I'm totally fucked."

Besides Luke, whose upbringing had been so dysfunctional, this was my first direct exposure to people whose backgrounds and status were so different from my own. Heather was probably the closest to me in terms of economic level, but only because she had recently been bumped down the ladder several rungs. I learned she had earned an MFA and had lived, when married, in a three-story Victorian mansion. But a nasty divorce had depleted her resources both financially and emotionally. She had custody of her ten-year-old daughter, while her husband had managed to keep her thirteen-year-old-son—and most of his sizable income as a dermatologist. She handled commercial sales for the agency with a blunt, take-it-or-leave-it attitude that seemed to work well in the business sector. Though I believe she was only in her midthirties, she already had permanent frown lines and a marked slump, as if she was actually toting her bag of woes around with her. She was so terse with me in the beginning that I just assumed she resented my presence in the cluttered office I shared with her and Linda.

"Your mom called while you out," I told her about a month after I'd started the job. "Three times."

"You don't have to keep track, Maddie. I kind of just assume she's called. And you don't have to chat with her the way you do. I know how much she repeats herself."

"I don't mind at all."

"Oh, please. You are such a Pollyanna!"

Linda, on the other hand, was eager to share the ongoing drama of her life with anyone who would listen. I'm not sure if she'd been this forthcoming before my arrival, because Heather always pointedly picked up the phone as soon as Linda began to talk. In any case, whenever Linda was in the office, we received regular updates about how her husband's career was starting to take off at Time Warner, that her brilliant daughter, Jeri, was torn between Ivy League colleges, why she loved her "double life" in the city and the small weekend place in Oakdale she used during the three days she was in the office. Her short-cropped dark hair had a flare of white at the right temple. She dressed with understated elegance in muted flowing tunics and large, striking necklaces and dangling earrings. Like Nana, she seemed to talk a mile a minute. And she made the same sort of assumptions Nana seemed to about my experience and background.

"So Jeri's decided on Purchase of all places! I know that seems so odd considering her choices. But apparently they have a really fabulous drama department there—and, who knew? She wants to get into the thee-a-tah! Not acting, thank God. I love my little lamb, but she has my big fat nose and little nasally voice. No, she's thinking about lighting. Isn't that interesting? She wants to be the next Jennifer Tipton or whatever. Well, I think Tipton's a genius, don't you? Did you see what she did this season for that new Paul Taylor piece?"

"It's great that Jeri already knows what she might want to do," I said, deflecting her questions. I was learning not to panic when I thought my ignorance might be exposed. I was getting good at skirting the truth, lying by omission. "I think so many kids probably go into college totally clueless about why they're there. And it's a pretty pricey way to try to find yourself."

"Absolutely. I'm really so proud of her."

Gradually, I got myself accepted, too. In many ways, my personality was cut right out for office life. I was so willing to please. I longed to fit in. I worked hard. I never complained. I molded myself to the needs of the moment, to whomever I was dealing with or talking to. I made myself indispensable to Nana. I organized her chaotic filing system. I helped keep her calendar, reminded her of appointments, and eventually started setting up showings for her. She was eager to teach me about the business, though her lesson plans were usually constructed around some variation on the theme of her own phenomenal success.

"Never forget that the client always comes first," Nana told me one evening when I'd put a call from her husband through to her before that of a client.

"Yes, but it was Mr. Osserman. . . ."

"Exactly. I could have called him back. But Jay Crandell is one tiny little push away from putting in a bid. It's precisely the moment when a call like this could make all the difference. The reason I've done so well is that I never forget that this is primarily a job of selling. Not showing. But selling, marketing, putting the best possible spin on whatever property is under consideration. And how do you go about doing that? Service, sweetie. That's the secret. Sales and service; they're really just flip sides of the same coin." She punched in a number while she was speaking, and without missing a beat, cried: "Jay, sweetie! I'm so sorry we got cut off. This is your cell phone, right? Hmmm . . . yes . . . I'm here for you twenty-four-seven—you know that. Of course, I totally understand . . ."

Within my first few weeks of working for her, my initial negative impression of Nana had faded away. Or, perhaps more to the point, I was able to get her in a better perspective. Yes, she was loud, but it no longer bothered me. After all, she had something to say. And she was outspoken in her praise for me. I was turning out to be a "godsend." Without being fully aware of it, I let go of my reservations and inhibitions and allowed Nana to disarm me with her energy and enthusiasm and sweep me up in her cyclonic orbit. And, finally, she began to push me to be more ambitious. More positive. Assertive. More like her.

"Anyone heard of a Roxley Lane in West Bairnbrook?" Nana asked as she entered the room Linda, Heather, and I shared. It was about three months after I started, an unusual morning as all four of us were actually in the office at the same time.

"I've never even heard of Bairnbrook," Linda said, turning in her chair to face Nana. "Let alone West whatever. What's there?"

"I just got a call from a couple who wants to sell," Nana said. "Though they'd like an estimate first, of course. I don't know, he sounded a little evasive. He didn't give me much to go on. Just the street address."

"West Bairnbrook's a suburb of Harringdale," I said. "It used to be a pretty nice area when the Untermeyer Paper Mill was still in operation. Now, though? I don't know. Harringdale's in a kind of transitional period. Hold on, and I'll look it up for you." I knew as soon as I clicked in for a close-up on the MapQuest site what the problem was. Roxley Lane was a tiny street off a series of short streets that formed a little constellation around what had once been a light industry site. I realized now that I'd passed through the neighborhood several times fairly recently; it was part of the shortcut I'd found on my way up to see Paul in the hospital.

"It's in a trailer park," I said, looking up from my computer. I saw the expression of horror that crossed Nana's face. Heather laughed out loud.

"Thank you, sweetie," Nana said. "You've spared me a totally unproductive afternoon."

"But what I would have given to see your face when you pulled up to that trailer!" Linda said. "Can you imagine? People actually living in one of those things?"

"I see them up in the woods around here," Heather said. "They mostly look abandoned, though, as far as I can tell."

"A lot of them are used by hunters," I said. "In the fall."

"And that's another thing I simply cannot conceive of," Linda went on. "People still hunting in this day and age. I don't know. It just seems so barbaric to me. Neanderthal."

"Oh, well," Nana said, crumpling up the pink message slip. "I thought it was too good to be true: a brand-new listing drifting in from nowhere."

I felt myself automatically sharing in Nana's disappointment. Exclusive listings, the lifeblood of every Realtor, were becoming harder and harder to come by. And no self-respecting broker would want to handle a house trailer, for heaven's sake! No wonder the man on Roxley Lane had sounded evasive. How embarrassing for Nana if she'd actually driven all the way up there, I thought. I felt a little flush of irritation that anyone would have thought Red River Realty might be interested in such a low-end property. That was how fast and far I'd come. That I would identify with Nana, Linda, and Heather so thoroughly, that I'd see the situation through their eyes, rather than my own. I, who had spent some of the happiest months of my life in an Elcona single-wide. *Can you imagine people actually living in one of those things?* At that moment, honestly, I really couldn't. I was halfway to believing that I actually was who the others imagined me to be: a local, yes, but someone really not too different from themselves. Educated, smart, experienced, a go-getter. The person I wanted to be.

So, yes, I longed to be something more, someone better. It often seemed to me that I'd spent my whole life looking behind me, worrying that the past was catching up. Deep down, I still lived with the fear that at any moment, someone might look at me and say: oh, *that* Maddie Alden. On some level, I knew that I would always have to hide who I really was. I would always need to pretend. But that didn't make my wanting to succeed any less imperative. It made it more so. And I saw that I could do this. I was quick and bright. Even Heather had softened toward me. She'd told me a few days earlier that she was pretty sure her mother was in the early stages of Alzheimer's; I'd confided to her about our problems with Clara. I felt a part of things now. And I loved the busyness of office life, the juggling of phones and messages, talking and typing at the same time, learning and doing. Planning ahead. Nana saw it before I did. How well the job suited me. Showing and selling. I was a pleaser. I was a people person. Clients first. Sales and service, 24/7.

32

Paul and I were both so busy now, I don't know what we would have done without Kathy and the new day-care center she started up that spring. I wouldn't normally have felt comfortable allowing my babies to be out of the house for so much of the day, but the farm was really like a second home to my daughters. Also, Lia was so confident and self-reliant. And Kathy was sensitive to Beanie's shyness; she knew when to let her just go and play on her own. Rachel now got off the school bus at the drop near the farm and hung out with Kathy and the younger children until I picked them all up after work. It was about this time that I began to appreciate what a sweet, responsible person my oldest daughter was turning out to be. Kathy noticed it, too.

"Rachel's so good with the kids," Kathy told me one night when two of her little charges ended up staying past their usual pickup times. "And they just love her! Look at Nate—he's that redhead over there. He's a total devil with me, but she's got him eating out of the palm of her hand. I'm going to advertise and try to expand some this summer. Do you think Rachel would want to help out? I'll pay her something, of course."

"I'm sure she'll want to. And I'm really happy to hear you're going to keep this going! It's gotten so busy at the office. I'll probably have to start going in on weekends now that we're heading into the really active selling season. And I want to start paying you for taking Lia and Beanie. You've been so great, Kath. But this is above and beyond the call of duty."

"I would never think of you or the girls as being a duty. You know that."

Paul agreed that we should start paying Kathy the going rate. We talked about it after dinner a few days later when I was doing the bills. I had the invoices, envelopes, and checkbook spread out on one end of the kitchen table. Paul had his own paperwork, including minutes from the various town select committees, in front of him.

"Oh, Christ," he said.

"What?"

"It's Rick's treasury report. I wasn't able to make the last meeting, but I heard something about this. The town's got three properties in tax title. They're planning on putting liens on them for unpaid back taxes. Guess who's on the list?"

"Don't tell me." Paul and I sometimes speculated about Luke's financial situation. We simply could not believe that he would be able to live off his meager earnings from selling his art pieces. The "sculpture garden" in front of his house rarely seemed to change, except when he added a new bizarre offering to the mix. Had his mother or another wealthy Barnett relation set up a small trust fund for him? Or did he just scrimp and save, living essentially off the grid, growing his own vegetables in the summer, cutting his own hair?

"Yeah, damn it. And I don't think he has any idea how serious this is. Do you know, if he doesn't pay this off in one year, the town can assume ownership of the property and put it up for sale? And they have every legal right to do it. But I can already hear Luke on this one, can't you?"

"Oh, yes. 'Why should I have to pay rent on something I already own?' Isn't that what he said last time this came up? So maybe it's not about the money, maybe it's just a matter of principle."

"There's no *just* a matter of principle with Luke, you know that. Principles are everything. I'm going to have to talk to him about this."

We fell silent then for a few moments, though Luke and his problems, as was so often the case, hung in the air between us.

"Do you think—" he began.

"If you need—" I said at the same time. We both laughed. We knew each other so well.

"How much do you think it is?" I asked.

"Well, my guess is a couple thousand maybe. He's been grousing about the tax increases ever since they went into effect—when was that? Almost a year ago now? I bet he hasn't paid anything since then."

"I think we could swing it, if we don't pay down the home equity line for a while," I said, looking over our bills. "Especially if Luke works out some kind of a payment schedule with the town, and we can help out in monthly increments. Rick and the committee will go for that, don't you think?"

"Yeah. But it's not them I'm worried about."

We decided to wrap the bitter pill inside the sweetest excuse we could think of. We often included Luke in the girls' birthday celebrations, and Beanie was turning three that coming weekend. Kathy, Bob, and the kids would be coming, too, though they tended to head home pretty early. Bob still kept farmer's hours, despite the fact that he had less and less real reason to do so.

"Do you think this looks okay on me, Mom?" Rachel asked that Sunday afternoon. I was in the kitchen, putting the finishing touches on Beanie's cake: carrot walnut with cream cheese icing—her favorite. Rachel stood in the doorway and turned around slowly. She'd shot up in the last year—and filled out. Though just thirteen, she could probably pass pretty easily for five years older than that. In the right light, dressed a certain way, she looked like a mature woman. As she did now. She had on the Gap halter dress that we'd bought at a clearance sale a few weeks before; it was made out of a silky pink material trimmed with pale pink lace. I hadn't paid much attention when she tried it on in the dressing room; we were both too busy scooping up the deeply discounted items. But now I realized that it looked more like a slip, really, or a negligee. How sweetly seductive it made her appear, her lush innocence on full, naive display. We never bothered to dress up for these family celebrations; I couldn't help but wonder why Rachel wanted to now.

"Mmmm. You look lovely," I said carefully. Lately, Rachel had become so touchy and defensive about her appearance. She worried that she was "fat," and went into a tailspin every time her acne started to flare up. I'd recently helped her buy her first real bra. And, with my approval, she'd begun to experiment with makeup. But each shaky step toward her inevitable adulthood was fraught with tension between us. She seemed to seek out my help and advice. But if I pushed my opinions a little too hard, suddenly I was "interfering and mean." She wanted my approval, but only if it was unqualified. "I think you'll probably need a sweater later, though. Which might spoil the look."

"No, I'll be fine," she said, twirling around in the doorframe. "But I think I'll try to put my hair up. It's almost long enough now."

I didn't have the energy or heart to challenge her. These days, with my job demanding so much of my time and attention, it seemed like a luxury just to be in my own kitchen. I was beginning to realize how lucky I'd been to be able to stay home all those years while Rachel was growing up. Though I loved working, I missed being with my girls all day long. The last thing I wanted at that moment was to fight with Rachel. Though her appearance stayed on my mind, like a tension headache, the rest of the afternoon.

It was early June. Already warm and humid. Paul had put the screen porch up a few weeks back. We hung balloons from the rafters and laid out *Finding Nemo* plates, cups, and napkins. Paul was grilling, of course, a Beanie favorite of jumbo shrimp, red pepper, and onion shish kebobs. Bob, Kathy, and the kids arrived around five and soon all the younger children were running through the sprinklers Paul had set up near the wildflower field. Luke pulled up about half an hour later, a bulky package wrapped in newspaper and string tilted against the backseat of the convertible. All of the adults went back so far together and knew each other so well. I don't remember what we talked about. Bob helped Paul with the grilling. Luke ran around with the hose, chasing the kids. Kathy and I could hear them squealing in delighted terror as we worked together in the kitchen, cooking the couscous and washing the lettuce for the salad. And then Rachel came downstairs. She'd arranged her thick honey-colored hair in a soft knot on the top of her head, little tendrils curling at her temples and around her nape. She must have been playing with my makeup; that glossy maroon lipstick was certainly not something I'd let her buy for herself.

"Oh, my," Kathy said when she saw her. "You look absolutely gorgeous. Like a movie star!"

Paul stopped short when he came into the kitchen carrying the big tray of grilled food, his startled gaze moving quickly from Rachel to me. I gave him a small shrug.

"You want to go out and round up the kids?" Paul told Rachel. "We're about ready to go here."

"I better check B.J.'s diaper before we sit down," Kathy said, following Rachel out through the porch.

"Jesus Christ!" Paul whispered. "Who the hell was that bombshell?"

"Your adolescent daughter. I don't want to ruin things by arguing with her, okay? Can we just let it go for tonight? I would not let her leave the house looking like that, believe me. But what harm can it do here? It's just family."

Except it wasn't, totally. There was Luke. And I realized almost as soon as we all sat down what prompted Rachel to get dressed up the way she had. I doubt she understood it herself. Why she insisted on sitting next to him. Or kept playing with her hair while she talked to him. She was so chatty, all lit up. The others didn't notice. Almost all of the attention was on Beanie, ensconced in her booster seat at the head of the table, a silver and pink plastic tiara spelling out "Birthday Princess" perched precariously on her head. But I found myself, sitting across from Rachel, eavesdropping on her conversation with Luke, attuned to the tug and pull of my oldest daughter's subconscious yearnings.

". . . but you're so lucky, you could go anywhere. Get in your convertible and just drive away!"

"But there's no other place I really want to be, Rach."

"I don't believe that!" she said, touching his arm. Luke had put on a white button-down shirt for the occasion and had rolled up the sleeves, revealing his deeply tanned forearms, the soft down of sun-bleached hair. Rachel left her hand there. I felt my heart aching for her. What drove her now was the same impulse that had prompted her to ask Luke, so many years ago, if he would like to marry her. He was her first love. And now her body, and I have no doubt her heart, too, was drawn to him with a sudden new urgency. She wanted something from him, though she didn't under-stand yet what it might be. I give Luke credit that he knew what she was asking. He realized what was happening. Women always wanted this from him. It was no mystery to him, no surprise. Though I believe that it shocked him that it would be coming from Rachel now. I picked up on Luke's sudden alertness, his caution, the careful way he pulled his arm free to reach across the table for a roll.

"When you're as old as I am you'll understand," he said. "That tired old line from the *Wizard of Oz* is one of the truest things ever written: there's no place like home. Even if it's just a run-down cottage by the side of the road."

"Yes, of course, I know that. But it would be fun to travel, don't you think? I'm allowed to go by myself to visit my cousins in Brookline this

summer. I was going to take the bus, but you could drive me in the Oldsmobile."

"Oh, baby," Luke said. "That old car's been through more lives than a
cat. I'll be lucky if it gets me home tonight."

"Okay." Rachel sighed, but she hadn't quite given up. "You didn't say anything about my new dress, Luke. Or my hair. Do you like it up this way?"

Luke turned and took her in. I saw him looking. It was such a long,
slow gaze—and so full of sadness! He loved her, of course. I knew that. She
represented everything he would never have in this world: daughter, family,
home. And, too, she was her own unique and lovely self. His fairy queen, his
growing girl. The best of himself reflected in her adoring gaze.

"Let me see," he said, tilting his head, making it look as though he
was giving her a considered, impartial appraisal. "Yes. I believe I do like it
that way."

Rachel helped me clear. As I was getting ready to light the candles on
the cake, she told me to hold on. She was getting chilly, after all, and was going to run upstairs and put on a sweater. We had cake and ice cream on the
porch; and then the evening coolness forced us inside to open the presents:
a tricycle with pink plastic handlebar tassels from Paul and me, a book on
horses from Rachel, and a *Finding Nemo* beach towel from Bob and Kathy.
Luke went outside and brought in his bulky gift. It turned out to be a large
cat, made from welded pieces of aluminum, which could turn in the wind,
like a weather vane.

"Or you could put it on a stake in the vegetable garden," Luke said. "You
know, kind of use it as a scarecrow."

"I love it!" Beanie said, hugging it to her as if it were a stuffed animal
or a living thing. "It's a very beautiful silver cat. And I'm going to keep it in
my room."

"Or that, too." Luke laughed, obviously pleased.

Bob, Kathy, and the kids went home soon after that. I took the girls up
to bed.

"Stay around for some tea," Paul told Luke. "I think we have some of
that god-awful organic stuff you like somewhere."

I knew Paul would wait until I came down again before broaching the
subject. When it came to Luke, I had always played the bad cop. I think
both men preferred it that way. They knew and cared about each other too

deeply. Any fight between them, however small, was brutal and damaging on both sides.

"That was sweet," Luke told me when I sat down across from him at the kitchen table. Paul had made me a mug of decaf, which I pulled toward me as Luke added: "Thanks for having me."

"If I didn't think it might wake her, I'd have you go up and take a look at Beanie. She's sleeping with your cat right beside her. That sure was a hit."

"Yeah." Luke smiled and looked down into his mug of tea. "I had fun making it for her. She's really something. And her vocabulary seems pretty amazing to me for three. She said: 'It's a very beautiful silver cat!' A perfect little sentence. Did you hear that?"

"Yeah, she's great," Paul said. I could tell he didn't want to get into it. That he wished the evening could stay just as it was: a happy time, a good memory. But we owed Luke more than that, didn't we?

"You know, Luke," I said. "I'm glad we have this chance to talk."

"Oh?" He was instantly alert to whatever he heard in my voice.

"I read about your overdue taxes," Paul said. "In the minutes from the finance committee."

"Isn't that kind of thing supposed to be private?"

"I'm a selectman now," Paul said. "It's part of my job to know these things. To help decide what to do. But I couldn't make the last meeting and they went ahead and decided this without me: you've got one year to pay things off. Then the town will take legal action."

"Which means what? It's my property. It's been in my family for almost three hundred years."

"Legally? They can take possession. They can sell it. They can do whatever the hell is necessary to get it back on the regular tax rolls."

"I don't believe it. That's insane."

"No, Luke. It's the law. It's always been the law. Now, what the fuck is going on with you? You don't have the money? Is that it?"

"Why should I pay rent for—"

"Oh, cut the crap, okay?"

"No. I do not have the money."

"Fine. We'll lend it to you," Paul said.

"Lend?" Luke laughed. "How am I supposed to pay you back? You know perfectly well you won't be lending it—you'll be—"

"We don't care," I told him. It felt so good to be able to say that! To have risen so far and, yes, to realize that Luke had allowed himself to sink so low.

"Well, I do," Luke said, looking across the table at me. "I care a whole lot. I'm not going to accept a handout from you guys. End of story."

"No, it's not," Paul replied. "What about the taxes? Are you going to wait until they serve you with an eviction notice? Talk about insane. You're the most goddamned stubborn—"

"Stop it, Paul," I told him. "Calling each other names isn't going to help."

"I'm sorry," Luke said. "I'm sorry to worry you both like this. I'm sorry to sound so ungrateful. I'm not. I'm really touched. I knew this thing was building, snowballing. It's my fault that I didn't figure out a way to cope with it before it got to this point."

"How much are we talking about?"

"Over three thousand dollars. That new appraisal they did two years ago? Suddenly my hovel has an estimated value of two hundred and fifty thousand dollars! Now that *is* insane, admit it."

"Yeah, well, they do most of that stuff on computers these days. It's because of all the building. The million-dollar places are driving up values everywhere."

"How many acres do you have, Luke?" I asked him.

"Around sixty, maybe a little more."

"Well, I have an idea," I said. "Why not sell some of it? You could get a hell of a lot of money for your land now. And it's really so beautiful. All rolling hills and meadows. Just what real estate brokers would kill for. Since I've been working for Nana Osserman I've come to realize how little desirable land is still left around here. Land that could be developed. You're sitting on a gold mine."

"Maddie's right, you know," Paul said. "You could sell and pay off your taxes, and you'd still have more than enough money to keep you in the clear for years."

Luke looked at Paul, then back to me.

"It would be like you guys selling one of your daughters. It's what I love best in this world. It's all I have."

"I'm not saying you should sell *all* of it," I told him. "Just what you don't need."

"No," Luke said. "I can't. Thanks for trying to help, though. I'll come up with something. Not the land, though."

Sitting in our kitchen after the party, Luke sounded so sure of himself, so positive that selling his land would be like selling his soul. So it was a surprise, to say the least, to hear his voice when I picked up my office phone the next day.

33

"Hey, Mad, it's me."

"Luke?"

"You know, I've been thinking about what you said last night. I know I sounded pretty negative, but I'd like to talk to you some more about it. How do we do this?"

"Well, why don't you come into the office and meet with us. Nana and me. When would be good?"

"Whenever. Now? This whole thing has been weighing on my mind. I'd like to get it settled."

"Okay. Sure. Hold on. Let me check with Nana and see if she's free."

She was, of course. She knew about the Barnett estate. In fact, I even got the impression that she knew why Luke was thinking of selling, though she certainly didn't hear it from me. I just said that he was an old friend, looking to cash in on the rising market.

"Well, sweetie, that's just fabulous. Good for you. Let's meet in my office. But you go ahead and take the lead on this one. I have to tell you I'm very impressed with your initiative."

"I didn't do anything but make a suggestion."

"Oh, no! Don't ever sell yourself short. Admit it: this was your idea, sweetie, and you sold him on it. I give you full credit. And I'm not one just to hand out praise. I'm not sure what it will be at this point, but if this all works out the way I hope, you'll be getting a very nice bonus, as well."

Later, of course, I would wonder many times over if what Nana said was true. It was what Luke accused me of, as well: that I'd orchestrated the whole thing. I'd manipulated Luke, persuaded him it was for his own good. And, all the while, I was really only doing it for myself. In the end, it did give my career a huge boost. Though I really don't think I ever consciously meant for that to happen. But, who knows? I've lived through enough now to believe we only vaguely understand what motivates us. And, too, my feelings for Luke have always been so conflicted and confused. I thought I was helping him. It looked like such an obvious solution in many ways. And it really did seem to come to me so spontaneously—*I have an idea: why not sell some of it?* But maybe, in fact, a darker, more aggressive plan had been building inside of me for months at that point.

Luke had showered and shaved for the meeting. Put on a clean shirt. But he still looked scruffy. His hair was way too long, and I noticed that his tan had a kind of ground-in look; sun mixed with dirt. He wore jeans and work boots: a lean, self-contained man who didn't fit into any of the usual categories. He seemed too aloof to be a local; too down-at-the-heel and eccentric for a weekender. I saw Nana sizing him up over her designer half-rim glasses as he greeted me in the hall outside her office.

"We're going to talk in here," I told him. "This is Nana Osserman, the owner. Nana, Luke Barnett."

"Delighted to meet you," Nana said, though I noticed that she kept her usual effusion in check. We took seats across from her. Nana looked at me and nodded. This was mine. She wanted to see how I would do.

"I'm not sure what you already might know about the Barnett family," I told her. "But Luke's forebears actually settled most of this county. The Barnett estate was part of the original land grant from the English—"

"*Was* is the operative word," Luke cut in. He sat forward in his chair, elbows on the armrests. He was very tense, I realized. He wanted to get this over with as quickly as possible. "All that's left now is about sixty acres and the mansion. I've decided that I want to keep just ten acres and the cottage I'm living in. Frankly, I can't afford to hold on to the rest of it anymore."

"Fifty acres? You really want to sell that much?" I asked him. "Are you sure?"

"Yes. I think so. What you said the other night? It really makes a lot of sense. What's the point of trying to keep it all now? It's just not practical, and from what you tell me this is the time to sell, right?"

Why was Luke doing this? What made him change his mind? I'm still not sure, but I doubt it was because he'd decided suddenly to start being practical. And he really wasn't the kind of person who paid much attention to market conditions. I don't doubt that the overdue back taxes worried him.

That he realized he couldn't keep scraping along as he'd been doing. But, honestly? I think the real reason he decided to go through with it—against every conviction that he held dear—was that he wanted to ease Paul's mind. He couldn't tolerate Paul's pity, just as he would never accept his charity. Yes, he needed to clear his name on the town tax rolls, but more important, he wanted to get straight with my husband.

"Maddie's absolutely right," Nana said. "You could not have picked a better moment. Now, I know Maddie's already familiar with your property, Mr. Barnett, but would you mind showing me around? We could take my car—or yours. Whatever's most convenient for you."

Luke looked down at his hands, clenched in his lap, and said, "Why don't you and Maddie do that together, okay? Let me know what you think when you've had a look. Maddie knows where to find me."

And that was that. Luke got up and shook Nana's hand. I walked him out to the Oldsmobile.

"Thank you for coming to me with this," I said to him as he opened the car door. "It means a lot to me."

"You mean I'll be a feather in your cap?"

"That, yes. If everything works out. But also that you would trust me—and Nana—to handle the sale for you. I know what a hard thing this must be for you, Luke."

"Do you?" he asked, looking up at me as he turned the key in the ignition. He left the question hanging as he backed around and drove out of the parking lot.

Nana and I took my secondhand Forrester and spent most of the afternoon exploring the Barnett property, starting with the mansion, which was literally starting to fall in over our heads.

"Good God, what happened here?" Nana asked as we made our way gingerly through the grand front rooms. The grandeur had more than faded. The place had been stripped bare. Luke had scavenged whatever wasn't too heavy to lift: Delft tiles had been jimmied from the fireplace, chandeliers picked clean of their crystal, vintage sconces torn out of the walls, even the inlaid molding from around the ceilings had been pried off. I looked upward from the foot of the double staircase and saw a ragged patch of sky above me.

"In the beginning, Luke put together most of those art pieces he creates from bits and pieces he found here," I told Nana. "I think it was his way of making some kind of ironic comment about the glory of the past."

"Ah, yes. I see. Like Ozymandias," Nana said. "Your friend certainly is an interesting character. But, I'll tell you, I don't think this place can be salvaged. I mean, maybe if all the beautiful original detailing was still in place, but even then I wouldn't count on it. People want new. Big. Designer-built. I'll have a reconstruction expert come by, but I seriously doubt it."

"The land is valuable, though, isn't it?" I asked her a little while later as we drove back down from the northern woods, where Luke and Paul had built the underground marijuana farm. That quarter-acre clearing was grown over now, maples and spruce sprouting up in what looked like nothing more noteworthy than a sunny meadow gone to seed.

"Oh, yes. I really think so. I'll want to talk to Frank and Nicky about it, of course, but I see this as a truly exclusive luxury development. Ten to fifteen acres per site. Fabulous homes. Top-of-the-line and fully loaded when we bring them to market. The potential is just enormous. And we owe it all to your initiative, Maddie."

It all happened pretty quickly. Nana, Nicky, and Frank Miles mapped out a tentative blueprint for subdividing Luke's fifty acres into six separate building parcels. They had a professional surveyor create a draft plan. Then they ran that by the Red River planning subcommittee that Paul now served on, and got an initial go-ahead. Nana suggested that I be the one to talk to Luke about the offer. "I get the feeling that he wants to keep this informal, just between friends," she told me. I invited Luke over that night. Paul took the girls up to bed, allowing me the chance to go over the preliminary survey with Luke alone. The computerized drawing looked like one of those constellation charts: an abstraction of iron pipe and rod settings, dotted-line streams and daisy-chain stone walls. I really couldn't tell much by looking at it, except that the plan clearly showed demarcations for six variously sized building sites. Luke and I were standing at the kitchen, where I'd spread out the vellum copy on the table.

"The smallest lot is seven acres. Right here," I told Luke, pointing to a squarish shape, about the size of a piece of toast, on the paper in front of us.

"You've gone to a lot of trouble," Luke said. "But I guess I don't really understand what this means. You plan to sell these individual lots? And what—I get paid as you make each sale?"

"No. Red River Development Partners—that is Nana, my boss; Nicky Polanski, who Paul works for; and Frank Miles the architect—intend to buy all the land from you at one time. Now. Then, over the next year or so they'll put their own money—the partnership's making a killing from the Tucker Hill project—into building spec houses. I think the plan is to start with two places and see how they move. But whatever happens, the point is this: they're not going to subdivide the land into dozens of little quarter-acre plots. These are all generous, well-thought-out sites, as you can see. And they're so spaced out; you probably won't even know they're there."

"Yes, I can see that, I guess," Luke said. "Though, honestly, I can't really imagine it. I've a feeling, even when these are built, that I won't be able to totally conceive of it. You know, my family used to own the area that's now called Cedar Grove?" Luke was referring to a neighborhood of mostly classic Colonial-style houses east of town. "My mom and I had to sell the land after my father died. But I'll drive by these days and not really be able to take in what's there. In my mind's eye it's all still the woods and fields I remember as a child."

"Well, these will be far more upscale than Cedar Grove," I assured Luke. "They'll be truly luxurious, really magnificent houses—more like the Tucker Hill places that Paul's working on."

"Oh, God, not those enormous things that are going up? You can't honestly tell me you think they're magnificent, Maddie! I thought you and I at least agreed on how really awful they are."

"I guess I've been seeing things a little differently since I started working for Nana," I told him. But he was right. And a big part of me still did agree with him. For a moment I thought I'd lost him. And in the end I might have, except Nana's offer just bowled him over.

"You've got to be kidding. That's a fortune."

"No. She's serious. The partnership sees a lot of potential in this project."

Luke laughed and shook his head.

"Well, I guess if I'm going to sell my soul, I might as well get good money for it."

"So? You think you might want to go ahead then?"

"Jesus, yes! Let's hurry. Before everybody comes to their senses."

"Well, you've got to hire a lawyer. Have someone look over the deed and get some feedback on the overall deal. This is a valuable piece of property, Luke. You'll want to make sure you're fully protected."

"And some high-priced lawyer's going to do that for me?" I remembered how much Luke distrusted the legal system. Between his father's law firm and his own checkered past, he'd built up an animosity to lawyers that was bordering on the pathological.

"Come on, Luke. Don't be penny-wise. You need someone to read through all the fine print, who understands the ins and outs of the selling process."

But in the end Luke didn't make any changes to the deed. And on the day of the closing, he arrived alone at the Red River Realty offices, where we'd arranged to have the signing.

"My guy couldn't make it," he said when Nana asked when his lawyer was arriving. "I'll be my own counsel."

"Oh, dear," Nana said, turning to Kenneth Firbank, who represented Red River Development Partners. "Isn't this a little bit . . . unusual?"

"Well, honestly, I've never—" Firbank began before Luke cut him off.

"It's what I want, okay? Take it or leave it. Now let's get this whole thing over with."

It turned out to be, according to Nana, one of the smoothest sales she'd ever been involved with. It was all over in less than fifteen minutes.

"Who'd like some champagne?" Nana asked, as Nicky, Frank Miles, and Luke finished signing the papers.

"Not me," Luke said. "I've got to go. Thanks, anyway."

Ken, Frank, and Nicky begged off, as well. So Nana insisted that Linda and Heather join us, instead. We sat around Nana's desk and she popped the cork and poured the smoking champagne into four flutes.

"I'd like to propose a toast," Nana said, holding up her glass.

"It's your party," Linda said.

"Okay, then." Nana turned to me with a smile and said, "To our new sales associate!"

Like almost every job, I suppose, I discovered that there really isn't a whole lot of mystery involved in learning how to sell real estate. The bonus Nana gave me for bringing Luke to the table helped pay for the three-day intensive course I took at the end of October up in the Harringdale high school auditorium. I'd already been studying a number of how-to books and test-prep guides that Nana had recommended. It helped a lot that Nana began to let me sit in on the weekly listing meeting, when she, Heather, and Linda went over the status of Red River Realty's exclusives and reviewed the current Multiple Listing Service postings for the area. I found that I already knew a lot about the basics of the business—title checks, loan applications and approvals, pest inspections—things I'd picked up naturally by helping Nana every day. My only real worry about taking the test was the math portion, but Linda sat down with me a couple of times and went over the fine points of calculating percentages and commissions, figuring monthly mortgage payments, and working out estimated closing costs. In the end, the actual test was something of a letdown. Nobody but me was the least bit surprised that I passed it the first time out. Paul framed the certificate that stated I had "successfully completed the requirements as a Real Estate Salesperson," and I hung it proudly on the wall above my desk.

Then the real work began. I was still the office manager, receptionist, and Nana's assistant. Now, too, though, I had to put in "floor time"—four-hour shifts at least twice a week when I was expected to handle any walk-in clients or phone inquiries. I also had to make myself better acquainted with the properties we handled, a process that meant driving around with Paul whenever we could for a couple of hours after work, at a time when we were both exhausted and short-tempered. But, frankly, all of these new challenges were easy compared to finding clients of my own. It didn't help my efforts that Red River Realty was considered by most of the locals as an agency that catered primarily to the upscale, second-home market. If you grew up in the area and wanted to sell or look around, you'd probably call Charlie Lowry at Millennium or Nancy Sanders over at North County. With Paul's help, I worked up a letter and mailed it to everybody I could think of. Paul did an e-mailing about me to his extensive list of friends and acquaintances. But escalating property values had already locked a lot of the people we knew out of the market. All the action and sales were being generated by buyers from Boston and New York. I was beginning to feel that I'd wasted my time, as well as Nana's.

Then, all at once, I got three active leads: from Paul's second cousin, who'd gotten a new job at Walco Propane and needed to relocate to Harringdale; from a walk-in I'd been wooing off and on for at least a month who finally decided he wanted me to "show him what I had"; and from a Marge Patterson, a good friend of my sister-in-law Louise.

"We've never done this before," Marge confided to me. "Gary's brother sold us the house we live in now when he relocated to Chicago, so it was all handled in a pretty informal way. And, between you and me, Gary gets his back up real easily about feeling cheated or taken advantage of. So it's been something of a struggle even getting him this far, to the talking stage."

"What *are* we talking about exactly, Marge? Do you have a sort of dream house in mind?" I asked. Friendly. Helpful. No pressure. Though I'd never thought it through before that moment, I knew right away that this was how I wanted to sound, how I intended to approach the whole thing.

"Yes. I want something classic, you know, like a big white clapboard farmhouse, or a Colonial. Only fairly new and in good condition. We have a ranch style now, and, frankly, I hate it. I want a house that *looks* like a home, you know? On some water, too, a little brook or a pond. Four bedrooms, three baths. Maybe two or three acres."

"That's great. A really good start," I told her. "Let me put some ideas together, okay? I'd like to make a date with you and Gary now, if I could. My calendar starts getting so filled up at the end of the week."

It didn't take off all at once. But things began to pick up. The alphabetical hanging file folders I'd set up for "prospects" and "active clients" were no longer empty. I was finally able to start a "closed transaction" file when I sold one of the condos over in Silver Acres to the grandparents of one of Kathy's day-care kids. What with liability insurance, office expenses, and splitting the commission with Nana, I was just about breaking even. It didn't matter. For the first time in my life, I felt I was finally getting somewhere. I was making my way. Nana seemed pleased. She called me her "baby broker." I basked in her approval. More than the sales and commissions, that was what thrilled me.

And then, in early April, when the earth began to soften, Red River Development Partners began logging and clearing the land for the first of the three spec houses they were building on the property that had, for as long as anyone could remember, belonged to the Barnett family.

34

"We've got a real problem here, Maddie." It was Paul, calling me at the office. Though it was officially spring, we'd had a flurry earlier that morning and snow still clung to trees that were just beginning to leaf out. Paul's tone was so grim that I immediately thought something had happened to him—or one of the girls.

"What? Where are you?" I stood up at my desk, ready to run to wherever I was needed.

"I'm up at the new site. Luke's here. We're—we have to talk. I need you to get up here. Can you do that?"

"What's happened? Is something wrong with Luke?"

"Maddie? Can you just come?" I realized then that Luke was right there, listening, and that Paul didn't want to discuss whatever the problem was in front of him. This was odd; Paul didn't hold much back from Luke.

Nana wasn't in yet. Heather was out on a call, and it was one of Linda's days to work from the city. I put the phone system on auto-answer and left a note for Nana. I made it sound as though I was meeting a client, which was not that far from the truth. The sun came out on the drive over, and the snow began melting away, exposing the stubble of greening fields, the pools of standing water in the low-lying meadows. I slowed down as I passed Luke's place, looking for the entrance to the construction site. Though I knew Nana had visited when the logging stage was complete, I hadn't yet been there. Paul's crew had only gone up for the first time the day before. He hadn't said much about it, just that he thought it was ironic that Red River Development was titling this building lot "Maple Rise," as the loggers had cleared at least an acre of hardwood trees, a great many of them sugar maples. I saw the mud tracks on the roadway before I saw the drive: it curved up through the woods behind Luke's cottage and then made a switchback up the hill. Though they'd laid down plenty of gravel, the surface was already heavily rutted, mud sucking in the rock. Even in my all-wheel drive, I felt the Forrester lose traction and churn on the softening curves.

A tableau of men and trucks awaited me at the top of the rise. There were four pickups, a small backhoe, and a much larger earthmover, its long neck suspended about fifteen feet above the cab and its shovel half open like the mouth of a dinosaur, the metal teeth streaked with dirt.

Paul and Luke stood apart from the half dozen men who were grouped together, talking and smoking, by a couple of newly unearthed boulders. I still blame myself that I didn't grasp what the problem was immediately. I think I imagined that Luke might be objecting to the noise, or the muddied highway. Under my parka, I was wearing one of my work outfits: a navy blue pantsuit and a pair of black leather boots that I was still breaking in. As I picked my way across the lot toward Paul and Luke, I remember feeling irritated that the heels of my new boots were sinking so deeply into the muck.

"What's going on?" I asked as I came up to them. Paul had the working plans wedged under his right arm.

"You tell me," Luke said, looking from me to Paul. "You see? She doesn't get it! I can't fucking believe that she doesn't—"

"Hold on," Paul said. "Just hold on. Maddie, turn around, okay? You see where the earthmover is? That's where the new house is sited to go in. Did you know that? I mean, I thought you and Luke went over these plans together."

"We went over the subdivision blueprint," I said, turning back and looking down the hill. From where we stood, facing south, with so many of the trees down, Luke's cottage was directly in our line of vision. "I haven't seen the actual building plans. Why would I? You know as well as I do that Frank only finished the designs this winter—months after Luke sold them the land." We were already starting to parcel out the blame, the two of us.

"Well, this just can't happen," Luke said. "I knew I should have come up here sooner. I should have walked up when the logging began. But I was just so fucking sick at heart to see all those stripped trunks being hauled away. And the noise! I kept telling myself it had to be farther up. That the hills just amplified the sound. But look at this disaster area. It's like a tornado came through."

"Frank was up here earlier and went over things with me," Paul said.

"This is definitely where he intends the site to be. What can we do?" He turned to me with the question, but I knew he was asking himself the same thing.

"Who's this Frank?" Luke asked.

"The architect," Paul told him. "Frank Miles. One of the partners."

"You met him at the closing," I said.

"Well, he's just going to have to rethink things," Luke said. "Didn't he see that my place is right down there? That this monstrosity will be looming over my house? Jesus Christ, Maddie, I remember you telling me that I wouldn't even know any of these houses were back here. What was that? Total bullshit? Your little way of getting me to agree to all this? Well, I'll tell you right now: I didn't sell my land to have this happen. It's got to be fixed. And, if you two won't help me, I'll—"

"Now, just hold on," Paul told him. "Of course we'll do what we can to help. And Maddie isn't responsible for any of this, okay? Come on, Luke! You know us better than that. We're going to do whatever we possibly can to get this changed. I'll take it up with Frank and Nicky. Maddie will talk to Nana. We'll work something out."

Luke turned and strode back down the hill, and Paul and I stood together watching him make his way unsteadily along the rutted roadway. Most construction sites are pretty ugly: a clutter of building equipment and materials scattered around a raw open hole in the ground. This one was made worse by the recently denuded landscape, now a mountainside of muddy debris. I could only guess how much money had been spent logging the site. How much more to regrade and lay in the drive. I'd talk to Nana, of course, but I already felt the hopelessness of the situation. I think Paul did, too, though he didn't let me see what he was feeling.

"How do you want to handle this?" he asked me. "Should we try to get the three of them together, maybe? Or do you want to talk to Nana on your own?"

"I think I'd do better one-on-one. Nana got to know Luke a little bit during the sale. She may have more sympathy than the others. God, I can't see Nicky giving a damn, can you?"

"No, but Frank might listen to reason. He's a pretty good guy, basically, once you get past that ego. And these are his designs, after all. I'm going to have to send the crew home, I guess. Then I'll try to track Frank down."

The office was still empty when I got back. But Nana arrived about half an hour later, and I went right in and laid the whole thing out to her. Her initial response was encouraging enough.

"I don't think any of us took that cottage into consideration. To be honest, sweetie, I forgot that anybody actually lived there. It just looks so run-down, almost abandoned. Your friend's a little—well—kooky, isn't he? I'm sorry he's so upset. Listen, I'll give Frank a call right now and see what we can do."

And it might have worked out except my kooky friend beat both Nana and Paul to the punch. Luke must have gone right home, looked up Frank Miles's address in the phone book, and driven immediately down to his architectural design offices in Northridge. I'd only met Frank a few times at that point. He's a tall, balding man in his midfifties who, according to Paul, spends an hour every morning lifting weights. He likes to touch himself when he talks, running his fingers appreciatively over his expensively clothed pecs and abs. But he's the single most respected and sought-after architect in our area, known for his sensitivity to the landscape and his promotion of environmentally responsible building materials. Despite his success, he seems friendly and easygoing enough—at least until his talent and authority are called into question. And, apparently, Luke had derided both in pretty short order. Frank was "in conference" when Nana first called him, but he phoned her back just as I was heading out her door to go back to my office. She waved at me to come back in.

"So, Frank, I—" Nana began, but then she had to stop and listen to the barrage of words that, even from across the room, was almost loud enough for me to hear.

"Yes, I know he's a little—

"But, don't you think he might have—

"No, I understand. Of course, it's your call. I know the gradient was tricky. Right. And the view from there . . . yes . . .

"He might try to fight it. But, legally, no, he doesn't have a leg to stand on. There weren't any covenants. Please, Frank, you know perfectly well this is your best work. Of course, you have my full support. . . ."

Nana at least seemed a little sorry. Frank was so furious that when Paul arrived at his office to plead Luke's case shortly after Luke had left, Frank threatened to fire him on the spot. Nicky was pissed off, too, especially when he found out that Paul had taken it upon himself to shut the work site down that morning.

"I think I was finally able to convince them both that I'd maybe done the right thing after all," Paul told me that night after the girls were in bed. We were sitting at the kitchen table, hunched over cups of cold decaf. It was a weekday night and we'd both have to get up at the crack of dawn, but neither of us was ready to head upstairs. We kept going over what had happened. "But, man, do I sense that Frank has his reservations about me right now. And Nicky's going to be riding my ass for the foreseeable future. God, what a mess. Why the hell didn't he let us handle things?"

This was the third or fourth time Paul had asked that question, and I kept pretending that I didn't know the answer. But it was obvious: Luke didn't trust us anymore. Neither one of us. Of course, I knew perfectly well that Luke blamed me for this disaster, but he knew without asking whose side Paul would be on. When the three of us stood together on that hillside, both Paul and I thought the situation could be salvaged, our friendship kept intact. But Luke knew better. He looked around him and saw that it was over. All those trees, some more than a hundred years old, gone, their trunks lumbered, the branches chipped into mulch. And he, too, had been stripped of direction, his bearings uprooted. And the world he had come to despise—represented by Frank's ambitious contemporary designs—rising up from the mud behind his home. He felt betrayed. And abandoned all over again. Except now he had lost so much of what he had once held dear. But he wasn't about to take what he saw as a massive injustice quietly. He was going to fight it every way he knew how—even if that meant fighting us, too.

Paul had decided to wait until the following day to talk to Luke; he said he needed to get a better grip on his own anger. What upset him most was that Luke had accused me of somehow talking him into selling the land. That Luke so obviously blamed me for what had happened.

"Nobody held a gun to his head when he signed those papers," Paul said. I should have taken some solace in the way Paul rallied to my defense.

But it gave me no joy. And the next morning Paul got a call from Owen Phelps: Luke was demanding a hearing of the select committee. He said that he'd hired a lawyer. He was talking about suing Red River Development Partners, the town, and the two of us.

"It sounds to me like he's really gone off the deep end," Owen told Paul.

I told Paul that I wanted to go to the special meeting, but he advised me against it.

"I think it would look as though you were there to defend yourself. You haven't done anything wrong. Luke's clearly worked up about this and he's bound to say some things—"

"That's exactly why I want to be there. It's his word against mine. I'm not afraid of anything he has to say, Paul. And I think it would look cowardly if I didn't show my face."

It was a Wednesday night. As usual, the committee met in the old high school gymnasium. Paul and Owen, three other selectmen, and the town clerk, Solly Heinrish, arranged themselves on folding chairs around a collapsible table. I sat in the back of the room on the bottom plank of the old bleachers. Owen called the meeting to order at 8:00. Luke arrived alone. I should have known his threat to hire a lawyer had been an empty one. Luke walked right over and stood in front of the group; I didn't think he saw me sitting behind him. Solly took notes on a long legal pad.

"We're here to address the concerns of Luke Barnett, relating to the construction project currently under way on property that he sold to Red River Development Partners last year. You should all have in front of you copies I had made of the blueprint that the planning committee signed off on at the time of the sale. Any questions before we let Luke take the floor? Okay then . . ."

"Good," Luke said. "You're looking at the same plan I was shown when I agreed to sell my land. I was told that there were going to be six big sites for possible development, as you can see there. And I was told that quote unquote I would probably not even know any houses were there because of the way things were laid out. Well, guess what? They're putting up the first one now and it's practically going to be sitting on top of my house. I mean it's right up there on the hillside directly behind my place. It's just incredible! I was lied to! That's why I'm—"

"Luke, I was looking over your file before you got here," Owen cut in, "and I didn't see any covenants."

"What's a covenant?"

Owen glanced at Paul before he replied. "It's something the seller stipulates as a condition of sale. For instance, people often say that they don't want any house trailers going in, or prefab homes. Or any building within a certain number of yards from the property line."

"I didn't know that I needed to do that."

"Well, it would have protected you from exactly the situation you're complaining about now. These deeds are legal contracts. You could have asked for as many covenants as you wanted, so long as the buyer agreed to them. But without anything in writing, there's really no way that we can act on this complaint."

"You're saying you won't do anything to stop this?"

"I'm saying I can't. We can't. There's no legal—"

"Oh, fuck you and your legal garbage, I—"

"I'd advise you to keep a civil tongue in your head."

"I don't believe this! I'm the one who should be civil? When you let these people just come marching into this town and rip it to shreds? Bulldoze the countryside to make way for these obscene houses? I'm the one who should be civil, when you thieves and liars—"

"Luke, please—" Paul said.

"Please what? Please don't make a fuss because you let your wife steamroll me into turning over my property—to be devastated! To have my home become like a prison—"

"Nobody steamrolled you into anything. You told Maddie—"

"Maddie! You and Maddie!" He turned around to stare at me. "I thought you were trying to help me. But you never told me anything about covenants, did you? You never warned me this might happen!"

"Luke," Paul said. "Leave Maddie out of this."

"I wish I could," Luke said, facing Paul again. "I wish to hell I had. But it's a little late for that, isn't it? And now, when my whole fucking life is being destroyed, you turn your back on me like the Judas you've always been—"

"Mr. Barnett," Owen interrupted him. "I think it best if you and Mr. Alden continue this more personal discussion elsewhere. Meeting adjourned."

Luke threw up his hands and, cursing, walked out of the room. Paul followed him.

I waited in the empty auditorium for ten minutes or so. Thinking back. To how Luke had reacted to the partnership's initial sale proposal. To the closing. To that business about his "guy not being able to make it." I finally realized just how deep his animosity toward the law really went: he'd only pretended to hire a lawyer when he sold his land. And now, too, when he'd hoped to fight what had happened. He held the law in such contempt. He thought he knew better. He was already broke. Why the hell should he pay good money for some lawyer's suspect advice? Once again, he'd let his prejudices, and now his anger, get in the way of his own best interests.

I can only guess what Luke and Paul said to each other when they faced off alone in the parking lot. Whatever it was, it hurt Paul so deeply that he's never spoken to me about it. I think, no, I know it had to do with me. I believe that was the moment—after a lifetime of holding back—when Luke finally told Paul what he thought of me. *Don't you see? She'd do anything to get what she wants, Paul. Anything.*

We drove home in silence. We didn't see Luke again for a long time after that. We did not talk about him in front of the girls. And, oddly, they didn't question us about why he was no longer in our lives. I think Rachel found out through school friends what had happened at the meeting; I'm sure the whole town was gossiping about it.

The construction continued. They broke ground farther up for the next site: Hemlock View. Sometime in July, a demolition crew came in and took apart and carted away what was left of the Barnett mansion. Paul managed to keep work ahead of schedule. By the end of the summer, Frank told Paul he was impressed by how well he was managing everything. All the ugliness on that first day of building was forgotten. At least by the others.

It was a busy fall. Both Paul and I were working so hard. Rachel and Beanie were back in school. After Christmas, I started Lia at the pre-K half days, dropping her off on my way to the office and picking her up at the end of the morning. She loved school, all those new kids to play with! She's like Paul that way; other people make her happy. She and I would have lunch together at home most days, just the two of us now, and she'd chatter on to me about her morning. I'd only half hear what she was saying—Angelina

Ballerina, and Gary said, then Mrs. Tyler got so mad—listening instead to the excitement in her voice, that thrill to be out there in the world. She was still going to Kathy's in the afternoons, but I could tell she would have been happier doing the full day at pre-K. Kathy's basement has a dank smell in the winter months and, even with all the overheads on, it can feel dim and claustrophobic. And Kathy herself had still not really recovered from that postpartum business she went through after Danny. I felt sometimes when I talked with her that she was not altogether there; her attention was fixed on something she couldn't explain, just over my shoulder.

I wonder sometimes about all the things we keep hidden from each other. Our little collections of shames and regrets that we hold so closely to our hearts. How bad are they really? How special? If we let them out—opened the window and unscrewed the lid—would they be any more terrible than bugs in a jar, fluttering away into the light? It's the darkness that makes them seem so important, isn't it? The fear? Paul and I didn't talk about Luke, but he was always there in the back of my mind. Now more than ever. As far as I knew, he'd cut himself off from everyone. He never even came into the general store to pick up the paper. But I kept thinking I would see him, or that I did see him: turning into the bank drive-up, or walking out of the post office. But it was always somebody else.

That morning started like any other, though we all had a hard time crawling out of bed; it was the beginning of daylight savings time and still pitch-dark at six thirty. We had to scramble to get out the door on time, but the bus was waiting at the end of our driveway for Rachel and Beanie, and I was actually only a few minutes late dropping Lia off at school. Heather called me on her cell phone about ten minutes after I opened the office. She was on the Mass Turnpike en route to Boston. Her mom and been found wandering half naked through the hallways of her apartment building the night before. Heather didn't know how long she'd be away; she'd decided to stay in Boston until she could get her mom into a nursing home. She'd try to make what calls she could from the road, but she went over a few things that she needed me to handle for her in the office.

The phone was ringing again as we were hanging up. It was Nana. She wouldn't be coming in either. Her allergies were acting up; she sounded terrible. She was upset to hear Heather was out, too. Because she knew Linda was going to be tied up with a closing. And Nana had an appointment to show Maple Rise, now in its finishing stages, to a new client that afternoon. It was a family from Manhattan. I would have to handle it. I could tell she was worried about how I'd do. And I was, too, honestly. But eager, as well. This was my first big break. A chance to prove I could be trusted with more than the quarter-acre in-towns or the condos at Silver Acres. Though I knew it wasn't really so much a question of what I was selling—but to whom.

Part Nine

35

The Zellers. Anne Zeller. She was lodged in my life now, painfully over-sized, monopolizing my attention. I didn't hear anything from her over the weekend after Richard had addressed the town meeting about Luke. What had Richard said when he got home that night? I couldn't stop thinking about her, and what I had told her about Luke. It stabbed at me. Had I been wrong to tell her? Had I betrayed Luke's trust? He'd begged me not to say anything to her, but surely it had been better coming from me rather than Richard. What was Anne thinking? What had I done?

The weather turned hot again: heavily humid with thunderstorms threatening every hour or so, gray clouds massing above the tree line, then sunlight suddenly slanting through and the heat rebuilding.

That Sunday, for the first time all summer, I didn't have any showings or appointments. Nana had been complaining that business was slacken-ing off, but I hadn't felt it myself until that weekend. This only added to my sense of uneasiness and foreboding. Late that afternoon, restless and uncomfortable, I called Paul on his cell and suggested that he meet us af-ter work at the lake for supper; we could cook some steaks on one of the outdoor grills there. The following weekend was Labor Day and we'd be expected at the farm for an Alden family get-together. Unbelievably, this was our last free Sunday of the summer.

"Sure," he said. "But I was going to stop off and see Luke after I'm done here. So I figure I'll get there around six or so, okay?"

"Just make sure you leave yourself enough time to go for a swim," I told him. He'd been working seven-day weeks at the Covington site, driv-ing himself and his crew to the point of exhaustion. It wasn't just that he was working too hard; he was throwing himself into the final stages of this project with a kind of fury. One of his men had actually walked off the job the day before, complaining that Paul had been verbally abusive. I think we both understood that his anger and drive had nothing to do with making that construction deadline.

Six o'clock came and went without Paul. The sun sank below the mountain ridge, casting our little crescent beach in sudden shadow. The other families started to pack up their folding chairs and towels. I lit the charcoal and Rachel began to set out our things on one of the picnic tables. Beanie and Lia had been laboring together for the last hour or so on an elaborate sand castle by the edge of the water, which was now mirrorlike and ethereal in the fading light. Rachel came over to me at the grill when she was done setting up for dinner.

"I was thinking about leaving for Bangor a little earlier than we talked about," she said. "I don't think Mrs. Zeller is going to need me this week."

"Is that because Mr. Zeller's home?"

"I guess so," Rachel said. "I checked the bus schedules already and they're the same for every weekday. I thought I'd go up on Wednesday instead of Friday."

I was trying to think of a way of asking her more about Anne and what was happening at the Zellers', so I wasn't really paying much attention to what she was saying about her long-anticipated trip to Maine to see Aaron.

"Are you sure that would be okay with Anne? I mean, didn't she already pay you for the whole month?" I knew she had, because I'd been there a week or so ago when Anne had handed Rachel a check made out to "cash" for over three hundred dollars, saying she was just trying to get her bills taken care of before Richard arrived. I'd suspected, though, that it was because she didn't want Richard to know how much she'd been relying on Rachel for help with the children and housework.

"She said she wouldn't be needing me anymore," Rachel replied. "And I did ask her about the money, Mom. She said I should keep it—like a bonus."

"Honestly, honey, that just seems to me like a lot—" And then an altogether different thought struck me. "Wasn't Aaron's dad going to pick you up at the station on Friday night on his way back from work in Boston? Who'll be there to meet you on Wednesday?"

"Maybe his dad's taking the week off?" Rachel said. It was because she answered me with another question that I realized she was lying. I suppose she thought that her "maybe" kept it from being a blatant deception, but it was a lie nevertheless. I knew it was a couple of hours from Bangor to the Neissens' house up on the coast. I supposed that Aaron would be there to get her, that perhaps they'd arranged to spend a night together somewhere. I guessed that Aaron was covering things up on his end, as well. This was the first time, at least that I knew of, that Rachel had ever willfully tried to deceive me. I felt sad—and guilty somehow. It seemed to me now that the summer had become overgrown with secrets and lies, an impossible tangle of good intentions, outsized hopes, neediness, and longing.

"I think I'd better give Aaron's mom a call then," I said. "Just to make sure that your being there a couple of days longer won't be an imposition."

"Please don't do that!" Rachel said.

"Why not?" I asked, turning to look at her. She was blushing. She knew that I knew.

"Just don't. You're right. It would be an imposition. I'll go Friday, the way we first planned."

It felt like a victory for me then. I believed I'd handled things with finesse—forcing the issue without provoking a confrontation with Rachel. Of course, I couldn't have known how much better it would have been for Rachel if she had left that Wednesday. If I'd allowed her what, in retrospect, would have been such a relatively harmless falsehood: a stolen night with a boy she imagined she loved. I wonder if she thinks about that, too. What might have been if she'd been able to lie to me a little better, if I hadn't known her quite so well.

At first I thought it was a deer or bear—a thrashing sound coming from the woods. I turned, alarmed, to see Paul come running through the underbrush, stripped to his bathing trunks, banging his chest like a gorilla and roaring, "Heeeeeeere I come, ready or not!" He ran across the beach as Beanie and Lia screamed, "Watch out for the castle! Daddy, be careful!"

But he leapt like the old hard-charging fullback he was over their little sand battlements, ran out several yards, and threw himself into the darkened waters. His antics broke the tense mood between Rachel and myself. By the time he'd had his swim, toweled off, and changed, the steaks were almost ready and it seemed to me that we were one happy family again.

"I had a good talk with Luke," he said after we'd all sat down. That he was even bringing this up in front of the girls was indication enough for me that the conversation had gone well.

"That's great," I said. "So he's agreed to clean things up?"

"He's already started! Can you believe it? He says that he's been clearing the place out all weekend. The basement's still a wreck but the downstairs looks almost presentable. I'm not sure what got into him, but he told me he's ready to start over. That this is going to be a whole new beginning for him. I can't tell you how relieved I am. It was really great to talk to him."

I could tell by Paul's unreserved enthusiasm that Luke hadn't confided in him why he was turning over this new leaf. But for the first time since my aborted phone conversation with Anne on Friday night, I allowed myself to believe that she was going to leave Richard after all. That she'd somehow communicated this to Luke; that he was readying his house for her and the children. Yes, this had to be what had happened! Perhaps Anne had slipped down there while Richard was asleep and they'd talked it all through: Luke explaining away his youthful missteps; Anne assuring him it didn't matter to her, nothing mattered but the two of them being together. Paul's obvious relief infused me with new confidence: it was all going to work out. Hadn't I always been too much of a worrier, a doubter? Later that night as we were getting ready for bed, I asked Paul, "Did you tell Luke about Richard Zeller—about what happened at the meeting?"

"No. But why else would he be doing what he was doing? Of course, he was adamant he was getting his act together for his own reasons. But I'd claim the same thing in his place. Nobody wants to feel pushed around by that asshole. I think he hates him as much as I do—no, maybe even more."

But, as Monday and Tuesday passed and I still hadn't heard from Anne, my uneasiness returned. I hadn't really thought about how often she'd taken to calling me at the office throughout the summer—chatting about some new store she'd found, checking in with me about Rachel's schedule, and, more recently, almost daily finding something to confide to me about Luke—until the phone calls so abruptly stopped. Late Tuesday afternoon, I decided to call her, something I very rarely did. But why not? I thought. It was another hot day and I'd promised the girls that we could go for a swim if I didn't get tied up at the office. I'd invite Anne and her kids to come along. Richard answered the phone.

"Who?" he replied when I gave him my name and asked to speak with Anne. He put down the phone and I heard his footsteps down the hall.

"Hello?"

"Hey, it's me. How are you?"

"I'm sorry. Who is this?"

"Anne, it's me. Maddie."

"Oh. Of course. I'm sorry. Richard told me it was Hallie."

"Is everything okay?"

"Yes."

"Good. That's great. Listen, I'm taking the girls up to the pond later, and I thought you guys might want to come."

"Oh. No. We can't. Sorry."

"You can't talk right now, can you?" I said. It was obvious she was uncomfortable; I sensed Richard in the background, listening.

"No. Sorry."

"That's okay. I understand. But you can always give me a call when it's better for you, okay? At work or home, it doesn't matter."

I felt a little better just hearing her voice. But I felt so bad for her. She clearly hadn't found the courage yet to tell Richard about Luke. I thought it must be agony for her, and I wished so much that I could help her somehow.

The office seemed eerily quiet on Wednesday; Heather was in Boston and Linda had started her vacation. Nana pointed out that a lot of people were away that week, the final one of the summer, which might account for the inactivity. But she looked preoccupied and left early that afternoon. It was Dan Osserman's seventy-fifth birthday the following day and Nana was putting on a big party for him at their house, complete with caterers traveling up from Manhattan and a jazz combo coming in from Boston. I wasn't surprised, or even hurt really, that Paul and I hadn't been invited. Though I think Nana is more egalitarian in her social dealings, Dan Osserman only mixes with the other wealthy second-home owners and the local monied class; Owen Phelps is a frequent golf partner of his.

It was a little busier Thursday morning because the new assistant, Alice Tolland, had long ago arranged with Nana to take the day off for a family wedding, and I was the only one in the office. I finalized the copy and digital photos for our listings in the September *Real Estate Buyer's Guide*. I rescheduled a closing for Linda.

When I went home for lunch, Lia asked me if she could go over and play at Kathy's that afternoon. Rachel had been so preoccupied getting ready for her trip to Maine the last few days that I think both her younger sisters felt a little abandoned by her. They'd loved having Rachel so involved with their daily lives over the course of the summer, sharing in all the attention and inventive fun she'd lavished on Katie and Max. But this week they'd been left to their own devices, and though Beanie was good at entertaining herself, I could tell that Lia was at loose ends. Kathy always welcomes drop-ins, so I didn't bother to call her: I just drove Lia and Beanie over there on my way back to work. I know I should have stopped and chatted, but I was already running late. I waved to Kathy from the car. She was in the backyard, surrounded by children, setting up the sprinkler hydrant. She looked unquestionably pregnant now and just plain heavy: her upper arms doughy in a sleeveless sundress.

The afternoon dragged on. I got a lot of filing done and killed some time checking out the latest listing updates on Promatch. The phone finally rang around four o'clock.

"Mom?" It was Rachel. "I'm sorry to bother you like this but Mrs. Zeller just called. She needs me to babysit for her tonight. Is that okay? And do you think you can drive me over there around six?"

"Sure," I said. I felt so relieved to hear from Anne again! Even though she'd called Rachel, I knew this was her way of reaching out to me, as well. "But I should hold the fort here until at least quarter of, so be ready to go when I get home, okay? I won't even get out of the car."

Rachel looked so pretty when she came running out to meet me. She'd lost some weight over the last few weeks, and her new slimness accentuated the fullness of her breasts under her flowered sundress. She had a pale lavender sweater tied loosely around her neck like a big scarf, a fashion trick she'd picked up from Anne. She'd had her hair cut and highlighted on Saturday in preparation for her visit to see Aaron; it tumbled around her shoulders as she ran, honey-colored, soft and thick.

"Thanks for doing this," she said as she slammed the door and I started to back out. "I was so sure she didn't need me that I left all my packing until tonight. So I've been scrambling to get everything ready. You know the bus leaves at seven thirty—and I can't miss it! You'll drive me down to Northridge, won't you? I'll set the alarm for six so we won't be late. And I'll make you a thermos of coffee."

"Did Mrs. Zeller say why she needed you?" I asked, as we turned onto the highway. "Are they going out?"

"No, she didn't say. Just that it would be great if I could help her. You know, I think I better set the alarm for five thirty to be safe."

Maybe it was because Luke was clearing things out inside the house, but, as we passed by, it seemed to me that the outside looked worse than ever: old boxes and empty bottles stacked on the front porch, a pile of stuffed garbage bags spilling down the steps. I thought I saw him as we made the turn—a flash of something in the doorway—but then the trees cut his house off from view. The Zeller property looked pristine in comparison. At Richard's insistence, Anne had hired a professional yard care and garden design outfit from Northridge that kept the long sloping lawn neatly mowed and watered; they'd also recently planted a garden of shrubs and hardy perennials around the front of the house. The vegetable garden that Bob had put in, its fence covered now by overgrown weeds, looked out of place, homegrown and rural in the middle of what was now a neatly manicured landscape.

I drove up to the house, circling in the turnaround, and stopped in front of the wide slate path. Rachel unbuckled her seat belt and opened the door.

"Thanks. I'll call you or Dad when it's time to pick me up. I'd rather it be you than Mr. Zeller, okay?"

"Sure, honey," I said as I looked beyond her to the house. It seemed so much more substantial and welcoming with the new garden, the lawn trimmed, the path weeded. Someone—could it have been Anne?—had put up one of those expensive butterfly houses at the top of the rise; it was circled by a newly planted mini-garden of Shasta daisies and echinacea. Then the front door opened, and I saw Anne standing there. On impulse, I turned the engine off. I followed Rachel up the pathway. Rachel said something to Anne, and then moved around her into the house.

"Hey," I said, walking up to the door. Anne stood there, her arms folded across her chest. She was wearing a sleeveless light blue silk sheath, printed with some kind of Oriental calligraphy in a shimmery silver. A braided silk cord holding an intricately carved piece of jade circled her neck; and, for the first time that I could remember, she was wearing a number of rings, including one with a diamond about the size of an almond. She shook her head.

She didn't say anything. Was Richard standing nearby? I wondered. Was this her way of warning me not to mention Luke?

"What a pretty dress!" I said. "Is it new?"

"What?" She looked down at what she was wearing. "No, it's not."

"But that necklace must be," I said. "It's so lovely. I don't think I've ever seen it before." I felt awkward standing there on the steps. I was about a foot below her, and she was looking down on me, though something seemed odd to me about her gaze. I remembered what Luke had told me about Richard's way of handling her problems: drugs, drugs, and more drugs. Was she a little out of it now?

"Anne?" I asked, lowering my voice. "Is everything okay?"

"Of course," she said, still not really looking at me. It was more that she was staring *through* me, the way I'd seen her gaze past people she didn't particularly want to notice. I couldn't believe that she really meant to look at me this way. Something else must be going on, I told myself. This couldn't be happening. But it was as if all the warmth, all the friendliness and interest, had been shut off. Like the flick of a switch! Gone!

"So, you and Richard are going out for the evening?" I knew it was a stupid thing to say, but I couldn't help myself. I think some childish part of me believed that if I kept asking questions, kept trying various combinations, I'd finally hit on the right one. The spell would be broken. The light would flash back on. And the door that had somehow become closed between us would open wide again.

"Yes, we're going to the Ossermans'," she said.

"Oh, right! Dan Osserman's big birthday party!"

"Is that what it is?" she said, her hand curling around the doorknob. "Don't tell me you're going, too?"

I stared at her, not believing what I had heard. It was the way that she'd said it—incredulous and yet somehow disinterested at the same time. But I knew she couldn't have meant her words to sound the way they did. Something was definitely wrong. It had to do with Richard, with her trying to make her break from him. I stood there, looking at her, desperately searching for something to say, for a way to make contact. What was she thinking? She'd spent the whole summer chattering away at me in a kind of stream-of-consciousness abandon, confiding intimacies, welcoming the same. And, in my own way, I'd given back, I'd shared, I'd opened my heart to her with a willingness I'd never felt with anyone but Paul before. It had been so freeing. Intoxicating. Seductive. I'd felt valued and, yes, even admired by someone I thought to be remarkable. In my mind, Anne had become more than just a friend; she was the epitome of everything I'd hoped to be. And it was primarily through her admiring eyes that I'd been able to see this new, possible, far more interesting self. Now she looked at me as though she barely recognized who I was.

"Anne?" I said, but I couldn't think how to ask what I needed to know.

"Anne?" Richard called from somewhere inside. "Where the fuck are my cuff links?"

"I'm coming," she called back.

36

Sometimes the past seems so real, doesn't it? Almost tangible. A place you could find your way back to if only you remembered the way. That's what I felt as I came down the Zellers' driveway and recalled, with disturbing clarity, walking up that same rise from the Barnetts' cottage so many years before. It had been all woods back then, the trees leafless in the late November light. I'd been anxious but also secretly thrilled: I'd never been inside the mansion before. The light then had been the way it was now: red-streaked, luminous, suspended between afternoon and evening. I'd known that something was wrong from Paul's tone of voice, his urgent *Wait for me there. Just go. Now.* But I'd really known all along that something wasn't right. Like alchemy, Paul and Luke were generating money from an overgrown quarter acre of nothing. I'd allowed myself to believe what Paul told me, while I skimmed over the surface of things, willfully unconcerned.

But then, when it all came crashing down, it was Paul who hit bottom, not me. He did everything he could to protect me from the fall. Yes, I was hurt by what happened. My life was never the same, but it didn't fundamentally change who I was—the way it did Paul. He stopped believing in anything but the here and now: me, a job, a roof over his head. The rest—God, faith, hope—became dangerous chimeras for him. He developed a tough and limited moral code: judge not, mind your own business, be a good neighbor, watch your back. But me? Though we lived by Paul's rules, I never really stopped yearning for more. To be more. Transformed. For years I waited for the chance: the thick vine beckoning me upward; the spinning wheel whispering: *come, touch me, spin.*

Luke stepped out of the shadows when I reached the bottom of the driveway. He was carrying a beat-up weed whacker over his shoulder but it didn't look to me as though he intended to do any trimming. The land on his side of the road was wildly overgrown, a dense bramble. I stopped the car and lowered the window.

"Did you see Anne?" he asked.

"Yes," I told him.

"Is she okay?" He was searching my face as if to see some trace of her there. "I've been worried."

"Why?"

"Because of what he might do to her," Luke said. Then he looked behind me up the hill. "I don't want him to see me here. Come back around to my place."

He disappeared into the undergrowth before I could say anything further. When I pulled up in front of the house, he was waiting for me on the front steps. He was smoking a cigarette.

"I thought you'd quit those things," I told him as I crossed the yard toward him. "Like about ten years ago."

"Yeah, well," he said, taking the cigarette from his mouth and dropping it on the step, where he ground it out with his boot heel. "I'll stop again as soon as we get settled. Come on in. I want you to see all the work I've been doing."

"No," I told him. "Let's just talk here, okay?"

"Sure. It's cooler out here anyway. Look what I found," he said, nodding to a pair of ancient metal chairs he'd unearthed from somewhere and set out on the porch. They had the salvaged look of something he'd originally intended to use for one of his art objects. The legs wobbled and creaked when we sat down on them.

"Paul told me you were clearing things out," I said.

"Well, I've been doing my best to get ready. I've gotten rid of most of the furniture inside and have been repainting the rooms. But I'd like Anne to arrange things the way she wants to, you know. When she moves down."

I stared out across Luke's porch to the piles of garbage bags and then, beyond, to the graveyard of rusting pieces posed across the shabby lawn: the flying hubcap tortoise, the scarecrow of molting broom heads and peeling handles, the enormous rabbit with its ancient TV antennae ears. Maybe it was the softening effect of the fading light, but Luke's sculptures no longer seemed so sinister to me, or even ugly, really. Instead, I think I finally understood their wacky humor, the sad, self-fulfilling prophecy behind their creation, how all our most cherished belongings come to this in the end. Ashes to ashes. Junk to junk. And our ambitions, too, I thought; everything we hold dear. It seemed to me that this is what Luke had always known, even as a boy; and why he'd always scared me. But he'd changed since meeting Anne. The irony and sarcasm that had once been so much a part of his character had diminished. In their place was this new earnestness. He seemed to have no edges to him anymore; instead he generated a kind of open-armed, unself-conscious optimism. He was like someone who'd found God or Zen. Except with Luke, what he'd found was Anne. It had humanized him, brought him down to earth. He didn't frighten me anymore. It was too late to wish that he would.

"So when is she leaving Richard?" I asked him. "What has she told you?"

"That's why I stopped you, Maddie. How did she seem to you when you saw her?"

"But you've seen her yourself, haven't you? You two have talked?" I asked, turning toward him. "Since Richard's been back?"

"No, we haven't. But you say she's okay? I hate to think of her up there with him. What he might do to her when she tells him about us."

"Just when do you think she's planning on telling him?"

"When it's right," Luke said. "I know Anne. This can't be easy for her, inflicting pain. She needs to find the right moment."

"Oh, come *on*, Luke," I said. "Richard's been back six days already! And do you want to know why I'm here? Why I went up there? To drop Rachel off so that she could babysit. Anne's all dressed up. They're going out to a dinner party."

"Maddie, what is it?" Luke asked, leaning over and peering at me through the gloom. "You sound so angry. What's going on?"

And I realized that, in fact, I *was* angry. No, I was furious. Burning with shame. The more I thought back on my conversation with Anne, the clearer it became that she was dropping me. She was ending the friendship. Was it because of what I'd told her about Luke? And if that was the case, how could I believe she was even planning to tell Richard about her affair—let alone go through with her decision to leave him? It had been almost a week, and what had she been doing?

"Anne knows," I said.

Luke slowly fished another cigarette out of his front shirt pocket and lit it. He didn't need to ask me what I meant.

"How did she find out?"

"Richard did some digging into your past. He rehashed the whole thing at the town meeting Friday night."

"Ah," Luke said. "I see. Oh, Jesus, poor Paul! Now I understand why he seemed so pathetically grateful when he dropped by here Sunday and saw what I was doing."

I was touched that Luke's first reaction would be concern for Paul rather than his own situation. I decided I had to tell him the whole truth, even if he ended up blaming me for everything.

"Richard came to the meeting directly from the city," I said. "So I guessed that Anne didn't know yet. I called her when Richard was on his way back to the house and told her before he got there. He'd been so nasty about you, Luke. I couldn't stand the thought of what he'd say to her, and I was hoping that—"

"I see. I understand. Thank you, Maddie. I'm sorry that this had to fall on you. But of course it's better now that it's all out in the open."

I was confused by how well he was taking this news. I would have thought he'd be furious. Frantic. But he actually seemed calmer and more confident now than when I first came upon him on the driveway.

"She was pretty upset," I said. "She didn't want to believe me."

"Well, of course not. We thought we'd told each other everything. But, you know, in some ways this will actually make things easier between us. More equal and balanced."

"I don't understand."

"No. And that's the way it should be. This is between Anne and me. But don't worry," he added as he got up from his chair. "Everything's going to be fine."

"You still believe she's going ahead with this?"

"Absolutely," he said as he led the way through the stacks of garbage bags. "There's no question in my mind." He walked me back to my car. It was dark now, inky black under the towering hemlocks. He took my elbow as he guided me around the side of the house.

"I want to have you guys over," he told me as I opened the car door, "as soon as Anne and the kids are settled in here, okay?"

I told him we'd be looking forward to it. He seemed to have such a clear vision of how things were going to be for them. Anne and him. For everyone he now included in their enchanted circle. I could almost imagine what he saw: the four of us, sitting down around his kitchen table, Anne pouring coffee, our children running around outside, their laughter drifting in an open window. But then, the future isn't ever much more than a dream, is it? Beckoning, elusive, disappearing down a sudden flight of stairs. Nothing about it is certain or clear, though—and this is what breaks your heart in the end—everything is always possible.

It was nearly seven thirty—an hour and a half past Kathy's usual day-care pickup time—when I finally turned into the driveway leading up to the farmhouse. Kathy never minded when I was late in the past, but things had changed between us now. We hadn't spoken much since BlueFest. I knew I'd been avoiding her. I understood that I'd let her down that summer; that in many ways I'd been failing her ever since I started working for Nana. I'd kept up with her in the beginning, chatting every day or so and seemingly staying in touch. But the truth was, I did what I could to remain on her good side because she was so helpful with the girls. She'd become useful to me, rather than close. And then we began to seem so different in my mind. She wasn't interested in my job, in hearing about Nana, my clients, the money I was making. Her world was circumscribed by the farm; Bob; her children—and mine. Honestly? I felt that I was leaving her behind. That I'd outgrown her. I'd met Anne. I didn't need Kathy anymore.

There was a Taurus I didn't recognize parked next to Bob's pickup; I figured I wasn't the only late parent, after all.

I made my way up the toy-strewn front walk and then around to the kitchen, where I saw lights on in the windows. I never knock, of course. I just pushed open the screen door. Bob and Kathy were sitting across the kitchen table from Charlie Lowry. Charlie had been a year behind me in high school; he was now a successful real estate agent at Millennium.

"Sorry I'm so late," I said, staring stupidly at the papers spread out across the table.

"Maddie!" Bob jumped up from his chair. "Hey. We were all just talking here. You know Charlie, right?" Charlie had shot up as well.

"Sure," he said, holding out his hand. "Of course. I think we were just finishing up, actually. What do you say, Bob? Kathy? I'll give you a call next week, okay?"

"No, please sit back down," I told the two men. Even without everyone's obvious embarrassment, it was clear to me that Bob and Kathy were talking to Charlie about selling the farm. It was a slap in the face—it felt to me like an actual blow—that they hadn't confided in Paul and me. And that they hadn't at least approached me about handling the sale. Kathy refused to meet my gaze; instead she stared intently into the coffee cup she was cradling between her fingers.

"I don't mean to interrupt," I said, breaking the awkward silence. "I'm just going to run downstairs and grab Lia and Beanie. We'll go out the basement way."

"No, honestly—" Charlie began to say, but Kathy cut him off.

"The kids are out back," she said, looking up. I felt the hostility in her gaze. "They're in the tree house with Charlie's daughter. I'd take a look at Beanie's ears, if I were you. She was complaining about them hurting her earlier this afternoon."

Lia prattled away on the drive back to the house. Beanie was quiet, which is nothing unusual, but I took her temperature when we got home: it was 102. I gave her some eardrops and made her lie down on the futon on the screened porch. We served her sherbet on a tray. She had a few bites, and then rolled over and fell asleep. Lia and I had dinner at the far end of the table, near Beanie. Around nine o'clock, after I'd done the dishes, Lia and I went back out to the porch. I sat down on the edge of the couch and shook Beanie's shoulder.

"Time for bed, honey. I want you and Lia to sleep inside tonight, so that I can keep an eye on you, okay?"

"I can't really hear you, Mommy," Beanie said, sitting up and shaking her head. Her voice was too loud. "You sound like you're talking from inside a cloud."

"It's probably just the drops," I told her, gathering her into my arms. She was hot and sweaty. It always comes as a surprise to me how light Beanie actually is. She's small-boned but long-limbed; it was like carrying a bundle of kindling up the stairs. I'd gotten both girls into their bunk and was giving Beanie a half caplet of Tylenol to help her sleep when we heard Paul come in downstairs. It was nine forty-five. I knew he must be exhausted.

"Come up and say good night to the girls," I called down to him. "I've got your dinner all ready."

I heard him climbing the stairs. Then I heard the whistle coming from the direction of the firehouse. This was the third time in the last month; the last two alarms had turned out to be prank calls. Probably teenagers, Paul had told me; Tom Langlois had insisted they install a caller ID system. I heard Paul swear and start back down the steps at a run.

"Grab a piece of that chicken on your way out!" I said, hurrying down the stairs after him. "You've got to be starving."

"I'll be back in ten minutes is my guess," he said. I was right behind him when he reached the kitchen door. When he turned around to say good-bye, he almost couldn't help but find me in his arms. That's where I wish we could have stayed, the two of us. With Lia asleep above us, and Beanie just drifting off. But where would that have left Rachel? No, it was already too late at that point. Sometimes I think it was always too late. Paul was halfway down the driveway when the phone rang. Damn, I thought. It was probably Dean or Jeb at the firehouse, calling to say it was just another false alarm. As I reached for the phone I decided I would say something to Paul later on about stepping down from the department. He did so much for the community anyway; it was time to let someone younger and less burdened deal with this sort of nonsense.

"Mommy?" For a confused moment I thought it was Beanie, somehow calling me from the upstairs phone. The voice sounded so young. She was crying.

"Rachel?"

"Mommy. Please come get me. Something bad has happened. Please come now."

37

I knew I couldn't risk leaving Beanie and Lia alone in the house. I carried them down separately and got them into their car seats. Lia woke up, protested briefly, and fell back to sleep. Beanie stayed knocked out. They looked like two life-sized rag dolls, arms and legs akimbo, hair flopped over their faces. The whole time I kept wondering what had happened at the Zellers'. My guess was that Anne and Richard had returned from the party already fighting, or had started in when they got back to the house. And then they'd continued their argument in front of my daughter. That Rachel had been forced to witness Anne's showdown with her husband somehow didn't surprise me. I could see Anne using Rachel as a kind of foil, both audience and witness. I didn't put much past Anne now, I realized. Fear forces us to compartmentalize our thoughts, I know. I guess that's why I didn't allow myself to think about Luke. Anne and Luke. How she might have been using him, too.

On certain nights, when there's the right amount of cloud cover, the lights of Albany glow above the hills to our west and north like a kind of low-rent aurora borealis. That's what I thought it was at first, though a part of me knew that the night was clear. I saw it as I made the turn onto River Road, although it was at least a half mile away: the fire trucks, the flashing lights, the billowing, obscuring smoke, and, above it all, roaring with triumphant abandon: the flames. Traffic was already backing up. I heard a siren behind me and saw lights circling in my rearview mirror. There's not much of a shoulder there, but I did what I could to pull off to the side of the road. Two fire trucks, a tanker, and a police cruiser sped past; they had come down from Covington.

It was then that I understood just how bad things really were, though I still didn't allow myself to think about what was happening. I just knew that

I had to find Rachel. The traffic wasn't moving in either direction; I realized they must have blocked it off at the scene of the fire. I made a U-turn and headed back into town. People were coming out of their houses now. A group had gathered in front of the general store, looking down River Road. I saw Phyllis Linden standing on her front porch, rocking her new baby on her hip. Her husband, Carl, serves with Paul on the volunteer fire force. I pulled into the driveway and ran up the front path to ask her if I could leave Lia and Beanie with her while I looked for Rachel.

"They're both asleep in the back. They can stay right there in the car seats, if you just keep an eye out for them from the porch."

"Sure, Maddie. I'm up anyway until Carl comes home." As I ran back down the path, she called after me:

"She's going to be okay."

Or maybe she said *We're going to be okay*. It doesn't matter. It's those unexpected small kindnesses that touch you the most when tragedy hits. I tried to walk back along River Road, but it was totally clogged. People had gotten out of their automobiles and were milling around, talking on their cell phones. I remembered that there used to be an old logging trail that ran more or less parallel to River Road; Paul and I had cross-country skied it the first winter we were married. I cut up through the woods. The path was still there, defined by an eerie pinkish glow. I ran toward the light.

Nobody knew for certain how it had started. A spark, perhaps, falling on a grease-stained rag resting on old newspapers. Luke, unaware of the growing conflagration, training his blowtorch at the scrap metal arranged on the worktable in front of him. Not noticing until it was too late. Or maybe it had been a cigarette. Left to smolder on some chipped saucer or Mason jar lid, scattering hot ash as it fell onto the litter-strewn floor. How the fire started, though, wasn't as important in the end as why it spread so quickly: raging upward to the floors above, roaring into the attic, engulfing the cottage in an inferno of smoke and flames. Luke's basement workroom had its share of solvents and flammables, but that wouldn't account for the speed with which the fire spread. Sadly, Paul came up with the answer for this, one that was eventually supported by the official investigation into the cause of the accident: it was the spray-in cellulose insulation that Luke had blown between the walls and rafters of the old house a few months after he'd moved down from the mansion for good. That had been years ago; the small amount of flame-retardant chemical applied to the insulation at the time would have long since lost its protective qualities.

By the time I reached the edge of the woods abutting Luke's property, the fire trucks had been forced to pull back from the house. Later, Paul would tell me that five towns had sent their fire equipment and emergency personnel. Dozens of firemen and EMS workers stood around and watched helplessly as flames shot through the rafters and cinders flew up into the smoke-filled night. I scrambled down into the underbrush, fighting my way through the brambles and weeds, and finally came out onto the soft green at the bottom of the Zeller property. From there I could see that several fire trucks had trained their hoses on the woods behind Luke's place, obviously working to keep the fire from spreading. I looked up at the Zellers'; it appeared as though every light in the place had been turned on. But then I realized that the windows were actually filled with the wavering, wanton light of the burning house below. I started up the driveway, but two firemen I didn't recognize stopped me before I'd made it twenty feet.

"We're blocking this area off," one of them told me. "You'll have to go back that way." He pointed west through the tree line.

"But my daughter's up there!" I said, pushing past them. "I've got to get her."

"No, ma'am. She's safe. The family just drove down, okay? Best head back that way. You're sure to find her down there."

A large crowd had gathered beyond the fire trucks: people had left their stranded vehicles and walked up to watch the show; neighbors had joined the spectacle. At the juncture of River Road and Maple Rise, I saw Richard Zeller standing by the front passenger door of his Lexus. He was talking to Chief Langlois, who was sitting in his cruiser, lights flashing. I made my way through the crowd toward them. Katie and Max were sitting cross-legged on the hood of the car; Anne was in the front seat, her short hair clearly outlined against the terrible light. I didn't see Rachel anywhere.

"Where's my daughter?" I asked when I reached Richard. "Didn't she come down with you?"

"Who?" Richard asked, turning toward me.

"She was right here, Maddie," Tom Langlois told me. "Don't worry. She's somewhere in this crowd."

"What about Luke?"

"We don't know yet," Tom told me. "We're doing everything we can."

I glanced over at Anne. She was sitting motionless in the front seat, her arms crossed on her chest. The window was up. I don't know if she saw or heard me; I'd stopped thinking I knew anything about her by then.

I turned back into the crowd, searching for Rachel. I kept seeing flashes of her—something blond or lavender, a familiar curve of shoulder, a freckled arm. I tried calling her name, but my voice was drowned by all the other voices, the roar of flame and water. I saw Paul in the midst of a group of firefighters, hauling a hose up the hill. Another truck was backing around and following them up the driveway. The effort seemed to be shifting now away from the house and up into the woods behind it. Firemen were stationed along the road, trying to get people to stay back. At one point, I heard a woman near me say, "God, no, who would live there? The place has been empty for years."

And then I saw Rachel: she was standing at the very front of the crowd, gazing up at the house, which was being allowed to self-destruct. I began pushing my way toward her, crying out to her, when the roof suddenly collapsed. Sparks flew up into the night and then showered back onto the crowd. A woman next to me screamed and stumbled into me. I slipped and fell. I lost sight of Rachel. People were shouting. I don't know how long it was, probably no more than a minute or two really, until I saw her again. She was only a few feet away, transfixed by the spectacle in front of her. The hemlocks were smoldering skeletons. Most of Luke's sculptures had been overturned; some burnt, others half melted. But a few still remained intact, black silhouettes—misfits every one—making a final, hopeless stand.

"Let's go, honey," I said, taking her hand.

"Where's Luke?" she asked, turning to me. "I've been looking for him. Have you seen him?"

"No, I haven't," I told her, pulling her away. "But we should go; it's dangerous. He wouldn't want you here." We made our way back to town along the side of the road. It was almost deserted now, except for the empty cars. Everyone had gone up to watch Luke's house burn down, as if it was some kind of fireworks display.

"I called 911 first. And then you," Rachel told me. "Then when the flames got so bad, I called Mrs. Zeller. They'd gone to the party after all. I didn't think she'd go, Mom. Not after everything."

I didn't understand what she was trying to tell me. I thought that Rachel must have somehow overheard Anne's and my conversation when I dropped her off to babysit. That "everything" was Anne's casual destruction of our friendship, my own anger and hurt feelings.

Phyllis Linden had carried Lia and Beanie into the house after Lia had woken up and begun to cry. Lia had fallen back asleep on the Lindens' living room couch, but Beanie was awake, sitting next to her sister, wide-eyed and mute.

"I tried to get her to have a cookie, or some milk, but she didn't seem to want anything," Phyllis told me. "She just keeps shaking her head."

"She's a little shy," I said.

"Let's go, Beanstalk," Rachel said, scooping her up. By the time I'd picked up Lia and thanked Phyllis, Rachel and Beanie were halfway to the car. I turned back to Phyllis. "Have you heard anything about Luke?"

"Carl called me about fifteen minutes ago. They're pretty sure he was in there. The fire started in the basement where he works. The place went up so fast, though, there's no way the guys could have reached him in time. And they'll have to wait until it's safe to go in. So until then, at least, I guess there's room for hope."

When we got home, Rachel helped me get Lia and Beanie upstairs, and then she went back down again. I stayed with Beanie for a while. She still had a temperature, and I could sense she knew something more serious than that was wrong with her world. I did what I could to soothe her. When she finally drifted off, I went downstairs to find Rachel on the couch on the porch.

"Are you okay?" I asked, sitting down next to her.

"Yes," she said. "I think so. But it's been the worst night of my life."

"I know," I told her. "I'm sorry."

"I don't like Mrs. Zeller anymore," Rachel told me. "In fact, I think I hate her."

I thought I understood. We had both been hurt by Anne.

"Sometimes people aren't who you think they are."

"Sometimes nobody's who I think they are."

"It's one of those awful lessons you learn when you grow up."

"Is that what you've been waiting for?" she asked, turning to me in the dark. "For me to grow up?"

"What do you mean?"

"Nothing. You're right. It's just one of those awful lessons."

I wasn't really listening to her; my mind was on something else. I felt I had to warn her. That she needed to be prepared.

"You know, you asked before about Luke? If anyone had seen him? There's a chance that he was there. In the house."

"No, he wasn't."

"Well, there's a chance. Nobody knows for sure yet. But I think you have to—"

"No. I don't care what you think, okay? Everything's ruined anyway."

"Rachel, honey—" I reached out for her.

"Oh, stop it!" she said, jumping up from the couch. "Just leave me alone. Why should I believe anything you have to say?"

38

The next two days were hell. Neither Paul nor I got any sleep. The night of the fire he was too wired and worked up even to think about going to bed. His usual self-control deserted him, and he spent the rest of that night going over the details of the accident with me again and again. I don't think I've ever seen him so angry. At Luke. How careless he'd been. How senseless the fire was. Stupid. It was in those desperate early-morning hours that he figured out that it must have been the blow-in insulation that had so accelerated the blaze. He latched on to that as if—altering this one part of the scenario—Paul could have somehow prevented the whole catastrophe.

"Luke's always so half-assed about safety! I told him not to use that cellulose shit. It's just a bunch of shredded newspapers, for chrissakes! But that's what he liked about it, you know. The fact that it was organic."

Paul's anguish was only exacerbated by Rachel's behavior. The next morning, she came down to the kitchen around six thirty, prettily dressed, dragging her large duffel. Paul had gone upstairs to lie down for an hour or so before heading up to Covington for the morning. He was planning to delegate as much of the critical last day of work at the site as he could, and try to be back at the fire scene by noon to help with the terrible business of sifting through the rubble.

"I'm ready," she said.

Rachel. I'd forgotten all about her plans to see Aaron. "You've got to know you won't be going now," I said.

"But you promised you'd take me down to the bus depot!" she replied, as if this was the only stumbling block to her enjoying her weekend away.

"But, Rachel. What are you thinking? Luke is—they haven't found him yet."

"He's fine, okay? Don't sound like that. And you promised to take me!"

"Honey, please. Your father and I were up all night. He's upstairs now, trying to get a little rest."

"Well, I don't care. I want to go. Now! I'm not going to let you make me miss that bus!"

This was so unlike Rachel that I didn't know what to do. I felt utterly exhausted and confused, but I also knew that something was seriously wrong with my eldest daughter, and that I'd have to pull myself together and approach the situation with care. Things might have worked out differently if Paul hadn't come clumping down the back stairs at that moment.

"Why are you yelling at your mother?" he demanded.

"Because she's going back on her word!"

"What is this?" Paul turned to me, his face gray with fatigue. "What's she talking about?"

"Her trip to Maine to see Aaron Neissen. I was supposed to take her down to the bus this morning first thing."

"What in the world's the matter with you?" Paul said, turning back to Rachel.

"With *me*?" she cried. "What's the matter with *me*? How about asking what the matter is with *you*! Both of you. Why should I believe anything either one of you has to tell me ever again!" She ran back up the stairs and slammed her door.

"Jesus," Paul said. "What the hell is going on around here?"

It only got worse after that. Rachel refused to leave her room. Beanie's earache got so bad she began to whimper around noontime and wouldn't stop. I had to call Kathy and ask her if I could drop Lia off at the farm so I could take Beanie down to our pediatrician in Northridge. It was a holiday weekend, about the only time Kathy got to have to herself. It made me so sad to feel that I was imposing.

Beanie, it turned out, had a bad ear infection, probably from some kind of bacteria she'd picked up at the pond. She'd forced herself to go under the water for the first time that summer, something I know she'd been desperately afraid of doing for the longest time. It seemed so unfair to me that she should be penalized for being brave.

Around seven that night, with the help of a special crew from Albany that included search dogs, a team of recovery workers was able to pull Luke's body from the ashes and rubble of his house. Paul helped them dig him out, and he traveled in the ambulance with Luke up to Harringdale, where the autopsy was to be performed. He called me from there.

"I think you should go ahead and tell the girls. I'm going to be too exhausted when I get home to do anything but collapse."

Breaking the news to Lia and Beanie was hard enough. They both started crying before I'd even gotten the words out. I thought I'd managed to keep them pretty sheltered from what was going on, but it's easy to forget how much kids pick up. They're like little sponges, soaking up all our excess hopes and fears. The three of us cried, right through a dinner that we didn't eat. I took them up to bed around nine, and then went and stood in front of Rachel's locked bedroom door.

"We need to talk," I said.

"Go ahead and talk," she said. At some point earlier in the evening, probably when the rest of us were having dinner, she'd left her room long enough to grab the cordless phone from our bedroom.

"I need to tell you something, Rachel, and I don't want to do it this way," I said. My words were greeted by silence. I felt I had no choice; this was one burden I knew I had to spare Paul.

"Luke's dead, Rachel. Your dad was on the crew that found his body."

"You're lying."

"No, I'm not." I felt so defeated. "Why would I want to lie to you about this?"

"Because you've been lying to me about everything. All my life."

Paul finally got home around midnight. He'd been holding himself together so tightly all day that he couldn't relax now. I made him sit out on the porch in the dark. I brought him a beer. He asked me how things had gone with the girls, and I told him it hadn't been easy. I didn't know what to tell him about Rachel, so I didn't say anything. His heart was already too heavy. The anger from last night had burned itself out. He sat staring out into the darkness. The last fireflies of the summer drifted over the wildflower field. For the first time in days I heard the crickets again, though they must have been singing the whole time: that endless sad song.

We didn't exactly fall asleep out there; my mind kept skittering back and forth over a fractured series of events, resting for a moment on my final conversation with Luke, then jumping ahead to Rachel's nastiness, flitting back to Anne staring past me on her doorstep, then returning to Luke walking me across his cluttered yard to my car. Sometime in the gray light of early morning, as the dew settled upon us with a narcotic heaviness, I felt myself falling. Just before hitting bottom, I woke with a jolt.

Richard Zeller answered the phone.

"Is Anne there?" I asked.

"Who's calling?"

"It's Maddie Alden. I need to talk to her."

"She can't talk to anyone right now."

"It's important. Tell her I'm driving over."

"No, really, she—" But I didn't wait to hear what excuse he'd find for her; I hung up the phone. It was Labor Day. The general store closed at noon, and the rest of the town seemed deserted. Up in the hills, across the lush meadows, the spacious, expensive new homes of weekenders and summer leasers were being cleared out, packed up. Children would be starting back to school in the city tomorrow, or the day after. I knew these people now; I'd sold several of them their houses. I'd made small talk with the husbands, kidded around with the children. I knew what the women were thinking: the summer had been lovely, almost relaxing for a time. But the children had become bored and had started to bicker. And there wasn't a decent hairstylist in the whole county. They'd found their perfect country getaways; filled their designer homes with expensive antiques, throw pillows, and quilts from the stores in Northridge. They'd be back for leaf-peeping in the fall and maybe a skiing weekend here and there, but this summer was over. The gas grill wheeled back into the pool house. A note left for the cleaning woman: she could take whatever perishables she wanted from the refrigerator.

As I drove past it, I couldn't allow myself to look at the charred ruin of Luke's cottage, but the smell of the fire seeped through my closed car windows: an acrid, earthy, rotting stink that made me want to gag. I turned sharply up the Zellers' driveway. The fire had claimed most of the woods between Luke's property and the Zellers', but their lawn was untouched: a rolling, well-kept carpet of green. A series of sprinklers, sunk into the sod, sprayed a fine mist over the sloping lawn. As I circled the turnaround and pulled up by the front path, Richard Zeller came out of the house and walked down to meet me.

"I'm here to see Anne," I told him, as I got out of the car.

"Well, she can't see anyone," he said. He stood on the path where it met the driveway, arms crossed above his belly, his heavy, imposing body essentially blocking me from going farther. It was one of the few times I'd ever seen him dressed casually. He was wearing a striped polo shirt and cargo-style shorts, and the effect was the opposite of what it should have been; he looked constrained and uncomfortable. It was hot in the open sun, and his thinning hair had separated into damp strands across his forehead. He had sunglasses on; the silver chain attached to them made two fussy loops behind his ears.

"This isn't a social call. I'm here because I'm worried about my daughter." When he looked down at me without any discernible reaction, I felt my anger building. "You know, Rachel? The girl who took care of your house and your children all summer?"

"Yes, I know Rachel," he said.

"Something happened here the night of the fire, and I want to know what it was. She's been acting—she hasn't been herself."

"Well, Anne's been having a bad time, too," he said. "Listen, I'm sure you've figured out by now that my wife's a little fragile. Unstable is probably a better word. I was hoping that a summer up here—away from everything that happened last spring—would help her. Get her back on track."

"What happened last spring?"

"She didn't tell you? And I thought the two of you were such great friends." Sighing, he took the dark glasses off and rubbed the bridge of his nose. "Well, I guess that just fits the pattern. Anne had an entirely inappropriate affair with a client at her advertising agency. He was the son of the owner of some sporting goods outfit the agency represented, a real loser from what I learned, whose judgment was about as sound as Anne's. They did nothing to hide what was going on. The agency lost the account. Anne was fired. It was pretty awful. For us. For me."

He could have been describing what happened to a total stranger. There was a definite sense of disapproval and distaste in his tone, but I didn't hear any anger or humiliation, little emotion, in fact, of any kind.

"She just told me she was taking a sabbatical. For the summer."

"Is that what she said?" He shook his head. "Well, now you know. And now this! After she was fired, I thought she'd finally learned her lesson. I actually began to believe that she'd gotten all this nonsense under control."

"What nonsense?"

"These affairs of hers," he said, sliding his sunglasses back on. "She has a history of hooking up with totally unacceptable people. Losers, liars, this—this drug dealer. She takes these people up, you know, and sweeps them into her orbit, building them up in her mind—and theirs—to be her equal. It always ends badly. I've got to say, though, this has been the worst."

It was as though he was complaining about his wife's bad taste in clothes or art. A certain tacky streak in her that he found objectionable. Evidently this was the "emotional problem" that Anne had alluded to many times—the vulnerability that attracted her to Richard in the first place. *This big, strong man wanted to take care of me.* And it was also what attracted Richard to her, I realized. There was something almost indulgent in the way he spoke about her faithlessness. I remembered what Anne had told me: *I'm really beginning to think that he wants me to stay troubled. It lets him remain in control, do you know what I mean?*

But whatever else Richard might have felt, he was wrong about Luke. Anne and Luke. Her affair with him had been something very different from whatever Anne had done in the past. I knew that. In spite of everything else, I still believed that.

I felt compelled to correct him.

"Your wife and Luke Barnett fell in love over the summer," I said. "She told him she was going to divorce you, leave you, for him."

"Oh, I'm sure she did," he said. "And she may have even convinced herself of it for a moment or two. But did you really believe her? Honestly? I mean, you must have known that the whole thing was ridiculous. Pathetic. Someone like Anne, leaving me for that crackpot? Come on!"

"What happened the other night after I dropped Rachel off?" I asked. This is what I had to know. Why I was there, forcing myself to talk to him. "Luke came up here, didn't he?"

"Yes, he came up here and told me what you just said; that he and Anne were in love and that she was going to leave me."

"And what did you say?"

"I told him he was delusional. That I'd told Anne all about him—and you and your husband. The kind of people you were. Criminals, for God's sake."

"And you said all this in front of my daughter?"

"Honestly, at that moment I forgot who she was; I was thinking of her just as our babysitter. Someone Anne had hired. I can't keep all you people straight."

I couldn't let him see how I felt. I had to keep my composure for just another second or two. One more question. And then I would never have to speak to Richard Zeller again.

"What did Anne say about all this?"

"Well, you know, she told me on Friday night that she'd had a relapse—that she'd slipped. That's how we think about it now. It's like an addiction on her part. I try my best to be sympathetic, helpful. Not that any of this has been easy on me, actually, but I've got my family to think about. My children. In any case, we'd already straightened the mess out between the two of us. She promised me that she'd go back into therapy this fall."

"But what did she say to Luke?"

"I think she said we had to get going, or we'd be late to the Ossermans'. Listen, I'm sorry about what happened to your friend. But remember I was the one who warned everyone that this could happen. That place was a firetrap. Isn't that exactly what I said?"

The tornado that swept across the county when I was nine years old left a path of destruction that in some places grew to be more than a half mile wide. The winds traveled across the length of Red River from north to south, uprooting trees, ripping roofs off houses and barns, upending trucks, trailers, and cars, and tossing household debris all over the countryside like so much confetti. Three people were killed. The gas station on Route 198 was demolished. I'd been up at the pond with my uncle Petie and aunt Adele and their three boys when what we thought was a bad thunderstorm roared through. But we drove back down Indian Hill Road to find the highway blocked by what looked like miles of fallen trees. The entire landscape had been altered—whole forests leveled—in less than fifteen minutes. We had to leave the car and pick our way around the fallen tree trunks and broken limbs. It took us four hours to reach my home.

The tornado had cut behind the house, leaving, at first sight, everything intact. Both my parents were safe, but deeply shaken. The twister had missed the house by yards but it had demolished the barn and tossed the henhouse halfway up into the haying field. Dead chickens, many of which

I'd stroked just that morning as I gathered eggs, lay about the property. In that one afternoon, my belief that life was essentially good—designed primarily for my happiness—was shattered.

As I made my way down the Zellers' drive I thought about that day. The acres of trees uprooted. The lives lost. I've always been afraid that it would happen again. And I've tried to be ready for it: herding the girls down to the basement with the first crack of thunder. But there's nothing you can do really, is there? To prepare, to protect? The storm will descend in its own time, without warning. It will roar and roar. It will rage through your heart and leave destruction in its wake.

I had not seen it coming at all. I had seen what I wanted to see: a beautiful, entitled woman who wanted me to be her friend. No, more than that: she wanted me to be her confidante. She'd whispered secrets to me. She'd complimented me on my family, my abilities, my looks. She'd entrusted my oldest daughter with her own children, flattering her, as well. Then she'd seen my husband's best friend and had taken him, too. Just reached out and grabbed. And I'd let her. I'd opened my life to her, welcomed her in. I'd admired her mercurial spirit. Her sense of fun. I'd seen what I wanted to see. I'd projected my own hopes and needs into her. She was a thing of light and surfaces. I hadn't understood that it was all an illusion, a dangerous one. That she was out of control. That she was driven by boredom and cravings, empty inside—a destructive force spiraling across our lives.

And Luke? He'd thought he'd found his first and only true love. He'd been searching all his life for this: the answering cry. And there she was: perfect in her beauty and in her brokenness. He was going to heal her, restore her to happiness, the way he never could his mother. For so many years, women had been trying to do the same for him, but that was not what Luke longed for. He never wanted to be the loved one. He wanted to be the one who loved. And there she was. It made it so much simpler that she wasn't real. That she was a mirror, reflecting back at him what he wanted to see. She was there when he most needed something. Someone. I remembered what he told me the night I'd first found out about the affair: *I felt like I was slowly going numb, losing all feeling. After things fell apart with you guys, I began to think, what the hell is the point? Who would really care if I didn't wake up some morning?*

And when he found out the truth about Anne, that she was false and unworthy, he had simply walked past her to something that had been waiting there in the shadows all along. Down the basement steps to the dark true flame that could not be extinguished, that was unconditional in its embrace. In time, the autopsy report would reveal that Luke had shot himself after starting the fire. I choose to believe that he set it in the uncertain hope that my husband and my daughters—and perhaps me, as well—would never have to know that his death hadn't been an accident. It was then that I finally found the courage to tell Paul about Luke and Anne. I knew that he would blame himself for Luke's death if I didn't. He had a way of taking responsibility for everything that went wrong in Luke's life. But this was one mistake that would rest forever on my shoulders.

The damage the tornado inflicted took years to heal. The trees had to be hauled away or shredded, stumps ground to sawdust. For months, blue tarpaulins flapped on what was left of houses. Even now, more than twenty-five years later, people walking back in the woods will come upon an old window frame, or a rusted kitchen object, or even a moldering family album, and think, how did these things come to be here?

The land where Luke's cottage stood won't take nearly so long to recover. The autumn leaves will blanket what is now no more than an open empty acre, intersected by a crumbling old stone wall bordering the roadway. Winter snow will pack the leaf debris down over the charred earth. And then, sometime in April, the first green shoots will poke up from under the ice: tickseed, milkweed, bull thistle. A mullein plant will rise up out of the mud. Then a pine sapling. A maple. And all will go on as before. As it always has. Mahican, Barnett, Alden, Zeller. It doesn't matter. The weeds grow back. The broken earth is covered over. It will go on, of course. Life. I know that. I know. Already, the air is clearer. The ash has settled. A crow flying over the rubble doesn't look down.

Liza Gyllenhaal spent many years in advertising and publishing. She lives with her husband in New York City and Western Massachusetts.

LOCAL KNOWLEDGE

LIZA GYLLENHAAL

This Conversation Guide is intended to enrich the
individual reading experience, as well as encourage us
to explore these topics together—because books,
and life, are meant for sharing.

A CONVERSATION
WITH LIZA GYLLENHAAL

Q. How did you come up with the idea for Local Knowledge? *Is it based on people and places you know in real life?*

A. Yes, the story is based on several different real-life elements, the most important being the tremendous building boom that occurred all across the country in the late 1990s. My husband and I have owned a small house in Massachusetts for many years in a lovely, welcoming town a bit like Red River. After 9/11, real estate values and second-home building escalated dramatically, fueled mainly by city dwellers. I found the clash of cultures between a primarily rural, close-knit community and the recently arrived upscale "weekenders" a rich vein to mine thematically.

Maddie is based very roughly on a woman I met for all of one hour, and I don't even remember her real name. She was a young real estate agent who was helping my younger sister and her husband find a weekend house not far from ours. My sister wanted our opinion of a place she had seen, and asked her agent to show it to us. When we climbed into the agent's car, I saw a kid's backpack and other signs of personal life. The woman told us that she had three girls and that she'd grown up in the area. She pointed out a dirt road that led up to "a pond where everyone goes to swim." The Zeller home is modeled on the striking contemporary house that we saw that day.

The other real elements—a marijuana farm discovered in a

nearby county in the late 1980s, a "sculpture garden" somewhat like Luke's, the collapse of dairy farming in our area—coalesced quickly after I saw the house and met the real estate agent who became Maddie. The story took on a life of its own from there.

Q. You've written Local Knowledge *in Maddie's voice. But your background in many ways—an advertising executive in New York City—is really more like Anne's. What made you choose Maddie's point of view?*

A. Well, I grew up in a small town in Pennsylvania, in an area that had been agricultural not that long ago. Over the years, I've watched the countryside be taken over—in a much more brutal way than Red River—by endless housing developments and strip malls. So I understand the sadness of knowing that "the forests and meadows of my girlhood . . . [are] all gone now and never to be recovered." More than that, though, I felt that this particular story had to be written in the voice of someone who was born in the town and loved the area—but who also aspired to something more. The only thing Maddie and Paul have is the land, and, ironically, both have to see it divided and torn up in order to succeed. As Luke says: "I feel like we're cannibalizing our birthright. The one good, beautiful thing we ever had."

I did feel I was taking some risks assuming Maddie's point of view. I had to empathize with her without being condescending. I had to try to *become* her, and one thing that really helped me was when I decided that it was okay to have her thoughts and feelings be conveyed in a more "sophisticated" way than through her everyday speaking voice. I believe we express our deepest and truest selves through the use of a special interior language.

Q. Anne is a complicated character. Did you find her hard to write?

A. Absolutely. She was by far the most difficult, because I wanted to have Maddie be really taken with her; at the same time, I needed to signal to the reader that Anne might have some real problems. So I had Paul, who in my mind is the moral center of the book, sound the alarm about her first. The reader, in turn, becomes aware of her erratic moods and questionable parenting, but Maddie keeps making excuses for her behavior. Anne's friendship comes to mean so much to Maddie that she's willing to turn a blind eye to her faults. By the time Maddie decides to let Rachel continue to babysit for the Zellers—despite knowing that Anne and Luke are having an affair—I hope it's plain that Maddie is making a serious mistake. I actually rewrote that chapter several times, each time trying to make it clearer that it was a critical turning point for Maddie.

Q. How did you learn about the real estate business? Did you do research? Do you talk to working real estate agents?

A. I did both. I was very lucky to find a bright young woman who was just starting out in real estate sales, who sat down with me several times and walked me through her workday, the computer programs her agency used, how she was going about building a client base, and so forth. At the end of one of our sessions, I met her boss, who told me she was proud of "her baby broker," which is what I had Nana call Maddie at one point.

I also spent a lot of time on the Internet (a godsend for researching just about anything in the world!), boning up on real estate classes and requirements for becoming a registered agent. And I bought and studied the kinds of test-prep books Maddie would have used to get her certification.

Q. You have Maddie say at one point: "I suppose every place on earth has its own version of royalty." Did the small town where you grew up have a version?

A. Oh, yes. The family was quite different from the Barnett clan, but also very wealthy, envied, and emulated. They also experienced a lot of tragedy over the years. I think American royalty is concerned primarily with money rather than bloodlines, but it doesn't make it any less real and powerful. I am drawn to writing about the dynamics of families and small towns, and I think this is a theme—in Fitzgerald's famous summation "the rich are different from you and me"—that is endlessly fascinating.

Q. *You don't have children, and yet you write about them with what seems like firsthand knowledge, Rachel especially. Where did she come from?*

A. I'm a very proud and happy aunt to a growing brood of kids, and I'm close enough to most of them to believe, as Maddie says early on, that they "come out of the box fully assembled for the most part." The fictional Alden children were like that for me, especially Beanie, though I think she is the most fictionalized of the three. I borrowed little bits and pieces of girls I know to help imagine Rachel, but she's not really at all like any teenager in my life now. If anything, she's probably more like me when I was that age. I've paid close attention when my friends talk about raising their teenage girls; that's primarily how I worked out Maddie and Rachel's relationship. I think a big part of learning how to write is knowing how to listen.

Q. *What authors do you like and did any one of them influence you in writing this book?*

A. I read a lot of fiction and poetry and my list of favorite writers is long, lowbrow, highfalutin, and all over the place. In no particular order, I love the fiction of Iris Murdoch, P. D. James, John Fowles, F. Scott and Penelope Fitzgerald, Susan Isaacs, and Alan Furst, and the poetry of Richard Wilbur, Mary Oliver, Elizabeth Bishop, and Theodore Roethke, to name just a very quick and beloved few. I've long admired the writing of Jane Smiley, from the early murder mystery

Duplicate Keys and the heartbreaking short stories in *Age of Grief* to her recent, enlightening nonfiction book *Thirteen Ways of Looking at a Novel*. I reread her Pulitzer Prize–winning *A Thousand Acres* recently. Among many other things, it tells the story of the demise of a farming community in the midwest. It remains, to my mind, one of the great novels of our time.

Q. Do you have a set writing routine?

A. I usually wake up early and reread whatever I've been working on. I revise constantly on the computer. (It continues to amaze me how Tolstoy could have written *War and Peace* in longhand!) Then I let the demands of daily life intervene for several hours and pick up again in the afternoon. Most days, I don't hit my stride until three o'clock or so, and then if I'm lucky get two or three good, productive hours in. I think a lot about what I'm working on when I'm not actually writing. When I'm running, for instance, or driving in my car back and forth from the city to the country. I try to work out problems—a scene I can't get off the ground, a character who refuses to behave—during that two-and-a half-hour stretch.

Q. Are you working on something new?

A. Yes, I'm working on something now, also about a small town, family, friendship, and a secret long buried in the past. In every other way, though, the new story is totally different from *Local Knowldege*.

QUESTIONS
FOR DISCUSSION

1. In the beginning of the first chapter, Maddie is driving over to the Zellers' place for the first time, and at the end of the last chapter she's driving back. From what point in time is Maddie actually telling the story?

2. Maddie's friendship with her sister-in-law Kathy begins to suffer when Anne and Maddie start to grow close. At one point Maddie admits to herself that she's been "using" Kathy. Do you see a parallel between what Maddie feels toward Kathy, and Anne toward Maddie? Have you ever "used" someone in the same way?

3. Maddie has a tendency to see other people initially through the prism of her own needs, hopes, and fears—then realize later that her perspective was somewhat skewed. Besides Anne, who else does Maddie change her views about over the course of the novel? Do your first impressions of others usually hold up over time?

4. Have you ever told yourself that you disliked someone—the way Maddie does Luke—when you secretly feel the opposite? Maddie admits that she's lied to herself about Luke in order to protect her true feelings. Does that explanation resonate with you?

5. When did you begin to suspect that Anne was not as "considerate and friendly" as Maddie first believed her to be?

6. Do you know someone who, like Paul, made some serious mistakes when he was young? How do you think that changes a person as he grows older?

7. The novel tells the story of two very different friendships: the one between Paul and Luke and that between Maddie and Anne. What do these contrasting relationships tell you about the people involved?

8. Similarly, the book explores two love affairs: the lifelong one between Maddie and Paul, and Luke and Anne's brief and fatal coming together. What do you think makes one relationship so stable—and the other so tragically volatile?

9. Have you ever kept a secret for a friend? Did you regret your decision, or did you believe that it was important to do so for the sake of the friendship?

10. Have you ever had a friend drop you, the way Anne does Maddie? How did that make you feel—and react? Were you able to forgive and forget in time?

11. Have you ever lied to—or kept the truth from—your husband or boyfriend for what you thought was his own good? Do you regret this?

12. Do you think Rachel knew what was going on between Anne and Luke? If so, what gave you that impression, and how do you think Rachel felt about these two adults having a love affair?

13. Do you think teenagers are entitled to their own secrets? For instance, was Maddie right to intervene when Rachel tried to arrange things so that she and Aaron could spend a night alone together? What would you have done?